continued . . .

ALSO BY LESLIE GLASS

Tracking Time
Stealing Time
Judging Time

Leslie Glass

THE SILENT BRIDE

AN ONYX BOOK

ONYX
Published by New American Library, a division of
Penguin Putnam Inc., 375 Hudson Street,
New York, New York 10014, U.S.A.
Penguin Books Ltd, 80 Strand,
London WC2R 0RL, England
Penguin Books Australia Ltd, Ringwood,
Victoria, Australia
Penguin Books Canada Ltd, 10 Alcorn Avenue,
Toronto, Ontario, Canada M4V 3B2
Penguin Books (N.Z.) Ltd, 182–190 Wairau Road,
Auckland 10, New Zealand

Penguin Books Ltd, Registered Offices:
Harmondsworth, Middlesex, England

First published by Onyx, an imprint of New American Library,
a division of Penguin Putnam Inc.

First Printing, June 2002
10 9 8 7 6 5 4 3 2 1

For Alex and Lindsey

ACKNOWLEDGMENTS

For a decade the officers of the New York City Police Department and the New York City Police Foundation have been my constant source of inspiration. Every year I have a greater appreciation for the people who serve and defend New York City. This year more than ever before, I want to acknowledge and commend the NYPD for the courage of its personnel in all its departments and their profound commitment to protect the citizens of New York City no matter how perilous the job.

Thanks especially to Commissioner Bernard Kerik and Deputy Commissioner Maureen Casey and all the top brass for their tireless caring for all the personnel in the department and for the people of New York in the toughest of times. I also want to thank Deputy Chief Dewey Fong for Chinese opera and the Borough of Queens, Inspector Barbara Sicilia for Hate, Detective Margaret Eng Wallace and Detective Ed Wallace for wedding photos and crime scene background, also Lieutenant Joe Blosis of the Crime Scene Unit. Thanks to Pam Delaney, Judy Dyna, Greg Roberts, and all my friends at Crime Stoppers and the Police Foundation for all the good they do.

Two years ago I ran a contest on my Web site. The prize: the winner would appear as a character in my next book. Seems a long time ago, but we do have a winner. His name is Anthony Price. He's a Welsh butler now living on the north shore of Long Island. I interviewed Anthony, changed his name from Price to Pryce, and made up a family for him. Here he is, probably not as sinister as he would like to be.

I am deeply grateful for the friendship and help of Dorothy Harris, director of the Leslie Glass Foundation and perpetual reader and advisor, for being with me every step of the way. Dr. Rosemary Perez Foster of New York University's Ehrenkranz School of Social Work, and Dr. Linda Mills of New York University's School of Law have provided insight into the psychology of traumatized immigrants and the Orthodox community. Claudia Oberweger, C.S.W., C.A.S.A.C., has taught me a great deal about substance and alcohol abuse. Thanks to Nancy Yost and Audrey LaFehr, Woo fans in all seasons.

One

On May ninth, at three-thirty in the afternoon, two months after her eighteenth birthday, Tovah Schoenfeld was getting dressed for her wedding and living the last half hour of her life. She was in a downstairs room of Temple Shalom, near where the caterers were fussing over the last details of the reception and dinner to come. She was perspiring in her heavy bridal gown and very nervous.

To get her married, Tovah's father and mother had tried to make all her dreams come true. Thus she was wearing a Tang Ling gown of white satin covered with lace and seed pearls, unlike anything her friends had ever seen. Her dream had been for a sleeveless gown, something cut down below the hollow in her neck, but exposing skin was not allowed. So this dress was a waterfall that completely enveloped her. Folds of it tumbled down from her shoulders in a wide swath of puddling, snowy silk that weighed a ton and completely hid her beautiful figure.

A jewel neckline tightly encircled her neck. The dress had no waist, and the princess style nipped in only the slightest bit under her breasts so that hardly a curve could be detected. Tovah's arms were encased to the wrists, and her veil, not yet attached to her hair, was outrageously voluminous and would cover her from head to foot. For such modesty the price had been nearly ten thousand dollars. Kim, the fitter from Tang Ling who'd made the dress and personally sewn on every pearl by hand, had come all the way out to Riverdale to dress her.

Tovah was supposed to reign supreme on her wedding day, and her hair was being styled to be seen in public for the last time in her life. Tovah had long fair hair that curled naturally, and she didn't want to cover it. Her mother had bought her a natural-looking shetl for more than three thousand dollars and begged her to put on the wig when she and Schmuel were alone for a few minutes after the ceremony. But Tovah wanted to save it for tomorrow night, the first of the traditional seven postwedding dinners that friends were giving for them. Tovah and her mother were still arguing about the wearing of the wig when her familiar nausea took hold of her.

The crowded room was cluttered with hanging racks of gowns and dresses for now and later, hair dryers, makeup cases, tables with mirrors, combs, containers of hair spray. Tovah's mother, Suri, was in there, her grandmother, Bubba, three of her five sisters, a photographer, a hairdresser, and a makeup artist. The girls were noisy. Tovah's mother was scolding them for running around. Bubba was scolding her for scolding. There wasn't enough air, and Tovah was worried about doing the right thing. Tovah didn't really want to get married. Had she chosen the right boy? She hardly knew him, and he'd looked so young when she'd seen him a week ago. He was shorter than she was; she couldn't even wear real heels with her wedding dress. And he didn't have to shave. She hadn't seemed to notice this the few times they'd dated. She'd been so frightened she could barely look at him.

Wendy, the party planner, was giving her a funny look, and suddenly she was fainting in the heat of the room. She was sweating in the dress. Her mother was getting more irritable. That look crossed Suri's face: *Don't make trouble, Tovah. Don't get sick and have a headache. Don't act crazy.*

"Kim, come in here," Wendy called out the door. "It's time to rock and roll."

Kim appeared at the door, smiling and bowing. "Everything all right, beautiful girl?" he asked. "Not worried anymore?"

Water filled Tovah's mouth. "Still worried," she whispered.

Suri and Bubba, in their own long gowns, both stopped yelling and exchanged looks. Surely, among the thousands of boys and girls matched up at the tender age of eighteen by their parents according to taste, disposition, and the financial worth of their parents, Tovah had to be about the most difficult. That was the story their rolling eyes told. Suri started scolding.

"Tovah, Schmuel and his family are here. The rabbi is waiting. Your father is waiting. You look beautiful; you're the luckiest bride in the world. It's time to get that veil on."

Tovah was white. But how could she be sure she was doing the right thing? The rule was you couldn't see or speak to your husband-to-be for a week before the wedding. Now she couldn't remember Schmuel's face or even recognize her own in the mirror in front of her. She'd never worn makeup before, just a little lipstick on their first date. Outside, she could hear people clinking glasses, talking loudly in the party room so extravagantly decorated. Guests who'd come from far away were already eating canapés and carrying on over the twenty varieties of roses and lilies in the centerpieces while they waited for the ceremony to start.

"Give her something sweet, a hard candy, quick." Bubba jockeyed for control.

"Beautiful girl, everyone is like this, nervous at first," Kim said softly.

Wendy grabbed Tovah's hands, chafed them. "Candy!" she commanded.

Suri pulled the wrapper off a lemon drop and stuffed it into Tovah's mouth. "There you go. Sweets for the sweet." She pushed the hairdresser out of the way. "Get out of the way, Penny. Give her some air. It's very hot in here."

"Penny, please step outside for a second. I'll get the veil on her." Wendy took over.

Then Tovah was on her feet. Wendy fluffed her hair and patted her on the back. Kim slid behind her and began fussing with the folds and the veil. While he worked, he murmured to Tovah as if she were a child, encouraging her and telling her she looked magnificent.

"Magnificent," Wendy agreed. "The best yet."

But something was wrong. Tovah was so numb she couldn't feel her feet moving her out of the room. She couldn't make real what was happening in the rabbi's study. She was aware of Schmuel, a skinny redheaded kid, dressed in a tuxedo that made him look more like a bar mitvah boy than a husband. He had blue eyes, too, chosen in part so they would have handsome, light-skinned children. His father was grinning. Her father too. The rest was a blank, the words, the signing of papers, the business being done. All she could feel was her cold sweat inside the magnificent dress. Why did she have to be the only girl in the world who didn't want to marry?

And then the business was done, and the rabbi ushered Schmuel and his mother and father out of his study. Tovah and her parents were following. Now she could hear the music. Her father was on one side of her. Her mother on the other. Each clutched one of her arms, almost holding her up. They began their walk. From the side door up the aisle of the women's section they came. The partition between the men's and women's sections had been removed so the whole congregation could see them: a magnificent trio, rich and beautiful. Tovah and her parents turned when they reached the back of the sanctuary, then headed for the center aisle that separated the men from the women.

There, the width of Tovah's dress prevented the parents and bride from walking abreast. Tovah's mother and father let go of her arms and moved down the aisle first. Because there were no flower girls, no ring bearer, no bridesmaids, Tovah walked alone. It was for this reason that her killer had a clear sight line of her. First her head, covered in lace and tulle, bobbed in the rifle's sights. All eyes were focused on her forward movement, not the empty lobby behind her where the doors were closed and no one was on guard in this safe, safe neighborhood. The bride's head was in the sights, then the cascade of silk falling from Tovah's shoulders. The shooter never shifted the rifle sights to the wall of men and boys in their black suits and skullcaps or the mass of women and children, agog at the richness of Tovah's gown. The people were all well fed and fat. So healthy and rich. Suddenly the barrel of the gun did shift to the crowd, but only for a moment. There was no choice but to fire. Even in five seconds it would be too late. Tovah would be surrounded. She'd be in front of the man with the black robes and white shawl, family on all sides. It would be too late.

No more pain in this life. Salvation was now. The short volley of shots came with a muffled sound. A kind of *phumfp*ing. The bullets slammed through the tulle and satin into Tovah's back. She pitched forward without uttering so much as a gurgle. A man in the first row jumped to help her up. At first no one guessed what had happened. It was so easy, so very easy. The bride went down, and it took almost a full minute for anyone to realize she'd been shot. The killer was out the door and gone before the screaming even started.

Two

Detective Sergeant April Woo fiddled with her chopsticks at a window table in Soong Fat's Best Noodle House on Main Street in Flushing, Queens. At four-fifteen on Sunday she was on a busman's holiday, doing a favor on her day off for her sister-cousin, Ching, who was neither a sister nor a cousin. Ching was the third daughter of her mother's friend, Mai Ma Dong, whom April had always called Auntie out of respect. She and Ching had known each other from birth, had shared the same crib, had played together as children, had stuffed themselves and yawned at countless family occasions, had stayed at each other's houses and been compared against each other enough by their highly competitive mothers to make them feel in equal measures the love and wrath of siblings.

Ching was very smart, had a business degree, and a great job at a stable Internet company. She was a rising star. If that wasn't enough to cause April's mother, Sai Yuan Woo, a serious loss of face in light of April's low-class work in law enforcement, Ching was getting married in two weeks to Matthew Tan, against whom April's own Latino lover, Lieutenant Mike Sanchez, stood as a poisonous threat to the

purity of all the Han peoples. Ching was getting married and April was doing her a favor. She'd agreed to
talk to Matthew's friend, Gao Wan, in the heart of
Queens on a Sunday because it was also a good place
to go food shopping for her mother.

April hadn't guessed that this favor would involve
listening to an endless, shaggy, Chinese dragon-
riding tale (illegal entry into the United States) that
was completely unbelievable not only because of the
manner of the telling, but also the telling itself. Usually illegal aliens did not inform authorities of their
plight.

"My mother was the daughter of a fisherman,"
he'd begun over an hour ago. "My father a river god."
Then the sly, appraising smile to see how she'd take
such a tall story.

Right then April had known this would take a
while. She appraised Gao right back. Could be he
was trying to make himself interesting. Could be he
didn't know who his father was. In any case, she was
no stranger to the most elaborate of superstitions.
Along with her ancestors, April herself half believed
that the skies were filled with ghosts and immortals
flying around making mischief in far greater measure
than good fortune. And she often thought her own
mother was the most powerful Chinese mythical
creature of all, a dragon capable of changing shape as
well as anything else that got in her way. Secretly, she
believed her Skinny Dragon Mother had invisible
armor on her body made up of far more aggressive
yang scales than kind and gentle yin ones. Further,
April had no doubt that her mother carried the precious pearl of long (possibly everlasting) life in her
mouth. The idea was terrifying to her.

"My mother drowned when her seducer took her to his river god home in the weeds. I was orphaned before birth," Gao went on cheerfully. "My uncle had a small café in a tourist town. I learned to cook there."

She watched his eyes as he described his teen years working in small restaurants and inns, then his horrific boat journey to the food mecca of the world, Hong Kong. He glossed over his years there, barely mentioning the sponsor who'd brought him here. And finally he hinted at a grave danger he faced from the gangsters who claimed they now owned his culinary gifts for life. April's classic oval face, almond eyes, and rosebud red lips remained neutral as she suppressed her irritation at this elaborate waste of her time.

She'd bet a month's salary that Gao's story was made up from beginning to end and that he had arrived not in the filthy hold of some Taiwanese tanker, but in the comfort of an American airliner, and no gangsters of any kind were after him.

April Woo might be an ABC—American-born Chinese—but she'd grown up in Chinatown and worked there in the Fifth Precinct on Elizabeth Street as a beat cop, then a detective for five years. She knew what was what. She listened to Gao's tall tale—as she did to all the others she heard in the course of her work—without letting any intelligence leak out of her eyes. She'd learned young to hide all emotion, to do her thinking behind the blank wall of a quiet, stupid-looking face. She let the man talk and talk, making the wheel go around. As they said in the Department, what goes around comes around. The way of Tao in the new world also happened to be the way of the NYPD. Eventually she'd learn why Ching had insisted on the meeting.

At nearly four-thirty she dropped her wrist under the table and glanced at her watch. Her *chico*, Lieutenant Mike Sanchez, commander of the Homicide Task Force, was working today, supervising a double homicide and suicide. This morning he'd told her he might not be free until late tonight, so she eyed the food on the table to give him later.

Gao Wan had cooked an impossibly big spread for her. It was late in the afternoon, and the feast was way too much even for a regularly scheduled meal. As her host, Gao wasn't eating a thing and, as honored guest, April could hardly pig out, either. Therefore, the fragrant steamed pork buns; wok-fried garlic tops; crisp scallion cakes; translucent Shanghai noodles, wide as a man's hand and swimming in spicy peanut sauce; clams with oyster sauce; mussels with fermented black beans; eggplant with garlic; shrimp balls; *shui mai*; and sweet/sour fish sat there cooling on their plates as April waited for Gao to say what he wanted from her.

Gao caught April's sidelong glance at the potential leftovers.

"Eat, eat, please," he urged for the fourteenth time. "You don't like?"

"Oh, I ate so much," April said politely. "I'm stuffed." She changed the subject. "How did you meet Matthew, by the way?" They were speaking in Cantonese.

She'd wondered about this because Matthew Tan, Gao's supposed "friend," was an ABC computer expert from California who'd met Ching Ma Dong at a convention in Tucson. Matthew's Chinese did not extend much beyond *kuai he!*, *xie xie*, and *cha*. *Drink up*, *thank you*, and *tea*. She'd be truly surprised if they'd ever met. April was spared having to wonder about it further by the ringing cell phone in her pocket. Caller ID said *private,* so she said, "Sergeant Woo."

"*Querida,* where are you?" Mike's voice sounded tense.

"Flushing, what's up?"

"We've got a synagogue shooting up in Riverdale; looks bad. . . ." His voice broke up.

"Mike?" April turned her body slightly away from Gao. "Riverdale where?"

"Burk . . . aou."

"Give me an address."

"Independence Ave. Exit Nineteen on the HH Parkway. Copy?"

"Yeah, I copy."

She wanted to know how many people were hit. Was anybody dead? But his siren was wailing, the radio in his car was squawking, and he'd hung up anyway.

The cop's life. April looked regretfully at Gao and the leftovers she wasn't going to get. "Sorry," she murmured. "Something's come up. I have to go."

Three

By the time April reached the restaurant door less than five feet away, she'd already forgotten Gao Wan. Crime always suspended real life. Didn't matter if it was her day off, or if she was in the middle of some important family occasion, a funeral or a wedding. When a call came, she hit the road.

Outside the restaurant, a riot of Asia greeted her on the busy Sunday afternoon. Colorful dual-alphabet and language signs for everything from acupuncture and ice cream to hair cutting and gourmet tea all screamed for attention on storefronts and in upstairs windows. Dresses, East and West style, hung outside store windows and in doorways. Merchandise—gewgaws of every kind imported from dozens of countries—jammed small storefronts. On the sidewalk, street vendors hawked a kaleidoscope of familiar products for homesick arrivals: plastic sandals, embroidered silk shoes, toys from China, incense, paper money, herbal cures.

Almost dizzying was the abundance of stalls featuring seductive, dewy-looking vegetables, long beans, cabbage, bok choy, radish, bean sprouts, bitter melon, oranges, Asian apples and pears. Nestled in their ice beds were cockles and clams, whole fish, shrimps, squid, baskets of clawing crabs still very much alive.

The sidewalk was jammed with mothers and children and whole families taking the day to eat and buy food. Everything Asian. Asian faces and products everywhere mixed with the overriding aroma of sizzling garlic and ginger. It all created the impression of a metropolis anywhere but Main Street, USA.

It was only a short block to the parking garage, but one that was clogged by hordes of people who were not in a hurry. April broke into sweat, dampening the armholes of the lime green shell under her lemon suit jacket. She stepped off the curb and dodged into the street, her shoulder bag slamming her hip as she ran. A bicycle messenger swerved to miss her when she dashed through a changing light.

"Fuck you!" he yelled at her in the only words she knew in Korean.

And then she was in her aging white Le Baron and on the road. For the next fifteen minutes she raced northwest, not even trying to rouse Mike on his cell. Beat officers on patrol had radios to communicate with dispatchers and bosses. Some detective units had cell phones or beepers as well so they could call each other directly. April's private car had no radio, and Mike was busy. She'd have to wait.

In less than half an hour, she found the local street in Riverdale off the Henry Hudson Parkway. Two uniforms, both female, were standing in the intersection, directing traffic beside their angle-parked blue-and-white. April resisted the urge to query them about the incident. She showed her ID and the uniforms waved her through.

Down the street half a dozen blue-and-whites

were double-parked in a line, some with their doors still open, as if their drivers had charged out. Four unmarked black sedans with shields in the windows indicated that brass had arrived. Two empty ambulances with their back doors closed stood like sentries. And all around was the pandemonium of deflated celebrants—all dressed up, bunched in groups outside their house of worship, stunned and angry, not yet released.

No matter how many times April walked out of everyday life into somebody's death chamber, into somebody's nightmare of grief, into a standoff of innocence against evil, it was always the same. It was a bungee jump into the hell where ghosts and devils lived. Right now there wasn't the frenzy and chaos of people in imminent danger, no hostages to save, no tense SWAT team taking positions against a sniper. No hovering choppers in the sky.

It looked as if a very big, expensive party had been interrupted. Maybe fifty or sixty elegantly dressed women, many of them stout and wearing flashy jewelry, their weight embraced by sparkly, bright-colored evening gowns. The same number of men in tuxedos with gold and red and bright blue cummerbunds and matching embroidered skullcaps. And there were children everywhere, dozens of them trying in vain to get some attention. Like the two sexes everywhere, the men and women had gathered in separate groups. The people were jittery and upset, but their attitude was marked by the kind of lassitude that comes when a tragedy has already taken place, when there's nothing left to do but go home. Whatever had occurred was over.

She parked the car, anxious to get there and do something.

"No more, no more, no more!" was the first thing she heard when she got out.

A woman was ranting, "Where were the police? This is not supposed to happen again."

Sweating heavily in her too-cheerful outfit, April felt her usual beginning-of-a-case sick feeling hit her hard. Headache, slight nausea. Hazard of the job. She was entering the fog of yin when everything was soft, hazy, unformed, and she had to keep her ears and eyes wide open to the sounds and sights around her. She could feel the presence of the immortals, the ghosts and demons churning in the air. It always made her a little queasy because she was an American and not supposed to believe in them. She shook them off and mapped the scene in her mind.

The synagogue was a two-story, rust-colored building flanked by blazing red azalea bushes over five feet tall and wide. It was adorned with only a Jewish star carved in stone over two sets of wide dark-wood doors. Down a short slope to the left, a parking lot was filled with enough prime product to make a used-car dealer a rich man. The street side of the lot was fronted by a four-foot evergreen fence, possibly to afford some shelter to the fortune sitting there. Behind the hedge, a number of valets in red jackets were smoking in a clump, not fetching cars for the women and children waiting for them.

April broke into a run when she heard snippets of angry conversation from the other side of the hedge. "Terrorists." "Israel." "Poor girl." The name "Tovah" and "car bomb."

Then she saw Mike. He was on the sidewalk in a

crowd far left of the building. His head was bent toward a precinct commander April had seen around but whose name she didn't know, two other high-ranking uniformed brass whose faces she also recognized, half a dozen stout men in tuxedos, and a small man in a black clerical gown with a blood-besmirched shawl around his shoulders. Her sunny suit caught Mike's eye, and he waved her over.

"Sergeant Woo, this is Rabbi Levi, Mr. Schoenfeld, the bride's grandfather, Mr. Schoenfeld, the bride's uncle. Mr. Ribikoff, the groom's father."

April nodded and murmured "Sir" after each of their names. Her face was neutral, but her head pounded with the shock of personal bad luck. To have a wedding case just when her almost-sister Ching was getting married was not good, not good at all. An irrational, uncoplike fear clutched her.

The rabbi's voice chilled her further. "I want every car on the street checked for explosives. Get your dogs, your Geiger counters, I don't care what. And the cars in the lot. Every one. I don't want a single one of my people getting into a car that hasn't been tested for a bomb."

My people! Oh, here we go. Already the lines were being drawn. That always ruffled feathers.

Mike took April's arm and led her toward the building before Chief Avise, the stern-looking chief of detectives, had a chance to respond. "*Querida*, you made good time."

"The traffic wasn't too bad."

"You okay?" Mike's almond eyes, not so very different from April's own, caught everything. Now he struck at her anxiety with the love look that had changed her life.

When they'd first sat at adjoining desks in the Two-oh, he'd seemed a bully out for the trophy of getting her in bed when no one else she worked with could. Each time he'd brought her in on a case or horned in on one of hers, she'd thought he was trying to control her, mess with her career. She'd taken a strong position against a cop couple working together, but he'd wanted her front and center, both in his professional and private life. And Mike always got what he wanted. Despite her mother's dire predictions about ethnic incompatibility, he turned out to be her rock.

"I'm okay." She tilted her head to one side. He looked out of place there with his mustache, leather jacket, and cowboy boots, but good to her.

"Enlighten me," she said softly.

His expression didn't change, even though he knew it would affect her. "Somebody shot the bride."

"Oh." April felt the kick of the catastrophe fill her own body. To be a bride, charged with all the hope and excitement for a happy life. Every cliché April both longed for and feared herself. She didn't ask if the girl was dead. She gathered the girl was dead. What bad luck! Bad, bad luck for every spring bride in New York. She shivered for Ching and all the families who would be spooked, even though it had nothing to do with them.

"The groom?" she murmured, scanning the tearful crowd of wedding guests.

"No, he didn't do it. He was standing at the altar waiting for her."

"I meant shot." April tried breathing again.

"No, no. Two other people got hit. A twelve-year-old lost an ear. Another one took a bullet in the shoulder, both males. Looks like the shooter was only after the bride. Chief Avise told me the parents went nuts when the paramedics cut her dress open."

"She's gone?" April asked. Meaning from the scene.

"Oh, yeah. The girl arrived DOA at the hospital."

"Did both officers go with her?"

"One went with her. Two more arrived almost at the same time. They're still here."

They moved closer to the building. The tapes were already up, barring the way up the front walk, but April and Mike would have skirted the bloodstained area anyway. This was going to be a challenge for the CSU unit. A hundred and fifty people stampeded out of the building, leaving footprints of blood, and other bits of themselves behind—tears, eyelashes, finger-prints, lint, fiber, even sequins from the fancy ball gowns.

More car doors slammed. April and Mike turned to see two pairs of German shepherds with trainers arrive and get out of their cars. April knew one of them from a bomb scare at Kennedy a few years back. Actually, it had been an American carrier flying to Tel Aviv, now that she thought about it. The rabbi's wish for an examination of each and every car was coming true. This was going to take a while.

"Any leads?"

Mike shook his head. "The father insists his daughter never dated anyone else," Mike said. "So it's not a boyfriend/girlfriend thing."

"No date? Ever?" April was surprised.

"They're Orthodox. The boys and girls don't min-gle. They don't even sit together. Men and women have separate sections here. The father also said no one outside the community knew her. She never left the four corners."

"The what?"

"That's what they call their neighborhood. I thought you knew Jews."

April rolled her eyes. What she knew about Jews could fill a teacup. A Chinese teacup. "What about the parents?" she asked.

"Wealthy. Very."

"I mean, do they leave the four corners?"

"It's a very tight group. I gather they don't mix socially outside, but Schoenfeld, the bride's father, has his business in Manhattan. He claims he has no enemies. He doesn't believe his daughter could be a target. He thinks the shooting was just an attempt to get everybody running to their cars so they'd be blown up in the parking lot."

"Imaginative theory. Is that why they're all in the parking lot now?"

Mike shrugged. Everybody knew by now that terrorists didn't do two-stage operations in a single site. They always made one hit with the hope of getting as many people as possible. They wouldn't shoot one female in a large crowd and leave all the men sitting there. What sense was there in that? Also, shooting and bombing were two different activities, involving different planning, psychology, and equipment. The shooting of a bride at a wedding had to be a personal thing. Somebody wanted her, and only her, not living happily ever after. April shivered.

Since Skinny Dragon Mother had told April in no uncertain terms that she'd rather see her only child dead on her wedding day than married to a non-

Chinese, that sort of thing felt quite reasonable to her in a totally crazy kind of way.

Police were everywhere now, moving people out of the parking lot, taking down names and statements, and starting to check the cars. Forty minutes from the 911 call, the CSU pulled up in two blue-and-white station wagons, and the investigation team was in place. It was a very high-profile case.

Four

"Looks like we have all the big guns here. How ya doin', April, Mike." Captain Dan D'Amato, commander of the CSU unit, looked a lot like an actor playing a cop. Handsome guy, six feet tall, slim build. Styled hair, blue eyes that didn't miss a thing.

He strode up with Detective Vic Walters, known as the architect because he had a degree in the field and was their structure specialist. Not that any of the forty-two CSU detectives considered themselves specialists in only one area. They were evidence collectors, supposed to know everything. Some of them were accredited scientists, like Vic, who analyzed the items they found and drew the pictures for the DA and the juries. Others photographed, sketched, collected thousands of bits and pieces of paint and soil and fiber and dust and markings of all kinds, handwriting, impressions like footprints, tire marks—everything imaginable for the scientists to match.

"Dan, Vic." Mike held out his hand, and the three men shook. Vic greeted April in a similar fashion.

"Sergeant. Long time."

"Good to see you," April replied.

Handsome Dan looked her over. "Always good to

work with the best," he said curtly. "Nice outfit," he added, awarding her a quick smile.

By the time April smiled back, he was already past the small-talk stage. "What do we got?" he asked.

Mike answered. "One homicide, two injuries, and a nightmare scene. Did you know it was a wedding party?" Mike pointed at the building. "A hundred and fifty people were seated in there. The wedding march was playing. Never been any trouble here, so there was no security—" He shrugged to shake off some tension.

"How many people went in? You?" Dan interrupted before he could go on.

Mike held his hands out, palms up. "Not me. I'm just relaying the pertinent here. Girl was shot in the back. First officers on the scene went in. Chaos in there. Panic. EMS went in to work on her. A lot of people were moving around, trying to get out. . . ."

"Okay, been there, done this." He was impatient to go in and look.

"You want to take a minute to hear, or not?"

"Yeah, yeah, I'll hear."

"It's better to have the picture." Mike combed the ends of his mustache.

"Okay, I know. Go ahead, give me the picture."

"The shooter must have come in after everybody was inside. But who knows, maybe he was one of them and ducked out. The lobby is a closed space. Our guess is he stood there for some time, several minutes at least, waiting for the bride to walk down the aisle. She was late." Mike glanced at April. It was all news to her. She had nothing to add.

"As I said, he shot her just before she reached the altar. Maybe you'll get something off the doors."

Captain D'Amato nodded seriously. "Definitely. We could get lucky. Magic is coming. Vic will stay. Who knows?" Now he shrugged. They were all big shruggers.

April stood on the bottom step and let her thoughts wander over to the parking lot. Hundreds of people to interview in this case. She liked that. Somebody was going to know, and that individual who knew would tell her. Somebody always knew. A brother, a sister, a drinking buddy, a friend. There were very few killers who didn't scratch the itch to brag.

This crowd in the parking lot was a particular windfall. A hundred and fifty guests well acquainted with the bride and groom. It wasn't going to be a mystery, she assured herself. They'd nail the killer fast, and the community would heal.

April was absorbed in the bubble of her own thoughts. It was clear to her that this was no random killing, a child caught in the cross fire of a political act. More likely the shooter was someone close to the bride and her family, not a stranger. It had to be someone, unlike herself, who would fit in, not be noticeable. Someone who knew the way in and out, what moment to strike. Someone very, very close to her.

Lost in her speculations, April suddenly realized that she was staring at a woman about her age wearing a pink-and-light-blue, large flower–print dress with long sleeves, many tiny tucks in the bodice, and a skirt that fell to her ankles. Around her neck was a thick collar of gold, and her hair was as black and thick as April's. The hair looked like a lacquered helmet, hard against the soft flesh of her face and the soft colors of the dress. There was something a little perplexing about it. The hair got April's attention.

Skinny Dragon Mother was always complaining about her hair getting thinner and thinner, losing weight with the years as she was. Skinny's white scalp showed through; she hated that. Soon she would have only three, four hairs on her head, Skinny grumbled. It seemed like every week she bought more herbal medicine from a fake doctor to make her hair grow thicker.

April slowly realized the hair of the woman in the parking lot was a wig, and one that happened to be not so different from the wigs strippers wore in bare bars. A big and brassy wig. Short but wide and high, and definitely sassy. April was further astonished that this woman's wig wasn't the only one. Lots of women were wearing them. She wondered if there was some cancer epidemic among them, and they'd all had chemotherapy.

The woman's chin jutted defensively at April's scrutiny. April turned away, sorry that curiosity and surprise had shown in her face. She didn't want to be disrespectful. Forget the wigs. She had a job to do. She made a big show of searching in her purse for her notebook. She had long been in the habit of taking extensive notes. Every stage, every interview in an investigation, required reports called DD-5s. Some people found the writing a chore, but April was addicted to correctly documenting information so that later she could recover her process accurately. This was a requirement of the job, but she was even more thorough than most. She had private notebooks for her own private thoughts.

On the operative level she worked for the DA and

the court case that came down the road. Her particular investigative nightmare was not the squirmy stuff, finding the bodies, even touching them when she had to—although Chinese feared the ghosts of corpses and avoided contact with them as much possible. April's nightmare was more along the line of many months, even years later, having some defense lawyer cause her to lose face by losing the case in front of the DA and the jury. So she wrote everything down, even the tiny details of crucial first impressions that often got lost in an avalanche of information that came later when the parameters of an investigation invariably widened.

Now she wrote down her time of arrival, who and what vehicles had been on the scene. It was Sunday. What was the significance of Sunday? The daughter of restaurant workers herself, she considered not only the cops on the scene, and the guests, but also the staff. How much of a staff did this temple have? Who was here today? Maybe some individual who worked here had a grudge. She knew that Jews hired non-Jews to work on the Sabbath, turn on and off the lights, lock and unlock the doors, clean up. What about them?

Mike was still talking. "The other two injured individuals are both males. Possibly by bullets that went through the victim. This guy knew what he was doing. Hey, Ken, Artie, how ya doin'."

Detective Kenneth Souter, a short, dark-haired, broad-chested, mustached thirty-eight-year-old with an intense expression showed up with Arthur Hayle, known as Bacon because of his large size, not his views or habits. Each carried two heavy black suitcases that contained the equipment. Ken particularly

had received a lot of attention after he'd lifted a partial thumbprint from the back of a bench in Central
Park. That partial was entered in the computer bank
in Albany, and a match popped up of a guy who'd
been arrested and printed for turnstile jumping. The
print led to the arrest of the killer of four individuals
in unconnected cases. Zero tolerance for quality-of-
life crimes had led to printing everyone arrested for
anything. It worked wonders to shake real criminals
out of the trees and enraged everyone else printed for
the small stuff.

Mike finished his account. The commander and
three CSU detectives immediately donned Tyvek over-
alls that covered them from head to foot and went
into the building to evaluate the scene before a team
of two would get down to work.

The brass had finished their look-see and were
getting ready to leave. One caught Mike's eye to call
him over. A few minutes later, they were heading for
their cars, and Mike jerked his chin at April.

She moved to his side, and he touched her hand,
sending a shiver up her arm. "The rabbi has some
concerns. The chief wants you to work with him until
Poppy gets here," he said.

"Okay." April's face was unreadable, but she was
surprised. Inspector Poppy Bellaqua was commander of the Hate Crimes Unit.

Mike gazed over her shoulder. "You're on it. We'll
get organized later."

Usually April loved getting out of her Midtown
North precinct detective unit for a high-profile case,
but this one felt like a curse leveled at her. A young
bride murdered in front of her husband-to-be, her
parents, brothers and sisters, and friends. All reason

rejected a crime so cruel. She didn't want anyone she loved to be tainted by it. Superstition! She shook off the selfish reaction and obeyed the command to work with the rabbi.

"I'm Sergeant Woo. I'll be working on the case with Lieutenant Sanchez," she introduced herself a minute later.

Rabbi Levi was a small, ascetic-looking man in black robes. He did not look at her or respond.

"Anything you need, any questions you have about procedure, I'll do my best to help," she continued politely.

"Are you the liaison they were talking about?" He tilted his head as if the wind, not a person, were speaking to him.

"For now, yes. Anything you need, you can run it by me and I'll see what can be done."

At this the rabbi separated himself from the other men and gestured with a finger for April to follow at a short distance.

"I do have some issues I told the officer—I don't know your ranks. Not the precinct commander. The heavy . . . I think he was a chief." He waved his hand impatiently at his memory, letting the identification go. "Can we talk in my study?"

"No, we can't go in. Crime Scene is not finished with the building yet," April said apologetically.

"What kind of investigation is this?" he demanded.

"It's routine," she assured him.

"The killer came into the lobby, that's all. He shot through the door. I was there. Everybody was there. What routine could take the police into my study?" he asked softly.

"I don't know that they will go into your study, Rabbi Levi. It's more a question of preserving the integrity of the crime scene."

"Is that a cruel joke?"

"Sir?"

"You're telling me about integrity?"

April rephrased. "They don't want people walking there, touching things until they're finished with it."

"Everybody walked there," he said angrily.

"Yes, sir."

"Well, there is a side entrance. Can I use that?"

"As soon as they say so."

"And how long will that be? We have evening prayers. . . . The caterers want to clean up."

"The reception was here?"

"Yes, the party is always here."

Ah. Then there were caterers, too. "I understand. Is there a particular time you need to pray, and if necessary is there another place you could pray tonight? This will take several hours at least." Maybe several days. She didn't want to tell him that now.

"How many hours?"

"It's a large space. Sometimes it takes as long as five hours. Sometimes longer."

"Why so long?"

"The Crime Scene Unit is very thorough. It can make a difference later."

"What kind of difference? The harm's already been done." Then he threw up his hands in another gesture of impatient compliance and changed the subject.

"That chief told me there is no way to prevent an autopsy."

"No, it's the law with homicides."

He managed to keep his eyes focused inward. "No way to oppose it?"

"No. I'm sorry. I know how difficult it is. If it's any solace to you, the autopsy may help us find Tovah's killer. I know you want that as much as we do."

"We have our laws, too."

"I understand."

"Our laws say she must never be alone. She must be cared for by us. Her father and mother want to stay with her. Her body must not be defiled. We must have her back today. We will bury her tomorrow."

April blinked. These were impossible requests.

"And we need her gown tomorrow," he said firmly.

April didn't want to query the need for the gown and lose face by betraying her ignorance of unfamiliar customs. She pressed her lips together. The other things could be negotiated, but the gown happened to be evidence in a homicide. From the bullet holes, exact calculations could be made about the movement of the victim and the people around her when the shots were fired. The path of the bullets could determine where the shooter stood and even his height. Sometimes the prosecution even dressed a mannequin in the victim's clothes to make some point to the jury. A wedding dress would have profound emotional impact in a courtroom. They'd never get it.

"We need the gown tomorrow," Rabbi Levi insisted. "No compromises. And the veil, too."

A sudden fear that they intended to bury the poor girl in her bloody wedding dress brought April's fist to her lips. Such profound cruelty would be devastating for Tovah's ghost. No Chinese ghost would ever be coaxed into a peaceful afterlife with such a gruesome eternal reminder of her violent end.

"And we need any other items of her clothing that were stained with her blood." The rabbi punched the air with his finger to show he meant it. The rabbi's shawl was bloody. Did that count, too? April wondered.

She felt sick. She worked for the dead but had no authority to negotiate for peace in their afterlives. The Jews clearly had a different idea from the Chinese of how their dead should be treated. What could she say? Of course they would release the body as soon as they could, possibly as early as tonight if an autopsy could be done immediately. Forensic work had to be done on the dress, however. Sometimes it took weeks, and she'd have to check that with the DA's office. Items that pertained to a crime were always kept in a secure location, introduced into evidence in court, and not released until after a trial. If a suspect wasn't apprehended, they remained in custody indefinitely. She didn't know if returning any forensic evidence before trial would be possible.

"I'll see what I can do," she promised. "Is this a religious requirement?"

"Yes, absolute requirement."

"I can contact the scientists at the lab to let them know about your time constraints," she said quickly. "But this may be an issue for the DA's office."

"The girl has to be buried with everything that came out of her. We have to have all of her there. Anything else would dishonor her memory. Can I go into my study now?"

"I'll ask," April promised.

Five

Three hours later April finished talking with the five valets. She'd taken down names and counted forty-two women wearing wigs. She'd spoken to ten snuffling, wig-wearing women in some detail. All ten were convinced the tragedy was another Arab plot. When questioned a little more deeply on the subject, they denied any possibility of the family's doing business or being acquainted with any Arabs, so their reasoning about how the Schoenfelds might have been singled out for an Arab attack remained unclear. She did not feel it was appropriate to ask about the wigs.

As time passed and cars were swept for bombs, the guests from the wedding party went home. When all were finally gone, April and Mike marched up the steps to the tall front doors of the synagogue and entered the crime scene for the first time. Inside the doors, a carpeted lobby about ten feet deep spread across the width of the building. April slowly absorbed the site. A clump of dark stains on the light brown Berber carpet in front of the two middle inner doors suggested that blood from the victims had been carried out this far on people's shoes, or else the shooter had somehow cut himself.

To the left, well away from the bloodstains on the main entrance path, Ken and Vic had made a little "trash pile" of their used materials so that items they'd brought to the scene wouldn't be confused with articles that had been there before they arrived. Empty film packs, blood-testing materials, used gloves, and soda cans sat on a newspaper blanket in the corner, indicating the CSU team had finished out here.

To the right of the third pair of doors the lobby angled into a hallway like a backward L, wide enough to serve as a landing at the top of a sweeping circular staircase that wound back down to the ground floor. Mike chose these side doors near the stairs for his point of entry to the sanctuary.

"Okay to come in?" he called out.

"Who is it?" Vic Walters called, as if he didn't know.

"Sanchez and Woo," Mike said, smiling a little at April.

"You guys sound like some kind of fusion law firm. Yeah. But come around the other side and don't touch anything in my grid. I haven't done over there yet."

Close to Mike, April breathed in the signature cologne that wafted deliciously from his shirt and jacket and was distracted for a moment. The spicy scent that April's father complained was a hundred times too sweet for a man used to set April's teeth on edge. A few times she'd tried to identify it at perfume counters. The aroma that permeated Mike was a deeper brew than bay rum, complex, but not as musky as patchouli. It evoked orange-lemon-jasmine-cinnabar-scented summer beaches, sex, and coconut-fruity drinks. None of which had Mike personally experienced growing up on 234th Street in the Bronx, which happened to be only a few miles east of where they were at the moment.

"Uh-oh. This is going to be a marathon," she said.

"Looks like." He touched her arm as if she needed reminding to step around the flagged areas on the floor. She knew he just liked touching her.

Through the far left doors they entered both the least and most adorned house of worship April had ever seen. Compared to the show of fancy cars outside, this synagogue was not fancy. Like a younger version of the Lower East Side turn-of-the-century immigrant synagogues, this could not be favorably compared to the uptown temples April had seen in Manhattan. Its auditorium had plain, even dingy walls, unexceptional windows, standard wooden pews, and a raised stage. On the stage were eight armchairs covered with shabby needlepoint, a wooden altar, an ark that April knew housed their Bible (written in the Hebrew alphabet and rolled into a scroll). She'd had a case in the Fifth Precinct years ago involving the burglary of an old man who sold them, so she knew what they were. Above the ark was a Jewish star and the flickering light they called the eternal light. This much about Judaism April knew.

What had been added today for the wedding was a tentlike structure over the altar that was completely covered with real leaves and many varieties of flowers. Even the four poles that supported the canopy were twined with white lilies and the palest pink and white roses. An amazing display. For April, however, white was the color of death. A Chinese wedding might have a bride in white, but only for the ceremony and only to satisfy Western convention. Every other decoration would be in the lucky colors of red and gold. Though Mike liked to tease her with bride magazines full of white dresses, April herself secretly hoped that if the day ever came for her she would wear lucky red.

In the temple, the magnificent white flower bower alone was not so shocking. What was shocking were the signs of flight. Articles of clothes left behind, ribbon-and-cinnamon-and-white bouquets on stands knocked every which way. Lilies and roses crushed underfoot and mixed with blood. It was a pitiful sight, but probably more fragrant than any crime scene in New York history. Vic and Ken were working furiously to record it all. Strobes of light flashed as Vic meticulously set his measuring instruments and shot photo after photo to document exactly how the sanctuary had been set up and looked. His suitcase contained a number of expensive cameras and lenses for different needs, as well as a video cam, which he was not using at the moment. Ken was nowhere in sight.

"Hey, April, you want to get us some food?" Vic called out.

April let annoyance roll off her back. "How long are you going to be? The rabbi needs to clean up. The men want to pray here before sundown."

Vic lowered the camera to check his watch. "Sundown? That's about an hour from now . . . no way. Look at the size of this place. We're not half done. You know that."

"Do you have an estimate? They start prayers here at five in the morning. *That* going to be okay?" She knew that was not going to be okay either.

Big sigh. "Oh, that's nearly ten hours from now. We've never gone twelve on a case."

"We'll be long gone by then. We're not staying here all night!" Ken called out.

"Don't mind him. We're on an eighteen-hour tour. We can stay on it. If the place is in continuous use, this is going to be our only shot." Vic had a reputation for being a pain in the ass on the subject of leaving before he was satisfied he had everything he could possibly get from a scene.

"A lot of physics to work out here, and physics takes time. How about some of that food downstairs? Can you arrange that?" Vic was back on the food.

April shook her head. They always wanted the females on the job to play mother. She outranked him and wasn't buying into it. Not that she was paranoid, or a stickler. She pointed at the froth of white stuffed under a pew down the center aisle, then caught her breath. It was a long swath of veil, glinting diamonds and pearls in the soft light. The wedding veil.

"Got anything interesting so far?" Mike asked.

"You won't believe this. I lifted a left ear print from the door out there." It was Ken's excited voice.

"An ear? Who do you think you're kidding?" April scoffed, still a little put off by the food request. Not that she was paranoid about it. Uh-uh. She trotted down the aisle to find him, saw his white-covered knees and shoes, and stood up again.

"Don't laugh. We're talking *ear print*. We're talking *second* ear print in history. I lifted it with superglue fumes."

"What's it good for?" April couldn't help teasing a little.

"You don't get it, do you?"

"Yes, we get it; you lifted an ear," Mike said, laughing with her.

"Okay, hotshots, how many body parts are absolutely unique?"

Mike didn't want to play. He took a little tour of the space, careful where he stepped and keeping his hands to himself.

"Okay, April, you don't know this; you should."

April answered. "Fine, I'll bite. Teeth." She counted one. "Fingerprints, footprints. DNA. That's four. What is this, anyway, school?"

"That's not all. What else?"

"Totally unique?" April glanced at Mike, now half an auditorium away. "Eyes?" she guessed.

Ken's voice thundered back. "Retina, yeah, that's five. What else?"

"Okay—ear, I got it. Ear." April thought about it. Okay, she'd concede. If they had the ear of a guy, they had something. She perked up a little. They had an ear. Great.

"And lips. I'll give you five of the seven. You didn't get ear and lips. That's a C in my book. You should do some forensic work."

"Lips. You can always change your lips with a little collagen. You don't happen to have a lip print, too?"

"You got a fucking C, Sarge. Don't make fun."

"Hey, watch the language around the lady," Mike said. Always the gentleman.

"You want an educated guess? Here's what we're thinking. The shooter has his head pressed against the door. He doesn't want to open the door even a crack until the victim is walking down the aisle, all eyes on her. The outside doors are closed. Maybe he's assembling his rifle."

Vic snapped more shots.

"You have something on the weapon?" Mike asked.

"Uh-huh," Ken said. "There was a discharged shell casing on the floor under where I lifted the ear print. It must have rolled back against the door, and he missed it when he picked up the others." His voice was cautiously optimistic. "Maybe we'll get a print from the casing. We got a couple dozen prints and partials from that door alone. Couple of partial palm prints. We're doing the whole damn place. It's a nightmare, but it may pay off later if the guy was ever in here."

Ken was wedged into the narrow space between two pews, about three-quarters of the way down the middle aisle. On his knees with his head down, he was carefully digging at a hole in the blood-spattered wood in front of him.

"Got it," he said suddenly. Clumsy in the tight space, he wiggled his bulk to his feet and displayed his trophy on the end of calipers, viewing it with his flashlight before bagging it in a paper bag and labeling it with all the appropriate numbers.

"Might be a hollow-point, and looks like there's something in it," he reported. "I hope it's not just a splinter of wood. Right here, I picked up a piece of the second victim's ear." He pointed, sniffed, took off his gloves, threw them aside, wiped his nose, donned a new pair of gloves.

April swallowed uneasily, thinking about the piece of ear, the ear print. What was this, an ear case?

Nothing to a Chinese was without some cosmic significance.

"Any idea how many shots were fired?" Vic slid across a row of pews to peer into the bag at the hollow in the crushed piece of lead. "Looks like fiber to me. Hmmm."

"We asked the witnesses what they heard. Not even the pop of a silencer. They said it was like a movie. The music was playing; the bride fell down," Mike said, taking his turn to look at what was left of the crushed bullet.

"You know, I'm wondering if there were two shooters." Vic returned to his photographing.

"How do you figure that?"

"The first shot hit her in the back. But another one hit her in the side of the face."

"She must have twisted as she fell. . . ." April murmured.

"Twisted *toward* the first shot, not away? Uh-uh."

April shrugged. They'd have to figure the path of shots from the dress and body. But none of them had seen the body. Until they saw Tovah's injuries for themselves, everything was speculation. The physics of the thing reminded her of the rabbi's asking for the return of the wedding gown tomorrow. This made her nervous. Everything had to be measured and reconstructed. These things took time. Vic worked with strings of different lengths to map the projectiles of the bullets.

No, no, the shots couldn't have come from two sources, she thought. More than three people would have been hit. Odds were it was one shooter. If they were lucky, he'd bled, or left some DNA somewhere.

Who knew if an ear print would be admissible evidence in court. She'd have to ask the DA.

She shook her head at the bad luck of a Yankees game. None of the five valets who'd parked the cars had seen anyone come out of the building before the screaming started. They had been listening to a baseball game, drinking sodas, and smoking under the beach umbrella set up for them. They'd not been aware of anything wrong until people started screaming and running out.

"Do you think the perp could have joined the crowd?" Mike echoed April's thought.

"What are the odds of that?"

"Why not? He could have stashed the gun and run down the stairs," Ken said.

Vic put down the camera and scanned the ceiling.

"What?" April asked.

"I don't know. Seems pretty clear to me the shots came from the lobby. We have the one bullet here. I got one from the pillar over there. Three people were hit. You don't know how many he got with each shot. Always look up," he murmured.

"You going to need a ladder?" April asked.

"Yeah, I'm going to need a ladder."

And this was going to take all night, she thought.

She left the three men talking and returned to the lobby to contemplate the door where the shooter might have left his signature ear. Ken had used tape and fumes, not powder, to lift the ear and many fingerprints from the door. There was nothing to see on it now.

She went down the winding stairs, scrutinizing the steps for blood or evidence. She didn't see anything big enough to catch her attention on the carpet, but Vic would no doubt comb it for fibers. A piece of gum was stuck under the banister. She didn't touch it. At the bottom of the stairs, she caught her breath at a sudden display of wealth. Palm trees and fruit trees with real oranges on them marked the passage from the ho-hum to the extraordinary.

Not broken down yet because the caterers had not been allowed back inside, the party room still had its fifteen tables set with lace tablecloths, silver flatware and silver goblets, crystal glasses, floral arrangements so striking in their appearance it was impossible to imagine anyone thinking them up. *Tovah and Schmuel* was printed on white ribbons that wrapped the party favors. Blue Tiffany boxes were on the plates in front of many seats. Dishes full of candies were scattered around. On one of the many stations where food had been set out, a large ice sculpture of a bridal couple was slowly melting.

Sad, very sad. A few minutes later, April found the dressing room with the gowns hanging on a rolling coatrack, the table scattered with some hairpins, a comb and brush, containers of makeup, a mirror, and other odds and ends, including a honey blond wig on a white Styrofoam head. The head was labeled *Tovah Ribikoff*. Another wig. April caught her breath.

Six

At eight-thirty April was on the road, heading back to Queens. At this hour the ground was in total darkness, the sky was her favorite deep blue, still backlit just a little by the dying sun, and the traffic wasn't too bad going south. Her mood was queasy, queasy. Mike was attending the autopsy without her. She didn't want to admit that she was glad. She had these groceries to take home. Then she was meeting Mike at his place. She felt unsettled. With Ching's wedding coming up, her family would be upset about the murder. Every bride in New York would be.

Her cell phone rang. With one hand on the wheel she fumbled around in her annoying purse that just couldn't stay organized with its numerous pairs of rubber gloves, her private notebooks and the Department-issue notebooks called Rosarios, her all-important address book, powder, lipstick, blush, hand cream, tissues, pens, .38 Chief's Special. Ah, right at the bottom she found the precious StarTAC. She flipped it open on the fourth ring.

"Sergeant Woo," she said, hoping it was Mike even though they'd parted only a few minutes ago.

"Hi, it's Ching. What's up?"

"Ching, how are you?" April said cautiously.

"You sound weird. Where are you?" Ching demanded.

"Oh, on the road."

"Working?"

"Yeah. What's going on?"

"Just wondering how it went with Gao. Am I a brilliant genius or what?"

April didn't answer. She knew Ching was a brilliant genius, but not why in this instance. She sighed as her lane suddenly slowed nearly to a stop.

"April, you *did* have lunch with Gao Wan, didn't you?" came the perky, happy voice of the one person in the world she didn't want to alarm right now.

"Oh, yeah. Sorry, it's been a long day." Seemed like a month.

"Nice guy, huh?" Ching prompted.

"Very nice," April said. Neutral.

"You don't have to do anything for him. I was just thinking he might be useful to you."

April sighed again. How could the off-the-boat be useful to her? People had such funny ideas. "I'm sorry, Ching. It's been one of those days."

"Oh, God. Don't make me feel guilty. I thought you were on your day off."

"I was, but something came up."

"A murder like the Wendy's?" Ching said, a little breathless now because the cop stuff always scared her to death. "The Wendy's" was a seven-person homicide and the worst case April had ever seen.

"No! No, no, nothing like that," she said hastily.

"What, then?"

"Nothing to worry about. Just a police matter." The lane opened up, and she hit the gas.

"You all right?" Ching sounded worried.

"Yes, of course. Talk to me. I'm sorry about Gao."

April hit a dead zone and the connection broke. Nothing came out of her phone but a reminder of a phantom ear print. She tossed the phone back in her bag, vowing to call Ching back when she got home.

Then she was back on ears, reviewing what she knew about prints. Not a whole lot. Skin on the hands and soles of the feet had their distinctive swirls and ridges but no oil glands, which meant the telltale marks often invisible to the naked eye that were left behind on certain, but not all, surfaces by "sweaty" palms and fingers were in fact 98.5 to 99.5 percent secreted water. The thing was, not everybody secreted equally. Some people didn't secrete enough moisture to leave prints, and cold hands didn't secrete either. April pondered the issue of secreting ears. Ken had fumed the moisture from this ear almost from the air itself. Impressive, but hardly conclusive.

The ear in question turned out to be located at such a low height, less than five feet, that Ken had to admit in the end that it might have come from a child, hiding out from the service. Or alternatively, the shooter was a young boy, or a girl. This was another idea that reason resisted. Yet April knew well enough that kids could kill. Or the shooter could have been hunched down, crouched, even kneeling. He said it was a very attractive ear, pretty as a seashell.

At ten to nine she pulled up in front of her personal albatross, the Woo family house in Astoria, Queens. Two stories high and red brick, it was a cookie-cutter copy of the five best, but all distinctly modest, houses on the block. Her rooms were on the second floor. The living room faced a small backyard where the tiny French poodle called Dim Sum ran around and did her business. April's small bedroom, large enough for a chair, a bureau, and a single bed, faced the street. Separating the two rooms was a tiny kitchen where she never cooked. Her full bathroom was well stocked with flowery bath-and-body products.

From the outside the only notable feature of the house was a bit of decoration over the windows that had been installed by the previous owners. Shaped like the NBC logo, the "awnings" were useless. They provided no shade against the southern exposure of the morning sun and caught rain with all the noise of a tin roof in the tropics. The fans were purely for show, as was April's signature on the mortgage, since she had debt but no title to the property.

Every time she looked at it, she was reminded that at the time of purchase she had not been included in the selection or the location of the house. She hadn't even known the transaction was in the works until she was pressured into the double bondage of using her savings for the down payment and assuming the mortgage so that her parents would be secure in their old age. At just twenty-one and new in the cops, she'd assumed a thirty-year debt. Nearly ten years later, she'd learned a lot. She'd discovered that many grown children could say no to their parents in bigger ways than choosing a career they didn't like. But somehow she wasn't turning out to be one of them. She'd fallen in love with Mike, but was afraid to tell him about the debt hanging over her head. Even worse, she was afraid of her mother's curse should she marry him. Her fears and her family loyalty made her ten thousand times a jerk, for no one was happy with her lack of decisive action. Her least of all.

With these thoughts in her head again, she slowed the car. The pathway of small red-for-luck azalea bushes that her father had planted on each side of the walk two years ago hadn't bloomed the year of their planting. Four days ago when April had last seen them, they'd still been covered with buds. Now they were finally, spectacularly in flower and every bit as delightful as he had predicted. Sighing, she parked in her usual space in front of the house and killed the engine.

Skinny Dragon Mother, who must have been waiting for her by the window, came running out before she'd opened the car door.

"Ayeeai, ayeeai! You so late," she screamed. "Nothing for dinner." Skinny was wearing one of her mismatched outfits. Plaid pants, flowered shirt, knitted vest, all of different colors, as if she'd picked them up willy-nilly from a Goodwill pile at a disaster site.

Chinese people could be very noisy, or very quiet. Either way could be trouble. Tonight was noisy. "Where you been?" the dragon screamed.

"Hi, Ma," April said, trying to think of a story that would not spook her.

"You said five o'clock. Now nine o'clock." Sai Yuan Woo ran toward the car, sniffing at her daughter as if she were a dog that had gotten into the garbage.

"I'm really sorry, Ma. Something came up."

"Today day off," Skinny grumbled.

"I know." April opened the back doors and started

gathering the plastic bags of staples she'd been careful to purchase before her meeting with Gao, just in case she didn't feel like it later. Lucky it hadn't been too hot a day and she hadn't bought a squirming fish that her mother would definitely reject now. Everything else looked okay.

"*Bu hao*. Murder every day." Skinny correctly intuited murder even though April had not touched the corpse.

"I know, Ma." How many times could she say she was sorry? One time for every leaf in all the trees in the neighborhood. One time for every star in the sky. Ten billion times, more than the national debt, would not be enough.

"Look what I got you, Ma. Fresh litchis, baby bok choy."

"Murder more important than sick old mother?"

"No, Ma. You're the most important thing in the whole world." April crossed her fingers.

Skinny scoffed at the bags stuffed with two pounds of adorable baby bok choy only two inches long, and the fat bean sprouts, better even than the ones from Chinatown. Enough to eat for a week and still make the pickled vegetables she loved.

"If you so important, how come not on TV?"

There was no way to win with Skinny. If she was on TV, her mother thought she looked bad. Which always was true. April trotted an armful of groceries into the house. In the kitchen she found her father sitting at the chipped linoleum table she kept trying to replace. By Ja Fa Woo's side was the ubiquitous bottle of Rémy Martin cognac that had replaced his former choice of Johnnie Walker Black Label. He was reading one of the four Chinese newspapers with opposing political views that came out every day. He was smoking a cigarette. A Chinese program was playing on cable TV. He was enjoying his day off with the poodle on his lap.

April's father was maybe five feet tall on a good day and had absolutely no flesh on his bones. Despite his profession as a chef, Ja Fa Woo was a walking skeleton, and he was bald except for a few stray hairs scattered over the top of his head. He wore glasses with big black frames and had a wide, toothy grin that revealed two bicuspids of twenty-two-carat Hong Kong gold. Although they were not the worst of her father's collection of features and characteristics, those gold teeth embarrassed April mightily at promotions and on other ceremonial occasions when police brass were present.

When she came into the kitchen, both the dog and her father came to life. The dog barked and Ja Fa Woo jumped up to give his only child what passed for a hug. He was a little drunk, but not so bad that he staggered. The ashtray was full of butts. She worried that he drank too much and was rotting his liver, that he'd fall down one night in the subway, that he'd get lung cancer from smoking all those cigarettes. All of the above.

"Beautiful girl," he said, lighting up now. "What want for dinner?"

With both Mother and Father Woo standing there so hopeful they'd have her at least for the night, she was at a complete loss for the right words to tell them she loved them a lot, really. But something had come up, and she had to leave.

Seven

On Monday at six-ten, when the cloudless sky outside his twenty-second-floor Forest Hills apartment was already brightly heralding the new day, Lieutenant Mike Sanchez was awakened by a throbbing erection. In his dream his body was pressed against April's. She was wearing a bikini, not much of one, yellow like her pantsuit. They were lying together, baking in the heat of a Mexican beach. Maybe a Caribbean beach. Hawaiian. Somewhere far away. He was caressing her flat tummy, the bare skin on her neck, her shoulders, her arms. Hugging her tight. Kissing her. April's skin was so smooth that he never got tired of stroking and admiring it. Smoother than any skin he'd ever felt before, and he'd felt plenty.

"Alpha hydroxy is the secret," she told him.

"Ha-ha." The very idea broke him up every time.

His mother, Maria Sanchez, complained that *la china* was too skinny and didn't eat enough (wasn't a Catholic), but her body was all roundness and generosity to Mike. Although she was not Catholic, April's spirit was just right, too. She was gutsy and tough, but not hard. How could he explain it to his mother, his priest? April's virtue came from doing right, not from fear of hell. Totally unusual where he came from.

Another difference was that her emotions didn't erupt when she was angry. She didn't get loud and hysterical like the other girls he'd known. She didn't try to eat him up from the inside or own him. How could he explain it? Oh, he throbbed with longing. April aroused so much feeling in him that he wanted to merge with her, be so completely together that their thoughts and bodies became one. This passion for her made him crazy because she would not marry him. And marriage was on his mind, on his mother's mind.

Mike knew his feelings for his lover, the woman he wanted as his wife, were both nuts and not nuts at all. Nuts because they were so intense, beyond anything he'd felt for anyone in his life. And not nuts because every day he was handed death on a platter. And every day his mother nagged at him to get married.

"Almost thirty-seven, *un adulto, casate, dame niños*," Maria Sanchez complained. *Give me some babies!*

But the only babies Mike saw were dead newborns stuffed in garbage cans. Young children burned to death in fires. Girls of all ages raped and strangled. College students mugged and drowned in the rivers. Almost every day some loon dreamed up an unimaginable horror to perpetrate on innocent humans. The World Trade Towers. How could a person absorb such horror? Mike often wondered how God could let such terrible things happen.

And he worried that he could never have a good life when this life he led of death every day destroyed so many marriages, including his own. His first wife had left him many years ago, then died of leukemia in Mexico. Mike was beginning to think April would never marry him and save him from that terrible failure.

But in his dream, he and April had escaped. They'd jumped all the hurdles. The snipers had missed them at their own wedding, and finally they were on the honeymoon seashore, set for life. He was breathing the tea rose smell of her, licking piña colada from her lips, and she was murmuring in his ear, urging him to hurry up . . . hurry up and come inside her. Oh, he was throbbing.

"*Querida*," he moaned.

"Hurry up, lover boy. It's your turn in the bathroom." It was April's voice, but not in any dream.

He smelled coffee, opened his eyes, realized that he was hugging a pillow. And she was standing with a cup in her hand, laughing at him. He reached out to grab her.

"*Chico*. Time to get up!"

"Uh-uh." He didn't want to come back from heaven. He rolled over, turning his back on her.

"Fine." She walked around the bed, then put the mug down beside his nose.

He muttered, grumbled. Bleary-eyed and deflating quickly, he sat up. As in his dream he was naked. But unlike his dream, he was not married, and not on a beach. He was in his queen-size bed, twisted up in the blue sheets that April had bought and he liked so much. The sun was orange in the sky, and all the tragic events of yesterday crashed back on him in a single arid breaker. "*Que hora?*" he asked.

"Six-fifteen."

"Mierda." He peered at her through a haze of sleep and groaned again. April was already dressed. She was wearing a light cotton wrap skirt, navy blue, and over it a slightly brighter blue jacket, smartly tailored, but loose enough to conceal the 9mm Glock she wore holstered at her waist. The jacket wasn't buttoned now. Her blouse was white. She was a very traditional girl, wearing a brand-new outfit for the first time. The skirt was not too long, not too short. Her face was fresh; her hair was newly blow-dried. She looked good. The woman he loved was a beauty. *Cómo no?*

Peering down at him, she refrained from scolding. He always had more trouble getting up in the morning than she did. This morning he looked so wasted that she took pity on him. She sat on the bed and began to rub the stiffness out of his neck and shoulders.

"Ohhh. Ohhh. Nice." He let his head roll around in her hands for about two seconds. Then, since she was now close enough to grab, he tried kissing her to get her to lie down again. This was not so easy to accomplish with an expert in karate who also wore a gun.

"Stop it and tell me about last night."

End of neck rubbing. End of nice sitting on the bed. She was back on her feet, fussing with the duvet and pillows that had fallen on the floor.

"We had a nice party, you and I. Come back."

"Too late." She threw a pillow at his head, then another, tidying up for the day.

He sighed and reached for the coffee, secretly pleased. She'd made coffee just the way he liked it, thick and sweet. He swallowed gratefully. "Angel from heaven, when are we getting married?"

"I had a dream about that girl last night," April said, pulling up the sheet to cover his lap. Modesty.

He laughed. "Was the dream a special message for you, *querida*?" As his dream had been for him.

"Probably. Why didn't you want to talk about it last night when you got home?" she accused.

"Where did you learn to make such good coffee, *querida*?" He couldn't help changing the subject, wanting the credit for having taught her himself. The case could wait three seconds, just three.

"I worried all night. You got home late, wouldn't talk." The sound of her complaining like her mother was enough to make him laugh some more. She wouldn't let up.

"Thank you for the coffee," he said.

April dipped her head in acknowledgment. She didn't drink coffee in the morning. Hot water with lemon. Or just hot water. He was grateful for her making the effort for him and gave up a little information.

"Tovah Schoenfeld had a malformation in her brain. That was about it." The autopsy on the young bride had given Mike a squirmy feeling.

Before Dr. Gloss, the ME, peeled back Tovah's scalp and sawed off the top half of her skull as if it were nothing more than the cap of a boiled egg, the girl had been lovely, a real stunner. It had been creepy to discover that had she lived, she might have died prematurely anyway.

"Really, what kind of malformation?" April asked.

"A little thing, like an aneurysm. It could have popped at any time. Weird, huh?"

"But that wasn't the COD?" April sat on the bed again and took his hand because she could see that he felt as bad as she did. Shit, a bride! This case was personally upsetting to both of them.

Mike shook his head. "You know how Gloss likes coming up with the special touches. He thought the brain thing was an interesting anomaly, since it might have caused her a problem at a later date. She'd had her appendix out. She wasn't pregnant." He swallowed the last of the coffee. "She was still a virgin. That's about it."

He gave her hand a last squeeze, then reached for his watch on the table and snapped it on his wrist. His three seconds of normal life were over. Now he was charged. His business was to catch a killer. It was his primary focus, and he was ready to go.

"That's one theory out the window." April took the empty cup to the kitchen.

"Boyfriend/girlfriend? Well, maybe."

"Would a spurned lover kill a virgin?"

"Maybe," Mike said again, disappearing into the bathroom.

"How many hits? What about the gun?" April fired questions at him through the door.

"I'll tell you in the car," he called out.

He stood under the hot water in the shower, scrubbing with the rough green seaweed soap April said purified his skin and increased his *qi*. He didn't know what his *qi* was. He suspected it was one of those things he had enough of already. In any case, he didn't think it was stimulated by laceration. He preferred soothing sensations, so he finished up quickly, jumped out, shaved, trimmed the ends of his lush mustache, and doused himself in aftershave. Then he put his clothes on in a hurry because April always complained it took him longer than a girl to choose his outfits. He changed his tie only three times, preoccupied by plans for the investigation. He was determined to clear this awful case in a day, two at the most.

Eight

Wendy Lotte's phone started ringing off the hook before seven. The phone was so persistent it felt as if the whole world was out to get her, not just a client this time. She pulled her beautiful duvet over her head and lay in bed, sniffing the stale scent of fear that emanated from all the pores in her body. Seven rings, then silence when voice messaging picked up. Then it started again. Wendy was frightened. Who else could it be but that detective again? This might be her busy season, but please. No one called this early.

She knew enough about cops to be afraid. She didn't want to go through another ordeal. Her life was good now. She'd stayed out of trouble all these years. But yesterday she almost lost it when the detective with the mustache started pushing her around. The bastard wouldn't let her leave, wouldn't believe her story and let her just go home, even though she was a pro at lying. He even searched her *car*. It freaked her out.

All night in a seriously inebriated state Wendy worried about the questions people would ask today. She worried about having to attend the funeral. Just the thought of a second funeral in less than a year

made her puke. She puked a lot during the night and
didn't sleep at all. Hanging over the cool porcelain
bowl in her bathroom, she agonized over her past
and future and gagged in equal proportions.

This morning she was so dizzy she couldn't get
up. She writhed under the covers, trying to calm
down and overcome the worst hangover she'd had
since high school. She'd dreamed this exact thing so
many times. Only weeks from the big four-oh, she
was the only person in the world who wasn't being
celebrated, wasn't getting a party, wasn't married
with children.

How many brides had she married over the years?
A generation of them. Literally hundreds of times
she'd worked through every single reception thing:
from the lists, to the invitations, to the gowns, to the
organization of registries in the appropriate stores,
the categorizing of gifts when they arrived, the
thank-you notes. The prewedding dinners, often
with their impossible blending of bride-and-groom
ill-fitting families. The tantrums over flowers and
ballrooms and bands. The bridesmaids who got so
drunk they couldn't stand up (and worse). The seating plans, the timing of everything so it all went off
each time just like a NASA space shot. Now she was
doing the sweet sixteens and the debutante parties
for the children of couples whose weddings she'd
worked on twenty years ago. Some of them were on
their second marriages. From sea to shining sea
Wendy had walked in brides' shoes through every
single phase of it. Every phase but one. She was almost forty years old and she hadn't pulled it off
herself.

Practically all her life she'd dreamed of being a

bride—the center of attention—feted and endured in all her demands and jitters. A big diamond sparkling on her finger. She'd dreamed every detail, the dress, the room, the flowers. Other girls found men—or their mothers found them—why not her? Sometimes, when she had to smile for hours and hours at other girls' weddings, it was so painful that her face felt like a pinched nerve.

Tovah Schoenfeld's death was a cautionary tale in a way, because she didn't deserve to be a wife. She didn't want to be a wife. The marriage would have been a flop, another fake. Wendy was sorry about the resulting chaos, though. The last thing she needed was to be questioned, to attend the funeral, to have her name in the newspapers.

Wendy had a firm rule: She never drank on the job. Never! A bottle of leftover celebratory Veuve Clicquot *might* find its way into her large carryall after an event and she *might* sip it slowly at home. But last night after police had checked her bag for the gun that had murdered poor Tovah, she'd been so upset that she'd slipped back into the party room and taken two bottles. Two were all she'd been able to rescue. No gifts had been on display, and she didn't want the trinkets in the little Tiffany boxes. There had been nothing else to rescue. It turned out that the Schoenfelds, who looked as if they were throwing money all over the place, were actually careful to the extreme about getting ripped off. The expensive gifts had always been elsewhere.

The phone rang seven times and was silent, seven times and was silent. Wendy's selfish assistant, Lori, had taken a vacation so there was no one to answer the phones and be her buffer against the world.

Wendy hated having no cover. Now she had to do a second event by herself. It wasn't fair. Reluctantly, she turned her thoughts to the wedding of Prudence Hay, who happened to be another undeserving, spoiled brat with a mother who doted on her. Wendy had no choice but to get a move on. With an aching head, she dragged herself out of bed, put Tovah behind her and Prudence to the fore.

Nine

The Long Island Expressway was already jammed by the time Mike and April hit the road at seven.

"You mind telling me where we're going?" April asked.

"One PP."

"Oh, yeah. I thought we were going to the Bronx."

"We're meeting Inspector Bellaqua first. Know her?"

"Not personally," April said.

"Good woman."

Satisfied for the moment, April pulled out her cell phone and called into Midtown North to get her messages. Then she roused her boss, Lieutenant Iriarte, on his cell while he was on the road driving in from his home in Westchester. He yelled at her for about ten minutes.

"Trouble?" Mike asked as soon as she finished the call.

"The usual bullshit." She dialed Woody Baum, her protégé and sometime driver, and talked to him for a while. When she finished that call she was quiet.

"*Querida,* you okay?" Mike asked after a minute or two.

Her response was a Chinese silence he didn't try to decipher. He took the Midtown Tunnel, then the

FDR down to the bridge exit. The traffic wasn't too bad. At eight-oh-nine, he flashed his gold at the patrol officer guarding the triangle around headquarters. The uniform waved them through the many barriers into the fortress of One Police Plaza, otherwise known as the puzzle palace. A number of department vehicles, black Crown Victorias, blue-and-white cruisers, and vans were parked inside the triangle. There was no place for Mike's ancient Camaro. At the ramp leading down to the garage in the building, he flashed his shield again, then drove in and found a parking place far from the elevators. From the garage they went straight up on a slow elevator that filled on the way. Mike said hello to a few people with whom he'd worked over the years, but he and April stood well apart and didn't speak to each other.

Everybody knew the elevators had ears, and theirs was a situation ripe for gossip. On the eleventh floor they got off and turned right. The Hate Crimes Unit was on the southwest corridor, last door on the left. *Bias Unit* read the outdated sign on the frosted glass–topped door. Mike went in first.

The area was set up just like dozens of other special units in the building. The main room was an open space crammed with desks and computers, filing cabinets, a few narrow lockers. On the far end a bank of windows faced downtown, where the sun was streaking in from Long Island. Narrow pathways between islands of four pushed-together desks barely allowed navigation through the room. Mike followed the path to the inspector's office. Bellaqua had a corner office with windows on two sides, a bookcase, an attractive desk, a small circular conference table, all the accouterments of a modern business executive. She was on the phone. As soon as she saw Mike, she finished up and waved him in.

"Hey, Mike. Right on time," she said. "Some night last night, huh?"

"Yes, it was. Inspector, this is Sergeant April Woo from Midtown North." Mike turned to April, who was right behind him.

"My old precinct. I've heard about you, April. Is Iriarte still in command over there?" Inspector Bellaqua was one of the higher-ranking women in the Department. She was about April's height, with a fuller, womanly figure and a round, youthful face. Dark hair, sharp eyes. Fresh lipstick, well applied and not too red. She regarded April with interest.

"Yes, ma'am." April responded with a no-frills answer. She always took things real slow with new people.

"Let's see, Arturo took over from me, what, four years ago?" Bellaqua mused.

"More." Mike jerked up his chin with a little smile. "The place was never the same after you left."

"Thanks." Bellaqua went on reminiscing, "That's right, almost four and a half now. We had some good times, busy place. How are you doin' over there, April?" The inspector gave April a long, speculative look, trying to read her.

"Good," April replied, flat as a pancake.

"It's a good command. You want some coffee, doughnuts?" Unperturbed, Bellaqua moved right on.

Hospitality at NYPD meant offering the official food of the department any time of day. Twenty-four/seven, doughnuts were highly acceptable.

"I sent out for a box. What kind do you like?" she asked.

"Thanks, we like them all," Mike said.

"Coffee?"

"Sure, that would be great," Mike said.

"Take a seat, please." The inspector rose. She was wearing a black pantsuit. She'd been up all night with the Schoenfeld family, but didn't look sleep-deprived. As she left the room, April assessed her back.

"Good woman. You should have seen her working with those people last night. A real inspiration." Mike took a seat on a new-looking chair in front of the desk.

"Good, we need some inspiration," April murmured.

When the inspector returned, her expression had changed. She was through with nice. Now came management. The Detective Bureau consisted of more than six thousand people working in precincts and special units all over the city, also in the puzzle palace of headquarters. In big cases like this detectives were pulled in from different units to work together, often displacing the precinct detectives on whose turf the crime occurred. The rivalry between precinct detectives and special-units detectives was well known. Everybody jockeyed to keep important information in his own court, to be the one to break the case and get the credit for himself and his own unit.

"Tovah Schoenfeld's body was released early this morning. Mike, you know this. I've never seen a victim move through the system so fast." Bellaqua put her index finger against her cheek and tapped. "I'm telling you, it was a very emotional scene at the ME's office. You know how it can get."

"What happened?" April asked.

"The family refused to leave without the body. The family staged a sit-in. They didn't want to leave the body alone. They also tried to get the gown released to bury her in." Bellaqua shook her head.

"How did they do on that?" April asked.

"An offer of a possible forty-eight hours was made. I don't know how real that was," Mike jumped in.

"Well, Jimmy might have been able to do the ballistics work in forty-eight, but the DA's office would have taken a stand that the dress was direct evidence in the case. When it was put to them that way, the family decided not to delay the funeral. They're putting her in the ground this morning. They've requested security at the funeral," Bellaqua said. "And they're getting a lot of it. The cemetery is in Queens."

"What's the rush?" April asked.

"They're very religious. They wanted her in the ground as soon as possible." The inspector lifted a shoulder. *You know how it is.*

"So what's the muscle?"

"Money. Riverdale. Real estate. Take your pick. You don't think ultra-Orthodox when you think of the area, do you?"

April glanced at Mike. He smiled. No one had to tell Mike about Riverdale. He'd grown up there, just a block or two from the Five-oh. But he let his superior talk.

"It's always been an enclave, classy. But pretty much of a mixed neighborhood. You got your pockets of Hasidic Jews in Brooklyn, in Morningside Heights. Upstate, of course, out in Port Washington, in Queens. Riverdale's Orthodox population has been growing lately. It's upscale, quiet, and, most important for them, geographically a confined space."

Mike nodded thoughtfully, as if he'd never heard this before, as if Poppy Bellaqua, who'd worked with him on several occasions, didn't know perfectly well where he came from.

"This neighborhood is bounded by the Henry Hudson Parkway and the Hudson River, from as far south as Spuyten Duyvil and up to the Two-forties. The synagogue is up on the parkway, Independence Avenue. You were there yesterday. Yes, thank you."

A very good-looking Latina, young, with about a ton of curly black hair and a red jacket, came in carrying a loaded cardboard tray.

"Right here." Bellaqua patted a space on her desk. "Detective Linda Perez, Sergeant Woo, Lieutenant Sanchez," she did the honors.

"Nice to know you." Detective Perez put the tray down. Three coffees in blue mugs, white-lettered with *Bias Unit*, a bakery box of assorted Dunkin' Donuts. A container of milk and a pile of sugar packets, both regular and Sweet 'n Low. Napkins, white plastic spoons.

The inspector examined it quickly. "Thank you, Linda. Go ahead, take," to Mike and April.

She grabbed a mug herself, passed on the container of milk, the sugars, and the doughnuts. *Dieting*, April thought. "You got everything you need here, Mike, April?" she asked.

Mike reached for a jelly doughnut. April hesitated. Bellaqua stared at her until she selected one, then waited for them to flavor their coffees before she went on.

"Okay, so they own a lot of real estate in the area

and have become something of a political force out there." The inspector paused to swallow some black coffee, grimacing only a little.

"This is what we know so far. They're Orthodox. Tovah just celebrated her eighteenth birthday two months ago. According to the custom, this was an arranged marriage." Bellaqua paused for effect.

"Wow." April put down her half-eaten doughnut, glanced at Mike again.

"Not an everyday situation, right?" Bellaqua tapped her cheek.

"I can see how it would be a parent's dream," Mike tossed back, clearly referring to April's parents.

"Not many can pull it off these days, though. And something went very wrong here. Who knows, this may be a family thing. It may not be. We're going to have to use our common sense here, go at it several ways. Frankly, they pulled me in on this; but I don't see the profile of a hate crime. I'm sure you've talked about this between you. April, you were on the scene yesterday, any preliminary thoughts?"

"I'm not an expert on bias cases," April murmured. She was way behind the curve on this.

"Well, it may not be a bias case. We'll break it down this way. My people will take the bias angle. We'll canvass the neighborhood. Mike, you and April can start with the families and see what we can come up with there. Finish your doughnut," she directed April.

April took another bite.

Her hostess duties satisfied, Bellaqua went on. "You may want to do some research on customs and practices. But here's the general background the way I understand it. This community is real tight. They keep the boys and girls apart. Marry them young before they have a chance to fool around. They don't go for sex out of marriage. This was confirmed in the prelim report. Tovah was a virgin."

This Mike had reported. Always fast with the sex details. April took out her notebook and pen.

"So the way it works is the mothers do the matching themselves when the kids graduate high school. The girls' mothers put out the word their daughters are looking and what they're looking for. The boys' mothers show interest. Both sides have lists of potential candidates. Let me tell you, the background checks are very detailed. If a boy gets into trouble being rebellious at camp or not saying his prayers, it goes on his record that he's a delinquent and it affects his marriage prospects. Same with the girls. They're watched and gossiped about." Bellaqua did not smile. This was no joke.

"It's very serious business to them and well organized. The kids all have blood tests but don't know what's up until their mothers tell them there's somebody for them to meet. Tovah and Schmuel went through this process two months ago and became engaged almost immediately. Maybe someone was against the match." Bellaqua shrugged.

"Had they dated anyone else before they met?" April asked.

"Schmuel apparently rejected two candidates before he met Tovah. That means he went out with each one once and told his mother no. Tovah had never been out with a boy before. That's their claim."

"But surely she knew other boys from school. . . ."

"She went to a girls' school, did not go to camp." Bellaqua shrugged again. "The Schoenfelds live in a house on Alderbrook Road, very nice. I've got a background check going on them."

"Let's return to the bias question for a moment," Mike said. "Has there been any anti-Semitic activity in the area? Any property complaints?" He licked a dusting of powdered sugar off his fingers.

The inspector nodded. "Nothing stands out here. In a typical hate crime profile there would be plenty of signs, cases of property damage. Swastikas, slashed tires, broken windows, that kind of thing. Perpetrators of hate crimes use terrorist tactics to isolate people, make them afraid to go out. Have another, please." Bellaqua waved at the doughnuts.

"No, no, thanks. One was great."

"We had a case of a hit-and-run not too long ago. African-American girl was hit by a van filled with Hasidic schoolboys out in Brooklyn. At first it looked like a prejudice thing. Unfortunately, the girl died of her injuries." Bellaqua shook her head, then went on. "We investigated. Turns out the van didn't stop to help her because it was against their code of ethics to touch or have eye contact with a non–family member female. You may have heard about it. The case inspired a lot of anti-Semitic feeling. We had complaints from both sides about harassment, assault, and property damage arising from it. What we're talking about in Riverdale is not that extreme. It's an Orthodox community that doesn't mix, but is not ultra-Orthodox like the Hasidim. You'll see. Anything else?"

April thawed a little. "Thanks for breakfast."

"Oh, and you'll be working out of the Five-oh. They'll take the statements of the various vendors, caterers, etc. You'll want to work closely with them.

Follow up on everything. Could be somebody who serviced the wedding. You never know. Push it. Keep in touch. We've got to nail this guy fast."

The interview was over.

Ten

By a little after ten April and Mike were on the Major Deegan, heading up to the Bronx. Mike found his voice and was finally talking freely. He told April about the Schoenfelds' agonized vigil at the medical examiner's office during Tovah's autopsy. He described his own feelings seeing Tovah on the autopsy table in her bloody wedding gown that spilled off the metal table onto the floor. She was photographed clothed to show where the bullets had entered her body through her clothing, then naked with the bullet holes in her back. The dress had been difficult for the attendants to manage because there was so much of it. In spots the blood was still wet on the heavy silk and lace. The gown was a ruin, slashed open from neck to knee. But the small holes in the back, with a minimal amount of blood edging them, showed clearly where on her body the bullets had entered. Only from the back, it turned out. Her front and back were photographed and then the attendants removed all of her articles of clothing and bagged them. The bridal gown, white lace bra and panties, white panty hose.

Six people were in the cold room, all suited up from head to toe, all wearing respirators, nobody making small talk. April knew Mike was usually cool in autopsies no matter how frightful the condition of the corpse. She was surprised to hear him admit that this time he'd almost puked.

"A hollow-point chewed up her heart and lungs like hamburger meat," he said, then got quiet thinking about it.

Not that he and April hadn't seen these horrors many times before. Hollow-point bullets left small holes where they entered the body, and exploded on impact like bursting bombs once they got inside. Usually they lodged in their victims and didn't exit at all. Hollow-points caused the worst damage and were the bullets cops feared most from guns out on the street. For the second time April was glad she hadn't been there to see Tovah's body, as Mike described it. She didn't need any more nightmares, but neither did he. She tried to divert him.

"He must have used a light rifle, something that can easily be broken down," she suggested.

"Yeah. Maybe a nine-shot with a short barrel," Mike agreed.

"Not so easy to hide in a space like that. Anybody could have seen him at any moment."

"Maybe somebody did see him but doesn't know it."

April nodded. Sometimes you don't see what you're not expecting to see.

"If this had happened at a church, right now I'd be thinking the shooter might have been somebody wearing a liturgical robe, maybe disguised as a nun, a priest, an altar boy. That would play. But I saw only two people wearing robes, the rabbi and the cantor," Mike went on.

April remembered them. One big and fat, one small and thin.

"Or it could have been a woman. There were a lot of women in long gowns," he added.

April considered the idea of a female sniper in an evening gown shooting a bride down in a synagogue full of people. "Gee, I don't know about that." It wasn't exactly a female kind of crime.

"It could have been a man dressed as a woman. Lot of wigs there, too."

She nodded, liking that better. "There you go."

She put her face out the car window into the wind and breathed the spring air. It wasn't good that both of them were so spooked by this homicide. Maybe Mike was troubled because it occurred near his old home, a section of the Bronx that crime-wise had always been quiet. In his day it had been staunchly middle- and upper-middle-class. Now a lot of newcomers to the city lived there. The neighborhood had changed from white-collar to blue-collar. Even Mike's mother, Maria Sanchez, who'd been a newcomer herself thirty years ago, complained about the immigrants who flocked to the buildings on Broadway. But still, the Five-oh was one of the safest precincts in the city. Crime-wise, it was sleepy.

The Deegan cut through the Bronx to Westchester. Apartment buildings were rooted in the hills on the east and west sides of the highway. The older ones were ten stories high, square, unrelieved red brick, one after another laddered in the hills. The newer ones were twenty, thirty stories high, towering on the bluffs.

April turned her thoughts to the funeral. They'd go. They'd see who was there saying good-bye.

Killers frequently went to the funerals of their victims. If the funeral was at one, they'd go over to the house and talk with Tovah's family in the late afternoon, around five. She didn't relish the prospect of interviewing the family. This was going to be a long day, but what day wasn't? Mike interrupted her timing calculations.

"I think we should get married. What do you say, *querida*? How about we finally set a date?" he asked suddenly.

"Let's not compete with Ching's wedding." *Or a homicide*, she thought.

"How is that competing?" He put his foot on the gas, reacting to the evasion.

"There's just a lot going on right now, that's all." April shook her head; he'd driven right out of her comfort zone. And now he was speeding.

"There's always a lot going on," he countered.

"What's the sudden hurry, *chico*?" she said softly. *Don't push me at a bad time.*

"The hurry is, I have a bad feeling."

"About what?" Her heart spiked as he changed lanes too fast. He was definitely pissed at her. She hated that, too.

"About this bride shooting. About being together but not married. Not being married feels wrong now, like bad luck. That's it. It feels like bad luck." He turned to look at her as he said it, and his expression was fierce, showing that he really meant it.

Bad luck! April felt the kick of those two highly charged words. Right in the gut where she was most vulnerable. Only yesterday he'd been content being together on any basis. Now he was thinking it was bad luck. That hurt, because April's constant nagging worry was that worse luck would result from their marrying. So far she'd been able to avert really bad luck by nonaction. Now he was suggesting nonaction itself was dangerous.

"I think you're in a funky mood," she said.

"And I think you have a problem, April."

Oh, now she had a problem. This cold reading sent her feelings careening from hurt, to anger, to anxiety about truth and untruth and what she had to do about it. The feelings vied for supremacy. *She* had a problem! He didn't understand the complexities of her life. *He* was her problem.

She wanted to lash out at him but had to contain herself. It wouldn't be fair to make a scene in his home territory. From the second he exited the highway and crossed the overpass to Broadway he always got funny, thinking his childhood was looking him in the eye. There, the skating rink from his youth. It was now a Loehmann's. There, where it used to be the Dale movie theater, now a bank. There, the Stella D'oro factory with the air still percolating with baking anisette and almond cookies. And Pauline's was still a grungy bar down the block from the precinct. McDonald's was still next door. Stop and Shop was across Broadway. Van Cortlandt Park a few blocks down. Two hundred thirty-eighth Street, still the end of the line for the Broadway El. And his mother within hailing distance. She couldn't say a word with his mother's ghost so close by.

April simmered on low as Mike parked outside the Five-oh, not a bad house, as precincts went. The blue building was three stories high and had been built within the last twenty years. But it was far from her home base back in Manhattan.

Mike got out and stretched. *"Todo bien, querida?"* he asked, as if he didn't know perfectly well that he'd ruined her day and she couldn't do a thing about it.

"Oh, yeah, everything's just hunky." April didn't lash out. She pulled herself out of the car, smoothed the wrinkles out of her blue skirt, adjusted her gun, her jacket, her brains. And she jerked herself back into line. There was no place for private feelings in police work. Anyway, she always got butterflies in a house not her own where she didn't know the personalities and no one wanted them there. She was far from hunky right now, but what else was new?

Cool as could be after laying his cards squarely on the table, Mike clipped on his ID and headed for the detective squad. It was in the usual spot on the second floor, had the usual components of holding cell, locker room with table for eating, a TV. Six desks that were home for twelve detectives, now scrambling because they hadn't had a homicide in quite a while. Suddenly smiling broadly as a man coming home, Mike raised his hand in salute to the worried-looking sergeant on command, and the guy dipped his head in acknowledgment.

"Hey, Sanchez, look at the big shot now. A lieutenant, hogging all the good cases. How ya doin'?" Sergeant Hollis held out his hand, oozing friendship.

"Hey, shut up. Let me think here," Hollis barked at the crowd in the room. No one shut up or moved out of the way, so he had to push through them.

Hollis was a man just over forty, five-ten, medium build, thinning ginger hair, light dusting of freckles across his nose and cheeks, blue eyes, a mustache almost as lush as Mike's own. A man in a quiet house, used to an easy life. He was wearing jeans and a Mickey Mouse tie.

"Jimmy, good to see you." Mike clasped the hand and made quick introductions. "This is Sergeant April Woo. Jimmy was my boss when I came in. April worked with me in the Two-oh."

Hollis nodded. "I know. Another hotshot. I've seen your picture, both you guys. How's Dev, see much of him these days?"

"From time to time." Mike's smile turned a little chilly. His old partner was a big boozer, always got him in trouble.

"This is a bad one," Jimmy said, getting right down to the case. "We're lucky on the other injuries. You hear about the kid in the hospital?"

"Anything new?" Mike asked.

"Twelve-year-old lost his ear. Could have been worse. The other one, bullet went right through him. He was lucky."

Right through him? April thought. *Another hollow-point went through someone?* That was rare.

"Any ideas?" Mike asked.

"Not yet. Everybody in the victim's family was in front of her in plain view. So was her intended and all his family. That excludes family members. We've been in contact with the wedding planner. She has a guest list and vendor list."

April glanced at Mike. They had a wedding planner.

Hollis smiled. "This is Riverdale," he told her. "They have somebody to do everything. The wedding planner, a woman called Wendy Lotte, has all the details, knows everybody's name and everybody's story. She was there the whole time. She can fill you in on personalities. Doesn't have an alibi for the moment of the shooting. Claims she was in the ladies' room." He arched an eyebrow. "I'm still talking to her."

"Really? She a suspect?" April found the idea downright weird. It wasn't a woman's crime.

"I don't know. She gives me a creepy feeling, what can I say?" He lifted a shoulder. "Nobody else stands out."

April frowned. "Motive, background check?"

"Oh, yeah, working on both."

"Okay, what about the community, any anti-Semitic stuff going on here?" Mike's question.

"Inspector Bellaqua's been all over me about this." Hollis flipped the Mickey Mouse tie up and down. "Nothing. Believe me, we'd be on it if there were anything in it."

Mike glanced around at the crowded space and the noisy detectives all pretending to ignore them. "Where do you want to set up the charts? Let's figure out how wide we have to go on this."

"Yeah, no problem."

They were down to business.

Eleven

Anthony Pryce shot the cuffs in his summer uniform and adjusted his chauffeur's hat. He was a tall, slender Welshman, good-looking, with intelligent blue eyes and sandy hair that straggled over his collar in a London-late-Beatles-era shag. His gray uniform was just as smart as the wing collar, striped trousers, and tails that he wore when butlering in the house. He finished prepping himself for the ride to Manhattan and went down the back stairs to see to the cars. He couldn't stop thinking about that bride on the news, shot dead in the Bronx just before she took her vows. He moved through his chores, feeling an odd tingle of excitement about the possibilities such a murder presented: If someone wanted revenge on any bride in New York, now was the time to get it. It was all about knowing everything.

Anthony had worked on the Hay North Shore estate for eleven years, ever since his twenty-first birthday. And there was nothing he did not know. He was the butler, the driver, the cook when only Hays pater and mater were at home. He was the horticultural expert who directed the gardener in all his endeavors, the official head of the kitchen garden, and expert in all areas of social protocol. Along with Wendy Lotte, he was practically in charge of Prudence's wedding.

Anthony's knowledge of the family's doings extended to the secret places where in jealous rages Alfred, the toy poodle, tinkled against the priceless antiques. He knew that Lucinda Hay hid packages of forbidden foods like Twinkies and Ding Dongs along with acceptable ones in her room and nibbled between her hearty breakfast, tea, luncheon, tea, cocktails, and dinner. Mrs. Hay had once been a great beauty as well as a socialite, Anthony was proud of telling his friends. Now, alas, she had run to fat.

Anthony also knew that Terence senior was very rich and loved the bottle at least as much as his wife, and Terence junior was following in his father's footsteps, with hardly a sober moment since his junior year in boarding school, despite a sterling record at Yale and Harvard Law School. The Irish legacy. He now worked at the venerable firm of Hathaway, Harold, and Dean on Wall Street. What Anthony knew about Prudence was everything. And more than anything in the world, he hated the idea of her marrying that creep Thomas, an unexciting boiled potato of a young man, who knew nothing about her at all. And cared less. Anthony hated the idea, but it was fixed. It was done. There was nothing he could do about it. He couldn't very well marry her himself, now, could he?

In the kitchen he slowed only for a second to check on Nora, the Peruvian housekeeper. She didn't speak a word of English, but she kept going all day long like one of those bunnies in TV commercials. She liked to clean and he didn't, so from morning 'til night he had her dusting and polishing silver and the brass lamps and stair rails in the circular staircase. He had her cleaning the crystal in the three great room chandeliers and all the bowls in the bathrooms. Right now she was doing the flatware, humming happily.

"*Hasta la vista*, Nora," he said as he charged out the back door.

"*Que la vía bien*," she replied. She knew he was on his way to the city and would be back by dinnertime.

On the mud porch, Anthony checked to see if the dry cleaner had been by yet to pick up Mr. Hay's suits and the quilt from the master bedroom that needed cleaning. Pampers had been by for the pickup. He checked his watch, ten-oh-two. Getting on the road between rush hours was both an art and a science. Anthony took personally long waits in halted traffic. Even now, when he hated what the family was doing to his girl—his Pru—he still couldn't help trying to make their lives perfect.

As he sailed out the back door, he noticed that the bird feeder was empty. It was hung on clothesline rope from a large oak limb over the brick-walled service area where the five cars were parked. The birds didn't really need seed in the spring and summer, but Mrs. Hay liked to see them constantly flying in for a feed, so he was careful to make sure it was well stocked in all seasons.

Anthony chose the Bentley for the drive into the city. At exactly ten-oh-five he drove out of the service entrance of Casa Capricorn and into the drive next to it. He circled the row of magnificent Kousa dogwoods, the late-blooming kind that stayed in flower all the way into July, and stopped by the brick mansion's front door.

Minutes later, he had Pru and Mrs. Hay settled in

the car, and they were headed toward 25A and the Grand Central Parkway. Mrs. Hay spoke up from the backseat.

"Anthony, the Denihan wedding." She picked up from where she'd left off yesterday, comparing all the weddings of their large acquaintance.

"Yes, Mrs. Hay." Anthony glanced in the rearview mirror. He could see Pru blowing on her engagement ring, polishing it on her sleeve even though he'd just cleaned it for her again this morning. Three carats, classic Tiffany solitaire. He kept telling her not to take it off and leave it on every sink everywhere she washed her hands. He knew she couldn't live on her own without him to care for her. She didn't know how to do a thing.

"Louis did the Denihan wedding, of course. What did you think of it?"

He was expected to answer even though they'd been over the Denihan wedding numerous times before. "Very pretty, but half the guests were overcome," he reminded her.

In fact, St. Thomas had been so glutted with lilies that people had coughed and sneezed throughout. Not only that, Mary Denihan had not allowed a single arrangement to be moved from the church to the reception, so that Louis had to repeat the fragrance debacle at the Pierre, where people sneezed all through dinner as well. The famous florist-to-the-stars had ended up acquiring every single Casablanca lily in the city for the event. That was the kind of thing Louis's clients liked him to do. Anthony would not mention it, however, for it would only fuel the competitive fires in Lucinda Hay's ever-spreading bosom. Lucinda Hay wanted Pru married well, and she wanted an over-the-top wedding. She was getting both.

"I'm glad we didn't do lilies, aren't you, Pru?" Mrs. Hay said loftily.

"I've always hated lilies, makes me think of funerals," Pru replied, just a touch sulky. She'd always had a crush on Teddy Denihan, a far more dashing boy than lackluster Thomas Fenton.

"But you *liked* the Angels' wedding, Anthony?"

"The violets were lovely." All two thousand bunches of them, all flown in from Africa. No more need be said.

"Yes, we thought so, too," Mrs. Hay said.

Anthony knew a great deal about weddings, funerals, engagement parties, et cetera, because his services were often requested for events requiring strict attention to detail in the moving around, announcing, and making comfortable of important guests. Claire Angel, now Collins, and all her twelve bridesmaids, who'd been dressed like something out of *A Midsummer Night's Dream* with crowns of fresh violets and gowns of tulle layered over lace over an array of sorbet-colored satins, had not stopped with the four-letter words and the inelegant cursing from the moment she'd gotten engaged. Her verbiage had been a scandal.

Anthony couldn't imagine how the young gentleman could put up with her prewedding, much less the rest of his blinking life. Bad behavior in a bride was unconscionable, Anthony thought. Still, the flowers had been delightful. Louis had found wildflowers out of season, and the guests had raved.

He glanced at Pru in the mirror. She'd turned out a beauty, after all, but was now chewing savagely on the side of her thumb. Recently she'd started mangling her cuticles so badly that the skin was ripped to shreds and her fingers bled. He knew she was nervous as a cat about getting hitched forever to boring Thomas. He caught her eye and she looked quickly away.

"I don't know what's the matter with Wendy. I've called her a dozen times this morning and she just isn't picking up," she said irritably.

"Don't worry. We'll see her at the fitting." Mrs. Hay had a certain tone for talking to her daughter. A combination of soothing and wheedling that always set Pru off.

"I have concerns. I want to talk to her now!"

Pru had to be managed. Lucinda managed her.

"Now, Pru, you know we'll get through this. Right here is fine, Anthony," she told him, as if he didn't know where to stop for Tang Ling's.

Anthony did not park in front of the Tang Ling store to wait for the Hay women to emerge. Instead, he drove the Bentley down Park Avenue and around to the St. Regis Hotel. As soon as he slowed to a stop, the doorman leaned in the car's open passenger window.

"Oh, Anthony, there you are. Ready for the big day?"

"Hello, George. We're working on it." Anthony knew some of the staff at the St. Regis because Mr. Hay and Terence drank at the bar there. Over the years he'd sat in this position chatting with this and other doormen for many happy hours. "You're not going to have any problem with the cars on Saturday now, are you?" he asked.

"None at all." George was an old-timer on the post. He gave the driver a knowing smile. "Are they taking rooms here or dressing at the apartment?"

"The apartment, but we'll leave the car here during the ceremony. They'll need me there, of course. As soon as they exchange vows, I'll run up to get it. Should be about noon, maybe twelve-thirty. You mind if I leave it here now for a few?"

"No problem." George was never unhappy with the maroon Bentley at his curb.

Anthony closed the window, dropped his gloves and chauffeur's hat on the front seat. Then he got out, sniffing disdainfully at the bloomed-out spring flowers in the window boxes. He'd have to have a word with Mrs. Hay about it.

"How long will you be, then?" George asked.

Anthony checked his watch. It was eleven-nineteen. "Ten, maybe twelve minutes."

"Good-oh."

Anthony patted the car as if parting from an old friend. He walked briskly to Fifth Avenue and down the few blocks to St. Patrick's Cathedral. There, he skipped up the steps to the side door on Fifty-first Street. The door was locked, and he wondered if security had been beefed up since the attack on the cardinal during a Mass a few months ago.

"The front entrance is open," a thin priest standing nearby chatting with an old lady called out, and waved him toward Fifth.

"Thank you, Father." Anthony about-faced and marched down the block, frowning at the hordes of office workers gathered on the front steps. The sun always brought people out of the buildings all around. They came to the cathedral for special occasions and also just to have their lunch on the warm steps in an open space. Tourists were also out in droves. Anthony clicked his tongue at the sound of so many foreign languages. The crowd boded ill for Saturday. This was what happened when a choice was made for the wrong reasons.

He ducked inside the huge doors and let himself enjoy for a few seconds the lovely coolness of stone and the comfort of flickering candles. Then he was overcome again with irritation at the tourists. On Saturday there would be no abatement of them. What if they wandered in and out during the Mass, during the exchange of vows? And here the wedding party of two hundred would look small and insignificant.

If it had been Anthony's wedding, he would have chosen a smaller church where the guests could feel comfortable, not ogled at, and where it was totally private and safe. But the Hays wanted to make a splash, have the best of everything. The best groom. *Idiots.* He shook his head at the great size of the place, at the women answering questions at the information tables up front, at the TV monitors mounted on the pillars for congregants in the back pews. Anything could happen in a place like this. He shivered and lit a candle, saying a quick prayer for his own salvation.

Twelve

Ching Ma Dong took the subway to Manhattan without her mother, or her sister-cousin April, or anyone else knowing she was going there. She was full of happy secrets, excited about the chance to spend a few private moments with her old friend Tang Ling, who was giving her a wedding gown at an absolutely unheard-of price: free, for nothing. And they hadn't even been close friends for more than a decade. Why had the famous Tang Ling made such a gesture? Ching guessed it was just for old times' sake, to show off how great she'd become. As if Ching didn't know.

Tang and Ching had met when Tang was just a young woman studying economics to please her parents, but secretly cutting out patterns for fantasy dresses on her bedroom floor. Tang had wanted to be a designer. Ching was the one with the head for business. The two had drifted apart long ago—Tang into glamour, Ching into the world of the Internet. Ching had been awed by Tang's flare for self-promotion ever since.

Tang Ling had been the first Asian designer to become a household name in the special-occasion dress business. She was the first to set up shop on Madison

Avenue, the first to have a worldwide clientele. Her broad peasant face was the first female Asian seen in AmEx commercials. She was a phenom. Everybody wanted a Tang Ling dress. The gowns were slinky, spare, understated, often cut on the bias. And the rage all over the world. Born and raised in Hong Kong, educated at Stanford and FIT, Tang Ling had been in the business for fifteen years, subsidized in her ambition by a wealthy grandfather and even wealthier father. She had a reputation as the close friend of celebrities, personally creating gowns for their Oscar night, Emmy night, and Golden Globe appearances. Her photo was in *People* magazine almost as often as theirs.

When Ching got engaged, she called Tang on a lark. She was well aware that Tang traveled in limos, knew all the movie people and politicos, was out every night. But even celebrities and people in the field paid through the nose to wear her clothes. She knew that, too. Tang had always been tightfisted and socially ambitious. She was Chinese, after all.

So Ching certainly had no expectations that a long-ago friendship would yield any special attention from Tang. She wasn't even sure that Tang would remember her at all. She called to say she was getting married. She was that happy and proud of herself and just wanted to share her news. Tang's instant positive response had taken her completely by surprise. It was as if no time had passed at all.

"Tell me all about the wedding," Tang had gushed as if they were still in a college dorm and no business meetings and important people were waiting while she chattered on the phone in her office.

"It's just a simple banquet at the Crystal Palace," Ching told her shyly. "Nothing special."

"Oh, that's perfect. I love Chinatown weddings. They're my favorite. You'll have to wear one of my gowns." Tang enthused over the idea as if Ching had thousands of dollars to spend, like all the stars with whom she mingled.

"I'd love to," Ching said slowly, but she couldn't possibly afford such a luxury. Not a chance. She didn't want to get embroiled in something that would cause her embarrassment.

"Yes, yes. Come into the shop. I insist. I'm sure we can find just the right gown for you. And don't worry about a thing; we're doing inventory now."

Ching was silent, didn't know what to say. Then Tang surprised her again.

"I'm giving you one, silly," she said. "You can't refuse."

So she didn't refuse. Ching had visited the magnificent shop on Madison Avenue, and Tang found a sample from last summer that they weren't making anymore.

Here Tang showed her true colors. No free lunch for anyone. She offered Ching a gown that had a large coffee stain in the train and was a size too big for her. Tang was queenly about her offer and promised Ching the gown would be perfect when they were finished working on it.

Ching was Chinese, too, and showed no distress over the gesture, or the tiny flaw in it. The dress had been, after all, five thousand dollars last year. That was a great deal of a gift, even if the item was unsellable now. Ching's athletic figure was far from delicate, and she had a robust appetite she'd never attempted to curb. Tang's sculpted sheath with pink pearls dancing across the bodice and tulip sleeves would skim her curves and give her stature and grace.

It also made her ambitious. Suddenly she wondered if there was another dress among the thousands Tang didn't need for her stubborn sister-cousin, April Woo. Nothing too fancy. Just the same fashion glory for them both, so they could shine together like real sisters on Ching's great day. April would object, of course. For sure she would object to being Ching's maid of honor. April didn't like standing out in any way whatsoever. That was the reason Ching hadn't told her yet. But if April had a magnificent gown, she wouldn't be able to refuse being maid of honor. She'd have to stand up with Ching and give a speech.

Secrets, manipulations, and most of all scheming was the only way to work with the stubborn Woos and also the Tangs of the world. When Ching got off the subway at the Hunter College stop, she was smiling at all her manipulations on April's behalf and hoping against hope that Tang would indulge her just a little more. It was a gorgeous day, only three blocks to Madison, and she wanted that dress.

When Ching climbed the stairs to Tang Ling's ultrachic second-floor showroom, however, she was disappointed to find Tang herself deeply engaged in a cantankerous bridal fitting for a noisy mother-daughter duo. Fittings with Tang were unusual. She was always so busy designing a new line for each season and traveling around the world that only the rarefied few received her personal attention after the choice of a gown was made.

"Prudence, stand still!" the mother shrilled loudly.

"I am standing still," protested a slender girl who seemed to Ching awfully young to be a bride. She was encased in alençon lace from shoulder to toe and eight feet beyond, dolled up like a Barbie of the fifties and looking every bit the part with a dip of real blond hair over one amethyst eye. All she needed was the white mink shrug of Doris Day to make her perfectly retro.

It was a daunting sight, and Ching was discouraged. She'd expected to have Tang to herself for at least a few minutes. She knew Tang had an important meeting at noon. So the young bride and her mother, and the friend they had with them, were an annoying setback. Time was passing, and they filled the ball-roomlike showroom—usually large enough for more than one party to parade around in at the same time—making it clear how important they were in the scheme of things.

"*Ni hao*, Ching," Tang called out when she saw her. "Have a seat. I'll be with you soon." She glanced at her watch, a large one, heavily studded with diamonds.

Ching nodded and sat on a slipper chair by the elevator to watch the maestro work. After she'd been there for fifteen minutes, she had to hand it to Tang. The most famous of all special-occasion designers knew how to work the crowd and steer clear of disaster. The bride was slender; the mother was stout. Ching's own mother was chubby, but this woman was huge, her chest as big as a ship's prow. Tang took control of them.

Both women were wearing white gowns. The mother's had a long chiffon skirt that softened her bulk, but she wasn't happy with it. The neckline was cut low enough to reveal a great expanse of soft, crepey skin on her neck and abundant chest. That, however, wasn't what bothered this MOB.

"It's too plain," she complained, eyeing her daughter's extravaganza.

"Ah, yes, it definitely needs something, don't you agree, Wendy?" Tang said.

The third woman nodded. "A beaded bolero?" she suggested.

"Maybe not beads," Tang said slowly.

Kim, the fitter, shook his head. "Better just a handkerchief of the same material."

"What do you think, Pru?" The MOB turned to her daughter. "Is it too plain?" she demanded.

"I don't know," the girl replied crossly. She turned her back on her mother and marched across the room to the window on Madison, dragging her train behind her. When she got there she stared out at the street blankly while Tang ordered one of the salesgirls to gather some jackets, scarves, and other accessories to enhance the MOB's dress.

"What's the matter, Pru?" The mother tried to rouse her daughter out of her sulk, but got no response for her effort.

"Wedding jitters?" teased the woman Tang had called Wendy.

"No," came the petulant reply.

"Maybe she doesn't want to get married so quick." This from Kim.

"Kim!" Tang's voice was sharp. "What are you talking about? Of course she wants to get married."

"No," came the sulky voice again.

"We don't want to get married! God, give me strength." The MOB clamped a hand on her chest.

"I can't wait until the ordeal is over. My God, I'm sick of all these freaking details."

"Ah, here we are," Tang said cheerfully.

The saleswoman arrived almost staggering under a load of shimmering, glittering merchandise.

Ching groaned to herself. This was going to take forever. Then she watched with utter fascination as Tang, the woman called Wendy, and Kim all skillfully steered the discontented MOB toward a stunning embroidered and beribboned bolero that served three purposes: it camouflaged the offending chest skin, allowed the mother to *almost* outshine her daughter, and cost an additional seven thousand dollars.

"The Hay women and their wedding planner," Tang said with a wan smile when they finally left. "Ching, I'm sorry to keep you waiting."

"No, no. It's nothing." Ching would never in a million years complain. "It was wonderful to watch you work. I never realized how hard it is."

"You can't even begin to imagine." Tang rolled her eyes, and immediately the salesgirl brought in Ching's gown.

Another girl came into the room and whispered loudly, "Your car is downstairs. You have two minutes."

"Ching, you look so great! I only have two minutes."

"Thank you." But Ching knew she didn't look great at all. Tang was the one who looked great. Thin, dressed all in Armani. Slide shoes, hair dyed red. Red nail polish. Pearls as large as marbles around her neck. And she'd had her eyes done! Almost Western eyes in a very Asian face. Ching had to admit it was a good job, even if she disapproved of surgery. She smiled. "You're the glamour girl."

"Not such a glamour girl today." Tang's customer demeanor dropped away, and she wilted visibly.

"Tired," Ching said sympathetically.

"No, didn't you hear? One of my brides was murdered yesterday," Tang told her with an angry look.

"No!" Ching put her hand to her mouth.

"Terrible thing," Kim said, his eyes tearing up.

"What happened?" Horrified, Ching looked from one to the other.

"Someone shot her as she was going down the aisle." Tang glanced at her watch. "Hurry up. I have one minute."

But Ching was still trying to digest the news. A bride shot! Suddenly she felt dizzy and wondered what April knew about it. Poor Tang. "Did you know her?" Ching asked.

"Of course I knew her. We dressed her, made her gown. Special order. A big one," Tang said impatiently. "It's just terrible! And they haven't paid the bill yet."

"What?" Ching was shocked by the concern about money, but the tragedy gave her an idea. It occurred to her that she had an important relation in the police department. Maybe she could help Tang somehow by offering April to assist her. Then maybe Tang would give her a free dress for her trouble.

"My best friend, my maid of honor, in fact, is a very important detective in the police department," Ching said slowly. Tang read her mind before she was even finished getting the sentence out.

"You aren't going to ask for a free dress for *her*, are you?" she said quickly. "I can't afford any more freebies."

Ching blushed hotly. "No, no. Of course not. You've already been so generous. I just thought maybe she can do something to help."

"Well, thanks anyway, Ching. But no cops. I just want to stay as far from this as possible. The last thing I need is this kind of attention."

"Miss Ling, you're going to be late." The girl was back. "I have your purse."

"No, no, take it back upstairs. I have some calls to make." Tang hurried out the door. "See you, Ching."

Suddenly Ching felt queasy. After the news of a murdered bride in a Tang gown and Tang's attitude, Ching's joy of being an insider with a free wedding dress dissipated fast. She felt like the poor college girl of the old days, someone getting leftovers. And the murder troubled her more than she wanted to admit. She felt funny putting on the gown, even though Kim had altered it to fit her perfectly.

She evaluated herself in front of the mirror. The train with the coffee stain was gone. The hem dipped just enough in back now to puddle a few inches on the floor. Kim had added more bobbing pearls to the bodice, adding to its luster. But Ching was a plain, no-nonsense kind of girl, not in any way the beauty that her friend April was, and her expression showed that she wasn't happy in her gift.

"What's the matter, girl, you don't want to get married?" Kim said, smoothing his hand along her waist speculatively. He took a tuck, careful not to stick her with the pin.

"No, no. I love the dress. Kim, you did an amazing job. Really."

"It was my design," he said modestly.

But he didn't think it was perfect. A few minutes later Ching left without the dress. Kim had insisted on another fitting.

Thirteen

At four-forty-five that afternoon April tapped at the closed door of Rabbi Levi's study in Temple Shalom. "It's Lieutenant Sanchez and Sergeant Woo," she said.

"Yes, they told me you were here. Come in," the rabbi said in a tired voice.

Mike opened the door, took a quick look around, then let her go in first. Coming from the brightness of the well-lit hall to the darkness of the paneled room, April's eyes didn't register a person in there at first. In his black suit Rabbi Levi was a small figure sitting motionless in a dark leather chair behind a large desk. On this sunny Monday afternoon his study was in dusk. Lined on three sides with leather-bound and dark-covered books, the room looked like an ancient library from another world. This atmosphere was enhanced by the folded newspaper in Hebrew that was all the paper visible on his desk. The sorrowful, gray-haired man seemed much reduced from yesterday. His expression clearly said it was happening again: His people were being embroiled in a brand-new holocaust in the year 2002, right there in Riverdale, New York.

Without looking at the two detectives, he gestured

for them to enter the office. "We had almost a thousand people at the funeral. They came from all over. A sizable demonstration of respect."

"Yes, and thank God there was no trouble," April murmured.

There had been no anti-Israel demonstrations and none of the anti-Semitic sentiment from the African-American and Middle Eastern factions in the city that the rabbi had predicted. April's instincts appeared to be on target. This killing was a personal thing. And the news media thought so, too. The media bulldozers were already moving the earth around the wealthy Schoenfeld family, searching for their underpinnings. The news vans were out in droves. Dozens of reporters from agencies all over the world had been at the funeral, plus the dozens of still cameras, clicking away. Tovah's murder was topping the worldwide charts as America's freak-of-the-week crime horror. The mayor was going nuts, the police commissioner, too.

A lot of people were asking again: What kind of city was this where somebody could shoot down an eighteen-year-old bride in front of hundreds of people? Several vans were outside the temple even now. Mike and April had been videoed going in. The press couldn't be stopped.

The rabbi bristled at April's remark that the funeral had gone without a hitch. "There's lots of trouble, maybe not the kind you mean. The girl, bless her soul, is in the ground now. No one else can hurt her. But that can't be said of rest of us." His anger escalated as he spoke. He was a man used to lecturing. "Do you know who did this terrible thing to us?"

To Tovah, April wanted to correct him. The victim

was a person with a name. Others could have been killed very easily, but no one else had been killed. It had been a careful hit. The murder was not a message for the universal *them*. April wished she could lecture right back and tell this mourning rabbi that Tovah was the one they had to think of now. They had to focus on what had made her a target in her happiest moment on her happiest day—not the day before, not the day after. She refrained from saying this. She wanted his help, not his ire.

"Your people left a mess. It's a disgrace," the rabbi went on, changing the subject so quickly April wasn't sure for a second what he meant.

"In the synagogue?" she asked, glancing at Mike, who'd asked her to conduct the interview.

"Everywhere. Those yellow tapes. Bloody floors."

Ah. Sometimes people went on the offensive when they were hurt. They threatened to hire lawyers, to sue anyone and everyone they could think of. The rabbi was a complainer. April nodded sympathetically. She knew that the Crime Scene Unit had taken all the refuse from their own materials with them, but he didn't mean that. He'd wanted the place cleaned up last night after they'd finished. Literally the floors and pews washed so they could have their services in the sanctuary today.

April had already checked out the situation. There were several other synagogues in the area where people could pray today and tomorrow. That was as far as she could go. In the movies, you might see bad guys cleaning up their murder scenes, but the police were the good guys. They provided other services.

"I know you talked with Inspector Bellaqua about anti-Semitism in the community," she murmured.

The rabbi leaned forward and looked hard at Mike for the first time. "Good, hardworking people live here. I told the inspector we had a small incident last year—a swastika in shaving cream on one of the windows. Not even spray paint. A prank. Since then, a broken window. A few things . . ." He seemed of two minds about pursuing it. If he let that angle go, where would the police look next?

"That's what Sergeant Hollis told us," April said.

"He's a good policeman. We had a car theft once. He was helpful." Rabbi Levi looked away. He'd played the hate crime card. Experienced bias detectives were all over the place. They were turning the area upside down. They would continue with every lead they could dig up. But not a lot was there. No follow-up to the crime had occurred so far. The killer had gone to ground. That put the motive back in the family arena. Rabbi Levi clearly wasn't comfortable with it.

April glanced at Mike again. He'd told her to lead, but the rabbi didn't want to acknowledge a female. Or maybe it was the Chinese thing. Maybe both. Some people didn't think a Chinese female could investigate a crime. Mike wasn't going to jump in and help. April made a note to call Dr. Jason Frank, a psychoanalyst and the only Jew she knew well enough to ask about how the Orthodox thought.

She changed the subject. "Tell us about your staff here. Any problems with them?"

Rabbi Levi gummed the insides of his cheeks as he recited the information. "We have a large staff, teachers in the school. They are all part of our community. We have cleaning people, same. Only one person is not of the tribe. He's a good man."

"You're talking about Harold Walker?" April asked.

"Yes, a good man," he said wearily.

"Never had any trouble with him?" April probed a bit more. In fact, a background check on the dignified Jamaican revealed that he'd been arrested twice for assault in bar fights. At the time Mr. Walker had only good things to say about Rabbi Levi. But he had a temper. Maybe he wasn't treated as well as he claimed and had a beef.

Rabbi Levi hesitated a long time. Finally he shook his head. "No trouble."

So there were some little things about Harold. Okay, they'd come back to it. She saw a slight movement of Mike's hand. He wanted her to move on.

"We need a list of everyone who works in the building, everybody who has a key. We'll be talking to everyone connected to the synagogue as well as everyone who attended the event. What about the photographers? Was anyone filming at the time the shots were fired?"

"No, it's strictly forbidden during services. They did videos in the party room and of the girls getting ready." He lifted his shoulders.

Too bad. It would have helped them to have a video of all the people in all the rows so they could know for sure who they could eliminate as suspects. The rabbi went on.

"Do whatever you have to do. I don't know everyone who was here. I just met the boy and his people last week."

"What did you think of them? Was it a good match?" The word didn't trip easily off April's tongue. *Match.* What was a good match, anyway? Mike was listening, taking notes. She could feel his warmth, smell his aftershave in the airless room, almost hear his thoughts churning.

"They did some upsetting things yesterday. I'm sure you heard." Now he was speaking to the bookcase.

April hadn't heard. "What things?"

"A terrible thing. When the ambulance got here, people were screaming. You couldn't tell what was going on. The technicians—whatever you call them—they came in and cut her dress open down the front." He demonstrated with his finger down his own front. "Terrible."

April nodded.

"They were trying to save her. Her parents were crazy. No one knew she was dying. People were afraid to go out the front doors; they were panicked." He talked without looking at her.

"When the girl was on the stretcher, and they were about to wheel her out, the boy's father reached over and pulled the ring off her finger." Rabbi Levi put a liver-spotted hand over his eyes.

"The ring?"

"The engagement ring," he said impatiently, as if she were some kind of oaf who didn't know that nice people had two rings.

"Did anyone try to stop him?"

"No, no. He did it quickly. The ring fit the girl's left hand, but it was big on her right hand. Ribikoff yanked it off and put it in his pocket." He shook his head. "I've seen many disputes over property of deceased loved ones in my time, but I have never seen anybody grab a piece of jewelry off a dying girl." He looked shocked all over again.

April, however, had seen these things. She'd seen

two sobbing relatives on the street stop grieving long enough to fight over which should get the watch of the man just murdered in front of them. She'd seen a widow, out of control on the scene of a traffic accident in which her husband had died, suddenly notice with pleasure that her best friend who'd emerged from the crash unscathed was wearing the diamond bracelet she'd wanted for her birthday.

"Do you think the ring has any relevance?" she asked.

"No, probably not. You just asked me about the people who were there, and I was thinking that the boy's people are from Brooklyn. I don't have much information about them, don't even know how Suri found them. The mothers don't always seek my advice in these matters. The women, they do it their own way." He went on, after a reflective pause. "I can tell you it was a large function. We have so many happy occasions to celebrate here, a bar mitzvah or a wedding almost every week. But this was the most elaborate party we've ever had here. Too bad, too bad." Rabbi Levi leaned back in his chair, contemplating the irony of a murder occurring at the most elaborate function the synagogue had ever had.

"Rabbi, tell me about the Schoenfelds."

He shook his head. "What is there to say? They are a wonderful family, very observant, generous people." He spread his fingers and touched his newspaper with a pinkie.

"You must have known Tovah well."

"Yes, since she was born. A very sweet girl, a wonderful girl." He nodded as if to confirm that to himself.

"What was she like?"

"Like?" He seemed puzzled by the question.

"Her personality, her likes and dislikes. Her hopes and dreams for her life with her husband. Did she love him? Was she excited?"

His features didn't register this line of questioning.

"Did she have boyfriends, someone who might have been disappointed?" April tried again.

"No, no, no," he answered sharply. "I told him yesterday." He pointed at Mike. "She was a good girl. No boyfriends. She didn't know anyone outside of here."

April had the feeling Tovah's spiritual leader hadn't known her very well, or maybe hadn't liked her. It was just a feeling.

"Somebody didn't like her enough to kill her, Rabbi. Somebody didn't want her married."

He made an angry gesture with his hand. "The girl was eighteen years old. She was beautiful. Who wouldn't like her?"

April shifted in her chair. The girl was beautiful. That was all he could say. Was beauty a motive to kill? Well, sometimes it was.

"Tell me some more about your congregation. You have many wealthy members." She tried another tack.

"Wealthy, no. Comfortable maybe . . ."

"But the Schoenfelds are wealthy."

The rabbi's fingers played with the newspaper. He glanced at Mike. It was clear he didn't want to talk to April. She waited, sweating a little at the snub. He was pale; he was small. He looked as if he hadn't eaten anything for a long time. "When can we clean up?" he asked.

"Soon," she said. "Can you tell me anything more about the party?"

"Ah." He became more animated with that subject. "We try not to encourage too much display here. Competition excites envy. People get hurt feelings when they can't do for their children what their wealthier neighbors are doing. But what can you do when people want to share their good fortune?" Again the shoulders went up.

"You should have seen today. Our custom in funerals is the opposite of the joyous occasions. In death we are always simple, modest. The remains of our loved ones are washed by our own members. You'd be amazed the people who choose to do it. The remains are wrapped in white cloth. They go into the ground in a plain wooden box. Everyone the same." His eyes strayed for a moment directly into April's face, and she was surprised to find herself blushing. This was how the women must feel when the men took notice of them. Trapped for a moment in the light.

"We were at the funeral," she murmured. And competition was the same everywhere.

She thought of Ching's upcoming wedding at the Crystal Pavilion on Mott Street. In Chinatown there was the eight-course wedding, the twelve-course wedding, and the twenty-course wedding. Ching was having the twelve-course feast, and she planned to change her clothes three times while the guests stuffed themselves. No one would remember the last two dresses because they'd all be drunk by the time she got them on, but the photos would last forever.

During her years as a cop, April must have seen hundreds of wedding parties coming out of churches and temples all over the city. She'd seen the brides in their white gowns and the men in their tuxedos, but she knew very little about them.

"Can you tell me anything about the wedding that was unusual beyond the extravagance?" April asked.

"They had a wedding planner. That was unusual, since Suri Schoenfeld is such a competent woman."

"Why did they, do you know?"

"I don't know; that woman put everything out of proportion. There was bad feeling about it. The spending was crazy. They had real flowers, real silver. The girl had her own gown from some store in Manhattan. Party favors for everyone. Such a waste."

"I don't know your customs, Rabbi. How is it generally done?" April asked.

"With our large families most people don't go in for too many extras. The trend is for the girls to rent their gowns, use the caterer's centerpieces. They're not real flowers, but they look very good. They might have one or two arrangements of real flowers in the sanctuary. And of course, there's always lots of food." A small smile lit up his eyes at the mention of food.

April nodded. Just like Chinatown. In Chinatown flowers were for funerals. At weddings, the families of the happy couple gave a wedding feast with lots of Scotch or cognac, plum wine, beer, soda. The decorations consisted of a few red carnations set on red tablecloths. For special show there might be red-lacquered chopsticks instead of the generic wooden ones. Personalized banners with slogans for good luck and long life in Chinese characters hung from the ceiling and were stuck on the walls with Scotch tape. Everything was red and gold. And cash went from friends to happy couple. As much cash as possible. The guests went away drunk and full but not with gifts and party favors.

April remembered the baskets of candy, the large floral arrangements so strongly scented, both in the sanctuary and on the tables: the palm trees, the orange trees with real oranges on them, the silver flatware, the gold-rimmed crystal glasses, the blue Tiffany boxes at many of the seats. They'd had favors from Tiffany!

"This party must have excited a lot of envy," April murmured.

"A lot of talk," the rabbi admitted. "Usually our own people make our parties. We've never had trouble before."

Afterward, the two detectives conferred about what they'd learned. April didn't like the way the rabbi kept calling Tovah "the girl" and the groom "the boy," so she was careful to keep Tovah's name in her mind as she made notes to herself.

Fourteen

Just before five Louis the Sun King sent his assistant, Tito, out in the van with the completed order for the benefit at Tavern on the Green in Central Park. Then he collapsed in a damp heap on the green Victorian wrought-iron settee in his hothouse of a garden, angry as a hornet at Wendy Lotte.

The sun was as hot as summer. Usually he felt blessed that the town houses around him were low enough for the sun to creep into all the corners of his walled refuge, but today he was exhausted and discouraged, so the heat seemed like just another blight on his world. Still, it was better outside than it would be inside, dealing with the ankle-deep mess of cut stems and leaves that Tito had left on the floor of the shop and Jama wasn't there to pick up because he'd gone to ground.

Louis did not want to be inside and visible to any hapless visitor who might want to get in to buy something. He was through for the day. If someone came and he was forced to speak, he would just scream. His irascibility had cost him bundles in the past, and he knew he mustn't revert to type because of a murder.

In the past Louis had done several funerals where

the estate lawyers didn't get around to paying him for over a year because the IRS questioned the expense. He had a policy against working for dead people. And now he'd just sunk more than fifty-five thousand dollars into a wedding for a dead person. He was going to sit there, sweating and cursing Wendy Lotte, until she showed up and reassured him that his investment was not lost.

Louis the Sun King's shop consisted of the first floor and garden of a town house in the East Sixties between Lexington and Park. His establishment was surrounded by antique shops, jewelry shops, a high-end chocolatier, a lingerie boutique, a custom tailor, and a number of pricey restaurants frequented by Eurotrash with titles from long-defunct monarchies, social pretensions, and lots of money. It was close enough to Bloomingdale's, Williams-Sonoma, Caviarteria, and Barneys for any kind of instant shopping pick-me-up, and Louis loved it.

Hardly any plants were for sale there. Garden antiques and collectible containers in many materials were for sale. Cement and bronze planters and painted Italian pottery that presently contained palm trees were for sale. Nineteenth-century Chinese export porcelain, Japanese Imari, sculptured Lalique, opaline, Venetian, and other forms of art-glass vases were for sale, as well as curios of all kinds and hard-to-identify objets d'art on lacquered Chinese and Italian mosaic tables. Screens that cleverly created cunning alcoves were for sale. The garden chairs around the large center table in the extension where the work of planning parties was done were not.

Last, in a corner of the shop, screened by a stand of bamboo in brass planters, Louis's boyfriend Jorge had set up a hair-coloring salon at one of the sinks Tito used for soaking and trimming flowers. Jorge recently commandeered the sink when he quit his job at one of the best hair salons in the city and refused to look for another.

Louis the Sun King was known for designing terrace gardens, greenhouse displays, weddings, benefits, and parties of all kinds. Two major hotels used his services for seasonal decorations of their lobbies. Nearly everything he did was a special order, and a lot of people who thought they knew the street well had no idea it contained a florist.

It was not a long wait. Wendy banged on the locked door at quarter past five. "Louie, Louie, it's me," she cried. Bang. Bang. Bang.

He buzzed her in. She marched through the shop and found him outside. Wendy Lotte was a tall, blond, self-important anorectic of impeccable credentials. She'd come up on Park Avenue. She'd graduated from Miss Porter's and Smith College. She'd been in the Sotheby's human resources department for a year after college, then worked for a giant PR company for five years after that as an event planner. She was keen on making a lot of money because her divorced parents had both married again, one more than once, and had new families to support. She was always expensively dressed and coiffed, and was attractive to people who liked fast-talking, slightly horsey, stiff-hipped kinds of girls.

"I've never had a day like this in my whole life." She sat and launched in without a pause. "You wouldn't have believed the scene there yesterday. Blood everywhere. People screaming, thinking it was another terrorist attack. It was so awful it was funny.

One woman's wig fell off, and she almost went crazy trying to find it. Hysteria beyond belief. All your little boys ran away, and that detective is harassing me. He called on my *cell* while I was with Prudence and Lucinda. Why do I have to take the flak?"

"Oh, please." Louie threw up a hand. "Wherever you are is trouble."

"No, really, Louie, this is not a joke. This Bronx idiot, with an accent so thick I can't understand a word, is harassing me."

Louis put his hand to his pompadour, smoothing it back. "Why?"

"I have no idea. He's a complete asshole. He doesn't like me, and I was perfectly nice to him until he tried to get into my purse."

"They searched your purse? Poor Wendy, you never learn."

"Oh, shut up, Louis. He didn't find anything. But this is all going to be in the papers. My name is coming up everywhere. You can't imagine how crazy it is. An agent called me twice while I was out with Pru and Lucinda. Somebody wants to do a TV movie. The *Enquirer* wants to pay me fifty thousand dollars for a story. 'Arranged marriage ends in murder. The wedding planner tells all.' Can you believe it?"

"Why not? It's a great story. That wretched girl was married like a cow." Louis fanned his face with a big hand.

"Louie, don't start with that."

He made an angry noise. "It was slavery, face it."

"Stop! You don't know anything about it."

Louis glared at her. "Anybody who knows that girl knows that the last thing she wanted was to marry."

"Not your business, Louie, just not your business."

"Well, did you shoot her? Or is your specialty cats?" He laughed.

Wendy leaned forward and grabbed his arm. "Look, Lori's on vacation this week. I'm alone in the office. I'm stressed beyond belief. Don't start with me."

"Hello, it's me, Wendy." He gazed at the sky. "Never forget how much I know about you."

"What are you talking about? Is this a threat?"

"No, no. But I don't need a spotlight on me right now."

"I gave you all this work. I thought we were friends. And now you're *blaming* me for a very unfortunate situation."

"Wendy, people want your story. *Hello,* now you've got the attention you've always craved. Your fifteen minutes of fame. How could I not be concerned—"

Wendy's face paled. "You shit!"

"Maybe. But I'm all you have. I'd say you were one of my riskiest projects." He gave her a bleak smile. "So. Tell me about Prudence Hay; is *she* going to make it to her wedding day?"

"You cold bastard." Wendy's eyes filled with tears. "How could you be so cruel when things are so crazy, and I'm under such pressure—without even *Lori* to help me?"

"Oh, please, look who's talking."

"It could have been you. It could have been any one of your boys. Don't look at me. Just don't look at me." Wendy covered her face. "I'm out of here," she announced. "I'm just gone. Don't try to call me. I hate you."

Fifteen

April burst outside into the radiant, early-evening light, grateful for the sweet breeze off the Hudson River. The whole time she'd been in Rabbi Levi's office she'd felt a tightness in her chest, as if Tovah's angry ghost were still trapped in the place where she'd died.

The rabbi had used the word *terrible* many times. That was what stuck in April's mind as she and Mike drove the few short blocks to the Schoenfeld house on Alderbrook Road. It was a terrible thing to interview a family before a funeral. It was just as terrible to interview a family after a funeral. Tomorrow, next week. A year from now it would still be terrible.

"What did you think of the rabbi?" she asked Mike.

"He didn't know her," he replied instantly.

"That's what I thought. He really pinpointed the wedding planner. May be an angle there," April mused.

"*Te quiero, te amo, querida,*" Mike said suddenly. He loved her.

"*Cómo no?*" she murmured, meeting his eye with just about her first smile of the day.

Mike was a handsome, sexy man, and even

though he'd criticized her earlier, he still loved her.
The thought gave her a warm feeling in the middle of
a mess. Bias, Bronx, and the Homicide Task Force
were all taking a piece of this case. Mike was Homicide. She was the monkey in the middle. Hollis was
already trying to steal their thunder. She'd have to
watch him. And her boss, Lieutenant Iriarte, would
be hoping for the worst. She had to find a way to let
him in so he wouldn't punish her later. But Mike was
back on the subject of love.

"I really do, *querida*. I love you more and more. I
don't know what I'd do if someone shot you on our
wedding day."

"No one's going to shoot me, wedding day or any
other time," April said, uneasy about making a promise no one could keep.

Skinny Dragon believed people owned each other.
The dragon believed that because she'd given birth to
April, she owned her daughter for life. But people
didn't own each other. Things happened, they fell in
love with the wrong people, got hurt, got sick, died.
Shooting wasn't the only bad thing that happened.

"*Yo rezo*," he said curtly, as if reading her mind.

Well, she prayed also, just to different gods. His
sudden Spanish made the point that in the Bronx he
was home. And at home there were certain things
you just didn't do in English. Praying and loving
were two. April knew how it was. At her home the
thing you didn't do was feel anything but guilt. Guilt
was the operative feeling. You had to make money
and save face, that was it. *Face* translated into Spanish as *macho*, and *macho* translated into English as
honor. As far as April was concerned all of it made
trouble.

"Next time, don't go to autopsies of brides in the middle of the night. Makes you morbid." She ended the conversation. He was tough, but it had gotten to him, no question about it.

Independence Avenue was only six blocks long, from 239th to 247th streets. It ran parallel to the Henry Hudson Parkway and the Hudson River, located halfway between the HH Parkway and the Palisades. Lining the parkway like soldiers in a parade were miles of luxury apartment buildings. Behind them was the old Riverdale, practically untouched. A real suburb only a few minutes from Manhattan, this area had narrow, hilly roads and gracious brick Tudor and stucco Mediterranean-style houses, overarched by the branches of venerable trees. Around them, landscaped yards with walks and arbors were studded with flowering shrubs and brilliantly hued spring flowers. The houses on the Hudson had the bonus of a majestic view of the mighty river and the green palisades of New Jersey.

"Wow." April whistled as they came to the tiny dead-end road of Alderbrook, a lane so narrow it didn't look wide enough for a moving van to get in or out. Tucked into a cul de sac that dated from early in the last century were six old houses. Parked cars and TV vans blocked the road and lined the roads around it. Mike had to backtrack and leave his unmarked vehicle in the circle of a giant apartment complex two blocks away. They plowed through a bunch of reporters who tried to get them to say something.

The Schoenfelds' house was at the end, in the curve of the U. It was a sturdy structure, built for a family just the size of theirs. It was pale gray–painted stucco with an orange-tiled roof and a covered veranda in the front. More reporters jammed the front lawn. Mike shook his head at them.

"You take the girl's family," he murmured to April.

"Tovah," April corrected softly. *Tovah*, she repeated to herself as she rang the bell.

Less than a minute later Mr. Schoenfeld opened the door. He was a tall, heavyset man, at least six-two. He didn't appear to be in good shape, but he looked young for a man with a daughter of marriageable age. He had curly light brown hair on a big head, a Roman nose, a strong chin thickly packed into a roll underneath, angry blue eyes.

"This is not a good time. We're sitting shivah," he said curtly.

"We're sorry to intrude," Mike told him.

Schoenfeld glanced quickly at April, dismissed her. "That other detective was already here. Isn't that enough for one day?"

"We have a few more questions."

Schoenfeld blocked the door. "What exactly do you want to know?"

"We need information about the party vendors," April said, not wanting to get his back up about their looking into his daughter's activities in the last few months, weeks, days, hours of her life.

"My wife and my daughter would be the ones who dealt with the . . ." He hiccuped and closed his eyes, swaying on his feet like a big tree caught in a wind. April saw that he'd been drinking.

He blinked, recovered his focus and balance, pushed away the hand the Mike held out to him. "Come in," he said abruptly.

The smell of food twitched at April's empty belly as she followed him into the kind of home she'd seen often on Central Park West. The living room was furnished with many traditional chairs she recognized as antiques and fat sofas upholstered in heavy brocade. A thick, patterned carpet partially covered the wide-planked wood floor. Voluminous drapes with tassel fringe, crystal lamps, inlaid tables, and gilded mirrors on the walls, now obscured by a soapy film, finished the look. From another part of the house came the muted sound of children's voices. About thirty well-dressed males sat and stood around with plates of food in their hands.

In the dining room, a spread of party food was laid out on a huge slab of a table, a crowd of women were loading their plates, and a heavy woman with a blond wig was directing traffic. April had forgotten the Styrofoam head with Tovah's wig on it, but she remembered it now. Her mother had one, too.

"Suri, these detectives want to talk to you," Schoenfeld said to the woman. Then he returned to the living room, where the men were.

"We're sorry to intrude. I'm Sergeant Woo; this is Lieutenant Sanchez," April said.

The woman put her hand out to a smaller woman near her, wiry with steely blue hair and a hard expression. "My mother," she said faintly.

"I'm Belle Levine."

The two women led the way through the kitchen out of the house onto the back porch, where there was outdoor furniture, a large table, a love seat, chairs, and a glider. There Mrs. Schoenfeld started to cry. "Why would anyone do this?"

"Tell me about your daughter, Mrs. Schoenfeld,"

April said gently. Mike gave April a sympathetic look and went into the house.

"She was a beautiful girl. Eighteen years old, nothing but childhood behind her, her whole life in front of her. What is there to tell?" her mother said.

"What was Tovah like? Who did she know?"

"A girl who led a quiet life, didn't know anybody, never dated a single boy but Schmuel," her grandmother said.

"He was a terrible choice. I'll never forgive myself," Tovah's mother sobbed.

"A terrible choice?" April murmured.

Suri Schoenfeld stopped crying abruptly. "Are you Chinese?" she demanded.

"Yes," April told her.

"You people have arranged marriages, don't you?"

"Some do," April admitted.

"You see." Suri pounded the arm of her chair. "I wanted the best for my daughter. Who wouldn't?" A wail escaped her.

"Suri," her mother said sharply. "Don't blame yourself. Tovah chose *him*."

"But I chose the family. Terrible family. Look. They won't show their faces here. It's a *shanda*. You should check those people. They're criminals, Russians with relatives in the mob."

"Suri, you don't know that," her mother said sharply.

"They took the ring off a dying girl's finger!" Suri's grief poured out. "What kind of people would do that? Now there's a curse on all my children. I'll never marry any of them. Murderers," she wailed.

"Tell me about the last two weeks," April said gently. "Tell me everything you did."

Suri wanted to talk. She told about Tovah's visit to the *mikvah* last Thursday, the ritual bath. April made a note to ask Jason Frank about it.

"And the wig maker to pick up the wig, also Thursday."

April finally had the chance to ask about the wigs. She opened her mouth to ask, but Suri Schoenfeld anticipated the question.

"We cover our hair after marriage," Suri said. "Modesty."

"Ah." April glanced at Suri's mother, with her own steely blue hair.

"Not all of us," Belle said pointedly, ending the inquiry.

Then Suri told her about the many calls back and forth to Wendy Lotte, the wedding planner, because the Ribikoffs had been so difficult about the final lists. People who hadn't been invited were coming. People who said they were coming couldn't come. Not only that, Schmuel's father was allergic to fish, nuts, and gluten and didn't want anything with those ingredients at the dinner. That was about as difficult as people could get.

"Nothing with flour!" Suri was still reeling over it. "It was a nightmare. Why couldn't they have told us that before?"

April noted everything, their trips to Manhattan to meet with the florist, a person improbably called Louis the Sun King, and with the caterer to constantly revamp the menu. Their meetings with Wendy Lotte, and their visits with Tang Ling and her fitter Kim. Suri went with her mother, Belle, most often. When necessary, they took Tovah with them.

"Tovah didn't always go with you?" April asked.

"It was so tiring." The two women exchanged glances.

"Tiring? Tovah was a young woman."

"She had migraines."

"What was her mood in the last few days?"

"Except for the migraines, she was fine."

"Was she anxious about getting married? You said she had no experience with boys."

Suri looked exasperated. "I went to college. I dated. What's so great?"

"She was not anxious," the grandmother insisted. "Every girl wants to get married. Who wants to be an old maid?"

April hid her ringless ring finger under her notebook. *But maybe not everybody wants to be married at eighteen.* April had barely graduated from high school at eighteen.

Then Suri launched into an explanation of their preparations for the Sabbath, the reason she'd hired a party planner. "I start on Wednesday. For a family this size, we need ten loaves of bread, six chickens, fish. I cook everything myself and always do five courses. I couldn't do that and a wedding too," she explained.

Such elaborate cooking and arrangements for a twenty-four-hour period every week! It was as bad as being Chinese.

"This was my first break in nineteen years. My husband owed it to me," Suri said tearfully.

"Can you think of anyone who disliked your daughter, Mrs. Schoenfeld?"

"Rich and pretty girls always excite envy," Suri said smoothly. "I know that from my own experience. But it couldn't be one of us. Jews don't have guns." She was certain about that.

"One more thing. Did you notice anyone leaving the sanctuary before the ceremony? Someone from either family missing?"

"Oh, I have no idea. The only person I couldn't find when we came in was Wendy. I needed her to do something. I looked for her, but she wasn't around. Can I go back in the house now?"

Wendy again. April nodded. "How long do you sit shivah?"

"Seven days," Suri said. "I don't know how I'll get through it."

"You will," April assured her. Somehow they always did.

Sixteen

Ching didn't watch Channel Twelve all day to keep track of all the terrible crimes that happened in New York City and April's role in solving them, but her mother Mai Ma Dong did. Mai followed April's career with avid interest, collecting the news clippings about her cases and recounting her successes in the police department to her daughter and anyone else who would listen. To Mai, her own daughter was a difficult rebel, but Sai's daughter was a real star. Sai, of course, felt exactly the opposite.

When they were little, the two best-friend mothers took turns dragging Ching and April to Chinese school on weekends to learn calligraphy and other Chinese arts. They'd taken them to martial-arts classes and taught them to cook traditional meals. Ching had incurred her mother's wrath by not being interested in any of it. She'd been the math genius and longed for escape from the narrowness of Chinatown. April had been the fighting beauty, the black belt who won all the matches—the stay-at-home who supported her parents and went to college at night. To Mai, who'd missed Ching when she was away in California for many years, April remained the loyal daughter and became the famous cop she saw on TV.

Mai was the one who sighted April and Mike during the coverage of the terrible shooting in the Bronx. They were coming out of the house of a murdered bride shaking their heads. "No comment at this time." And right away she called Ching at work to warn her.

"Bad luck," she cried. "Terrible luck to happen just before your wedding."

Oh, God. This was the last thing Ching wanted to think about. "It's the Bronx, Ma. A Jewish wedding. Nothing to do with us."

"Poor April," Mai wailed. "Bad luck for her."

"No, no, Ma. Don't say that."

"Yes, yes, now she'll never get married," Mai predicted unhappily.

"But this is her job. One thing has nothing to do with the other!" Ching argued.

"I don't know. Bad luck," Mai insisted.

The reasoning was nuts. "Come on, terrible things happen every day; that doesn't mean they'll happen to us."

"You better call April," Mai concluded. "Tell her."

"Tell her what, Ma?"

"No more murders before the wedding," Mai said.

Ching groaned. Oh, sure, as if April could keep the whole city crimeless for ten whole days.

"Okay, Ma. I'll tell her." She hung up and scratched the side of her mouth the way she did when she was troubled. Her mother was a management problem at the best of times. April was not so easy, either. All Ching wanted to do was keep her mother quiet for a few more days, and get April away from her work long enough to be her maid of honor. She wanted to have a happy wedding, and go on her well-deserved honeymoon to Venice.

Seventeen

Wendy checked her caller ID. When she saw it was Kim again, she smiled at the two detectives in her living room and dropped the ringing cell phone back in her pocket.

"I'm devastated to have missed the funeral. I called this morning to see what I could do to help, but no one picked up." Wendy appraised the two cops. A Chinese woman, young, very attractive. No wedding ring. She noticed these things. A Hispanic man with a mustache like the other detective. No wedding ring either. Like the Bronx detective, these two were dressed in plain clothes and didn't look terribly intelligent. Wendy didn't know she was just slightly dulled with drink. She always felt she could talk her way through anything no matter how much hooch was in her. And she'd had plenty of experience with both cops and vodka.

"I had no idea they'd bury her so fast. It's so difficult with all these restrictions." She hurriedly ticked them off on her fingers. "No communication on Friday after dark until Saturday after dark. That's twenty-four whole hours of every week out the window. Believe me, that can be quite a hurdle when you have details that need attention. I had to learn all this. I've never done Orthodox before. You know anything about them?"

"No, tell us," the Chinese said.

"No answering the phone when you're in mourning. Who would think of it? I can't imagine how the arrangements get done." Wendy lifted her eyes heavenward. "Not that I'm judgmental about customs. I work with all kinds of people," she amended quickly. Now the phone rang in her office. She ignored it.

"How do arrangements get done?"

"I gather there's some sort of temple fellowship that takes care of everything so the family doesn't have to think about it. They don't allow flowers." Wendy glanced at her watch, blew air out of her mouth to control her impatience.

"I asked the caterer to help. They're a very nice kosher couple, by the way. They wanted to know what to do with the food from yesterday. No one ate. Mr. Schoenfeld didn't want to *pay* for it after what happened, so I told the Goldsteins to take that food right over to the house and set it up for the shivah." Wendy was proud of this maneuver. The delivery of the food was done in the guise of kindness, and she knew Mr. Schoenfeld would have no choice about paying for it now. Luckily she'd learned a long time ago to take her own cuts up front and in commissions along the way. A lot of vendors could go unpaid for this kind of disaster.

"And the Goldsteins did it?"

"Oh, yes. Smart people always take my advice. Thinking ahead is the key to my business." Wendy wanted to be alone and wondered what she should do to make these two cops happy and go away.

"Would you like something to drink, a glass of

champagne?" she offered. She was longing for a glass herself.

"No, thanks."

"Are you sure, April?"

Wendy was good at names. April Woo. She wouldn't forget it. Mike Sanchez. She wouldn't forget that, either. They were sitting there like two Dobermans, waiting for a reason to attack. She could see the gun on one of them, but they weren't acting like any cop from any cop show she'd ever seen on TV, or like that Bronx detective who kept calling and harassing her just because she was out of sight for ten lousy minutes.

She glanced pointedly at her watch again. Nearly eight-thirty and she had fifty messages to return. *Please go home now,* her smile said. No such luck. At the sound of her name the Chinese frowned. Wendy's agreeable expression didn't change. She knew that look. Chip-on-the-shoulder look. *I'm a sergeant. Don't call me by my first name.* All that garbage.

"Then how about a glass of water, Sergeant?" Wendy sweetened her tone, aware that she was taller than both cops, had good breeding, was well dressed. All that made her feel in control.

"Maybe later," the sergeant replied.

Wendy smiled at the rebuff and crossed her legs for Lieutenant Latino, who was staring at her with undisguised interest. Wendy had good long legs. She was wearing a short skirt and beige-and-camel alligator pumps, good copies of the real Hermès ones. She thought of herself as a beautiful woman and sat at ease on her modern modular sofa. She'd had a few drinks to calm down after her fight with Louis. But not too many to lose her edge, she thought. Like her mother and father, she could hold her liquor. And then she'd opened her last bottle of Tovah's wedding champagne. Alcohol didn't bother her. She was still in control.

The telltale signs of her solitary tippling—the open bottle and empty crystal flute—were on the cocktail table, but they didn't bother her, either. She was in her own home; there was no law against having a glass of bubbly at the end of a long day.

She smiled again at the Latino wearing cowboy boots. "How about you, Lieutenant?"

"Nice place you have," he remarked.

"Thank you." But Wendy knew it was just okay. She lived on Seventy-second Street and Lexington Avenue. Her five rooms were light and airy. Her wood floors were pickled white and her decor was modern. Beige was the darkest color in her decorating palette. But it wasn't Park Avenue. Not at all what she would have if she married someone who could double her income. She tapped her foot, anxious for them to go.

"Do you mind if I use the bathroom?" the Latino asked.

"Of course not. Right this way." She led him through the office. He went into her second bathroom and closed the door. She hesitated at the desk, listening for the sound of water in the bowl. She waited in there for the toilet to flush. She did not want him opening her closets or files, or messing with her computer. The toilet flushed. He took some time running water. She began to worry about the cop in her living room. Which one should she watch? Finally he opened the door.

"May I look in your albums? I'm getting married myself," he said.

"Congratulations," she said curtly. "Why don't you bring it into the drawing room with you?"

He picked one up and took his time slowly turning the pages of an album featuring table settings with elaborate centerpieces. Wendy ducked out the door and was alarmed not to see the Chinese in the living room. She hurried out of the office to find her, then exhaled with relief. Woo was standing at the window, studying the photos in a *Bride*. Sanchez came out of her office with two albums. "Sergeant, this may interest you," he said.

The two of them put their heads together, flipping the pages of an album that showed the whole process: invites, table settings, menus, decorations of churches and other sites, tents, favors, wedding gowns and tuxedos. They seemed impressed.

"Okay, now that you know what I do. I told you I was in the ladies' room when it happened; are we all square now?" Wendy was finished being nice.

The Woo woman looked up, puzzled.

"Isn't the ceremony the most important moment in a wedding?"

"Not for me. We practice the walk together, but then there comes the moment when they just have to muddle through themselves." Wendy slid over the single facet of her job that made her queasy.

"You went to the ladies' room?"

"Yes. I told you that." Wendy showed irritation for the first time. "I'd been there all day. Not only with the florist to supervise setting up the *huppah*—I'm sure you noticed it; it was huge—and the caterers setting up the party space *and* the seating plan for the tables. And they dressed and had their hair and makeup done right there in the temple! It was a madhouse with all those girls assembled there. Crowded and hot, tempers volatile. Six girls in there! The mother and the grandmother." Wendy shuddered at the chaos.

"But you went to the ladies' room at the exact moment when the service started. Isn't that unusual?"

Wendy made an impatient noise. "Not for me. Look, don't you people coordinate? I told that other detective that I needed to pee. I hadn't had a moment to myself all afternoon. So I went *then*. It seemed a good time."

"What about the family?"

"Oh, don't get me started. It was weird. This big production for a girl who wasn't all there."

"What do you mean?"

"It was sad. When we were going through the planning stages, Tovah was kind of out of it. Her mother and grandmother pulled all the strings."

The Chinese was interested. "Do you think maybe Tovah was coerced into the marriage? Did she have another boyfriend?"

"Oh, no. It was more like she was on drugs or something," Wendy said slowly.

"Drugs?"

"Yes, she had a kind of stoned look, maybe tranquilizers." Wendy lifted her shoulders, glancing at the champagne. At least half a bottle remained. Her buzz was dulling. She needed a lift.

"Was there anybody else in the bathroom with you?"

"Oh, I don't remember." Wendy shook her foot. They were back on the bathroom. "Let's see, yes. I think there were. Several people. Look, it's really late. . . ."

"One last question. If I understand this correctly, you were downstairs in the party room when the family was getting ready. Then the family went upstairs and spent about twenty minutes in the rabbi's study before the ceremony, signing papers and doing the business before the procession got under way. Where were you then?" Woo asked.

Wendy blinked. "I don't understand the question."

"What were you doing before you went to the bathroom?"

"Oh, I was outside having a cigarette," she said quickly.

"Thank you. We're about done for the moment. I'd like a list of your events for the last year or so," Woo said.

"Why?" Wendy was stunned.

"Routine," the cop said. "And then we'll get out of your hair."

Eighteen

"Thanks for the diversion, *chico*." April glanced at the menu at the uptown Evergreen, known for its good dim sum.

"You're welcome. Find anything interesting?"

"The woman's a pack rat. You running a check on her?"

"Yeah. I get the feeling something's off there. She wanted to come into the bathroom with me."

"Since when is that a negative with you?" April tried to laugh off some nervous energy.

"She didn't want me alone in her office," he elaborated.

"What didn't she want you to see?"

He shrugged. "You got her client list."

She nodded. "She certainly didn't want me to have it. If you think there's something in her place, we can always get a search warrant. I'm really bothered by her time frame. She said she was out having a cigarette while the Schoenfelds were in the rabbi's study. But she's no smoker."

There had been no ashtrays, no lighters, or cigarette butts in her apartment. No odor of smoke in her clothes. Smokers smelled; their homes smelled, too.

No amount of scented candles or bowls of potpourri could quite cover it.

"Besides, if she needed to pee, wouldn't she do that first and then go out for a smoke?"

"She's a boozer. Maybe she slipped out for a drink."

"Yeah, she's a drinker," April agreed.

"I don't want Hollis in there," Mike was saying. "He's got his own thing going here. Maybe he's checking guests and staff for someone who saw her in the bathroom. Maybe he knows something we don't know."

"Maybe, but I still don't see her as our killer." April shook her head at the thought. "Twenty-some minutes is a long time to disappear, but what would be her motive? The Schoenfelds were clients of hers. She was trying to get that Orthodox business."

"Maybe she was playing another angle."

"What?" April knew a lot of Chinese like Wendy—self-important people who never stopped talking and arranging things *their* way. The political ones made trouble. Manipulators. Look how Wendy had engineered getting the wedding food to the funeral.

Not only that, Wendy looked as if she were all set for her own wedding, with cupboards stocked with many pairs of candlesticks, crystal glasses, bowls and plates all with their labels still affixed. Stacks of table linens: napkins and place mats still tied in white ribbons. Lot of stuff in there. The woman was a pack rat, a hamster. What did she get, free samples?

Mike was busy with his Department minicomputer. April sighed, grateful that the long day was over. She lifted her hot hair off her neck and clipped it into a ponytail, pleased that it had been her turn to win the daily debate between Chinese and Mexican food. This reminded her of the wedding food on the banquet table at the Schoenfelds' house. Funeral food now. She knew a little about Jewish cuisine from her days on the Lower East Side. Smoked fish and meats, pickles and pickled herring. Knishes, noodle pudding. Gefilte fish. Chopped liver, all heavy stuff.

She mused about Mike's taste for meats and chicken that had been stewed all day so you couldn't tell what it was or how old it had been when it went into the pot. He loved melted cheese and weird-tasting sauces made with ingredients the Chinese never used: ground seeds, green tomatoes, red tomatoes, many types of dried peppers, cocoa, beans, avocado, cumin.

Like many Chinese, April thought even the freshest, mildest cheese smelled bad and that Mexican sauces left a gritty taste in the mouth. When she married, her parents and friends would expect a Chinese banquet. Fifteen to twenty-two courses, without mole.

A skinny waiter set a teapot on the table. The Chinese believed twenty cups of green tea a day was a necessity for good health. Yesterday she'd come up fourteen short. April poured and downed her first cup of today. Nineteen to go.

"Come up with anything?" she asked.

Mike had one of those gizmos only the top brass had. About the size of a Palm Pilot, the thing beeped, then printed on the screen every major crime as the dispatchers called them in. Already a shooting in Brooklyn and two rapes in the Bronx that day. Mondays were usually pretty quiet.

"I'm running a warrant check on Wendy. It's

showing an error." Mike fiddled some more, then put the thing in his pocket.

The skinny waiter reappeared. He and April consulted in Chinese. "Any special requests?" she asked Mike.

"Yeah." He pocketed the computer and turned serious. "Tell me your problem, *querida*."

"My problem?" The question surprised her.

"Uh-huh. You're not truthful. You say you trust me, but you don't trust anybody." Mike had the expression he used for suspects—the bad ones, not the not-so-bad ones.

April's face reddened in front of the hovering waiter. She placed an order in rapid Chinese.

"What are you talking about?" she asked as soon as he was gone.

"Tell me what picture you see in this case." Changing tack rapidly was one of Mike's effective interview techniques.

"Okay. The wedding was for show for sure. They hired a party planner to pull off a Broadway production. What?" He was giving her a funny look.

"I mean about the girl." Again with *the girl*.

"Oh. Tovah." They kept calling her *the girl*. That really bothered her. "Her name was Tovah," she said.

"Tell me about Tovah then," he said, chewing on his mustache.

"She was marrying a boy she didn't know well because her family didn't want her dating. She had a zoned appearance. The party planner thought she was on drugs, is that what you mean?" April raised her delicate eyebrows. "Drug angle?"

"Why don't you tell the truth to a man you know

well, who loves you very much and wants to marry you?"

Who needed this tonight of all nights? Twice in one day was too much. April tossed her head. They'd been through it all before. Certain things were facts of life. Their differences. She didn't want to go into it again.

"Don't you get it?" he demanded. "You're nearly twice that girl's age. You talk about getting married. You think about the menu and your dress, but that's about it. What are you waiting for? A death in the family?"

"Mike!" April inhaled sharply, taking a direct hit from the man she'd always counted on to be a good sport.

"You know your mother is not going to die to release you. She'll probably outlive us both. Why can't you do what's right for you and me?" His face was angry. He meant it.

April stared at him, annoyed that he'd just tossed away any chance for a happy moment at the end of a very difficult day.

"Why bring this up now?" She poured more tea for health. Drank her second cup of the day, immediately needed to pee.

Mike put his hands on the table. "A relationship has to move forward or end. That's it, April. I'm telling you right now."

"What's this, an ultimatum?" Her cheeks flushed hotter.

"Look, I've tried everything to show I love you. How many years now? I'm discouraged. I have bad dreams." Mike shook his head. "And now this case."

April was tired and just as upset by the case as

he was. The press was doing its usual dirty work, blaming the victim for the crime. The Ribikoffs and Schoenfelds were being held up as child abusers for arranging the marriage of teenage children. April wished her lover would stay focused on the crime. It wasn't about them.

"You'd be insulted if a man lived with you forever without setting a date." He drank some water, then called the waiter over and ordered a beer.

"This case is doing something to you," she said finally.

"Maybe, but it isn't only the case. It's a lot of things coming together. You've been stalling. You only think about your point of view, never mine."

"I think about you all the time," she protested.

"Look. Last week when you went home I had dinner with *Mamita*. You know what she said?"

"I can guess." April put a hand to the medal Maria Sanchez had given her to make her a Catholic. It was the patron saint of soldiers and policemen. St. Some-thingorother.

"*Mamita* has a boyfriend who wants to marry her."

April nodded. Nothing new there.

"She's telling people she's thirty-eight, two years older than me; that's going some on the Virgin Mother. And she loves that what's-his-name." Mike waved his hand, unable to remember the name of his mother's lover. "*Mami* says she can't marry him until I'm married."

Oy. Diego Alambra, believe it or not, was an Italian maître d' who wanted to marry Mike's Spanish mother, a widow of five years. She was over fifty. What was she waiting for? Figure it out.

"*Mamita* says she's living in sin. She says we're living in sin. And the truth is, I wouldn't live endlessly with someone who wouldn't marry *me*. Would you?" Mike gave her a clear-eyed stare, and April finally drew breath.

There was a Chinese saying: A relationship can endure anything but disrespect. So now they had a pride situation: the pride of Maria Sanchez against the face of Sai Yuan Woo. A pathetic situation. Maria Sanchez had plans of her own, and now she had muscle. She'd found the right words to influence her son. Pride and honor for the Spanish ran as deep as face for the Chinese. Mike had to defend his honor now, and now that April saw it his way, she couldn't deny he was right. Jimmy Wong, who'd been her sometime boyfriend for several years before Mike, had frequently promised to marry her. When he hadn't made good on his promise, she'd dumped him. Mike always told her she was the love of his life, but right now she could see that pride was gaining strength. Certainly in Chinese, face for millions of people was more important than love.

The waiter returned with some pickled vegetables, a plate of steamed vegetable dumplings, and *shui mai*. April poured herself another cup of tea. She'd lost her appetite. Poor Tovah had gone along with her mother's wish for her to marry a boy she didn't know in a big production. This was something only poor and hopeless Chinese women did these days. Independent people didn't marry to suit their parents. It wasn't as though April didn't *know* this.

"Querida?"

Mike wanted an answer. She owed him one. She wasn't a girl like Tovah with no will of her own, a wuss, a sop, a weakling afraid to defy her parents.

There were consequences for everything. So she decided to tell him and let him figure it out. She put her hand to her forehead and blurted her secret. "I hold the mortgage on the house."

"Your house?" Mike frowned. What did that have to do with anything?

"Yes."

"That's it? That's your reason for not getting married?"

April pressed her lips together. Not quite, but pretty much that was it.

"So . . . you owe, what, sixty thousand dollars? Seventy?" It wasn't that great a property; how much could it be? Mike frowned, trying to figure it out. It was just across the bridge from Manhattan, but small, had no garage. They'd bought it before the Queens real estate boom. There wasn't even a dishwasher in the kitchen.

"Seventy-three," April admitted. "It has a thirty-year mortgage, and the house is probably worth more now."

"Lots more now. I don't get this. You don't want to get married because you owe seventy-three thousand dollars?" He was incredulous. She made more than that in a year. Together they made more than twice that every year. He already had more than fifteen years in. He was being recruited to the private sector practically every day. Plenty of jobs out there for a lot more money.

"The house is probably worth two hundred now. Maybe more," he said. What was her problem?

"I don't own it, only the mortgage." April's bladder was bursting. She needed a bathroom.

"That's it?" he repeated, frowning some more.

"Yeah." She lifted a shoulder. It was a lot of money, and she couldn't force her parents to sell. The way she saw it, Mike supported his mother. That was two rents in his column. Her father helped with the house, but not a lot, and Skinny Dragon not at all. Both of April's parents were tightfisted in the extreme. They were saving for their old age, afraid of an empty belly. April's head ached. Money and filial piety, and love for Mike. Those were her conflicts. She'd almost gotten over the whole ambition thing. Almost.

"I'll be right back." She jumped out of her chair, charged to the bathroom, and peed copiously, sighing with relief. Then the case popped back in her mind. So much for lack of ambition.

Wendy may or may not have had a cigarette or a drink and then gone to pee during the ceremony. But she had opportunity. She was the manipulator here, the one who knew everything. April made a note to herself to have a word with Hollis to stay out of it and let her handle the questioning. She wanted to go over the client list, do her own background check of Wendy. There was something there, but she didn't know what it was.

When April got back to the table, Mike was sipping his beer, deep in thought. He picked up a dumpling with his chopsticks and smiled at her enigmatically. "Pretty good," he said about the food.

"I'm glad you like it." April waited for his next words. But none were forthcoming. She gathered that the ball was in her court now. She poured her fourth cup of tea. Now for health she had only sixteen to go.

Nineteen

At eleven-thirty that night April picked up her home phone on the first ring. It was Ching.

"Ching. How ya doin'?" April was disappointed. She'd hoped it was Mike, calling to say he was sorry he'd been so tough on her.

Ching started wailing right away. "Oh, God, April. This is a terrible thing. Who killed that poor girl? Ma saw it on TV and she's going nuts."

"I don't know. It's an odd, sad case, but it doesn't have anything to do with you. Tell your mother."

"I told her, but she thinks it's bad luck."

April sighed. "How can a stranger's murder be bad luck for you?"

"Well, not only me, April. You, too."

"Oh, God," April muttered.

"She thinks you'll never get married. Did you call Gao back?"

"Huh? Gao?"

"He's the chef you had lunch with yesterday."

Oh, Jesus. April closed her eyes. She didn't have time for this. "Sorry, Ching, I remember. You know I can't fix parking tickets. I have no 'in' with Immigration. He wants a green card, get a lawyer, whatever.

If he's been collared I'll check it out. But not right now."

"He hasn't been collared," Ching said.

"Good." Anything having to do with a hostage or kidnaping she could get Special Case detectives on it. She didn't want to sound harsh, but her plate was full and her influence limited.

"No, no, it's nothing like that. He wants to better himself is all. He's a good guy, relative of a relative of Matthew's. And he's really good, trust me."

"Ching, can't this wait?" April wailed.

"No, it can't wait. I know your father is slowing down," Ching told her.

April groaned. She had to look at Wendy's client list, see if there was anything funny about any of the other weddings she'd done. She had to stay focused on finding Tovah's killer. But she couldn't resist the sore subject of her father slowing down. It would be a disaster if he retired.

"Who says?" she demanded. Her father looked pretty good to her. As long as she could remember he'd been bald and skinny, had worn thick glasses, and stumbled around with his buddies after drinking too much Johnnie Walker. As far as she could tell, he was still energetic on the two-P.M. to two-A.M. schedule.

"This is what I heard. You with me? Gao is interested in meeting him. He's very good. They come from the same area, you know, speak the same language. I thought it might help you out."

April didn't see how it would help her out.

"April?"

"Yeah."

"You're very stubborn, anybody ever tell you that?"

"Yeah." Everybody told her that. Her parents, her bosses, Mike, now her sister-cousin. What were they talking about? She wasn't stubborn. She was the essence of flexible.

"Look, I don't want you to have bad luck. Be an old maid. Do I have to spell this out for you?" Ching was getting impatient.

"I don't have any idea what you're talking about," April said huffily.

"Oh, come on, April. I wanted to marry an American. I *intended* to marry an American. My parents flipped; I'm not kidding. Boy, did we fight. Every time we talked it was a fight."

"I remember. But you didn't marry an American." End of argument.

"Where Matthew grew up, he was like the only Chinese in school, okay? He's as American as they come, hot dogs and pizza every day, no Chinese food at all, and he doesn't speak a word."

"Ching, I have to get up early tomorrow."

"And frankly, he didn't want to marry Chinese any more than I did. He thinks Chinese girls are bossy. Our falling in love was an accident."

"Ching! Stop already."

"You love fighting with your ma. Get over it. Just make it happen. Take control. Listen to the *I Ching*, April."

April snorted. The *I Ching* was the Chinese oracle, possibly the world's oldest fortune-telling device and guide to correct behavior. April did consult the *I Ching* from time to time, but it never gave her any advice she wanted to have. Patience, patience, patience. That was about it. But that wasn't the *I Ching* Ching meant.

"Look, you and I go back a long way," Ching said.

True, all the way back to birth. Ching had a fat mother. April had a skinny one. In middle school they used to roll around in bed laughing about it. Same mother, different sizes. Ching ended up going to college in California and dating a bunch of American boys. She'd gotten out. April had always been jealous. Now Ching was marrying a Chinese after all and was considered the good and golden daughter by everyone. April's concessions to her parents left her with nothing but the unpleasant label "worm daughter" because she wasn't doing better.

"Stubborn!" Ching repeated. "If your dad retires without choosing his replacement, he'll have no one owing him. He'll get nothing out of it."

"So you're thinking of Gao as his replacement," April said slowly. That would mean she wouldn't have to take care of him and Skinny in their retirement, as they threatened every time she talked about marrying Mike.

"Do I have to spell it out for you?"

"Ah, so. Replace me," she murmured thoughtfully.

"Yes, replace you," Ching said. "Duh!"

April wondered why she hadn't thought of this before. Outsourcing children was a ten-thousand-year-old Chinese tradition. No son, adopt a son. When April started dating Mike, she'd given Skinny Dragon the poodle Dim Sum as a peace offering. The dog was cute but couldn't pay the rent or fix the toilets, couldn't have a grandchild. Brilliant, Americanized sister-cousin understood Chinese manipulation better than she. Interesting.

"Gao had a good position in Hong Kong. He just

threw it off and came here with the wrong people. You know your dad's a good guy. If he thinks Gao is a comer, he'll help out. If Gao caters to your mom, she'll like him. You leave. Gao takes your place and pays the mortgage."

"Does he have the money?" April said finally, a little breathless with the possibility of escape.

"He will as soon as he gets the job."

"Ching, you're amazing." In all the years that April's father and mother had schemed and plotted to get her to do what they wanted it never occurred to April that she might actively manipulate her parents right back. Ching interrupted her reflection on the subject.

"April, you know that murdered girl?"

Again *that girl.* "Her name was Tovah," April said softly.

"She was wearing a Tang Ling gown. I saw Tang today. She's very upset about it, but doesn't want her name in the paper. It's bad luck for her too."

"Jesus." April was stunned. She'd forgotten Ching's acquaintance with the famous designer. "Did Tang know her?"

"Yes. It was a custom gown. She'd met the girl and her mother. It's just so terrible."

"Yes, it is, Ching," April murmured.

"One more thing," Ching said, suddenly hesitant.

"What's that?"

"Tang offered me a gown," she said meekly.

"Wow. Lucky you," April said lightly, though her head spun a little with the happy news. Not only a Chinese groom, and a Chinese wedding, but a famous Chinese designer gown, too! Skinny was going to have a field day with this.

"My mother doesn't know. She's going to kill me because she wants a traditional wedding, the whole bit. No white gown."

"No, no, Ching. Don't worry. It's your day. You get to choose. Mai will understand. Everything's going to be fine," April told her. The magic words finally got the happy bride off the phone.

Twenty

On Tuesday morning at quarter to eight April called in for her messages at Midtown North. Lieutenant Iriarte himself instantly came on the line.

"You in today?" he demanded.

"No, sir."

He grunted. "What's the story with that bride case?"

"Unclear," she murmured, wondering whether she should ask for his help.

"Had a gypsy case a few years back," he mused, trying to be friendly. "Let me tell you, those Romanies sell their girls, too. At the weddings, they take over a trailer park or a motel. Relatives come from all over. Crime goes way up in the area. People don't know what hit them. They get ripped off every which way. You hear about that?"

"Yes, sir, there was a seminar about it a few years ago," April replied. Gypsies posing as plumbers, driveway pavers, phone repairmen, utility workers, went into people's houses, got them all confused, stole their money and everything else they could carry away. The victims were mostly old people, no longer sharp and thinking defensively. It didn't apply to midtown Manhattan, or to Riverdale.

"I could go on and on about those Romanies. Their weddings are just an excuse for a big brawl. They get drunk, gamble money and women, knife each other. When we bring them in, they run riot over the precinct. They have it all over us. I'm telling you these people have no rule of law. We've seen some pretty bad stuff. Killings, knifings, rapes . . ."

"Yes, sir," April said. But it didn't have anything to do with her law-abiding Orthodox Jews.

"Anybody who'd sell a little girl is sick in the head. You got a line on that?" he said finally.

"Not yet." But after a late-night conversation with Inspector Bellaqua, April did have a slightly different take on the matter. Turns out it was the girls' families that enticed the boys' families. They didn't *sell* their daughters; they bought husbands for them. Quite the opposite of the Chinese way. During a restless night, April tried to imagine her parents putting out a nickel to impress a son-in-law. She thought about Ching agonizing over wearing an extravagant Tang Ling gown, and her auntie Mai worrying that she would never get married. This started her thinking about something Mike had said last night, but she couldn't tease out what it was.

"Thanks for the input, sir, I'll look into it," she said about the gypsies. Should she ask him?

"And you're getting behind here. That's not good," he grumbled, abandoning friendly. "Don't drop the ball."

"No, sir," April said.

Iriarte was always worried about her dropping the ball. But she never did. Last week she'd been working a car theft. A tourist from Tennessee had left his Mercedes unattended on Sixth Avenue in front of

Radio City Music Hall. She also had a home invasion on Central Park West. A white male posing as the decorator had forced his way into a co-op, tied up the maid, and stolen some expensive jewelry and silver that turned out to be the owner's family heirlooms. Neither exactly major crimes. She also had a court appearance on another case for which the DA's office needed to prep her. But it was nothing hot-button like this major homicide racing toward the forty-eight-hour mark with no resolution in sight. Should she ask him?

"Oh, and by the way, you got Doled," Iriarte said.

"What! Are you sure?" Was he pranking her?

"Dead sure. The notification's for today, so you gotta go, you hear me?" he demanded.

"Yes, sir," she said.

She was in her car on her way up to the Bronx to warn Hollis off Wendy before meeting Mike and Poppy Bellaqua at headquarters to view the wedding video, which had been viewed so far only at the Five-oh. She'd left Queens and just entered the Bronx going west on the Major Deegan Expressway toward Riverdale. Now she had to get off, turn around, and head back around the heel of the Bronx to the Bruckner Expressway that followed a northeasterly course in the direction of White Plains and New England. *Shit.*

Dole was random drug testing. This was the one Department order that put all other orders, including major homicides, on the back burner. There was no getting around it, no missed appointments, no changing days, and nobody was exempt, from the police commissioner on down. Names were drawn every day, and the day you were picked you had to go up to Health Services and pee into two vials. The second vial was kept in case there was a challenge on the first one. If the drug test was positive, you were fired. Period.

It was absolutely firm that you had to go that day so there was no chance for the passage of time to get anything funny out of your system. And there was no chance of cheating because someone came into the room with you and watched you provide your sample. In April's case, this was a particular agony because she had a major peeing-in-public phobia. Major. Everybody else breezed right through the nothing ordeal, but to April it was not a nothing ordeal. She didn't like even a female person in there with her, didn't like it at all.

"Listen, you could help me out," she said slowly.

"Oh, yeah?" Iriarte's voice brightened.

"You could save us some time and have Charlie do some background work for me."

"You got a suspect?"

"Could be."

"You got a name on that suspect?"

"Yeah. Wendy Lotte. That's Lincoln, Oliver, double Tom, Eleanor. Got it?"

"Yeah, yeah. Lot with two Ts and an E. Would that be Gwendolyn?"

"No, just the W."

"Would there be anything else?"

"Tang Ling."

"The dress designer?"

"Yeah. The bride was wearing a Tang gown. Just indulge me a little."

"Okay, can do."

The Schoenfelds had five girls and four boys. April

finished her Dole in record time and spent an hour in the Schoenfelds' finished basement, talking in turn with all five girls and two of the boys while upstairs more sitting shivah was going on, and outside a dozen reporters were taking photos of mourners and trying to get them to speak.

April had totally expected to waste her time. Unlike in the movies, investigative interviews were never wrapped up in five minutes. First of all, it took hours of traveling time, across a bridge, two bridges, traffic all the way. When she got wherever she was going, sometimes the person she wanted was available, sometimes not. If she was really lucky, the person was there and willing to talk. But a lot of people thought they didn't know anything worthwhile and didn't want to talk. April had learned a long time ago that she couldn't ever go anywhere cold. She had to do some homework first, had to have some idea of what kind of information she wanted to elicit. And she had to know something about the person she wanted to question so a connection could be made.

Usually it took hours and she went away with a little something, a tiny tidbit that might be important down the line and might not. What April knew about Tovah was that she was spacey, not all there. She wanted to know what that meant.

At the same time Mike traveled to the Ribikoffs' three-story brick house in Flatbush, Brooklyn. He hadn't slept well without April. But after their dim sum dinner last night, he hadn't felt like spending the night with her and took her right home. A first. Now he was wide-awake and focused on his interview with the groom's family.

He'd done some research on the family, and the background check had uncovered an uneventful life. The Ribikoffs were registered Republicans, had traveled to Israel in 1998 and 2000. They paid taxes every year and had never been audited. Their credit cards were far from maxed out. They owned their house and '94 Ford Explorer. No vehicular violations. They had four children of which Schmuel was the second. Their oldest child was a girl, married last year, now living upstate. The wedding had cost in the neighborhood of twenty thousand dollars, about ten percent of what the Schoenfelds had put out for Tovah's. The Ribikoffs' two younger boys were still in high school. Neither of them had ever been in trouble, nor had Schmuel, who was highly regarded by his teachers and classmates. The family business was real estate—not big-time like the Schoenfelds—but the Ribikoffs were not doing badly, either. They were connected to some recent Russian émigrés, who hadn't been invited to the wedding. Was that good enough motive to kill the bride? Mike didn't think so.

Unlike the Schoenfeld house, this one was comfortable but had little display of major wealth. Mr. Ribikoff himself answered the door. Thin, balding, sad-looking, and small, he didn't look like the kind of man who would seize a valuable diamond ring off a dying girl.

"I don't know how I can help you. I told the detective yesterday I don't know why anyone would do something like this," he said, reluctantly offering Mike a seat in his living room.

"How well did your son know Tovah?" Mike got to the point right away.

Ribikoff lifted a hand. "The boy saw her picture.

She was a pretty girl." The almost-father-in-law's face became animated for a moment as he thought of how pretty his son's wife would have been. "A nice, quiet girl, not a chatterbox. He liked her; what else did he need to know?"

"How did they meet?"

"My wife's friend, Ruth Lasker, she had the photo. My wife, she liked the girl's face, too. I liked her. Rebecca told Ruth we were interested." He dipped his chin. "Then he came to take a look at Schmuel praying."

Mike frowned. "Who?"

"Schoenfeld. He came to the Yeshiva, looked at the boy, liked what he saw." Mr. Ribikoff had moment of pride for his son, who'd attracted the interest of a rich and important family.

"Then what happened?"

"Naturally my wife wanted to go to the house, have a cup of coffee, eat a piece of cake, and see the girl before they started to date. But Suri Schoenfeld refused. That's the kind of person she is."

"Why?"

"She didn't want us telling Schmuel what to do. She insisted it was up to the children to decide if they liked each other." He rolled his eyes. "My wife is not like Suri Schoenfeld with the airs, but she does have a mind of her own. Why are you asking this? Who do you suspect?"

"We're looking for anything unusual."

"Oh, there was plenty unusual." Ribikoff made a face. "We live in a tight community here. You can get everything you need here. You never have to leave. Everybody understands the rules. My wife complains that the whole world knows your business, knows your kids' business. They see you coming, they see you going, and the talk keeps up all day long. That's why it's a tradition to find new blood for the children, people outside your own four corners. But new blood that's the same blood. You know what I'm talking?"

Mike nodded. He knew exactly what Ribikoff was talking.

"Tovah was a religious girl and the family would have been good for Schmuel, but they polluted us."

"Polluted?"

"Yes, we do things simply, in a family way. We stick with the people we know. We don't bring in goyim—*shfartzes* from Africa to arrange the flowers. No offense, but you see what I'm saying? Look at the shame they've brought us," he said sadly.

Mike changed the subject. "Tell me about Tovah's ring," he said.

"It was a very costly ring. That's all I'm going to say." His eyes strayed toward the ceiling.

"Why did you remove it from Tovah's finger?"

Ribikoff closed his eyes, opened them, avoided the steady gaze of the detective. "It has nothing to do with this."

"Did you think the girl was dead?" Mike persisted. Did he want the girl dead?

"I didn't know. I wasn't thinking." Ribikoff crossed his legs.

"It seems an odd reaction."

Ribikoff clicked his tongue. "It was what it was."

"You just wanted it back?" Mike probed softly.

The man erupted. "Well, of course I wanted it back. The boy couldn't have married her after that, could he?" he said angrily.

Mike frowned. "Even if she'd recovered?"

Ribikoff shook his head as if only a dummy would think otherwise, then jabbed his chin belligerently at Mike. "It was a costly item. They would never have given it back."

Mike was chilled by these answers. He had his suspicions about the whole arrangement. Bad feeling rocketed back and forth between the two families. The Ribikoffs were not sitting shivah with the Schoenfelds. Something was way off the normal about the Ribikoffs, but that didn't make them killers. Mike questioned Schmuel and his mother closely but learned nothing really useful.

Twenty-one

Just before noon April, Mike, and Inspector Bellaqua met in the video section at One Police Plaza to view the video of Tovah Schoenfeld's wedding preparations. It was crowded in the room where usually only one person pored over surveillance tapes of banks, stores, fast-food chains, and the elevators of housing projects where crimes had been committed. This was an eerie first. Not many homicide detectives got to see their victim alive and the murder scene being constructed.

The video opens on the synagogue with its two bloodred azalea bushes out front, then cuts to a Caucasian male, five-ten, heavy build. Distinguishing feature: a blond pompadour that stood up a good three inches. He's wearing a pink silk shirt and fusses with the *huppah*, his lips moving as he waves away the camera. *Get out of here*, he's saying.

There is no audio or time frame. The next sequence shows a good-looking, skinny Latino, five-five, five-six, wearing tight jeans. His thick black hair is in a short ponytail. He's adjusting flowers in the party room, sashaying from table to table, aware of the camera. He sticks a lily stem between his teeth and poses. Cut. Next, waitresses are setting the tables

with glasses, silver, napkins, plates. Three women—
all have thick curly hair and gold Jewish stars around
their necks. Cut to a short take of an African American, black as midnight, a big man, around six-two.
He's standing by the exit door between two orange
trees with an unreadable expression on his face. Cut
to an elaborate ice sculpture on the food table, not yet
beginning to melt. Cut to . . .

"There she is," Bellaqua said.

Tovah appears, disconcertingly alive with her hair
in rollers under a hair dryer. Her hands are splayed
in front of her on a table. Only the back of the manicurist is seen as she bends over her task of painting
Tovah's nails are pearl pink. The manicurist has red
hair. On the table beside Tovah is the blond wig on a
Styrofoam head. Behind her are many colorful
dresses hanging on a clothes rack, among them her
wedding gown and veil in two plastic bags. Tovah
looks at the camera as if she doesn't see it.

"She looks drugged," April commented.

"Mmmm," Bellaqua agreed.

"Weird," Mike murmured.

Cut to a little girl on the floor crying. Tovah leans
over to hug her, hands her a hard candy. The little girl
takes the candy, puts it in her mouth, and stops crying. Tovah smiles.

"There. She looks okay there," Mike said. "Pretty
girl. Likes children."

Cut to Tovah and her mother and grandmother
arm in arm. Tovah's hair and nails are done. She's
smiling here, too.

"She looks fine here. Eyes are okay," April said.

Cut to . . .

"Ah," Bellaqua sighed.

"Just look at that!" Mike marveled.

At last, Tovah is wearing her voluminous wedding dress. A small Asian male stoops to arrange the folds of the dress, then steps back and tosses a cloud of white over her. A fog drops over her. The veil makes Tovah look as if she's trapped inside a tent of mosquito netting.

"Jesus. That's something. Who's that guy?" April said.

"Name's Kim. He's from the dress store."

"She sent someone?" April said, incredulous. Tang again. Not good. The presence of Ching's famous friend in this case was beginning to bother her.

"Guess so."

Cut to Tovah in her ten-thousand-dollar tent walking out of the room—not into the party room, but into the corridor on the other side that leads to the elevator that leads to the rabbi's study on the second floor. The camera follows her and her mother into the study, where Rabbi Levi waits with her father and the Ribikoffs. Nothing can be seen of Tovah through her veil as an illustrated scroll of some kind is brought out and displayed. Papers are signed.

It's a long movie. Then the camera follows the bride, her train, and her family downstairs to the corridor outside the sanctuary. Cut. The film ends at the open door of the sanctuary. They groaned and played the video two more times.

"Let's get stills of all the non–family members," April said. "We'll see if anyone saw them."

"Yep. And backgrounds on all of them. It's time to widen the net. Maybe one of these people hates Jews enough to kill one," Bellaqua said. "Ugly," she murmured. "Let's break for some lunch."

They left headquarters and walked across the street for a hamburger at the Metropolitan. While they ate Mike recounted his interview with the Ribikoffs. April did not say a word about going up to COOP City to pee in a cup, but she did describe her visit to the Schoenfelds.

"Tovah was a very nervous girl, probably had an anxiety disorder that was treated with antacids and bed rest. She liked shopping trips in the city with her mother and grandmother, but didn't do well with the strict adherence to rules. Apparently Tovah didn't like controls and direction. Her sisters said she was the only one who consistently wiggled out of tasks and schoolwork and anything else she didn't want to do. She had headaches and tuned out a lot."

Bellaqua shook her head. "So we've got zip on the families and their friends."

"No one who was present had opportunity. Everybody was accounted for, but . . ." Mike shrugged.

"But what?" April asked.

"The families were at odds before the incident. Ribikoff took the ring because he didn't trust the Schoenfelds to give it back, and he didn't want his son marrying a damaged item. He was thinking very clearly, almost as if he had a plan."

"Oy." Bellaqua picked up the tab, thought about it for a minute.

"Okay, let's take it further, then. We'll run a check on everyone Ribikoff knows, every call he made in the last month, every withdrawal from his bank. See what he was up to." She rolled her eyes. "It's a hell of a way to break off an engagement, but we'll follow it through."

Mike nodded as she paid the bill. "Thanks. They make good burgers here."

Bellaqua didn't answer. She and April were heading for the door. Already on to the next thing.

After lunch, Mike checked with Ballistics to see what they had on the gun. He couldn't make contact with the right person so he and April headed uptown to see the blond guy in the video, the florist who called himself Louis like one of the French kings. On the way April told him about her two-minute conversation with Hollis. "I told him we'd deal with Wendy ourselves. Do our own background on her."

"How did he take it?"

"Seemed fine with it."

Louis's shop was icy, and they almost walked out when they saw a woman with little packages of foil in rows all over her head sitting under a hair dryer reading a magazine. Then they saw Louis.

"Come on in. We do hair on Wednesdays," he said.

"Sergeant Woo, Lieutenant Sanchez," Mike said.

"Louis the Sun King. What can I do for you?" Louis's hair was yellow. It stood straight up. His shirt was purple. Stuck in the open collar was an ascot. Bright red and yellow spilled out. His nails were manicured, shiny. His accent was slightly, incongruously British. He tilted his head and looked, for a second, like a huge, curious canary.

"We're investigating the Tovah Schoenfeld homicide," Mike took the lead.

"A terrible tragedy. Come out in the garden where we can talk." Officiously, he patted his astonishing pompadour.

As they walked through the shop, April glanced

around at the planters and display of glass and
porcelain vases. Everything looked expensive. Outside, Louis plopped himself on a garden chair in the
shade of the building next door and indicated to
Mike and April the two chairs in the sun. Mike
moved them into the shade and waited for April to
sit down.

"I've already made a statement. What else do you
want to know?" Louis said, leaning back in his chair.

"Details. A lot more details."

"Why? Do you suspect me?" Louis laughed
loudly.

Mike sniffed delicately and took out his notebook.
"How did you get the Schoenfeld job?" he asked.

"They came in one day. They wanted something
no one else they know had done. And, of course, the
more the better. The Schoenfelds were not hard to
please."

"People just come in off the street?" Mike said
incredulously.

"Some do."

"How do they know about you?"

"Oh, the magazines. I've been written up in all
the industry rags. Plus the *New York Times, Town and
Country.* Word of mouth." Again the hand went to his
hair.

"I understand you have a waiting list. And people
offer to change their dates just to get you." This from
April.

"The spring is a busy time," Louis said modestly.

"So people don't just come off the street," she said.

"Well." He lifted a shoulder.

"Who referred the Schoenfelds?" Mike again.

"I'll have to check. Maybe it was Wendy Lotte. I've been doing a lot of work with Wendy lately."

April glanced at Mike. Wendy again.

"Does Wendy get a commission?" she asked.

Louis looked surprised. "Why do you ask?"

"Decorators get commissions on everything they provide for a job. I just wondered if party planning works the same way." April was all over it. She'd checked it out. Party planners got a commission on everything.

"No, I have one fee. The principals pay me directly. It doesn't go through Wendy," he said glibly.

She made a note that he was a liar. "Does Wendy use other people?" she asked.

"Oh, of course. And so do I."

Mike grew silent as April took over and led Louis through his movements the two days before the Schoenfeld event. It took a while. They got an earful on the difficulties of working with suppliers of all kinds. This week, for example, Louis needed fresh coconut palm fronds. He had to order out of state. He showed them the plans for the Hay wedding.

"The Hays wanted whole grass huts constructed, but the St. Regis refused, so they had to settle on thatched umbrellas with twinkling lights."

Mike and April saw how a ballroom got transformed into a fantasy place.

"Sometimes a client wants to create a real night sky complete with the Big Dipper and the Milky Way. I use theater techies for lighting, and carpentry. They're the best." Louis's hand went to his hair again. "I love the theater, don't you?"

"Absolutely," April said.

Then Mike asked where Louis's staff had been at the time of the shooting.

"We were gone long before the guests began arriving," Louis said.

Mike asked a few more questions about his relationship to Wendy, then collected the names and addresses of the "boys" in the video. Tito wasn't there at the moment, but Louis explained where he could be reached.

"Ah, and Jama?"

"Jama isn't his real name," Louis said. "I call him Jama because he's from Africa. That's how they say hello there."

April knew Louis was misinformed about that or lying again. "What's his real name, then?" she asked.

"I have no idea. He didn't tell me," Louis said loftily.

"Where is he now?"

"Home sick."

"What's wrong with him?"

"He's scared to death of cops. Wouldn't you be if someone was murdered and you were the only one on the scene who happened to be black?"

Mike took the man's address and stuffed his notebook back in his jacket pocket. From the car April called Poppy on her cell.

The inspector didn't have anything on the others yet, but a computer check on Louis's social security number revealed his real name as Steve Creese.

"Guy comes from western Connecticut, near Hartford. At the age of six, he and his older brother, David, were removed from their parents. An arsonist, possibly their estranged father, burned down the house, severely injuring their mother. Steve grew up in a number of foster homes, got in trouble in middle school, straightened himself out in high school. He turned up running an art gallery in Hawaii in the early eighties. Returned to California in the late eighties, where he dressed sets for movies. Migrated back east and became the assistant to Jack Eldridge, a well-known florist whose inspiration was the regimented shrubs and gardens of Louis the Fourteenth. Jack Eldridge died of AIDS in 'ninety-three. Steve Creese inherited the shop and the business and reinvented himself as Louis the Sun King."

April handed the phone to Mike. He heard it all again. Then she dialed the lab out in Jamaica. Still no word on the gun. The rest of the day was busy, but uneventful. Just after ten April headed home to Queens alone, disappointed when Mike didn't mention spending the night together.

Twenty-two

Prudence Hay woke up on Wednesday morning with the dreads, the same dreads she'd had for the few last months about whether she really wanted to marry Thomas Fenton, or not really. The dreads were nauseating. Dizzy making. She'd also had too much to drink last night, trying to goad some life into him. She pulled her face out from under a mountain of pillows, rolled over on her back, and tried to make the room stop spinning. *OhGodithurt.*

Her thoughts were as agonizing as her hangover. They spun with the room, for Thomas was perfect on paper but not so perfect in real life. *I want to get married. I don't want to get married.* Oh, Prudence felt sick. She was in her bed in the Sutton Place apartment where they were staying all week until the wedding—barely three days away. Her room was all pink and apple green. *Girlie* was the only word for it. She groaned. She adored her mother even though her mother was sometimes silly and extravagant. Her mother had been loyal to her no matter what she did, and she'd had her share of scrapes growing up. Her mother wanted her to marry Thomas Fenton: he was tall, dark, handsome, suitable in every way. Her father was her rock, her advisor, and her friend. She was his only daughter, and he wanted her to marry Thomas Fenton: his family was prominent and wealthy. He trusted Thomas to take good care of her. Already Thomas had bought an apartment for them and was making it absolutely perfect. Everything with Thomas had to be perfect except himself.

He didn't like travel, didn't like going out and having fun. Didn't play golf or tennis, didn't finish work before ten or eleven even on weekends. And he didn't get hard when he hugged her. That was the problem. He had no passion, no juice. Still, he was every girl's dream. He was on partner track, had money in the bank. He was a perfectionist who personally oversaw every detail of the apartment renovations so that she didn't have to worry about a thing. Thomas wanted her totally free of worry, just a happy-go-lucky wife with nothing much to do. When he wasn't fussing with the contractors, he was working to make money all the time so she could have a perfect life. A hammer beat in Pru's head as she imagined Thomas's vision for her perfect, orderly life. She was twenty-four. He was thirty-two and certain she was the One. Everyone she knew thought he was an absolute doll. All twelve of her bridesmaids thought so. Thomas kissed her on the street, insisted on holding hands all the time, and no one knew their infrequent sex together took less than two minutes. He had no staying power. She wasn't sure how much it should matter to her.

"How about some coffee?"

"Jesus! Get out of here, Anthony!" Prudence yelped. "It creeps me out when you do that." She sat up, clutching her throbbing head. Why did Anthony do that! "Jesus! Are you crazy!" she said, furious at him for yet another intrusion into her private space. He had no right to come into her room.

"Wendy is here opening your gifts. I'd worry about it if I were you," he said, neutral as always.

"You aren't me," she said. "I trust Wendy completely. What is she going to do, take something?"

"You should open your own gifts," he told her. "If you were a happy girl, you'd be taking an interest."

"I'm a happy *woman*. And it's not your business. Haven't you heard of the intercom?" she added.

"I'm worried about you, and you don't answer the intercom."

"I told you I don't like your bugging me." Prudence sighed. "I'm not a little girl anymore."

Anthony humphed about that. He didn't move. He stood in the doorway, looking at her. She hated that.

"Wendy wants to go over the guest list and the seating plan with you. Your mother wants you to go over to Louis's after your fitting. She'll meet you at the florist's. Hurry up. It's getting late."

"All right, all right. I'm coming. Close the door, will you?"

"Is everything all right, Pru? You look so unhappy—"

"Close the door, Anthony."

"I'll get your coffee."

"Fine, but don't bring it here. I'll have it in the dining room."

"Very good." Anthony backed out and closed the door.

Unhappy? She didn't like him saying that. She wasn't unhappy. She just had a hangover. Prudence threw back the covers all the way. She was wearing a peach slip and nothing else. Groaning, she dragged herself out of bed. *Ohshitohshitohshit. I feel like dog food.* Muttering this, she stumbled to the bathroom, where she tossed down two aspirin without water, then squinted at herself in the mirror. She breathed noisily through her nose as she assessed the damage. Did she look unhappy? No, she did not. But she did look pretty wasted. Thomas wouldn't like seeing her like that. She didn't want Wendy seeing her wasted, either. Spoiled her glow.

She splashed cold water on her face. *Hello.* She was back in the world, about to be Mrs. Thomas Fenton. Never mind that that her head hurt like hell, and she sometimes had a niggling worry. Life was great. It would all work out. She knew it would. She threw on jeans and a T-shirt and padded into the dining room, where Wendy sat with a mountain of opened blue Tiffany boxes.

"Okay, I'm ready," Prudence said brightly, smiling and happy again. "Bring it on."

Twenty-three

Wendy's life fell apart when she was ten, after a jolt of pure terror forged together a jumble of images. War was on the news, and though science was on her mind, war was in her heart, too. That day she'd killed the gardener's pet rabbit to feed the shark.

Feeding the shark had not been her smart idea. Her brother Randy wanted to see if a shark would eat a rabbit. But Randy was with Daddy on a hunting trip in Alaska and she'd been left alone for many days, so she'd decided to do some hunting herself. She killed the big tame white rabbit that was a prize from a local magic show, then put it in a garbage bag and hid it under the dock.

Later, she saw stunned little bundles on the news—children with missing hands or legs wrapped in rags. Maybe land mines. Maybe civil war. Wendy didn't know what it was. Little faces bobbed over the shoulders of grown-ups who were walking in a long line away from the popping-corn sound of bullets. Some of the bundles were on the ground, not moving, wrapped up tightly so that nothing showed. It scared her. She thought she was next.

When it was dark, she took the spear gun and underwater light from the rack of scuba gear in the mudroom. Outside, the sky was a light show with a three-quarter moon so bright she didn't need the flashlight to make her way down to the saltwater pond. She walked across the wet grass of the broad lawn that sloped down to the water, then through the trees following the path through the sea grass down to the dock, trying to be brave without her brothers. She hated being left behind.

The ocean crept in here at high tide, rising to meet the dock at the farthest end, more than a mile from the cut that made it a suitable breeding ground for clams and mussels and scallops. That night was so quiet and windless that the water barely lapped at the wedge of rocky sand on the shoreline where the biggest clams dug in deep; the crabs scuttled along, pincers ready to grab at anything that crossed their path; and the razor clams were as sharp and lethal as their name.

From here, the mainland lights joined together as a soft glow against black land. The few pale white halos that could be seen around the pond marked the nearest summer houses, far down unconnected dirt roads. The Lotte farm was a lonely spot.

When Wendy finally turned on the light and shone it on the inky water, right away she saw the dark shape of the dog shark that came in with the tide at night. It circled in the shallows near the dock, possibly looking for lobster bait, or a place to spawn. She dumped the rabbit into the water. It hit with a splash and sank quickly into the black, then bobbed up in the shallows. The shark swam in, close to the shore, almost close enough for her to reach out and touch with the tip of her spear gun. It circled and circled but would not strike the dead rabbit. Wendy was scared.

If the tide didn't draw the rabbit out to deeper water by morning, everyone would know what she had done. She crept back to her room, certain she'd be caught and punished. She was sorry, really. When she heard the *chop chop chop* of a bird in the sky, she thought the helicopter was war coming to her from far away. Her punishment. A strobe flashed into her room, lighting it brighter than ten flashes of lightning on a nor'easter night.

"Mummy!" She wanted to hide in the attic. Instead, she ran down the hall calling for her mother.

"Ssshh, it's just the Coast Guard. There must have been a boating accident. Go to bed, sweetheart, everything's all right."

But Wendy didn't want to go to bed. She could see someone in there. Daddy was back; her brothers were back. They'd know it wasn't a boating accident. The strobe lit the room again, and she realized the man with her mother was not her daddy. After that night, she knew the divorce that ruined everything was all her fault.

Twenty-four

"What happened to it? I don't understand." Prudence had lost her good spirits. She was getting weepy. Her wedding gown was too tight. It wouldn't zip up, an impossible situation. She stamped her foot. "What are we going to do?" she demanded. "I want to talk to Tang."

"Oh, no, that's not necessary." Wendy was eager to prevent her from making a scene. "Don't worry so much, dear. We can get this fixed."

Wendy sounded cheery, but she was seething inside. This should have taken five minutes, should have been a nothing visit. Instead, Prudence was flipping out. Wendy didn't need this. She glanced at her watch, then looked up in time to see Tang herself sweep down the stairs to the second-floor showroom from her private office on the floor above. Her ice blue spring suit was a stunner.

"Prudence, I heard you were here," she said with a smile.

Her assistant, Tessa, a tall, blond girl wearing a sober suit, followed Tang, carrying an alligator briefcase and matching purse. Tessa was briefing her boss in a fully audible whisper.

"You have four minutes right now. Remember,

you have to leave the leadership luncheon in an hour. You have to be at CBS for your taping at two. I booked makeup for one-thirty. Ben doesn't have a lot of time for you today; he's doing Hillary. . . . Don't worry about leaving the dais. They know you can't stay for dessert. After your taping, your husband will pick you up at the studio. His plane leaves at eight. You only have time for a quick drink, but he insists—"

"That's enough." Tang raised her hand, and Tessa shut her mouth. Wendy knew Tang needed constant reminders about her schedule and clearly enjoyed the running monologue. She raged at her own Lori for taking such an inconvenient vacation.

"Tang, how are you?" Wendy said, rising quickly to her feet.

Tang tapped at her diamond watch. She didn't have time to comment for Wendy.

"How does your mother like her jacket?" she asked Prudence, all smiles for *her*.

Prudence, however, could barely respond. She was that close to tears. "I don't know. I think it's all right. But Tang, this gown is a complete mess. My underwear shouldn't show. I expected better than this from you."

Tang frowned. "Let me see. Oh, my goodness, you're right. Have you been partying a little too much, Prudence?" she teased.

"Two minutes. The car is waiting," Tessa reminded.

Wendy glared at her. Tang made the silence signal with the back of her hand, then pushed the fitter out of the way so she could poke at the back seam of

Pru's gown, with its long zipper and two hundred tiny buttons that wouldn't close.

"Oh, this is not a problem. Kim can fix this in a second." She turned to Kim, her honey voice turning to acid. "Fix it in a second, Kim."

He nodded. "No problem."

"It's a problem for Miss Hay. Don't disappoint her," Tang said coldly. Then the honey voice again. "You'll have it tomorrow. Say hello to your mother for me." Tang turned to the open elevator and got in, followed by Tessa, already talking again.

Wendy smiled until the elevator doors closed and Prudence disappeared into a dressing room. Then she let loose.

"What's wrong with you? I wanted that dress done today!" she fumed, so furious at Kim she could barely control the tremor in her voice. "The gown was way too tight. The bustier showed. You upset Prudence and Tang."

"Don't yell at me, Wendy." Kim couldn't take it when people were upset with him.

"You did it on purpose," she ranted. "Why?"

"She got fatter," he protested.

"She did not get fatter. You fucked up her dress. Are you crazy? Don't you understand we can't afford having anyone suspicious now?"

Suspicious? He looked as her sideways. "Why you mad at me, Wendy? I don't understand. No one's suspicious."

"Don't give me that shit. The cops are all over me. You understand perfectly what's at stake. What do you think you're doing messing with that dress?"

"Clio so mad with me I'm scared she'll kill me in my sleep," he said. He was holding the heavy dress and long train in a plastic bag. It dipped to the carpet when Wendy took him by his two shoulders and shook him hard.

"You messed up Tovah's dress. You shouldn't have fucking been there. Don't you understand!" she hissed at him. "Now Prudence's. What are you thinking! Do you want us all in trouble?"

"Don't be mad with me, Wendy." Kim's teeth clacked with her shaking.

Wendy stopped shaking and dug her fingernails into his upper arms. "Yes, I'm mad at you."

"You're hurting me," he said.

She let him go. "What's Clio's problem?"

"Clio hates Tang. She don't pay me. I do extra work. She don't pay me."

"Oh, please. You make extra work on purpose. You want a tip, isn't that it?"

"Clio hate those rich girls." He swiped at his nose. "She hates them. She's not happy with me," he added sadly.

"Well, hello. Surprise, what did she expect?"

"Every day more mad. The police ask so many questions. Help me, Wendy. Tell Clio don't be mad."

"The police ask questions, doesn't mean they know what they're doing. Remember poor Andrea? God knows that was bad enough. . . ." Wendy let him go, her heart racing at the threat of Kim messing up those dresses just so he could do more work and get a tip. "What did you tell them?" she demanded.

"Oh, police?" Kim lifted his shoulders with the meek smile that was his trademark. "I don't understand English," he said softly. "Hardly a word."

"What did Clio tell them?" Wendy demanded.

"Clio crazy," he said. "She told me she'll kill me in my sleep."

Wendy blew air out of her mouth to stop herself from laughing at Clio's dilemma. She'd married a gay seamstress, hoping he'd become a heterosexual waiter. It wasn't going to happen.

"Look, keep me out of your troubles, Kim. Just keep my name out of it. And get that dress finished tomorrow the latest, you hear me? Make it perfect."

"Wendy, I gave Tang the plant you suggested. She's not mad with me, is she?"

"How should I know?"

Prudence came out of the dressing room, wearing her street clothes.

"There you are." Wendy smiled.

At three-thirty, after Prudence and Lucinda left the shop, Louis collapsed at his conference table, surrounded by the sketches for Pru's wedding. He was creating Hawaii again with real blooming passion-flower vines, and a water wall studded with birds-of-paradise. A hundred and fifty Hawaiian Sunset cattleyas would bloom in real seashell centerpieces on the tables, and even the band members would be dressed in leis and tropical shirts.

"What's the matter with you?" Wendy demanded as soon as they were alone. Everybody was in a funk today.

"Why bother asking? I thought you hated me." Louis's stormy gray eyes raked her over.

"What are you talking about?" Wendy tossed her head at the ridiculous idea.

"You stormed out on Monday, shrieking that you hate me, don't you remember?"

Wendy laughed. "Getting paranoid again, are we? Forgetting to take our medicine?"

"Oh, very funny." Louis made an irritated face and patted his hair uneasily.

"We're in this together, so don't freak on me. Prudence is having her prewedding jitters."

"Not exactly my problem. You're the Hay manager," Louis said.

"Uh-uh-uh. It's all our problem. Kim made her dress too tight. Her bustier showed. Lucinda is freaking out because of what happened to Tovah. We can't afford anyone acting out now."

"Well, I don't like her, either," Louis said sullenly.

"Who?"

"Spoiled, silly Prudence."

"Oh, for God's sake! Prudence is a lovely girl. . . . What's that face supposed to mean?"

"The police were here again."

Wendy's stomach heaved. "Which one?"

"The one with the mustache," he said, rolling his eyes.

"They all have mustaches," she said, impatiently.

"This one was in cowboy boots, quite attractive but a terrible dresser."

"Oh, the Spanish one. What did he want?"

"He had his Chinese sidekick with him," Louis added.

"Oh, Jesus." Wendy didn't like this. She needed a little drink to give her a lift, wished Lori were around to take over.

"They wanted to know who went up to the Bronx with me and how long we were there and what time I left. Same things they asked before. I told them what they asked."

"They haven't a clue," Wendy said angrily. "Everyone is freaking out."

"And now Jama is out there somewhere. He hasn't turned up since Sunday. My nerves are shot. I could just jump out of my skin."

"Well, tell the police about him. Let them deal with it," Wendy told him.

"I did." Louis groaned. "I told them where he lives. I hope they get him fast, so I can calm down and do St. Pat's. Now I'm down one helper. I should have six people working for me." *Pat pat* to the pompadour.

Wendy snorted. It was Louis's own fault that he didn't hire regular people to work for him instead of his pretty boys, all those runaways from civil war in those oh-so-faraway countries. The drama of the misplaced and traumatized every single day—that was Louis's thing. Who could even think of having people like that in their lives? Who needed it? Louis was a one-man social work agency. He had no fear.

And every boy Louis "helped" with work was a beautiful, troubled specimen. Only six months ago one of them had stolen fifty thousand dollars worth of art glass. Louis didn't know which boy was the thief, so he'd fired them both. Now he had Jama, an African near mute who'd never seen a town, much less a city, before he'd arrived in New York. Tito was an Argentinean whose family were among the disappeared. And Jorge, the Argentinean hair colorist, was another one. Who even knew his story? Louis could read her mind.

"Jorge wants to make a permanent spot for himself in the shop. Is the place big enough for two of us? Is it? I don't know. Tito is threatening to quit because there's too much work." Louis was frantic. "I don't know how I bear it."

Wendy changed the subject back to Pru's wedding. "How are the Sunset cats doing?"

He didn't answer. The orchids had a color palette of rust, lavender, white, and purple and were supposed to bloom in large seashells. But they were fragile and had a bloom time of exactly two and a half days. Only a lot of luck would make them absolutely perfect for the wedding luncheon on Saturday.

"How are your fifteen minutes of fame going? You selling your story to the *National Enquirer*?" Louis asked instead.

"Not yet. They haven't come up with enough to get me." Wendy smiled. Fifty thousand dollars to tell about the secret rituals of matchmaking among Orthodox Jews in America? *Please*. It was tempting, but not anywhere near enough. She wanted a quarter of a million for her story, an escalating story for sure. Wendy's hands were trembling. She needed a drink.

"Be nice to Prudence, will you? She's having a hard time," was her parting remark.

Twenty-five

After a second night sleeping apart, April and Mike worked separately on Wednesday morning. Mike and a detective from Homicide interviewed Louis's helper Tito for many hours. Tito stuck to the same story as Louis. Either they were both telling the truth or both of them were lying. April drove up to Riverdale to the Five-oh to talk with one of the detectives who'd visited Kim and his wife out in Queens on Sunday night.

"Kim is a real cutie, and his wife gives him a solid alibi," he said confidently. Detective Calvin Hill was maybe twelve and a half years old and newly promoted to the bureau. He held a copy of his DD-5, but April shook her head.

"I want to hear it from you. What do you mean, cutie?" she said.

He flapped his wrist. "The wife, Clio, definitely wears the pants in the family. Much older than he. Kim doesn't speak English. I think he speaks Philippine. Wife wouldn't let him talk. She says she drove him and the dress out to Riverdale in their car on Sunday afternoon."

April frowned. "He brought the wedding gown to his home? When and how did he get it there?"

Calvin shook his head. He hadn't asked that question.

"Why did he deliver the dress so late?" she asked.

"Kim's wife said the gown needed last-minute alterations. She says Mrs. Schoenfeld asked him to deliver the gown and help Tovah get dressed."

"Where did he do these alterations?"

Calvin shook his head again. He hadn't been interested in the movements of the dress, only the fitter.

April had the case file on the desk in front of her. It was already stuffed with hundreds of statements and interviews, but there were gaps everywhere. And the information they had didn't add up. The story of the gown didn't play to April at all.

"So Kim's wife drove him to Riverdale. Where did she park the car?" she said, back on Calvin's report.

"Down the block. There was no room in front of the synagogue. And Clio said she didn't want to get stuck in the lot because so many cars were moving in."

"Which way?" April asked.

"Excuse me?"

"Which way down the block?" she said impatiently.

"She didn't know," he said.

April blinked.

"I asked her, but she didn't know the area. She said she moved the car down the block, waited an hour for him to come out."

"I want to know where the car was parked. What time was that?" She moved on to the next question.

"Two P.M.," he said.

April scratched her head some more. "Two P.M.

they arrived? Two P.M. they parked? I need a more precise time frame here."

"I think they arrived at two P.M."

April was silent. *He thought* was not good enough.

Cavin consulted his notes. "She waited for him for an hour. He came out and the two of them drove home to Queens."

"That put the time at . . . ?"

"She said they left just after three. The shooting occurred twenty-five minutes later."

"What make of car? Did you take a look at the car?" April snapped.

Calvin shook his head.

"Find out what make of car. Where the two drove from. I want to know what time that couple arrived and where the car was parked. Every single thing about that car. And the gown. I want to know where it was. Who handled it, what time . . ." April couldn't contain her annoyance at the incomplete interview.

"Right here you had two people, husband and wife, who had the opportunity to get close to Tovah and the means to get away. I want to know everything about them." Her voice was hard. "Today."

Calvin gave her a stunned look. "Yes, ma'am."

A little while later she got a call from Lieutenant Iriarte on her cell phone.

"What do you have on Wendy Lotte?" he said.

Across the room April could see Hollis talking on the phone.

"You got something." She knew her boss, could hear excitement in his voice.

"Oh, yeah. We got a lot. She's a sport shooter, almost went to the Olympics. And she has a sheet."

"No kidding!"

"She was arrested for shoplifting three times in college, then shot her fiancé up on Martha's Vineyard. All these incidents occurred in Massachusetts. The family is prominent there. She was not charged in the shooting, got suspended sentences on the thefts. In the shooting incident, the young man was treated and released. They broke up. That was seventeen years ago. Funny thing, she's been clean as a whistle since."

April stared at Sergeant Hollis, knowing he'd held out on her. "Lieutenant, could you put that in written form and fax it to Inspector Bellaqua?"

"Uh-huh, already working on it. You owe me big." He hung up before she could ask him about Tang. Okay, looked like Wendy was it again.

April got Bellaqua on the line in her office at One PP.

"Hey, April, what's up?" she asked.

"Turns out Wendy Lotte is a sport shooter and she has priors. Shoplifting in college. Shot her boyfriend. No charges were pressed. Nothing for seventeen years. At the time of Tovah's shooting, she was out of sight for twenty minutes."

"Yeah, I know. What's her story?"

"She says she was outside having a cigarette. Then she went inside and was in the ladies' room when she heard the screams."

"Motive?"

"I don't know, jealousy? She's an unmarried woman. Apparently she shot her own fiancé. I don't have the full story on that. It occurred in Massachusetts. I have the feeling she gets squirmy watching brides walk down the aisle."

"Yeah, well, a lot of us get squirmy watching brides

walk down the aisle, doesn't mean we shoot them."
Bellaqua snorted. "Have you spoken to the DA about
this?"

"Not yet. You're my first call. What about you, Inspector? Anything on the bias angle?" April asked,
switching gears for a moment.

"Nothing. The Schoenfelds are highly respected,
have no known enemies. Everyone loves them. Same
with the synagogue. The Ribikoffs have an ongoing
investigation on some of their relatives, but they
weren't at the wedding, and there seems to be no connection to this. Same with the real estate issue. Both
families are in real estate, but in different areas. That's
about it."

"Has the Riverdale canvass come up with anything?"

"One lady reported a flasher walking on Palisades
Avenue. Could have been Saturday, could have been
Sunday. She's not sure. According to her, he waved it
at her as she drove by. She says she swerved and almost went off the road, down the bluff, and into the
river. Mike is chasing down the missing African who
works for Louis. I heard from him an hour ago."

"Me, too. Anything else from Riverdale?"

"A number of people reported a parade of strange
cars in the area that day. But there's always a lot of activity around the synagogue. Saturdays, people walk.
But Sunday is wedding time. A lot of people from out
of the area drive in. We do have the plates of every
car in the lot. But the killer could have parked on the
street, even down on Palisades Avenue."

April flashed to Kim and his wife. They took off in
a car; Louis had a truck. Wendy had a car, too. Lots of
possibilities.

"Do you have anything on the weapon?" she asked.

"We're still looking for it."

"What about a computer check on the shell casings?"

"They're working on it. Look, I'll get with the DA about Wendy."

"Inspector, does anything strike you about this?"

"A lot of things. What's on your mind?"

"Psychologically, I mean. What's the message of the crime?"

"Strikes me as impersonal," Bellaqua said promptly.

"Yeah, I didn't think so at first, but now it has the feel of a public execution. I don't know. Maybe I'm dreaming here."

"Go on. You got a theory?"

"If it was a rage thing, wouldn't the killer have gotten up-close and personal? Done the thing in private so the victim could look in his face and know her killer? And they've been planning this wedding for, what—only two months? Isn't that kind of rushing things?" April mused. Matthew and Ching had been planning their wedding for eight months.

"So?"

"There were a hundred ways to do Tovah with a lot less risk. Where she lives is a cul de sac in a quiet neighborhood. She was a solitary girl, liked to sit on the back porch out of sight of the rest of her family and listen to her Walkman. Anybody who knew her knew that and could have picked her off anytime in her own backyard. We wouldn't have had a clue. What does that tell us about our killer?"

"Experienced sniper or maybe a country club shooter. Who knows? Whoever it was may not have known the girl, but knew all about the wedding. Wasn't afraid of crowds. Not a professional."

"Yeah, that's what I'm thinking. Our shooter didn't know the girl. That's why I'm curious about the weapon. Might be another homicide with the gun in the computer that we don't know about yet. Could give us a link."

"Yeah, get on them about the gun," Bellaqua agreed.

Twenty-six

It's afternoon. He doesn't know what time it is. Maybe dark. Maybe not. He's not moving. That's all he knows. He tells himself his story. He was a good boy, one of the good ones. He doesn't like it when people cheat, when they hurt each other. Ask Louis, he know. Ask anybody. Every day he help somebody. Somebody on the street. Tito. A little child. He say the prayers, and he don't do no bad things. This is what he tells himself when he's hiding.

He's hiding from Louis, from Tito, from all the policemen who could shoot him. He knows the policemen shoot Africans here. They told him that the first day. Don't get in no trouble in New York City. The policemen shoot black boys. Don't go for your wallet, passport. Whatever happens, don't start running.

He's hiding in the basement, afraid the police will shoot him. The men he shares the damp basement with know they're not supposed to open the door. Too many people live there, and they can't cook or wash. They all know the woman who lives upstairs and takes rent money from them can get in trouble. If they get caught living there, they can be sent back. None of them want to be sent back, so they never open the door.

He doesn't know what time it is when the woman from upstairs opens the door. He runs to hide behind the tank that makes the water hot for the apartment upstairs, squeezes himself in close to the crumbling wall, and prays no one will find him. Please, God, no one find him.

"Look, you can see for yourself no one's here," the woman said.

But two men came in and found him right away.

"Jama, come out, I won't hurt you," one of them says.

He starts to cry. He can't help crying. No one is with him now, no one to help him. No Louis, no Tito, no two brothers in Minnesota. The church people told him they only had room for two boys. So he had to stay here. And now he only does what Louis tells him. Then he comes back here. That's it. That's the life he has. He prays for the spirits of the dead. He drinks beer. Sometimes the stories in his head stop for a while and he falls asleep. Sometimes he wakes up sweating, crying. Other times he's screaming.

In the morning the noise is so loud in the subway. Too many people close together, pushing, looking at him. Laughing if he stumbles on the platform. He's still afraid the doors will close on him. Inside the train, he's scared the doors will open and someone will push him out on the tracks. He knows that happens, too. He's scared when the train stops in the tunnel and no one can get out. When that happens, he's sure they'll all be shot in the dark. Some of the people on the train look like people he used to know. The death soldiers.

Sometimes he's so scared in that shaking train he can hardly breathe. He's sure the death soldiers know

him. Even in the store noises bother him. Little Tito
coming up from behind when the hair dryer is on and
he doesn't know he's there. He's afraid of planes at-
tacking from the sky.

He puts the rose stems with the thorns in his pockets and takes them home. At night when he's in a
panic, he pokes himself all over his arms and hands
with the rose thorns until he's wearing a blanket of
blood. Like the blankets of blood on the dead where
he came from. He doesn't know why he pokes himself to bleed. He's not a walking dead. Not a boy
with stumps where hands and feet should be. He's a
whole boy, one of the lucky ones, one of the good
ones.

The man is talking to him, and he's trying to listen.
The man has a mustache. He watches the mustache
move. He's talking about Louis, something about
Louis. Asking what he does in the shop.

He tells the policeman what he does in the shop,
how he copies the way Louis puts the flowers together in the water. He shows him with his hands.
Yes, he likes doing that. He doesn't look at the man
when he says it.

He doesn't say he hates riding in the van when
Tito drives. It makes him remember things he doesn't
want to remember, but he doesn't say anything about
the van. He's so scared of the policeman he can feel
his eyes rolling around in his head.

He knows people here are afraid of him. They look
at him and move away on the street. In the subway
they move away. He knows the policeman has a gun.
He looks up for a second and sees the man's lips
moving. He doesn't know what the man is asking
him. He's trying to answer the man's question.

Now the man asks him if he has a gun.

He shakes his head, not anymore. He does know someone shot the girl. But he didn't do it. He doesn't hurt people. He sweats, worrying that the man might think he hurt people. He doesn't remember ever shooting anyone or doing anything bad. He sees the pictures in his head, the blood pouring out of screaming people, and the bloody blankets that covered them. But he's sure he was one of the good ones. He tells himself this every day. He was one of the good ones.

He doesn't know which militia killed the girl. He doesn't know how it works here. His voice starts making no-talk sounds. He's talking no-talk, cowering in front of the man, almost on his knees. Not saying that they came into a quiet place where there were fields and a few huts. They put the first men they saw on a truck, took them away. Later they came back for the women and children.

They didn't have a system, no list of names. It didn't matter who was who. It was always the same. Whatever side they were on, rebels or army, the enemy was the people in the huts. The enemy was the people in the fields, in the schools, whoever they wanted it to be. Wherever they went, wherever they were, anyone they didn't like the look of was the enemy. Anyone who didn't give them food. Anyone who talked back or resisted. They took those people away, or they killed them right there.

It always happened fast, like a storm coming up on a sunny day. No warning, no time to hide. They came in a truck or many trucks, waving guns in the air so everybody ran inside. The boys were in the fields, at school, with their fathers. Sometimes just by themselves away from their mothers. When the men in the trucks came, the girls stayed with their mothers. The boys ran away. That's what happened with him. His father and uncle and two of his cousins were killed. He saw their bodies in the field behind the house and ran away before the soldiers could find him. When the soldiers were gone, people came out of their huts to cry and bury their dead. But the trucks came back. In daylight, at night, didn't make a difference. When they came back they killed the little girls, the babies first; then they raped the bigger girls and the women. Sometimes they didn't rape them, just killed them.

The first time he came back to his mother. After the second time, he ran away and didn't come back. He was a little boy. He didn't know who shot his father, his uncle, cousins in the field. He didn't know who cut off his sisters' arms with a machete and sliced the baby out of his mother's big belly. He ran away and lived in the forest with other boys he called his brothers, places where no one came. They were sick and many boys died. They were frightened and naked and starving. When men in the trucks found them and gave them food and guns, they became killers, too.

All this fills his head, and his mouth is talking no-talk. He's peed in his pants. The policeman has strapped his wrists behind him. He sees the cuts on his arms and asks about the cuts. Then he asks more questions about his bloody clothes. His ID card. Where is it?

"What's your real name? Where are you from? Do you have a visa, a green card? Where's your passport?" The policeman asks him more questions.

He's so scared his eyes roll up in his head. He's forgotten what name is in his papers, what he's supposed to say.

"Brother," he says. His name is Brother. He knows he's going to be executed right here in this chair. He's big and he's strong and he knows how to fight.

He strikes out at the policeman with his boots, kicking him in the head so hard the man falls over. The straps holding his arms break apart, freeing him to fight for his life. The other policeman runs over to help. The first one struggles to get up. Now they're all fighting. But he's big. He's the biggest, and he doesn't want to die in this basement.

Twenty-seven

April and Inspector Bellaqua and her driver were waiting for Wendy outside her building in the inspector's unmarked four-by-four when she got home. Mike and his partner were off the radar screen somewhere in Brooklyn when Wendy strode up the block at nine-oh-five. The two cops slowly got out of the car. The driver stayed put.

"Oh, Sergeant Woo." Wendy flashed April an uneasy smile from her higher vantage point of natural height plus spike heels.

"You know Inspector Bellaqua," April said.

"Hello," she said, looking down on her, too. "What can I do for you?"

"We'd like to come inside and ask you a few questions," Poppy told her.

Wendy hesitated, glanced in both directions, then nodded. "Okay, I understand. Come inside, of course. Maybe you'd like a drink."

Maybe not. It looked like she'd already had a few. The three women went up in the elevator without exchanging another word. When they got to Wendy's floor, she unlocked her apartment and switched on the light. The place was neat and didn't look as if it had been gone over a few hours ago. If Wendy had any sense that her apartment had been searched while she was out, she didn't show it. She dropped her purse and briefcase on her dining/conference table, then moved purposefully across the living room to the window.

Bellaqua didn't react, but April's heart raced. Several years ago during an arrest, a female homicide suspect like this one—much larger than herself—had jumped out of a window and tried to pull April out with her. She'd hung on as long as she could before the woman finally twisted out of her grasp and fell four stories. The resulting broken legs did not prevent a jury from convicting her of the two stabbing murders she'd committed.

"Hold it right there," April barked.

Wendy stopped and raised her hands. "Okay, no problem. Don't get jumpy on me, ladies."

Bellaqua moved forward and grabbed the gauzy curtains. Nothing but an air conditioner behind them.

"Okay if I turn it on?" Wendy asked.

"Okay." April relaxed, but only a little.

"What's your problem?" The sheers billowed out in icy air and Wendy gave them a disgusted look as the room cooled. Then she sat on her beige sofa, crossing her excellent legs. "Your reaction is upsetting me."

Bellaqua's eyes swept the living room as if the search there might have missed something, nodding at April to take the lead. April pulled out her Rosario and read Wendy's words from her notes.

"The key to your business is planning. You orchestrate everything from beginning to end," she said.

"It's my living. I'm good at it." Wendy swung one long leg over the other and bobbed her foot. "I've already told both you and Sergeant Hollis everything I know. I gave him my statement."

"Well, you'd better start over, Miss Lotte," April told her breezily. "You left out a few things."

"Look, I answered all your questions. You can call me Wendy. Everyone else does," Wendy said calmly. She checked her manicure, as if unconcerned about what was coming.

"Wendy, I want to level with you. Someone with planning ability, expertise with a rifle, knowledge of the timing of the event, and the ability to move around without suspicion planned and carried out this shooting."

Wendy nodded seriously. "I'm aware of that. I've been thinking about it, too." She glanced at the inspector, who'd taken a call on her cell phone and wandered off into Wendy's office.

"And what are your thoughts on the matter?" April went on.

"I'm not sure. I don't know what to think."

"Do you think there's a religious basis for the killing?"

"Maybe. I don't want to go into it though." Wendy shook her foot, studied her nails.

"We know about your past. We know you can shoot," April said. "We know you can plan. We know you were there. Your story about where you were at the time of the shooting hasn't been verified. All we're missing on your case is the gun."

The foot stopped bobbing. Wendy clenched her fist. "Look, I know what you're getting at. I had an accident a long time ago. I was young. I was engaged.

I changed my mind. The man had other ideas and threatened me." Wendy's face showed pain. It looked pretty real to April except that was not the way the story went up in Massachusetts.

"I was afraid for my life, but I did not mean to shoot Barry. Even cops are allowed to shoot someone if they're afraid for their lives, isn't that right?" she asked defiantly.

April shook her head. Nope. They were not allowed to shoot. A good defense lawyer could get a cop off for killing someone sometimes. But allowed to shoot, uh-uh. Shooting someone was always a bad career move. "We're looking hard at you, Wendy. What do you have to say?"

Bellaqua wandered back into the room. Wendy gave her a hostile stare and bobbed her foot some more. "The bullet grazed his arm. He's still playing golf, has a twenty-four handicap. Believe me, if I'd meant to hurt him I would have taken his driving arm off." Wendy said this with a tight little smile, acknowledging her prowess.

April locked eyes with Bellaqua. This was a dangerous adversary, a competent person flawed in some fundamental way who could think in terms of taking a man's arm off to spoil his golf game if he angered her. It clicked again. Tovah's death had been an assassination. The perpetrator hadn't wanted her to see what was coming and be afraid. Sadists were people out for revenge and liked the face-to-face high of seeing their victims paralyzed, frantic with terror. They got their kick from the squirm, the fear. Tovah's murder had been a cold hit.

Wendy's mouth twitched. She was smiling now. "You really don't have anything at all, do you? You're going to keep harassing me even though I had nothing to do with it. And the maniac who did it is going to get away. It makes me sick."

Made them sick, too.

Bellaqua replied angrily, speaking for the first time. "This is how we run an investigation. We put the pieces together one by one. You have a better way, let us know."

"Well, it's a fucking insult. You know I didn't do it. Why would I kill that poor girl? I haven't shot a gun in years. I don't even *have* a gun anymore."

There. Bellaqua and April connected again. Smart people like Wendy became more sophisticated as they developed, but they didn't necessarily change in the fundamentals. She had guns, they were sure of it. The search of her apartment had not come up with any, but April guessed she still had some somewhere. People who loved guns didn't give them up. She also guessed that Wendy had been lifting things from the gift tables of her clients, judging from the merchandise that had been in her cupboards two days ago, but was missing this afternoon when the police did their search.

Wendy grimaced suddenly, and April knew that she was still a shooter, still a thief, but they didn't have what they needed to arrest her. It made the two detectives sick as they headed home for the night. Nothing from Mike in many hours. April was anxious with him out there in the wind.

Twenty-eight

M ike called on April's cell at midnight just as
April was pulling onto her street in Astoria.

"Thank God! I was getting worried. Are you
okay?" she asked when she heard his tired voice.

"Yeah, fine, why?"

"You sound funny." And she hadn't heard from
him. That made her uneasy, especially when she hadn't
seen him all day.

"Nah, I'm fine. What's up?"

"You first," she said.

"Okay. Something's way off about that guy Louis,
the florist. Everybody he has working for him has a
shadow past." Mike's voice crackled on the cell phone,
and she wondered where he was.

"What kind of shadow past?" The reference made
her think of Ching's chef Gao Wan and his tall tale
about the river god he claimed was his father. Immigrants frequently invented mythic histories for themselves. They all had shadow pasts.

"He hires young men who fought in wars."

April parked in front of her house, killed her engine,
doused the lights, and sat in her car in the dark. Boys
who fought in wars. Where was this going? "Any wars
in particular?" she asked after a pause.

"Nope. He's an equal-opportunity employer. He's had them all—Tutsis, Hutus, Bosnians, Angolans, Cambodians, Iraqis, Afghans."

"Jesus, Mike, what does that mean?" She shivered in the quiet of her Astoria street.

"It means he puts his clients in contact with a bunch of unstable young men with a history of violence. I called a social worker friend of mine about it. She said we've still got boys coming in from all over the world who participated in mass killings back where they came from, civil wars on many continents. Also survivors. There are a lot of traumatized EDPs out there who get through INS."

Were they back to terrorists? "Aren't we doing anything about screening who comes in?" April asked, checking the row of silent houses where most of her neighbors had already gone to bed. EDPs were emotionally disturbed persons.

Mike didn't answer, but April knew perfectly well that nothing the FBI, CIA, and INS did could stop the flood of people who sailed, flew, walked, swam, and were smuggled into the USA every day. Some of them were persecuted back home, some persecutors. There had never been a treatment protocol for killers, walk-in clinics for the tortured and traumatized. One of April's motives for becoming a cop long ago had been to help Chinese immigrants negotiate the system, get the services and protection they needed.

Mike's voice became stronger. "The guy we picked up calls himself Brother. He came in from Africa about six months ago through a church group. I haven't been able to contact them yet. They're based in Liberia. He's young, possibly psychotic. Louis told me he tried high school in Brooklyn for a few weeks, couldn't hack it.

Has very little English. He lives in a basement in Brooklyn with a bunch of other guys like him. It's not a healthy place. The Health Department's going to be all over it if any of them have TB.

"Louis seems to have a network of illegals going. He calls our guy Jama. We don't know what his real name is yet. He has scratches all over his body, and we found bloody clothes. Somebody may be torturing him, but the injuries look like they could be self-inflicted."

"What makes you think so?"

"It's a long story. Have you spoken to your shrink friend yet? This guy's a head case."

"No, I called his office on Monday. His voice mail said he's away for two weeks. Emma and the baby must be with him. Got the machine on the home phone, too."

"You know where he is?"

"Uh-uh." Psychiatrists didn't exactly leave their itineraries for their patients. "But he says self-mutilators hurt themselves, not others. Is Jama organized enough to be Tovah's killer?" April didn't want to get too excited.

"Probably not by himself. But somebody could have directed him to do it, supplied the gun, then took it away afterward. He appears to be in shock."

"Oh, God, I hope he's it. Anything new on the gun?"

"No, no. Nothing found yet. Nothing from FAS, either."

April didn't want to get out of the car, go into her house, sleep alone. She missed him. "FAS, what the hell is that?" she demanded.

"Firearms Analysis Section, don't you keep up?"

"No." She hated the Department's constant name changing. "It'll always be Ballistics to me. What about Tito?" she asked, still sitting in the dark.

"Tito's brothers were among the disappeared in Argentina."

"God, what's the connection with these people? Wendy has a shadow past of her own."

"Oh, yeah, anything new?"

"Her apartment came up clean for drugs and guns. Cupboards were pretty much emptied, though. Looks like she moved a lot of stuff out. We couldn't get anything out of her. I get the feeling she's holding back a lot, but she's toughing it out, hasn't gotten herself a lawyer."

April paused. She knew the type, the kind who thought they could handle anything. She went on, "Wendy's profile doesn't make her a perfect fit for this kind of hit. And there's no motive. But she has some empty cupboards. . . . Where are you now?"

"I'm finishing up at ER."

What! "What happened? Are you okay?"

"Oh, yeah, it's nothing."

"Mike, you want me to meet you? I could come over," April offered quickly.

"I need to crash for a few hours. Where are you?"

"I just got home. I'm still in my car. I could come over," she repeated. She wanted to clap eyes upon him, make sure he was all right. But he wasn't going to let her.

"Get some sleep. I'll pick you up at seven." His voice cracked and died.

"Damn."

The phone rang again and she answered, hoping it was Mike calling back to enlighten her.

"Sergeant Woo."

"April, thank God I got you. I've called and called. Are you all right?"

"Ching, of course I'm fine." April inhaled deeply.

"I hate not being able to reach you," Ching complained.

April crawled out of the car. "I'm on a homicide, you know how it is. But I'm here now, just got home. I'm walking up the walk. Talk to me."

"Have you arrested the killer?" Ching asked, breathless with hope. "There wasn't anything on the news."

"We're real close," April lied. She put her key in the lock, opened the door. Inside it was still quiet. Her parents had not returned from their little trip to New Jersey.

"It's been almost a week." Her voice sounded accusing. "How can you not know?"

"It's been only three days," April corrected her. It was a complicated case, a bizarre case. There was a lot to sort through. She didn't want to be defensive. "It's coming together," she said. "We'll nail it soon."

"Did you talk to Tang yet?"

"Not yet." April took the stairs to her apartment two at a time. "When is your next fitting? I want to go with you."

Ching hesitated. "Well, sure you can. But April, your dress isn't from Tang's," she confessed.

"My dress?" April kicked her door closed, hit the light switch, and collapsed on her pink sofa. She hadn't had time to think about dresses.

"I want you to be my maid of honor. I want you to stand at my side and say something at the reception," Ching blurted.

Maid of honor? Say something? April was stunned. She'd had no idea this was in the wind. "Did Mike have something to do with this?"

"Please, April. Just a short speech. It's time the girls stand up, not just the guys. The fathers, know what I mean?" Ching was pleading. "You're my sister. I want to honor you. You can't say no," Ching said.

April shuddered at the thought of being on display, making a speech. "I don't know." It was a bad time.

"I got you a drop-dead dress. It will be ready on Saturday. Will you pick it up?" Ching wheedled.

"Ching, I'm very touched, but you didn't have to do that." *I don't want a drop-dead dress.* She didn't say it. *I don't want to think about your wedding right now with Mike's ultimatum hanging over me.*

"Of course, I had to do it. My fitting at Tang's is Monday. Will the case be solved by then?"

That was four days away. "Absolutely," April promised.

"You'll pick up your dress on Saturday?"

"Okay, sure. I'll pick it up." She loved Ching. She didn't want to be selfish, thinking only of herself. Of course she would do whatever Ching asked.

"I'll come with you, okay? I want to see your face when you try it on."

"I love you, Ching," April said suddenly. "Don't be nervous. It's going to be a great wedding."

"Love you, too, April. I know it will." Ching hung up, and April was alone in the empty house. Skinny Dragon wasn't home, so there was no late-night conversation, no force-feeding. She didn't like the feeling.

Mike didn't answer either of his phones. He told her he'd picked up a suspect, Louis's African, Jama/Brother. Mike was in the ER, but who had the nothing? Just like him not to make a big deal of it! She brooded as she brushed her teeth and drank down three glasses of water, too tired to forage for food. She hoped Mike was all right, figured he was all right and just didn't want to be with her. That upset her, too. She knew she wasn't going to sleep at all. She got in bed and brooded. Jama had to be their man, had to be. Mike had broken the case. Maybe it was over. But where did that leave Wendy. . . . She fell asleep right away.

Twenty-nine

At seven A.M. sharp on Thursday morning Mike parked his Camaro in front of April's Le Baron and pulled himself out of the car with far less energy than usual. April had been waiting for him by the window and saw right away that his right cheekbone was bruised and a white bandage decorated his forehead. He hated showing wear and tear, so he held his hand over it as if shading the morning light. She had her answer. Brother must have resisted being taken in.

"Looks worse than it is," Mike said sheepishly as she ran out to give him a long hug.

"How's the other guy?" she asked lightly. Mike was on his feet, nothing in a sling. She knew better than to make a big deal about it if he didn't.

"Heavily sedated on the psych ward. Hungry?"

"Yes."

April didn't want to admit that she'd missed dinner and missed him, but at least last night there had been a reason. She gave him another hug and climbed into the car, making it a point not to press him for details as they headed up to the Bronx. They stopped for a big breakfast in a diner. Mike ordered bacon, eggs, hash browns, toast, lots of ketchup.

While they were waiting to be served she skirted the subject, keeping neutral. Was Brother their man? Come on, give.

"Stitches?" she asked about his forehead.

"Only six. Right along the hairline." He sugared his coffee heavily, then sipped. "Not as good as yours," he commented, giving her a crooked smile. "Are you missing me yet?"

She nodded. "What do you think? Is Brother our killer?"

Mike stirred in more sugar. Four packets made it a record. "I want to think we have him. He seemed pretty out of it last night, but drugs could do that. When he comes around, we'll see how connected he is to reality." He touched his forehead. "I'll tell you, he has a lethal kick. I wasn't expecting it," he admitted. "Careless."

April's heart thudded. Between the two of them, Mike was the dirtier *mano-a-mano* fighter, but she had it all over him in kickboxing and karate. She felt she should have been there. She didn't say a word. The food came. They started eating. Two fried eggs suddenly didn't seem like enough. Mike ordered pancakes, too.

"I hope he's our guy," she said. *Let Brother be our guy,* she prayed, pouring on the syrup with a heavy hand.

"Let's hope. I think Louis is involved somehow, but I don't see him as a killer. The question is, did the African leave in Louis's truck at two-thirty, as Tito and Louis said he did, or did he stay behind? If he stayed behind, how did he get back to the city? Subway? Bus? Did he ditch the gun in a garbage can? Did they wait for him?"

All the garbage cans in the area had been thoroughly searched on Sunday and Monday, but the killer could have dumped it in the Hudson River. There were many places to get rid of a gun.

They ate slowly, puzzling over different aspects of the case. The tangle of leads kept going back to the wedding people, none of whom were entirely what they seemed, but none of whom had a motive, either. April flashed to Ching's call last night and her request for April to be her maid of honor. She didn't want to discuss it with Mike right now. They had more important things to worry about.

"What's the matter, run out of steam?" he said.

"Yeah." The pancakes sat there in a lake of syrup.

Mike paid up and they were on time for their meeting with the Bronx DA, an older guy neither of them knew. Shad Apply was tall and skinny. His face was the color of window caulk, prematurely rutted with deep wrinkles. Two younger, gray-suited ADAs were in the office with him. All three showed signs of life when Mike told them about the suspect in custody.

"Where is he? We want to talk to him," Apply said, nodding with satisfaction at his henchmen, a chubby male who looked about thirty, and a long-haired female of indeterminate age. Both were intently taking notes on legal pads. Apparently between last night and now, no one had been in touch.

"Talking's a problem right now. He's in Bellevue," Mike told them.

"Is he injured?" Shad Apply frowned at Mike's bruise and the bandage on his head. "Did you hurt him?"

Mike shook his head. "Not as bad as he hurt me.

The guy's a head case. He went berserk in the middle of the interview. We're having him evaluated, but it may take some time. He'll have to wake up first."

The prosecutor's face organized itself into a smile. The good news outweighed the bad. The good news: A confused psychotic would be a big plus for everybody. They could nail him quickly and have done with an ugly case. The DA's office wouldn't have to dig too deeply for a motive. Crazies lived in worlds of their own; their circuit boards were down. The pathways to reason didn't connect.

There were other pluses. Incidents involving seriously mentally impaired people, though catastrophic for the victims and their families, were not that common. If the perpetrators happened to be wholly unconnected to reality, they couldn't plan, couldn't repeat a crime, couldn't get away. Such a resolution of the Tovah case would be ideal. The bad news: It would probably take quite a while. Psychotics didn't get stabilized overnight.

"Good job," Apply said, appraising Mike in a rosier light. "You're the one who brought him in?"

Mike nodded.

"Did he give you anything at all?"

"Not enough. He was scared to death, less than lucid. Also, his boss, the florist, made an initial statement saying he was with him at the time of the shooting. We have a little problem with that."

The DA pulled on his nose. "We can bring him in as a material witness, hold him for a while. That might jog his memory. I'd like to clean this up before the weekend. Okay, thanks. That should do it for now. I'll start talking to the attending shrink. You follow through on the background check." Apply unfolded from his chair.

"Excuse me, sir." April took a few minutes to fill them in on her and Bellaqua's work on Wendy.

He wasn't that interested. Her past misdemeanors were way too old to be admissible in any case against her. He looked fifteen years younger when they left.

By two in the afternoon Mike and April were on the phones at the Five-oh. Mike was trying to locate the church group that had brought the Liberian into the country. April was following through with her study of the seven-page printout that described each event Wendy had done since January, five months of completed events and a summer of parties to come. April also had an older file of events Wendy had managed, going back some five years, that had been printed out from her computer. She spent all day on it. Late in the afternoon she found something that pushed her alarm button.

Another of Wendy's brides-to-be hadn't made it to the altar. Andrea Straka. April recognized the name right away. Another sad case. The day before her wedding, Andrea Straka had jumped or fallen—or been pushed—off a subway platform in front of an oncoming train. She'd been killed instantly. The tragedy made all the newspapers. A horrible thing, a famous unsolved case. Had it been suicide, accident, homicide? No one knew for sure.

April's heart raced as she considered the possibilities this new death presented. One bride had died the day *before* her wedding, another bride on the day of her wedding. Eight months apart. April tended to think in threes. Another bride on the day *after* her wedding, sometime down the road? Or what about eight months *before* Andrea's death? Had there been another case—a young woman just engaged?

Maybe Tovah's murder meant that a killer was getting bolder, was coming out in the open. April shivered and shook herself. Her cynicism was getting ahead of the evidence. She had no reason yet to panic. Still, she had to take Andrea's death very seriously. Someone had to take another look at Andrea's file, reinterview the witnesses, the whole nine yards.

April also had to dig deeper to see if anyone else had died near a wedding date. Andrea's death could be a coincidence, but cops were suspicious. When it came to police work, April didn't believe in coincidences.

Thirty

Thunder rumbled over the city, and jagged shafts of lightning cracked the sky open like an eggshell. The clouds let loose, sending rain down in a long free fall, so heavy the water itself sounded like thunder and the thunder like artillery in a war.

Prudence Hay had settled into a state of peaceful sleep Thursday night, knowing that rain was on the way and they were fully prepared for it. Her father, Terence Hay, was a Weather Channel aficionado. Throughout every day of his life he consulted it frequently. He checked the weather in the morning and afternoon before traveling back and forth to Long Island, and even before he left his office for lunch. He followed storms the way he studied the stock market, trying to keep out of trouble on both fronts.

His concern about rain had affected his decision so many months ago to have a hotel wedding, not a tented affair out at the house where a heavy rain would dampen a good deal more than spirits. He had one daughter to give away, not five or six like his brothers and sisters. One beautiful girl, and he didn't trust the weather to do her proud. Although Prudence would have preferred to hold her reception at home among the spring flowers, her father was always right. The way he always took charge in so many ways had irritated her hugely when she was young. But now his planning contingencies for weather and other disasters made her feel safe. He always said she should let him do the worrying for all of them, so she did.

That was the reason she slept well through the thunder and lightning. Her gown was in the apartment, perfect now. Kim had embroidered a little angel in it. White on white, so it was very subtle. A nice touch, she thought. Tomorrow afternoon they would have their rehearsal in the cathedral and stay for Mass. Then they would have their prewedding dinner. It didn't matter if it rained. Her father's careful planning would become part of the story in the toasts. No one's feet would get wet in the grass. The lunch would not be cold. The St. Regis would bloom like Hawaii indoors. The rain came and washed her doubts away. She was confident she and Thomas would live happily ever after just like they were supposed to.

Thirty-one

Thursday marked the fourth night that April slept alone in her empty family house. Her parents were still away, and not even the poodle was there for company. Mike was taking a hard line with her, probably hurting more from his injuries than he'd ever admit. And Ching was insistent about the maid of honor thing. Nearly a week had passed since Tovah's murder, and now there was just a week to go until Ching's wedding. This uncomfortable juxtaposition of events worried April.

Two weeks—three weekends—meant they were almost in the mid-position of a triangle with tragedy on one side and great happiness for a loved one on the other. In Chinese philosophy numbers had a huge significance. To April, this mid-position of three was like the midsection of a hexagram in the *I Ching* in which things could change for the better or the worse, depending on the action or nonaction one took.

Whether from Confucius or Mencius, the Tao, or the smiling Buddha, the underlying principles for the superior person (or state) in Chinese thinking were three: whether or not to take action, when to take action, and how to take action. The Tao's absolute favorite course of action was perseverance in complete passivity, a nearly impossible path to travel if one happened to be a cop.

Since Mike's ultimatum about getting married and Ching's pronouncement that she was stubborn, April had steadily been taking stock of herself. She knew that people with whom she'd worked said she was inner-directed, like an ingrown toenail—frustrating and difficult to get to know. Such an assessment might well be in her record. And she knew it was there because she was neither fully Chinese nor perfectly American and couldn't be both at once.

As much as she'd longed to be all reason, April had always been guided by less rational laws of the universe—those of her own gut instincts and the wisdom of the ancients. The homicide of a bride, when Mike wanted her to be his bride and Skinny Dragon Mother wanted her to be anyone else's, brought it all into sharp focus. Tovah's murder had aggravated Chinese superstition (her own, Auntie Mai's, Ching's), and she was stuck trying to sort out reality from feeling.

In many of April's cases, synchronicity played a part. One unconnected event after another suddenly connected unexpectedly in a brutal murder, in catastrophe, and these evils created chaos. The abrupt, dreadful occurrences that changed lives forever were often completely random. The victim was in the wrong place at the wrong time. The randomness, the luck of the draw in so many aspects of life even in the twenty-first century, was at the core of Chinese superstition and was in complete opposition to Western belief in causality and reason.

What Westerners had always worshiped as cause

and effect passed almost unnoticed in the Chinese mind, which was ever preoccupied with chance. The immense importance of serendipity could not be underestimated in Chinese thinking, and with good reason. For the ancients, no amount of foresight or precaution could possibly protect either the state or individuals against the vagaries of disease, war, politics, and natural disasters like earthquakes, floods, and famine. Throughout time, the best shot a human had was to remain as solid as the earth, accepting all with a steadfast heart and praying for the good luck of safety and good fortune.

All her life, in the Chinese way, April had tried to avoid conflict with her parents. She didn't want them to lose face by her marrying a Mexican American. But this correct Asian passivity was highly incorrect and even considered self-destructive in Western culture. Self-destructive didn't even exist in Asian thinking, for the self was not regarded as a separate entity.

In the wee hours of Friday morning, nearing the exact midpoint between tragedy and celebration, April resorted to the *I Ching* and her Chinese heart to get a reading on her life and Tovah's case. The *I Ching*, or Book of Changes, charts the movement of all things: the sun, the moon, fire, earth, water; human activities, qualities, emotions, and good and bad actions. Though obscure to the Western mind, the *I Ching* offers to the informed questioner judgments on when to persevere, when to stand back, when to speak, and when to remain steadfastly silent. It foretells danger and success and reveals the way to act correctly in all situations, to gain wealth and inner peace.

As the rain let loose, April sat on her single bed

and prepared to throw the coins—five pennies and a dime—to get the judgment of the ancient oracle as to who was Tovah's killer and what she should do about her crisis with the man she thought it would be bad luck to marry. Like a gambler at a craps table, she blew on the pennies, then threw them out. The coins fell on the flowered quilt three heads, then three tails.

Three heads represented three straight lines one on top of another: heaven. Three tails represented three broken lines beneath the three straight ones: earth. Heaven over earth was the hexagram *P'i* (standstill or stagnation). The judgment was: Heaven and earth do not unite, and all beings fail to achieve union. Further, it said, The shadowy is within, the light is without. The way of the superior was falling. The way of the inferior was rising.

April was crushed. Her dime was in the fourth position, third line from the top. That meant her personal message was: He who acts at the command of the highest remains without blame. What was willed was done.

She was mulling over what it meant when Skinny Dragon opened her door without warning. Four days she'd been away and this was her greeting.

"*Ni* (you), I have food; you eat."

A wet Dim Sum ran into her room, yelping happily, and jumped on April's bed to lick her face. It was the middle of the night, but for once April was not unhappy to see her mother. Dragons had things they wanted to talk about, had trouble sleeping, wanted to be nice. And look, Skinny was smiling. She'd brought a ceremonial gift of oranges. Hastily, April gathered up the coins and her fancy Princeton edition of the *I Ching* and hid them under her pillow.

Thirty-two

Friday morning Mike and April were working downtown in Bellaqua's office when Mike finally located someone at God's Goodness out in Minneapolis who personally knew the man they had under restraints in Bellevue. Daniel Dody came on the line just before eleven o'clock. Mike put him on speakerphone so April and Bellaqua could listen in.

"Oh, yeah, Ubu Natzuma. I remember him. Big guy, real shy." Dody's strong Midwestern voice was cheerful. "Who are you again?"

"Lieutenant Sanchez, New York City Police Department, Inspector Bellaqua, Sergeant Woo."

"Three of you, I see. How can I help you?" The voice cooled down without losing its perkiness.

"I gather you have responsibility for Mr. Natzuma."

"Well, not exactly. We did sponsor him in a school program out here, but after his orientation, he decided to stay in New York."

"He decided to stay in New York? A real shy guy?"

"He didn't want to get caught in the middle," Dody said slowly.

"In the middle of what?" Mike asked.

"The country. A big landmass. He gets upset when he's frightened, so we didn't try to force him."

"He was upset, so you left him here?"

"Well, no, we didn't just leave him. We gave him some names and numbers, found a place for him to stay and a school for him."

"I need those names and numbers," Mike said. The notebooks were out.

"Uh, sure. I'll have to look them up, though. It may take some time. What is this all about?" Dody sounded a little less sure about those names.

"A woman was shot here in New York last week at her wedding. Mr. Natzuma may have been involved," Mike said flatly, doodling in his notebook, not glancing at April or Poppy.

"Oh, no. Not that one I read about in the paper? That Jewish girl?" The voice flattened out a little more.

"Yes, Tovah Schoenfeld. How does Mr. Natzuma feel about Jews?"

"Oh, goodness. I can't even imagine. I know he may have some primitive ideas, but I'm sure Ubu never even met a Jew."

"Tell me about him."

"I don't know where to begin. He experienced some real deprivation when he was very young. Malnutrition, abuse, just like almost everyone in his country. I don't know if you know anything about Liberia's wars, but he was in the middle of it. Landlocked and also trapped between warring factions, one of which killed his parents. He may have witnessed that." Dody ran out of steam.

"Do you have any dates on this?"

"Gee, let me think. We're pretty sure he was recruited into a militia when he was eleven or twelve, but before that he lived with a gang of boys, hiding out, for several years. His parents may have been killed when he was nine or ten. It's hard to put dates on anything. We can only piece together their histories from their own accounts. If he's eighteen now, we might be able to correlate events in his village nine years ago."

"Did you hear any accounts of an attack during a wedding? Maybe someone from his own family?" *Something he might be reliving a world away*, Mike didn't say out loud.

"Gee, I wouldn't know, but two of his brothers are with us out here. Maybe they would know."

"What about violence?"

"I don't know what you mean."

"You said he was recruited into a militia when he was eleven. I assume that doesn't mean he was a mascot."

"Ah, Lieutenant, we try to rehabilitate them; we don't ask them to relive their tragedies."

Very preachy. Mike glanced at April and Poppy. Their faces showed their dismay.

"You don't do any psychological testing before you let potential killers loose over here?"

"I don't like the sound of that. We don't take that view. Let me remind you that soldiers throughout the ages have returned to normal life when their wars were over. Our mission is to help these people do that through Jesus Christ."

"You think of Mr. Natzuma as a retired soldier then."

"A kind of solider, yes. As he was a member of a rebel militia group, we know he was a witness to the torture and killing of dozens of civilians on many different occasions. But as a participant . . . ?"

"But he can shoot a gun," Mike interrupted.

"Oh, that, certainly. Is there anything else I can help you with?"

"Oh, yes, this is just the beginning. We need to pin down if he shot any of those civilians, if he witnessed, or participated in, violence at a wedding. And if he hates Jews."

Dody was silent for a while. "He's had a sad life."

"Does that translate into a man too violent to take with you to your church in Minneapolis?"

"No, no, not violent, more like a management problem."

"Why didn't you send that management problem home?"

Dody was silent for a longer time. "We don't think in terms of sending them home. Our mission is to get them out. Bring them to safety, teach them the ways of Christ, our Lord."

"Mr. Dody, will you get those names and addresses for me? We're going to be sending someone out there to talk to you and Ubu's brothers. We'll be following up on this immediately."

Mike recited the squad number and his cell phone number and said, "Thanks, we appreciate your help," before hanging up.

He tried to frown and winced as his stitches pulled.

Thirty-three

L ouis the Sun King knew the drill. For the Hay wedding, St. Patrick's would be closed to the public for only two hours. He would not be allowed to work after the doors were closed for the night or before they were opened in the early morning. In fact, he was not allowed to work there at all. All he could do was deliver finished product. Same thing with the St. Regis. There was an event in the ballroom that night, so he couldn't get in there until Saturday morning.

Coordinating the two sites took master planning. Louis had to get the ten thirty-five-foot, gardenia-plugged ficus trees in place in the cathedral, the massive arrangements down at the altar, and the ribbons and baskets along the pews as soon as the cathedral doors were open Saturday morning. The trees had to be brought in by cherry pickers. The cherry pickers had to disappear, then reappear as soon as the bride and groom walked back down the aisle and out of the building. Everything related to the Hay wedding had to be out of the cathedral before two o'clock, then delivered immediately to the designated not-for-profit for the tax deduction.

What it meant was that the ten ficus trees had to be

plugged with five thousand blooming gardenias. Twenty-five giant seashells filled with perfectly blooming Hawaiian Sunset cats and other tropical and marine-type fauna. Twenty-five large umbrellas decanvased, palm fronded, and set with twinkling lights. Four arrangements for the altar and the baskets and ribbons for the pews had to be constructed. All this had to be done before nine. Saturday. The umbrellas had been done before the rain started. The police had stopped bugging him, Wendy was off his case, and he was feeling better.

Louis loved the magic of the party and missed the old days when only the richest people in the world could have what anyone could have now—masses of lilies, roses, lilac, orchids, tulips, hydrangea—anything at all any time of the year. Twenty years ago only the designers had real access to the growers and shippers and suppliers. He felt his business had been destroyed by Martha Stewart do-it-yourselfism coupled with the excessive wealth of the 1990s.

These days it was tough to make events truly unique when anyone could get what he could get. Flower growers had fields all over the world. FedEx flew in every day. Bloom-a-Million on the Internet. Call 1-800-FLOWERS. Roses of every hue, six dollars a dozen at every corner Korean market in the city.

At one time Louis's former partner had employed forty-five people full-time. Back in the day more than a hundred people might be involved in an event for hardly more than a hundred people. All that was gone forever. Now everything was canned, nothing was new. He'd done this before. He was bemoaning his difficulties made worse by the rain when his buzzer rang and he saw that the two detectives were back.

Groaning, he buzzed them in and pushed through the crush of extra helpers he'd hired for the day. "Morning," he said. "We're a little crowded in here today."

The Chinese nailed him with a look. "Ubu didn't really come home with you in the truck last Sunday, did he, Louis?" Respectful of his shop, she stood dripping on the doormat.

"I don't know what you mean," he said.

"Yes, you do. Three of you went to Riverdale, but only two of you came back."

Louis closed his eyes, then shook his head slowly. "He didn't want to be in the back of the truck. He wanted to walk home."

"You left him there, up in Riverdale all alone, a stranger to New York? How did you expect him to walk home to Brooklyn?"

Louis sighed. "It's complicated. We didn't just leave him on Independence Avenue. We took him to the subway. I told him, van or subway—you can't walk to Brooklyn. He chose subway. I haven't seen him since." He grimaced at the lieutenant's purpling cheek but didn't ask how he got it.

"Why didn't you tell us this before?"

"We left the synagogue before three. He didn't know the area. He couldn't have gotten back in time anyway. Why complicate things for everyone irrelevant?" Louis argued. He patted his hair nervously. He was sorry, okay.

"Does Andrea Straka complicate things for everybody, too?" the Chinese said suddenly.

"Jesus." Louis stopped being sorry and took a deep

breath. This was getting out of control. "I've never been on a subway in my life. I didn't have anything to do with Tovah's death. You now know everything I know. If you want to arrest me, arrest me. Otherwise, leave me alone. I have a wedding to do."

Thirty-four

It rained all Friday night, and it rained Saturday morning. A stranger sat in St. Patrick's, warm and dry at the long information table piled with pamphlets touting Catholicism in different languages. The long table, skirted with green felt, was set back far behind the front doors in the space before the pews began. A TV screen was mounted on a column nearby. Throughout the year different countries had their chance to disseminate at this coveted spot. Now it was the Philippines. Sometimes nuns in gray habits sat at the table with laywomen. Sometimes no nuns. Today there were none.

While a truck moved trees in and young men hurried around hanging baskets of flowers on the very first pews way down in the front, a nine o'clock Mass then a ten o'clock Mass played on the TV screen. At the end of each Mass the small congregation of celebrants who were close enough to each other offered the handshake of peace, and then they left. No one looked twice at the table by the doors where two people gossiped quietly, and a third clicked the beads of a rosary. No one noticed when the rosary went into a pocket, and the lone person got up to examine the chapels of each and every saint, the height of the rail-

ing, the darkness of the corners, pausing in front of
even the confessionals as if considering whether or
not to slip inside.

Whatever the weather, St. Patrick's attracted many
different kinds of people. Except on high holidays or
when the cardinal was present and politics raged over
one issue or another, no one worried about them. On
a rainy spring day with nothing political going on no
one was fearful.

The rifle was in a carryall under the skirt that hid
the legs of the table. No one had looked into it when
it was brought inside. When the two women at the
information table went out for a break, the rifle was
assembled one-two-three. It had a short stock and
barrel.

Once the barrel was raised there would be no way
to hide it, as there had been in the Bronx. There was
no enclosed space to slip into except one of the confessionals, or deep behind the railings in one of the
saints' chapels. This was too far away and too uncertain to get off a good shot. Only the front pews way
down in front were being used. Getting closer would
be a problem. A shot from the side might hit others,
especially if the guests rose for a better view of the
bride, as they often did. More than likely someone
else would get hit and the bride might be missed al-
together.

Saturday morning on a second day of rain, St.
Patrick's suddenly seemed all wrong. The side doors
were locked. If Prudence were shot as she entered,
the escape from one door would be blocked by her
own body. Church people were keeping the public
out of the other door. Without the public, there was
no way to blend in with the crowd. There was no way

to hide behind a column. All the signs were wrong; this was not the right place for killing even though Prudence was destined for a better place, like Tovah.

As the morning lengthened, it became clear that the cathedral would work only if all the pews were filled, if people were standing around the back. Many people. Now only a few people were there gawking at the trees and flowers, and they would have to leave before the wedding began. The killer's nerve faltered. The cathedral was too big, too empty. The rosary beads clicked, but no amount of prayers would fix this. Prudence could not be killed in St. Patrick's. She would have to live on a little while longer.

Thirty-five

Exhausted from the stress of the long week and her boyfriend's ultimatum, April slept in on Saturday morning. She came downstairs at the impossibly late hour of ten-thirty and found Dim Sum waiting for her at the bottom of the stairs whining to go out. She opened the door, but when the diminutive poodle saw the sleeting rain she changed her mind. April had to nudge her out into the waterlogged backyard, then find a towel to pat her dry after she trotted back in shaking water everywhere and sneezing her disapproval.

No time to eat anything or even leave a note for the Dragon, April showered and dressed quickly. Her hair was still wet as she hurried into the city to meet Ching at the Formal Wear shop on Bowery. A thousand thoughts barraged her as her tires splashed through the rain. The primary one was relief that they had Tovah's killer. Yesterday afternoon they'd clocked two officers from the Five-oh slogging in the wet up the hill to Independence Avenue from Broadway. The time was tight, but there was no doubt that Ubu could have made it in time to slip in and shoot Tovah.

Primary thought two was that Ubu may have been

up there. But proving he did it without a confession or a weapon would be another thing. April was glad that the killer wasn't Wendy or anyone involved with Tang, which would have made Ching nuts. She didn't dwell on Andrea Straka.

Her other primary thoughts centered on Ching: happiness for her, trepidation at having to perform at her wedding. Skinny Dragon's new defense maneuvers . . . The pouring rain and her thoughts didn't let up all the way across the BQE and the Brooklyn Bridge into Manhattan. April left the car in front of a fire hydrant on Bowery and dashed upstairs to the dress shop whose windows she'd been studying all her life.

Up on the second floor, above a huge lighting fixture store, Formal Wear was a veritable warehouse of bridal gowns, evening gowns, tuxedos, and traditional Chinese dresses, jackets, and pants. Every style and age was represented. Gray and heather and silver for the old, red and black and purple and green all shot with gold for the young. Ching was waiting for her.

"Hey, sister," she whooped, giving April a hug. "Thank you for coming. One week to go, can you believe it?"

April grinned and hugged her back. She gazed at Ching fondly. April's lifetime competition—Ching— the big brain with the chunky body, the glasses, and blunt haircut, was wearing contacts and had slimmed down quite a bit. And her face was beaming with delight.

"You look so different! I wouldn't even have recognized you," April cried.

"I'm wearing makeup," Ching confessed.

"I can see you are." April happened to be a big fan of makeup. "It's done wonders for you. Really."

Ching looked a little sheepish. Growing up she'd always been brilliant in school but awkward around the paintbox. And April had the looks. Now they were even—both smart, both beautiful.

"You only marry once, right? I had a makeover." She giggled. "Wait till you see my gown. It's going to be so perfect." She kissed her fingers Italian style. "Tang is having an angel embroidered in it for me; isn't that sweet?"

April nodded absently.

"You're late," an aged saleswoman grumbled in Chinese. "Very busy day. I expected you at ten." She pointed at the clock.

April saw that it was nearly eleven-thirty now. "Oh, my God, I'm sorry."

Ching made a face. "Don't worry; I told her eleven."

The woman went away. Ching hugged April again and didn't say a thing about April's hair, straight and still damp. As usual Ching shuddered when she was bumped by the gun holstered at April's waist, and April was thankful that she didn't probe the specifics of the case.

"Here it is." The ancient padded back. "This one's yours." She held up a see-though garment bag as if it contained solid gold.

April recognized it right away and shivered. The cheongsam Ching had ordered for her was a replica of one she and Ching had seen at a community center concert they'd gone to twenty years ago. The Chinese opera star wearing it had changed her dress four times. The dress in the bag, a horror of mismatched

colors and patterns, had been the number-one dress.
She and Ching had adored it. The dress was purple.
Purple like a pope's robe, purple like a spring hy-
acinth, the purplest purple on the color chart. Woven
into the solid-colored silk was a lavish pattern of
peonies, but the cheongsam's high neck, bodice, and
short sleeves were of a different silk, one printed with
red and pink and white peonies on a field of green
leaves. Purple piping around the red and pink married the two clashing fabrics. It was louder than any
dress April would dream of wearing, garish beyond
belief.

"Isn't it absolutely fabulous?" Ching crowed.

"You bet," April said.

"I could never wear anything like that," Ching
murmured.

Neither could I, April thought as she obediently
trotted into a dressing room to try it on. *How can I get
out of this?* she thought.

"Can't see like this. Why didn't you bring your
shoes?" the grandmother scolded in Chinese when
April clunked back in her work shoes and climbed
up on the fitting pedestal.

"I don't have them yet," April admitted. For sure
she didn't have *any* shoes that would go with this!
The dress was formfitting, very constricting, but
now very much back in fashion. She hadn't worn a
cheongsam in a long time, and never for Mike. Criti-
cally, she examined herself in the mirror.

"Just right!" Ching squealed. "Look at her,
perfect."

April took a deep breath and lifted her chin. She
looked surprisingly good in their little-girl fantasy
of ultimate elegance. It was like Cinderella, Chinese

style. Ching's choosing this dress sent a strong message April couldn't ignore. Even on her special day, Ching wanted April as visible as she and in a starring role beside her. How many real sisters were that generous?

"Ching, you're too much. Thank you." April couldn't help grinning at herself as she twirled around on the pedestal, high off the ground for fitting long evening gowns. She looked tall and slender in the dress, almost like a movie star. Small waist, small but well-rounded bottom. Long neck. Good legs. She had to admit it. She looked good. She lifted her eyebrows at herself as she kicked the slit open. It was high; every step would show her whole leg. Everyone would look. Generous, generous Ching. How could she repay? April shook her head, tearing up just a little. It had been an emotional week.

"Beautiful." Even the grumbling, overworked women in the shop admired her as she went to change.

"Ching, thank you for the dress, thank you so much. Got to go to work." In seconds April reappeared in her slacks and jacket, her red blouse for luck. She grabbed the precious package that was all ready to go.

"Same old, same old. No time for lunch," Ching complained, but for once her reproach had no bite.

Thirty-six

At noon, the rain still hammered down. The wind had kicked up several notches in the last several hours, driving hard from the north. It slammed water sideways at the long red canopy that covered a slash of sidewalk from Fifth Avenue and traveled all the way up the steps to the very doors of St. Patrick's. The canopy did not fully protect Prudence Hay's party-dressed guests as a steady stream of them emerged from limos starting at eleven-thirty.

Under a poncho that was gray as the stone of the cathedral, Tovah's killer saw a mess. Umbrellas moving this way and that, like in a movie, tilted against the wind. Across the street a sparse crowd huddled out of the rain under the awning at Saks Fifth Avenue. The disparate group, unsettled by the weather, had stopped to watch the parade of fancy people fighting their unruly umbrellas as they scurried to get out of the wet. It was a mess. In a big black slicker a uniformed cop stood on the corner of Fifty-first Street and Fifth. Just stood there doing nothing. Another was on the corner of Fiftieth Street. Both like statues getting pissed on.

The rain was bad luck for Prudence. She would get wet when she got out of her limousine. Her expensive veil would blow off her head. Her white-beaded pumps would get spattered. Nothing could stop it. The rain was bad luck for Prudence, but why not good luck for a killer? The picture was already spoiled; why wait for later?

The killer thought of how perfect Tovah had been for her march down the aisle straight to heaven. Tovah was an angel in heaven now, not a slave in a bad marriage. Why wait? The gun was under the poncho. The poncho hidden by an umbrella. Umbrellas were everywhere. Channel Thirteen umbrellas. Museum of Natural History umbrellas. Chase Bank umbrellas. Black ones, red ones, even American flag ones, touting patriotism. *Ha.* The killer didn't return to the church, and didn't walk away, either.

Prudence hadn't arrived yet. Every second felt like an hour. On Fifth Avenue, the line of limos was a lot longer. The cars were queued up along the block two deep with the windows closed and all fogged up. The killer watched even more cars arrive. The groom arrived. But no Prudence. Things must have gotten stalled by the weather.

Finally! The family and the bridesmaids arrived. The drivers got out to help the old people and the twelve girls in their colorful gowns and feathered headdresses. So gaudy and tasteless.

Suddenly chaos. The girls were running. They were running to the church, everybody was running. Tovah's killer emerged from the side of the cathedral as Prudence got out of the car.

All in white, no raincoat or anything, Prudence was supported by her portly father and the driver, both wearing tails. One was on each side. They were trying to hurry her along. But Prudence was being careful of her beaded shoes, of the train secured around her wrist by a satin-covered elastic band. She was holding back for her mother and the flurry of squeaking girls in their fluffy chiffon parrot dresses to all get inside first. She had a serene expression on her face despite the rain, as if she knew she was going to a better place. The killer's umbrella went down to hide the gun. Then went up when the shot was fired. It happened in seconds. The first shot grazed Prudence's neck, but it hit an artery and blood bubbled out.

She looked surprised. She stumbled, but was held aloft by the two men on either side of her. Still a good target. The next two shots hit her in the eye and chest. One of the men went down with her. Thunder rumbled in the distance as the screaming started. Prudence's killer had slipped away and war was back.

Thirty-seven

The phone on Bellaqua's desk rang. The task force was busy so she let it ring. Seconds later a detective from the Hate Squad hurried in.

"Inspector?"

"Yeah, Rudy, what you got?"

"There's been a shooting at St. Patrick's. Another bride is likely." *Likely* in police jargon meant likely to die.

"Oh, no." April put her hand to her heart, couldn't help herself. *Oh, shit.* They'd missed something.

"Jesus Christ!" Bellaqua swore. She reached for her purse. Mike said nothing. He was already on his feet. They were out the door.

Down in the garage, Inspector Bellaqua and her driver headed for her four-by-four. Mike wiggled his finger at April. She got into a shiny Crown Vic with him, and they followed the inspector out. Bellaqua's driver, a former helicopter pilot, drove like a maniac, occasionally popping the siren for a few seconds to get through a clot of stalled traffic.

April was quiet as Mike turned on the police radio. It crackled with other matters, the airwaves already shut down tight. As Mike wove the unit through traffic, she studied his tense profile.

"Spooky," she murmured.

"More than spooky." He didn't look over at her.

"Connected?"

Tovah's murder was supposed to be like every homicide, a tornado they couldn't have predicted. A second one was a disaster. April's stomach knotted as if it were all her fault. She shouldn't have slept in, shouldn't have gone shopping this morning, shouldn't have been thinking about herself.

Mike's voice came as a surprise. "Don't be so hard on yourself. Could be a copycat. Could have nothing to do with it."

"Hmmm." She could tell by the furrows in his forehead that he didn't think so, and the instant call to Inspector Bellaqua meant no one else thought so, either.

Ordinarily, no connection would be made between a homicide at a synagogue in the Bronx and a homicide at a church in Manhattan a week later. The fact that the victim was another bride on her wedding day yanked them and Bias right back in. It was a bride case, a certainty now that someone was killing brides. It wasn't religious. It wasn't personal. The trigger was the bride herself. Sick.

Mike got off the drive and headed across town to Fifth, where traffic was already showing the strain. Fifth Avenue was closed between Fifty-third and Forty-eighth streets. Fiftieth and Fifty-first Streets were closed between Fifth and Madison. Cars and buses were all snarled up on Madison. News vans with their satellite dishes had already begun to assemble, trying to get as close to the action as possible. Mike hit his siren to get through, then clipped his shield onto his jacket pocket for the two uniforms at the barricade on Fifty-third. April did the same.

The uniforms waved them through, and they drove down the three cleared blocks to Fiftieth. There, the entire front section of St. Patrick's had been cordoned off with yellow tape. At least two dozen officers and brass had assembled to view the first homicide in the Seventeenth Precinct in two years.

Mike parked the car on the west side of the avenue and they got out. The rain had finally stopped, and the sun was just beginning to stab through deep banks of clouds as April looked across the street and saw a body lying there on the red carpet. Mike crossed himself, and April's eyes instantly became a camera.

Click, at the line of limos on Fifth Avenue, their windows all steamed up. Click, at the drivers out of their cars talking to officers in front of Saks. Click, at the two ambulances, doors open. Click, at the two men in tails, one of them large, beefy, stunned-looking with his head cocked to one side as he listened to talking brass. The bride's father? The other man, tall, thin, was talking rapidly, gesticulating while a detective wrote down what he said.

They were earlier on the scene here, and organization happened faster than it had in the Bronx a week ago. The body had been isolated to prevent further contamination. All individuals present at the time of the incident had been separated to prevent them from talking to each other and influencing one another's memories. Also to keep them as far as possible from specialists arriving on the scene. There were always complaints about the callous-sounding greetings and gallows humor of police arriving on grisly scenes. April heard there had been complaints about it from Tovah's family.

Click. No wedding guests were milling around outside. They couldn't be gone already, so the officers must have closed the front doors of the cathedral to keep the entire wedding party contained inside. April's first thought pertained to meaning. Tovah had died surrounded by family and friends. This girl hadn't made it inside. Different message, different shooter?

Click. The girl's body lying there in plain view, right between St. Patrick's and Rockefeller Center. Sometimes victims were left in the open like that while family members stood by, helpless and numb. No matter how mutilated or disturbing the dead looked, they could not be moved until the obligatory forensic work was done. Loved ones—children, mothers, wives, husbands—were left just the way they'd been in the last seconds of their lives, after all hope of sustaining them was gone.

Click. A sheet from one of the EMS vehicles had been thrown over the body. The sheet was not big enough to cover the long swath of bloodied, lacy wedding gown train that hid the girl's feet. The train puddled out from under the operating-room-blue drape like an unchecked milk stain.

They moved closer, walking at a normal speed, fighting the instinct to run. Run and stop it. Save the girl. Chase the perp. April stumbled on the high curb on the other side. Mike reached out and touched her arm. Going into situations, partners had many forms of communication. This wasn't a *watch out*. It wasn't a *slow down*. It wasn't even a *Cuidado, careful now*. He touched her arm in a different way, almost as if to make sure she was still with him. Still alive, and still his.

"*Contigo.*" *I'm with you*, she murmured.

He squeezed her upper arm, then let go. *Okay.*

A few more steps across the sidewalk. Then, click, she saw the blood, almost black on the red carpet. Blood everywhere. Cops everywhere. Mike headed through rain puddles to the people in the know.

"Captain Coulter, Chief." Precinct captain. Chief of detectives, Avise. Present on a Saturday. They must have been gathered together for some event that was interrupted, April thought.

The two men looked grim. "Mike, glad you're here," the chief said. Today they didn't shake hands.

"You know Sergeant Woo."

"Sergeant." The chief nodded at her.

"Sir."

Two minutes later, Inspector Bellaqua turned up with wild hair. She shook her head when she saw that April and Mike had gotten there first. Her hotshot pilot wasn't such a hotshot after all. Humiliating for her. Then she saw the body.

"Who is it?" were her first words. She shot Mike and April a glance full of meaning neither understood, then listened as the chief answered.

"Prudence Hay. Her father's a big shot on Wall Street. Her husband-to-be is from Pittsburgh. Big money on both sides."

"Jesus. What's the story?"

The chief gestured. "The killer was waiting for her out here." He pointed to the cathedral door on the Saks side.

"We had two uniforms over there in front of Saks. Two more up there." He pointed toward Fifty-first.

They followed his finger as it swept in opposite directions.

"It was sheeting rain. None of them had a clear view. The shooter nailed her as she came toward him. In the face and neck. Ugly. She bled out in seconds."

"Any other witnesses?" Bellaqua appeared to be making some calculations. The body was half-off the sodden red carpet under the dripping canopy about thirty feet from the door. Close enough for both the limo drivers and her father to see something if they'd been looking.

Avise glanced back at the limos with their obscured windows. "It's like a steam room in those cars. None of them saw him."

"What about the father?"

"He was trying to keep his daughter dry. He didn't look up."

Bellaqua nodded. Then, smug as a cat, she took stock of each of them and dropped her bomb. "We have a break in the Tovah case."

April frowned at Mike. They did? When did that happen? He seemed as startled by the news as she was.

"You know that partial thumbprint on one of the shell casings they found at the scene? It took so much time because there was so little minutiae that the match couldn't be made by computer. The partial had to be eyeballed against the prints of every person connected with Tovah's wedding. But we do now have a possible match," Bellaqua reported. "I just heard from FAS."

"Anyone we know?" Mike asked.

Bellaqua paused, holding the moment. She looked at April with a slight shake of her head. That caused

Chief Avise to look at April. Mike looked at April. *What?*

April felt the chill of the query, even though directly above them the sun finally pierced through the gloom of a gray, gray day. It shot down from an opening patch of blue with such intensity that the last flurry of rain droplets, hanging wherever they could take purchase, were suddenly transformed into strings of sparkling diamonds. Diamonds hung all around the church, the canopy, and trees in front of it.

April saw the shimmering diamonds of light reflected all around her and got it in an instant. She'd known it on Wednesday. She should have been all over it. She had been thinking backward, not forward. Prudence Hay had been next on Wendy Lotte's party list. But they had cooled on Wendy by then, were hot on Ubu.

"Wendy Lotte," April said with a sinking heart. The print was Wendy's. "Is she here?"

"You tell us. You wanted to be her contact," the chief accused.

So she had. "She's the wedding planner. She should be here," April said faintly.

"Bring her in," he said.

"Yes, sir," April said. Why were they all looking at her? She wasn't the primary here. Both Bellaqua and Mike outranked her. April was sweating heavily. Her mouth filled with water. Nausea made her head spin. Already she was taking the fall.

"Let's get this resolved today," the chief said quietly.

"Yessir," the three detectives chorused.

Thirty-eight

The brides rose up in the air like ducks over a pond, like clay pigeons in a skeet shoot. Just as they were about to take their vows, those brides took flight. They lifted up, and as they ascended into the heavens, instead of getting smaller they got bigger and bigger until they were as pregnant as clouds. Beyond pregnant, they filled the whole sky, growing as vast as continents on a globe. Looking up, no one could miss those expanding girls. They lifted up into the sights of the waiting hunters, and the guns exploded. Boom, boom, boom. The bride balloons fell down to earth, and one by one deflated into tiny dead babies in christening gowns.

Wendy huddled in a back pew, having her visions again. Prudence was gone just like Tovah, and the people she was supposed to be tending so carefully— moving from ceremony to celebration—had become a bunch of miserable hostages. Even as a calming voice spoke to them over the microphones, telling them what happened and what they had to do, they were getting rebellious. There was no food, no water. How should she deal with this? For once Wendy didn't know.

Her hands were shaking. She needed a shot of

vodka, the whole bottle. The organ throbbed under the agitated buzz of voices. Some official was giving more instructions. She was doubled up and didn't hear what he was saying. She jumped when someone touched her arm.

"Wendy, please come with me."

Wendy looked up, but already knew the owner of that flat New York voice. Her misery turned to angry resentment when she saw the little Chinese detective standing over her, evaluating her with those slitted black eyes that were as cold as night. Behind her were two uniformed officers with 9mm Glocks and nightsticks dangling off their overburdened belts. Wendy felt the persecution keenly. Hundreds of people were swarming all over the place. Why single her out to embarrass?

"I was in here the whole time. I didn't see anything. I don't know what happened," she said defensively.

"That may be, but we need to talk anyway." The detective stepped back to make way for her.

Wendy got to her feet shaking her head. "I *can't* be a suspect, Sergeant . . . ?" For once she couldn't remember an important name. She was sick, couldn't the woman tell?

"Woo," the detective said over her shoulder.

Look, Woo, Wendy wanted to say. *The shooting happened* outside. She didn't know anything about it. Anybody with a brain could instantly deduce she had *nothing* to do with it. Obviously this cop had no brain. Her anger escalated as the small woman with the gun at her waist and the two officers marched her around the crowd, down the side of the building where the saints' chapels were and candles burned.

She wanted to cover her face. But she didn't have anything to use. She'd left her raincoat somewhere; she didn't know where.

She also wished she had a gun of her own hanging from her own belt to threaten those cops right back. How dare they . . . She kept her head down to avoid making eye contact with anyone, but even so she did manage to see Lucinda Hay flanked by her sons. She certainly *heard* Lucinda, as usual not exactly behaving with dignity. Lucinda was wailing, demanding to see her husband, her daughter. No one was doing anything about it.

Then Wendy and the cops were outside, amazingly in sunlight. Wendy was blinded by the sun. Intense blue sky after all that rain. She was on Fifty-first Street close to Madison, where nothing of the crime was visible. She was marched over to a police car. Her eyes blurred at the sight of the car. It looked like a regular car, but it was a police car. Someone opened the door and pushed her head down when she got in. She was shaking, but not with fear. With anger. The Chinese sergeant got in front and didn't talk to her. Another car with more police followed behind. She didn't see who was in it, but she heard the doors slamming. She weighed her options: Call a lawyer? No! Lawyers were a breed of compromisers, always wanted you to confess to *something* and make a deal. She wasn't doing that again. She could handle this herself. Just keep quiet. She needed to focus on keeping her life and her secrets to herself. She wasn't telling anyone anything. No matter what.

They traveled the blocks she knew so well as they headed east on Fifty-fourth Street. She was wondering if they were going downtown when the car suddenly stopped in front of the Seventeenth Precinct. Sergeant Woo got out of the car and walked back to talk to the people in the car behind them. They didn't get out and show their faces. Who did they think they were, treating her like this? Didn't they know that she was well connected? She knew a hundred lawyers, maybe more. She could sue if she had to, she thought. Her hands were shaking. She knew she had too many secrets to sue. Woo returned, took her out of the car, and led her up the stairs to the second floor, where the detective squad room was nearly empty. It was a disgusting place.

Ignoring her some more, the sergeant conferred with a detective. Together they moved an unwashed male and the fat detective who'd been questioning him out of a dirty room that said INTERVIEW ROOM on the door. Woo came back to Wendy and led the way in, glancing at the full wastebasket and abandoned cell phone on the floor.

"Gee, I'm sorry the place is such a mess," she murmured.

Wendy made a disgusted noise. She did not want to enter the malodorous room. She was wearing a very good silk shantung suit and didn't want to sit in either of the chairs just vacated. She smelled alcohol. She needed no reminders that she yearned for a drink.

Woo picked up the cell phone and left the room with it. Wendy looked up and noticed the mirror against one wall. With a sick feeling, she saw that four chairs had been set up in a line. Except for the table, the chairs took up nearly all the floor space in the room. What now, a lineup?

The sergeant returned with a tape recorder. She

did not seem distressed by the possibility of catching some disease in the room. She put the tape recorder down, rearranged the chairs around the table, then motioned for Wendy to sit. Wendy stood there. Next to the Chinese woman, she felt the power of her height. She was a tall and elegant girl from a good family. She did not deserve this treatment. Her eyes were puffy. She wasn't feeling well. She didn't like being pushed around by this little female cop, disliked it even more than when the male detectives had questioned her. The need for a drink circled her like a hungry shark.

"Have a seat," the cop told her.

Fine, Wendy sat. She could throw away the good suit. "Would you mind telling me why I'm here?"

Woo popped a cassette into the recorder.

Wendy looked down at her hands.

The cop smiled, friendly. "Wendy, you and I talked last week, remember?"

"Yes, of course I remember. You almost shot me when I went to turn on the air conditioner." Wendy ventured a little smirk.

"Remember I asked you if there was anything in the apartment there shouldn't be?" Woo said, still nice as pie.

Wendy's heart hammered harder. "Yes . . . so?"

"And you said there wasn't anything."

Wendy frowned. "That's right. Where's this leading? Did you go into my apartment? I'll sue you . . . I'll have your badge!"

April Woo didn't answer. She pushed the record button on the tape recorder, gave her ID, a lot of it. Wendy's ID, the place, the day, the date, and the hour. Who was in the room. Just the two of them. Wendy glanced sharply at her watch, suddenly aware of how late it was. Nearly one-forty-five. By now the guests should be well lubricated and the luncheon in full swing. There would be no luncheon. She touched her hair. It was still damp. She dropped her hand.

Woo led her through some simple questions, where she lived, what she did, her involvement in the Tovah Schoenfeld wedding. An hour passed. Easy questions. Wendy yawned. Woo seemed tireless. She turned the cassette over. Wendy asked for a Coke. The sergeant stepped to the door, called out for a uniform to bring a Coke. A moment later she had one. Woo punched the record button, repeated all the pertinent information. Still only two of them in the room.

"Wendy, in our talks last week you didn't tell me the whole truth about your part in Tovah Schoenfeld's murder."

"I told you I was in the ladies' room," Wendy said, flushing a deep red. How many times did they have to go over this? "There were witnesses who saw me there."

"Did you know that eyewitness testimony is among the most unreliable of all?" Woo said smoothly.

Wendy snorted. "What's reliable? You know I didn't kill Tovah. I couldn't have killed Prudence."

"What's reliable is physical evidence. It's incontestable; there's no way to fight it."

"I know the law," Wendy said angrily. "You can't intimidate me."

"Wendy, why is your hair wet?"

"What?"

"Your hair is wet," Woo said coldly.

"Uh, I was out in the rain."

"When were you out in the rain, while Prudence was shot?"

"Hey. It's been raining for two days. I couldn't get a cab this morning. You're intimidating me."

"Not at all. I'm just trying to get to facts we can all rely on. Did you know that conspiracy to commit murder and accessory to murder carry the same weight under the law as committing a murder?"

"Conspiracy?"

"Under the law it's called felony murder. Do you understand what I'm saying?"

"No!" Wendy spat out. "I'm completely in the dark. I haven't a clue what you're talking about, and that's the honest truth." Wendy sniffed. It bothered her that her hair was wet.

"Well, you've told me a few dishonest truths. Let's move to the honest truths now."

Wendy shook her head again. "I don't know what you're talking about." She glanced at the mirror. "Whoever you are back there, I don't know what she's talking about."

"Yes, you do, Wendy. You know exactly what I'm talking about. Prudence Hay was the next bride on your list."

"Look, I was inside the church the whole time. I was where you found me. I had nothing to do with it." She brushed her palms together, brushing off the accusation. They were trembling.

"There was Andrea. There was Tovah. And now Prudence. Prudence was the next bride on your list. You're the connection, Wendy—"

"What! Andrea! What are you saying?"

"Andrea Straka, pushed in front of a subway train the day before her wedding."

"Oh, no, I never take the subway. Just—no!" Tears stung Wendy's eyes. "I don't know."

"Yes, you're the link to all of them, Wendy. You know the who and the why."

"I don't. I'm as puzzled as you. If I knew, why would I protect a murderer?"

"That's a good question. Let's get this cleared up right now."

Wendy drank some Coke. "I'm not the only person who worked on all three weddings. Louis did, his boys did. Tang did. Tons of people . . . the calligrapher. I have an assistant."

"Her name?"

"Lori Wilson, she's on vacation."

"Where is Lori on vacation?"

"Martha's Vineyard. Can I go now?"

"No, Wendy. You can't go. You have to stay and help me out here. You're the link."

"What's your problem? I'm not the link," Wendy snapped. "I told you I don't know."

"And you're lying."

Wendy shook her head. "I don't feel well. I need to go home."

"In time. We have a lot to talk about."

Wendy kept shaking her head. "What is it that you think you have?"

"Your thumbprint on one of the discharged shell casings, one of the bullets that killed Tovah Schoenfeld."

Wendy's eyes widened. They jerked to the mirror behind which she was sure other detectives were watching her, maybe even filming her. Then to the closed door. No exit.

"Jesus Christ. I'm being framed," she cried.

"You're framing me." Panic filled her for the first time.

"That's not the way it happens. Tell me what you know. I'm here to listen and to help. There's nothing that can't be explained and worked out," Woo said.

Okay, yeah. Of course, everything could be explained. She calmed down. She knew how to spin her stories. Her stomach grumbled. She didn't know when she'd eaten last. She started thinking about food, then drink. She needed a drink. She'd explain fast so she could get that drink.

Thirty-nine

The recorder clicked. End side two, cassette three. April reached over and popped it out, her face showing patience she didn't feel. She had six cassettes. She could get more and sit there for the next two days if she had to. The first three contained a lot of sighing.

"Did you turn the recorder off so no one can hear you torture me?" Wendy slouched in her chair, looking more and more like a surly teenager.

April nodded. She was going to zap the suspect with a stun gun. She almost wished she could, because she was not having much luck finding a way into this irritating woman, and liking her less and less as the hours passed. The pressure for something to break was crushing, and she couldn't help thinking of Jason Frank having fun thousands of miles away, leaving her with a psycho case she couldn't seem to handle. April knew exactly how Jason jumped into the sea of misery with his patients, leading them back into the past and forward into the future at the same time. She'd seen him do it. And now she'd tried being like him, nicer in every way. And it wasn't working.

Wendy responded by slouching and sneering like

a big caged cat—or a guy. That was it, she was acting more guy than girl. Her coil of resistance was
strengthening. She'd become one hundred percent
yang, almost as if she knew for sure that nothing
could touch her. The arrogance pissed April off. She
felt ever more stressed by the ticking clock, by Bellaqua's and Mike's depending on her, and the chief's
personal command to get it done today. The story
was right here in the room. April could feel it just out
of reach. All she needed to do was push the right
button.

"Can I have a Coke, please?"

"Sure." April stepped outside. "Get me another
Coke, please."

Mike appeared. "Want me to take a crack at her?"

"Not yet. Let me keep it soft for a while. We can
try that. There's always time to muscle her. Anything
come up on Lori Wilson, the assistant?"

"Nothing yet. Her background looks clean, but
let's find out where she is."

April nodded, glanced at her watch.

"You sure you don't want me to hammer her?"

"Uh-uh. Thanks," to the uniform for the Coke.

She went back in. "Here you go." It was Coke
number five.

Wendy drank half of it in one gulp.

"Feeling better?"

"No."

"Look, don't push me away. I can help you out.
Whatever happened I know you had a reason. You
don't have to be a tough guy with me," April
soothed. "I'm on your side here."

Wendy snorted. "Oh, come on, you're treating me
as if I were a common crook, like that bum who was

in here before. You said I was a thief, you implied I was fired from my last job. You told me you have my fingerprints on shell casings. Ha-ha." She made the explosive sound of air extruded through closed lips. "I understand what you're doing."

"I want to help you go home, that's all."

"That's what they always say on cop shows." Wendy snorted.

"We're not in a movie here. At least three young women died on your watch. You're the link, Wendy. I need your help."

"I don't care what you need. It's not my problem." Wendy tapped her foot.

"Let me repeat that. Two beautiful young women were murdered at your weddings. A third died the day before her wedding. I'm not forgetting Andrea. Three of your weddings make it your problem."

"Not my weddings." Wendy made a face.

April caught the sudden slice of pain through bravado. "Of course, your weddings," she said lightly.

"Turn that thing back on." Wendy pointed to the recorder.

April lifted a shoulder and complied with a new cassette and the routine of coding in the pertinent information. The mood was shot again. Wendy was an expert at pushing away.

"Tell me about Barry," April said softly, starting at square one again.

Wendy swiped at her nose with the back of her hand. "It was an accident. How many times do I have to say it?"

"No, no. I mean what was he like?"

"What was he like?" She shifted position and gazed up at the cracks in the ceiling.

"Yeah, what happened? What went wrong?"

"It won't help you. It has nothing to do with this." She glanced down at April, then clicked her tongue as if she thought April was stupid.

"It's part of your history. It's part of what makes you tick."

"Why do you want to know what makes me tick?"

"You're in a lot of trouble. I want to help you."

"Sure you do."

"What went wrong with Barry?" April could push right back.

"Oh, please. The usual, what else? It happens all the time. A girl thinks she has someone; the guy has a different idea." She rolled her eyes, drawing the pain upward like smoke up a chimney.

"I know what it feels like. Yeah, men suck, don't they?" April murmured.

For the first time Wendy's eyes flashed interest. "Yes, that's about it."

"You got engaged, he cheated on you," April guessed.

Wendy shrugged wide, bony shoulders. "It's no big thing. They all do it. They'll do it the day before their wedding. They'll do it the night of their wedding. Shit, some of them will go out for a shave the morning after and fuck someone else before lunch."

"And you're in a position to know about that," April murmured.

"Oh, I know a lot about that," Wendy agreed, checked her nails this time.

April did not doubt it. She nodded. "Barry was a big disappointment."

"Barry is an asshole." Wendy's burst of laughter was contemptuous. "The jerk's been married twice since then. Doesn't that say it all?" She drank up the rest of the Coke.

"You were, what, twenty at the time?"

"Twenty-three. Old enough to know better," she said bitterly.

"Not really. Twenty-three is a very hopeful age. How did you meet him?"

Wendy chewed the inside of her lip, bobbed her head. "You really want the story of my life?"

"Absolutely, we have all time in the world."

"We have the time until I call my lawyer." Wendy laughed again.

April froze. She and her camera became still as stone. Wendy knew exactly what she was doing. The minute she demanded a lawyer it would be over. It would be either arrest her on the spot or let her go home. A partial print was weak, nothing more than a muscle to flex. April had lied about one thing: Even fingerprints could be contested. A paid expert could easily contest a partial. How much minutiae could they have, how many matching swirls? *Please*. Even if there was enough minutiae to suggest a match alone, the print was only a suggestion of guilt, a possibility. Aware of watchers behind the mirror, April pressed on.

"You met him . . . ?"

"Barry is my stepfather's son. He's my stepbrother."

"No kidding." A flag. Something new.

"Well, not at first. My mother didn't marry him until years later," Wendy amended. She glanced at her watch, at the ceiling, everywhere but at April.

"After you started going out, you mean?" April ignored an itch in an intimate place.

"Yes, I guess that's what I mean. They didn't get divorced right away." Wendy sucked in her lips and sighed as if bored.

"Right away when?"

"Oh, they knew each other a long time." Now she broke into a smile. Some little secret smile. The woman had swift mood changes.

Oh, this was a long game. April kept waiting.

"I knew Barry. My brothers liked his sister, Miff. It was all pretty friendly when we were growing up." Wendy paused; then her expression soured again. "They had a couple more kids. They're still together."

So Wendy shot a stepbrother and was now out in the cold, probably not so welcome at family reunions, at the very least. April wasn't a shrink, but psychologically speaking, it sounded as if alienation from her own family might be a component of Wendy's problem. April flashed to Jason again. Ha, she could do this.

"Where did the shooting incident occur?" she asked, feeling the excitement of a puzzle piece fitting.

"On Martha's Vineyard. We had a home there."

Click, Martha's Vineyard was also where Lori Wilson, Wendy's assistant, was on vacation. And she'd seen something else about Martha's Vineyard. What was it?

"Had?" she prompted.

"Oh, we lived in it when I was little. My mother got the house in the divorce," Wendy said, offhand.

"Does she live there now?"

Wendy shook her head. "No. They moved to Newport."

Rhode Island. Another resort area April knew nothing about. "Who owns the place now?"

"I don't know." Wendy gazed at the ceiling.

"What kind of shooting did you do?"

"Sport shooting." Flat.

"Oh, yeah, what exactly is that?"

Wendy gave her a look. "Sportsmen shoot bull's-eyes, either slow fire or rapid fire, but it's the opposite of what you do."

"Really. What do we do?"

"You just empty a magazine into the silhouette of a human as fast as you can. With a rifle or revolver. Combat shooting is pretty trashy. It's for the beer-drinking crowd. In sport shooting, the idea is to aim. You do any knockdowns?"

April shook her head. That was for the military.

"In sport shooting you go for silhouettes of game animals about twenty, thirty yards out. If you hit them, they fall over. Or we shoot clay, skeet. No humans." She said it with a nervous laugh. "Unlike you."

"What kind of rifles do you use?"

"It depends. A sporting clay, a skeet rifle. A trap gun. For competition you use a 308; that's a .30-caliber rifle."

"Shotguns." Now they were getting somewhere.

"Mm-hm. They have different chokes in them, seven-and-a-half-, eight-, or nine-size pellets, depending. You could cut somebody up pretty bad from twenty yards away but not kill them with that size shot, but as I said, we don't go out for humans like you do."

"How many guns do you have, Wendy?" April asked, unperturbed.

"I don't know."

"What do you mean, you don't know?"

"The house was burgled during the winter years ago. I don't even remember when. I had a few guns up there then; I don't remember how many." Wendy bobbed her foot.

April guessed that was where the murder weapon came from. She switched off the tape recorder and left the room without a word. She glanced at her watch. Jesus, nearly seven. She had to pee. And she had to go to Martha's Vineyard to find Lori Wilson and more about Wendy's missing guns.

Forty

"Hey, what's your hurry, *querida*?" Mike caught her as soon as she stepped into the squad room.

"Gotta pee. Be right back."

She brushed past him, found the lieutenant's bathroom, cursed because there was no tissue, used some from her purse. She washed her hands and face with the grimy soap chip on the sink. No paper towels, either. They didn't keep up the housekeeping here. Muttering, she glanced up for a moment to see how bad she looked. She was startled by the shadow of a dragon, snapping its tail deep inside the mirror behind her miserable reflection. She clapped her hands the way the noisemakers did on the Chinese New Year to chase away evil spirits. The clap jogged her memory. Wendy had done a wedding on Martha's Vineyard a month ago. Now her assistant was there on vacation. She flushed the toilet with her foot and forgot about applying lipstick. Something was up with Massachusetts.

Mike was waiting for her when she came out. "We located Tito and Louis, just in case you're interested," Mike said.

"Where?"

His lips disappeared in a grimace under his mustache. "At Louis's shop. The two alibi each other again. Louis says they worked half the night last night setting up, then returned to the shop around eleven. They've been there ever since." He lifted a shoulder.

"Very convenient, but he lied about that last time," April remarked.

"Right, we can't rule them out now. The Ubu story is up for grabs, too."

"We're way behind the curve, *chico*. You heard Wendy's fiancé was her stepbrother? Missed that one." She shook her head. "Missed a few other things, too."

"Uh-huh." Mike planted himself against a wall of wanted posters, looked pretty tired.

"The shooting must have broken up the family. The parents moved away a while ago. But Wendy still has ties. She did a wedding there a month ago."

"No kidding. April?"

"Yes. Mike?" April poked him to get by.

"Not you, *querida*, the month. Who gets married up there in cold, rainy April?" he mused, still keeping the wall up.

"Someone did. I have to go to Martha's Vineyard." April had stopped trembling. The female fog of yin had been replaced by the male energy of yang when she didn't need food, didn't need sleep. She could feel energy spiking her system. How long it would last she didn't know. She wanted to keep at it, though. She knew all these wedding people were intertwined somehow. Covering for each other. And the one who'd kicked Mike in the face, now on suicide watch at Bellevue. All in it together. The how and why was what they didn't know.

"You want to tell me why?" Mike said.

"Lori Wilson, the assistant. All these people and their movements. And the house. Houses are powerful things. I want to get a look at the house." She was certain Wendy had lied about the house.

"Okay." Mike watched her think.

"Look, we'll talk about it later. I want to get back to her."

Mike shook his head. "We're going to Sutton Place. Poppy wants to take a go at her now."

April shook her head, disappointed. "But I was getting somewhere."

"Let's go talk to Mr. Hay and his butler before their memories blur." Mike pushed off the wall.

"We were just establishing a rapport," April protested.

"She'll keep."

April frowned. "She won't keep. She'll shut down. I know this woman."

"But you're going with me," he said. "*Vamos.*" He smiled ruefully at the door. There was nothing he could do. Poppy was the boss.

"Fine." Frowning, she swung her purse over her shoulder. Sutton Place it was.

Forty-one

Anthony Pryce set out milk, sugar, and a plate of chocolate-chip cookies. He was wearing a crisply ironed pair of chinos and a white shirt. His eyes were red, but his face was composed and his movements quick and sure. Relegated to a yin position again, April's energy faded down to a shadow. Suddenly she was dead tired.

She watched Anthony's intense focus on correct service, her thoughts flashing like a neon sign to Martha's Vineyard. Martha's Vineyard. What a waste. After an hour with Mr. Hay, all they got from him was a deep conviction that the shooter was very tall. Who was tall? Louis and Wendy were tall. The African in a psych ward at Bellevue was tall. Why couldn't he remember anything else?

Anthony set down a white china coffeepot, a matching teapot, and a plate of cookies, arranging them just so on the table. Then he quickly attacked a wayward cookie crumb, brushing it off the polished wood into his hand. A perfectionist. Good. April's nose twitched at the deep and smoky aroma of Lapsang souchong infusing in the teapot.

She and Mike sat at a small table on the window end of the kitchen in a grand apartment that overlooked the East River. At eight o'clock it was dark outside. Over in Queens the lights twinkled on a cool and silvery city evening. Mike ate a few more cookies, deep in his own thoughts. April's paranoia uncoiled just enough to make her wonder if he knew something he wasn't sharing.

Anthony disappeared into the butler's pantry around the corner, then reappeared with two dessert plates and two linen napkins. He set down the plates, folded the napkins, went back for a pitcher of water and two glasses.

"We have food. I could make you a sandwich," he offered.

"No, thanks. This is terrific." The plate of cookies was nearly gone and so was Mike's coffee. "Have a seat," he said.

"It's no trouble." It was clear Anthony didn't want to take a seat. He poured more coffee in Mike's cup, continuing to hover.

Mike raised his eyebrows at April. Food?

"No, thanks," she echoed, dying for a sandwich but not enough to take the time for him to make one.

"I read about that other girl in the paper," Anthony said. He brushed at the crumbs that littered Mike's side of the table.

"Did you know her?" Mike asked.

"No, no, of course not. It was in the Bronx, wasn't it?" he kneaded his hands nervously.

"Yes, Riverdale."

"This is so upsetting. Who would do this?" His eyes filled. "Did the same person kill both girls?"

"It's a possibility," Mike said slowly.

"When that girl was shot, the first thing I did was go to St. Patrick's to look around."

"Why?" Mike was surprised.

Anthony finally sat down, his face suddenly animated. "Someone attacked the cardinal there. A few months back, do you remember that?"

"Yes. Were you expecting something to happen?"

"No, not expecting, really, but you have to be vigilant. People will do anything in these troubled times. We can't ever forget that, can we?" Anthony found another crumb.

"Did you have any special danger in mind?"

"The Hays are Irish."

Mike's eyebrows shot up like flags. *Ah, the Irish.* He caught April's eye. "Do you think there's an Irish connection to the shooting?"

"Everything's so political now, isn't it? One can't ignore the risks."

"Are you Irish yourself?" Mike asked. Everybody had a natural enemy these days.

"I've lived in Ireland, of course. That's where I met the Hays. But no, I'm Welsh," Anthony said proudly.

"So you think there may be some political motive at work here? Can you be more specific about your concerns?"

"I thought about it, that's all," Anthony said vaguely.

Mike glanced at April again. Her face was the Great Wall of China. Impenetrable.

"When you went to St. Patrick's, what were you looking for?" She spoke for the first time.

"I try to be thorough. It's my responsibility to see that things go smoothly." Anthony brushed the hair out of his eyes.

"You thought something could go wrong?"

"I told you, there was the other girl. And the cardinal. It worried me."

The phone in April's purse started to burble. She located it, checked caller ID. It was Ching. She turned the phone off, then tossed it back into the mess.

"Tovah Schoenfeld was not Irish. She was an Orthodox Jew," Mike pointed out.

"I heard something about that. It just made me think, that's all. People get ideas from these things. Politics, it makes sense, doesn't it?"

Not really. "What did you hope to find?" Mike asked.

"I was concerned about people walking in and out throughout the ceremony. I wanted to see how that would be."

"You didn't know it would be private?"

"No. And maybe he didn't either. That's why he shot her outside."

Click. Ah, it might have been someone who had been inside but went outside when the cathedral was cleared.

"Are you certain it was a he?"

"They've asked me that. I don't know. I didn't really see much. It was so sudden. I just saw the flash of gray, the raincoat. I never even saw the barrel of a gun. It might have been a revolver. There was just a little sound. More like a cough than a pop. She just . . ." Anthony shook his head as if it were his fault. "I just didn't see it coming."

"I know you've gone through this with the officers before, but we want to see what we can do to jog your memory. Just for a few seconds. Try to tell us what you saw, what you might not even know you saw. It's okay if you just give us impressions."

His color leached out as he searched his memory. "It's like a black hole in my mind—" He stopped. "All I can think of is I was struggling to keep the umbrella over her head, their heads. Then blood spurting out on her dress. So much blood. It covered her in a second. She drowned in it." He reached for his own neck.

April's heart thudded.

"It was so . . . horrible. *Horrible!* I was trying to hold the umbrella over them. The wind changed; it turned inside out. I let it go and I saw . . . her eye was gone." His shoulders shook. "All I know for sure was that the man's raincoat had a hood."

"Were you aware that Wendy Lotte was the party planner for both weddings?" April asked.

"Yes. After the first girl was killed, it was in the newspapers."

"Were the Hays concerned?"

"About their daughter, yes. About Wendy, no. They trusted her."

"How about you? Did you trust her?"

"No."

"Was that why you went to St. Patrick's?"

"No, I didn't trust her because she has light fingers," Anthony said.

"You mean she steals." A confirmation of what they knew. April glanced at Mike. His eyes flickered.

"I'm not accusing. It's just possible," Anthony said, neutral.

"How about the florist? Anything unusual about him?"

"I don't know anything about him. He never came to the house."

April began to revive with the tea. "Did you drive Prudence everywhere?"

"Pretty much."

"Great. Let's go back through the week. Everything she did, who she saw, that kind of thing."

Anthony nodded and poured more tea. It was going to take a while.

Forty-two

The dog was barking, and Kim was upset. Wendy wasn't answering her phone, and he had no one to talk to except his wife. Clio wouldn't let him near the phone. She stood in front of him, pushing the broom against him so he couldn't get to the phone without hurting her.

"You so bad person," she screamed.

This made Kim feel terrible, but he knew he wasn't a bad person. He did so many things for people. "Honey, I bought you a diamond ring," he reminded her, pushing a little at the broom.

"Only little one," she screamed, shoving back. "Who you calling, huh? After all I do for you? Who you calling? I hope that woman's business fall into the ground. I hope you lose your job."

"Don't say that. Tang's a great woman." This made Kim mad.

"I married you for nothing. I should throw you away today."

He bit his tongue because he didn't want to scream back. Whenever he fought back, she hit him.

"You don't give me money. I should divorce you. You can go right back to those ships."

Right now it didn't sound so bad to him. He'd had

some beer so he wasn't really listening to her. He was thinking of his poor sister beaten so bad by her husband. His not listening made her madder still.

"Why are you crying? I didn't hurt you." She poked him in the shoulder with the broom handle, almost knocking him over.

He shook his head. He wasn't crying.

"Yes, you're crying. Stop crying. You're not a child." She stamped her foot, mad enough to hit him some more.

People said Clio Alma was a beautiful woman. She had a round face with smooth skin, full lips, and not a bad figure for someone so old. But she was a cold woman, hard and angry all the time. She pushed him back against the wall, screaming at him.

"Why you so bad person? Why don't Tang give you more money? Huh, why not? Why you like her?" Clio was so mad her English broke up.

Kim was scared of her. Everyone said she was a nice woman, but he knew she was really a witch and not right in her head. He had bruises. His head hurt. He didn't just like Tang. He loved Tang. She was good to him. He didn't love Clio, it was true. She was mean to him. And even though he'd told her before they married that he could never give her a child, she was still mad that he wouldn't sleep in her bed. Three years and she wouldn't give up.

She wanted money. She wanted a child. She wanted to know where he was every minute of the day. Jealous of everybody. Who could live like that? He was only thirty and could not sleep even on the same floor with her. He had to be downstairs, near the door so he could get out whenever he had to. He felt choked to death, also contrite and sorry that she thought so much was wrong with him. He wanted to tell her he didn't like Tang that way, either. No girl.

Clio spat at him. "You didn't come home last night."

"Yes, I did," he whispered. But she always knew. He wiped her spit off his face with the back of his hand.

"Where were you?"

He was not going to tell her he was with his friend Bill, an old man who gave him money. She didn't like him having friends. She didn't like him getting money that she didn't know about. If he told her he had money, she always took it from him.

"Tell me," she demanded.

He put his lips together. He wouldn't say anything. Whatever he said made her madder.

"It's your fault he did it. You were supposed to come home and take him out. His mess is your fault." Now she was complaining about the dog.

He looked sorry. He was busy. He'd forgotten about the dog.

"Stop that; you're disgusting."

His face turned sullen.

"Stop it," she yelled.

He wasn't doing anything. He bit his lips. This angry woman who didn't get what she wanted burned him like acid. He wished he weren't such a good and tender person, so kind to her no matter what she did. She was the one who hid all the money. Even if she were hit by a subway train, he would never get any money.

"You're worse than the dog," she screamed. "You took my money. You took a thousand dollars."

He shook his head, his eyes rolling up. It was the

other way around. She took his money. He didn't even know where she hid it.

"Yes, you did. You took my money. Where is it?" she demanded.

"I didn't take your money. I have my own money." He couldn't help teasing her just a little.

"What money?" Her voice rose almost to a howl.

Sometimes Clio screamed so loud in this quiet Queens neighborhood that someone called the police to make her stop. As soon as the police came, she opened the door nice and calm and said she was so sorry. Her husband was a little crazy, but nothing she couldn't handle. She assured them he wouldn't hurt anyone, and no one ever looked to see if she hurt him. It made him feel bad that she would say the noise was his fault.

"No money. I was just kidding," he said, meek again. "I'll talk to you. What do you want me to say?"

"What money?" she yelled, hurting his ears. She let him go and started looking through his things for the money.

"No money, really," he cried. He didn't want her to take the money he'd gotten from the old man. He wanted to use it to buy more flowers for Tang. She'd been so happy with the last ones. Clio didn't find the money. He forgot he'd hidden it somewhere else. When she took the dog out he called Wendy. He wanted to tell her he'd found her gray raincoat, but she didn't answer her phone.

Forty-three

Candles burned. Dozens of them, all colors. Some smelled like wine, others like vanilla, oranges, root beer. The peculiar collection of scents assaulted April's nose when Louis the Sun King opened the door to his Beekman Place town house apartment. The warmth and aroma of candles reached out and choked the air in the second-floor hallway.

"I thought we were finished." He was wearing a white short-sleeved shirt with a pleated front, a Spanish shirt, and was surprised to see Mike again. From the look of him the party had been going on for a while. April glanced at Mike.

"Uh-uh, we're not finished," Mike told him.

Louis groaned and retreated into his highly stylized living room that was all clogged up with deep, soft sofas in orange and red, black and white Moroccan inlaid tables, oversize sari-covered pillows. Painted ostrich eggs, twig balls, vases and urns. Chairs and up-holstered stools filled every corner. Scrolls covered the walls. It was a busy place. The burning candles danced colors around like spangles in a kaleidoscope.

"We're coping as best as we can," Louis murmured, indicating the martini shaker. "Poor Prudence loved her martinis. Would you care to join us?"

April's eyes swept the room, taking in the objects and the boyfriend, handsome as a movie star.

"This is Jorge," Louis said proudly.

"Sergeant Woo," April introduced herself.

"I know. I know. Come in." Louis led the way to the sofa Jorge wasn't occupying. "Two in one week. This epidemic could ruin me."

"Two what?" April asked, playing the dummy.

"I already told him these dead girls are bad for business."

"What a joker," Mike remarked.

"Believe me, I'm not laughing. What do you want from me now?"

April didn't appreciate his attitude. "A better story than your last one."

"Oh, for Christ's sake, I'm just a civilian. I don't know what that means."

"Fine, let's start with Wendy."

"Oh, before it was poor Ubu and Tito and me. Now it's Wendy. Jorge, these people can't make up their minds." Louis threw himself on the sofa next to his friend, jogging him slightly with his foot. April tilted her head at Mike.

"Jorge, go to your room," he said.

"I don't live here," Jorge replied, reaching over to pour himself more drink.

"I don't care. 'Bye now." Mike squared himself off for a little Latin confrontation. Jorge evaluated the situation and said something—something probably not so nice in Portuguese. Then he downed the last of his martini and stood to go. His compliance indicated to April that he didn't have a green card.

"Hey, what do you think you're doing? You can't throw my friends out." Louis jumped up to follow

Jorge as he made for the exit. "Jorge, just walk around the block and come back, okay? This will only take a few minutes, I promise." They argued at the door for a moment. Louis's voice was pleading.

Then he came back into the room angry as a hornet. "What's the matter with you? Are you nuts? He didn't do anything."

"Let's impress upon you the seriousness of this matter, Louis. Two girls are dead, and none of us are sleeping until we find out who killed them. So let's not cha-cha around this anymore." April said it as nicely as she could.

"Believe me, I haven't forgotten. I did their weddings, their fucking wakes. I may go broke over this. It's hard enough to get paid when they *live*." He tossed his head, acting.

"Still joking," Mike said, annoyed enough for both of them. "Cut the crap; we don't have the patience."

"Humor is my crutch, okay? Doesn't mean I don't have feelings." Louis sank down on the sofa with a loving pat to the dent left there by his friend. "Quite aside from the personal, there's a financial component. I'm hurting here. This is going to cost me, maybe ruin me." He held both hands over his heart. "I'm not involved in any crimes."

"Oh, you're involved. You're right there at the top of the list."

This elicited a laugh. "Why? I've been written up everywhere. Didn't he tell you?" Louis pointed at Mike, still on his feet.

April was still on her feet, too. She didn't want to sink into that soft sofa and have trouble getting up down the road. "The killer is right here in your little group, Louis. It's one of you, or all of you. Let's face it. You know it's one of you."

He patted his pompadour, anxious. "I know. I know. I *know* you think that. I told the lieutenant here where I came from, about my parents. He knows. And poor Ubu, this has sent him over the edge. It's a fucking tragedy." He pointed at Mike. "Sit down, will you? You're making me nervous."

Mike obliged. April didn't.

"I told you. I have nothing to hide. I had a shitty past, okay? I took a new name and found a new life. And now I feel bad for kids who suffered like I did. I'm giving something back. You want to sue me because I help them, sue me." He was emoting all over the place, but dead serious and right on the nerve center of his life. April yawned.

"You think we're different, huh? Well, nobody escapes violence in this life, okay? I know that. Ask the shrinkers, they'll tell you. Everybody's been brutalized one way or another." *Pat pat* at the pompadour.

"I may be an aging queen, but I know a thing or two about this. Take Tito. Both his brothers disappeared in Argentina, just disappeared. Politics. The police didn't care, claimed they didn't know anything. Tito was the baby, the faggot the family beat up, and suddenly the sole male survivor. Now he's just a loony bedbug, positive those brothers aren't really dead. They're around every corner, coming back soon so he can go home again."

April watched his eyes and yawned again. How did this pertain? Louis shot her a bitter look.

"People don't talk about this stuff. They get nervous if you tell them that growing up you got fucked over every single day. People just plain don't like to hear it. Doesn't mean we turn out killers."

April yawned a third time.

"Fuck it, you don't give a shit," Louis grunted at her.

"Tell me about Wendy," she said.

"Huh. Do you have a year? She's a very complicated person."

"No, Louis, I have an hour. Come on, tell me something I need to know. Did you see her this morning?"

Louis dropped his head into his hands. "We spoke on the phone. You probably have all the phone records. You know we spoke. Where is she?"

"What did you talk about?" April asked.

"Nothing. Details. She was upset about the rain. She wanted to make sure we didn't line the red carpet with flower trees as we'd planned."

"Any particular reason?"

"Wendy is particular about everything. The winds were high. She knew the flowers would be spoiled. She was concerned the image of decay would give a bad impression."

"The image of decay?" April said, not believing a word of this.

"She always wanted her brides to have happy memories. It's ironic." He sniffed angrily.

"Because she knew Prudence would die? Were you the final say on the flowers, Louis?"

"No, no. Of course not. Mrs. Hay ordered them. I couldn't just not deliver them. I spoke to Mr. Hay about it. He was only too happy to cut them out. We donated all twenty-six flower trees. I'm praying they'll pay me. Maybe I should sue the city." He got up to move his glass, then sat again, eyes moving from one to the other.

"Did Wendy have anything else on her mind?" April asked.

"No, not that I remember." Louis's face was flushed almost purple from emotion, or drink. He looked about ready to have a stroke. "I already told him all this."

"Well, here comes something new. You're very close. You know her state of mind. So far, she's the key to the killings, and you're the key to her."

"No. I said this before. Wendy has her weaknesses, but she's not a killer."

April lifted a shoulder. "Nonetheless. You're the key to her."

Louis raised his hand. "I'm not the key to her. We do business. I wouldn't say we're close."

"Hey, don't play with me!" she said sharply. "I have the party list going back years. You've had your problems in the past. We know about that, too. So cut the cha-cha. You do a lot of business with Wendy."

"Okay, a lot. So what?" Louis's face went through a number of expressions: pissed, nervous, impatient.

"You did a wedding together on Martha's Vineyard a month ago?"

"Yes . . . ?" Now he was wary.

"How did you get there?"

"We took the van." Very surprised.

"Your van?"

"Of course my van."

"Who went?" April asked.

Louis pursed his lips. "Tito and me." He raised his shoulders.

"What about Wendy?"

"Wendy went in her own car."

"Did anybody go with Wendy?"

"I don't know, why?"

"Did you know Wendy was a marksman?"

"Of course."

"Did she brag about it?"

"Brag, no. It was a fact of life, like being left-handed."

"Is she left-handed?"

"No."

"What did her being a shooter mean to you?"

Up went that shoulder. "I don't know, nothing. Wendy's good at her job. That's all I think about."

"You're a smart man, Louis. Don't give me that. Did she ever talk about taking somebody out?" April kept pushing.

"Never."

"What about Tito?"

"I told you he's a bedbug, afraid of his own shadow."

"Like Ubu?"

"I don't know what you're talking about."

"Did you shoot the guns, Louis?" April demanded.

"Me, are you crazy?" His eyes bulged out.

"Oh, come on, it's fun. You know it's fun. Why not?" she prodded. "Everybody likes to shoot."

"I still don't know what you're talking about." He looked pained.

"I'm talking about the guns on the Vineyard. Wendy told me all about it. She said you all shot the guns."

Up went the shoulder.

"You remember it now?"

He shook his head. "I'm not sure. I don't remember. Maybe some of the others did." His face was draining now.

"Did you all stay at the house while you were there?"

"Wendy's house?"

April nodded, holding her breath.

"Yeah, we stayed at Wendy's house."

"Ubu, too?"

"Yeah."

April exhaled, and so did Mike. "You may go away for the rest of your life for not telling us about the guns sooner, Louis. You certainly could have saved Prudence. I don't know. Maybe you didn't want to save Prudence. I don't know, Mike, does this look like a conspiracy to you?"

"Could be. We'll have to see how the DA takes it."

"I never touched those guns."

"How many guns, Louis? One, two? An arsenal?"

"I don't know, a few," he said vaguely. "I don't like guns. I wasn't paying attention."

"Maybe you didn't touch them, but transported them."

He shook his head. "They never left the island. I'm sure of it."

"How can you be sure of it if you weren't paying attention?"

Silence.

"You took a big chance, Louis, and you're going to pay for it."

"The bigger chance was talking to you," he muttered.

"We're going to take a look around, that okay with you? If it isn't okay with you, we'll get a warrant. Which do you prefer?"

He shook his head. "You have my permission. Look away," he said.

Forty-four

M ike blew air out of his mouth. In big puffs like
someone practicing Lamaze. He was tired and
wanted April to come home with him. "You okay?"

"Oh, yeah, just thinking." April was writing
quickly in her notebook. Her to-do list. Go to
Martha's Vineyard Island. Do not pass Go. Do not
collect two hundred dollars.

He could see her thoughts churning. In a few
hours they'd covered a lot of bases. This time they'd
gone through Wendy's place themselves, and not
looking just for guns. They were after an address and
found one in a file with tax and electric and phone
and water bills for a house located at Chappaquon-
sett, Vineyard Haven, Mass. Bingo.

They also found the garage bill and located her car
in a garage on Third Avenue. It was a tomato BMW
538i. In the BMW, a bunch of empty Coke cans, a
couple of Steamship Authority ferry schedules—one
for winter and the latest, spring/summer, just out
this week. Also used ticket stubs for Tuesday, May
eleventh. After Tovah's killing and before Prudence's.
Killers were dumb. Nearly always. They never
thought their tracks could be followed. Why hadn't
they followed this track sooner? They guessed that

the gun used to shoot Tovah was back on Martha's Vineyard and possibly a different gun had been used to kill Prudence. Why? People who loved guns—people who shot them regularly—usually had more than one. Some had dozens; collectors had hundreds. They were betting that Wendy, of the tomato red BMW and many pairs of candlesticks and stemware with the stickers still on them, had many guns.

The Vineyard Haven sheriff said he'd meet them at the airport in the A.M. Barring fog at either end, they'd be there before ten. They'd already placed their bets on what they'd find in her house. Mike wanted his sweetheart home with him.

"*Querida?*"

"Hmmm?" She didn't look up.

"You want to eat?"

"The pizza was fine." Still writing.

"You didn't touch it."

"I ate the crust."

Cheese, she still wouldn't eat cheese. He blew out more air, remembering his perpetual warning to himself: *Women. You risk your life if you fall in love with one.* These Chinese girls were tough. Ching had warned him that he'd better be prepared for a long battle if he wanted to win.

April put the notebook down and looked up. "Tired?" she asked.

"No, I'm cool." They were now in the shiny Crown Vic headed down Second Avenue to Twenty-third Street, where his battered Camaro was parked. April's car was in the garage at One PP, all the way downtown. He'd have to take her down there to get her car; then they'd both head home in different cars on the BQE. Toughness was tough on logistics. He knew he was going to pick her up in the morning for the drive to La Guardia, but he didn't want to be separated from her for what remained of the night.

"I wish they'd held on to Wendy. I don't want to get yanked out of bed when she takes off in an hour." April yawned.

"Exactly what I was thinking," Mike said.

They'd held on to her for nearly ten hours. Some of that time she'd cooled her heels all alone in an interview room. They had her on video, chewing her nails, tapping her feet, twisting around in her chair, taking insignificant bites of three sandwiches then discarding them, and drinking more than a dozen Cokes. There was a saying in the cops that if you put three suspects in a cell for the night only the guilty one would sleep. The innocent ones would be scared shitless; the guilty one could relax because he knew who did it. Wendy was worried and pretty much hopping out of her skin. Without her guns connected to the homicides, though, they didn't have enough to arrest her. They needed the guns to connect the dots.

Mike left the Crown Vic at Twenty-third Street, and they both got in the Camaro. "You want to leave your car and come home with me tonight?" he asked. So much for toughness.

Forty-five

Skinny Dragon was waiting for April when she drove up at one-thirty-three A.M. April could see her fried-seaweed hair framed in the light of the living room window. Before April had even switched the headlights off, Skinny was out the front door in her pajamas, screaming as if there were no such thing as sleeping neighbors.

"Where you been, *ni*?" she cried. "So late. Thoughtless, thoughtless." Loud. Something April didn't catch, softer in Chinese. About a party she was supposed to go to, didn't get to. It wasn't clear which one of them Skinny meant.

April grabbed her purse and Ching's custom dress in its see-through plastic, then jumped wearily out of the car. "Hi, Ma. Sorry. I didn't know it would take so long."

"No good. Worry all day. Sorry not good enough," she scolded in Chinese.

Of course not. What could be good enough to appease a suffering mother? A hundred years of apology would not be enough.

"Where you been?" Skinny asked softer now, clearly relieved her only child was not dead, as she had feared. "What's that? You go shopping?"

As soon as Skinny struck a more normal furious tone, April didn't feel the need to run anymore. Her exhausted body crawled up the walk, acting like the worm her mother thought she was. She wished she could hide the dress. No such luck.

"How much you spend for that?" Skinny demanded.

"Nothing, it was free," April said.

"Free? What kind of dress is free?" Skinny moved closer for a better look. "You do monkey business for that dress, *ni*?" She peered at the dress, giving her daughter a poke in the ribs.

"Maaa!" April dodged her, dove through the front door. *Home sweet home.* But she didn't make it to the stairs leading to her apartment.

Skinny hurried in right behind her, now screaming with a worse idea. "You get that dress from ghost?" she demanded, poking the air with her finger, appalled that April could even consider taking an article of clothing from a dead person. But where else would such a thing come free? The Dragon was not a sophisticated thinker.

"Ma, relax. It was a gift," April assured her.

"Ha." That meant monkey business for sure. Skinny drew close to her daughter to sniff out the truth. She grabbed April's arm and held her in the old iron grip.

It was late and April longed to permanently wrench herself away from her difficult mother with the one-track mind. The problem was, Skinny had a nose worthy of one of those fake doctors in Chinatown who smelled their patients for symptoms. In fact, if Skinny had become a fake doctor, she'd have made a fortune and wouldn't need a daughter to torture and take care of her.

But April was too tired to wrench right now, and there Skinny went. Sniff, sniff, sniff at April's neck, her hair, the palms of her hands, sniffing for sex and murder. And April happened to have been exposed to both that day, the sex most recently. Where and how she would never tell. Mike had been hot; she had been hot. The long week without was more than either could take a second longer. Okay, they'd done it in a car. Okay, in both cars.

April tried to disengage so her mother wouldn't know, but it was too late.

"Aiyeeei," Skinny screamed.

"Ma, come on, I'll make you some tea. We'll talk," she said. "Look at my dress. Here, isn't it beautiful?"

Skinny staggered into the kitchen, too traumatized to think about the origins of a dress. Sex made her absolutely nuts. She was nuts for ten minutes; then the kitchen restored her to what passed in her for sanity. Like a windup toy she went directly to the refrigerator and started taking out the food, which was a good thing because April was really, really hungry.

Skinny's angry muttering while she cooked, however, soon drove April upstairs, where she threw her offending clothes on the floor, showered, and changed into a clean T-shirt and a pair of NYPD shorts. When she returned to the kitchen to mollify the Dragon with stories of Ching's kindness, the ham-and-scrambled-egg fried rice, pickled baby bok choy, and red-cook chicken was on the table. Relieved, April collapsed in one of three battered kitchen chairs and reached for her chopsticks.

"Eat," Skinny demanded, as if she weren't about to.

"Thanks, Ma. I'm starved." April snagged a bite of succulent wing meat, perfectly simmered in gingered soy and saki and still warm. Her favorite.

"Bad luck," Skinny said.

"Yum." April savored that first bite, then attacked the mound of hacked chicken on the plate. For a few seconds Prudence's murder pushed back just a few inches and her mother's comfort food made life as poignantly sweet as it had been in April's youngest years. Her body tingled with the afterglow of Mike's love and the excitement of leaving the city for her first on-the-job flight out of town.

"Bad luck," Skinny announced again, pouring tea.

April stopped gobbling long enough to swallow some. Delicious. She didn't want to ask what in particular was bad luck, since practically anything from the Dragon's point of view could be. She tried distraction.

"The dress came from Ching, Ma. Isn't it beautiful?"

"She gave it to you, why?" Skinny looked suspicious.

"She wants me to give a speech at her wedding."

"Why!" Skinny was flabbergasted.

April lifted a shoulder. A little break with tradition. Skinny didn't wait for an answer.

"Ching called five times," she announced. "Bad luck."

"Okay, Ma, what's the bad luck?"

"Tang Ling on TV. Big interview. You see?"

No, April did not have time to watch TV today, or any other day. "Is that what Ching called about?"

"Tang made Ching's dress."

"I know."

Skinny leaned over the table and took a bite off April's plate. "They're friends. She was invited to the wedding. You didn't know?"

"I know." April flashed to her garish Chinatown cheongsam. Too bad she didn't get a Tang Ling dress.

"Ching can't wear bad-luck dress! Tang very mad. Call her now," Skinny commanded.

April checked the kitchen clock. "It's almost two in the morning, Ma. I can't call her now."

"Tang very famous, *ni*."

"I know." April put her chopsticks down, her short-lived feeling of well-being totally gone. Had Prudence been wearing a Tang dress? That was something she hadn't asked.

Five minutes with her mother and the fog was back. She remembered that she could have stayed at Mike's place and avoided this complication. She should have stayed at Mike's. But her makeup case was here. Her clean clothes were here, and she hadn't wanted to leave town even for a few hours unequipped. Tang Ling wanted to talk to her, or maybe it was Ching who wanted Tang to talk to her. That meant Prudence's dress was a Tang. Another thread to follow.

"You solve case?"

"I hope so, Ma," April said wearily.

"Good girl. You solve," Skinny said, nodding with approval for the first time April could remember.

Forty-six

Too soon it was morning. Birds called outside April's window. She heard them before the click of her alarm, almost as soon as the sun had dragged itself out of the ocean and made its presence known in Queens. The chirping and chattering heightened as light slowly suffused her little room. She'd had a deep and dreamless night, thanks to the feeding philosophy of Skinny. Fill the belly to cease all functioning of the brain.

It worked for only a little while, though. The new day always kicked April's thinking back into gear. Yesterday, storms and catastrophe. Today, birdsong and optimism. Two young women were dead, and nature didn't give a shit. Groaning, she punched the pillow to find a cooler place for her face. That kept her calm for exactly fifteen seconds. After that, all possibility of sleep was gone. She rolled over to stretch her spine and muscles. She hadn't run yesterday or the day before. No martial arts for weeks. Last night, love in a hurry, hardly the sustained hard exercise her legs and spirit required. Today she didn't have time to give it to them, either.

Exactly a week ago Tovah Schoenfeld died. Yesterday Prudence Hay followed her into an uncertain afterlife. But peaceful afterlife wasn't her business. Fully alert now, she jumped out of bed and into the shower. No time for food or further thinking.

A few minutes before seven Mike pulled up in the Camaro. The second she heard the car begin to cough its way into her block, she charged down the stairs and out the door before her mother could ask her where she was going so early on a Sunday morning. The fact that she still had the habit of sneaking in and out at thirty-one years old would have filled her with her usual disgust if Mike hadn't been out of his car, standing by the passenger door. With his ample mustache, dark sunglasses, open-collared amber shirt, buff jacket, and cowboy boots he looked like a drug lord from Miami or *Miami Vice*, one or the other. One who'd been in a fight. But his open arms sent her heart sailing.

Seventy-one degrees, cerulean, nearly cloudless sky, and she was dressed for travel in all-American Gap. Navy polished-cotton trousers, matching blazerlike jacket, and underneath a lucky-red camp shirt, short-sleeved in case it got really hot later. On the job like Mike, she was wearing a Glock on her hip and dark shades. They kissed by the car. Mike's mustache prickled as his tongue nudged into her mouth. She sucked it in deeper, swaying a little in the embrace. Death and hunting: It always made them edgy and hot. She could have kept at the necking for some time, but they had a plane to catch. Reluctantly, she stepped back. Just in time to see her mother's face with its sour expression in the window. Freedom hit her like a drug, and she smiled.

"You're late. Will we make it?" she asked.

"Sure. It's only ten minutes from here." He closed

the door gently and paused just long enough to wave gallantly at the Dragon. Then he got in, revved up the noisy car, and peeled out into the quiet street. Fresh spring air blew in from the open windows, bringing the thrill of escape. Mike raced through the back streets of Queens, avoiding the highway. He pulled into the short-term parking lot at La Guardia nine minutes later.

All was quiet there on May sixteenth for the American Eagle seven-fifty A.M. flight to Martha's Vineyard until they arrived—the couple on the job with four guns, one on the hip, one in a shoulder holster, one in the shoulder bag, and one in a cowboy boot. April and Mike had their boarding passes in hand, but before they'd pulled their gold and authorization to fly armed, the new, beefed-up security teams converged on them like birds to bread crumbs.

"Police," Mike announced, quickly producing the paperwork.

A uniformed officer and the four security persons manning the two metal detectors and conveyor belts each checked out Bellaqua's letter before falling away. The other passengers had backed away for the confrontation.

April's heavy shoulder bag with the .38 and extra ammunition never hit the belt. She kept her sunglasses on, trying to act cool when actually she felt as excited as a kid. City cops rarely traveled out of state on the job, and on those occasions it was usually to escort a prisoner or a suspect back. This trip was also a quickie. They were booked on a three o'clock flight back.

"*Chico*, ever travel on business before?" April asked as they walked out on the tarmac into a stiffening breeze toward the tiny propeller job that was their conveyance.

He nodded. "Wasn't fun like this, though. I had to go down to South Carolina to pick up a guy who'd hacked up his wife. We had to sedate him pretty heavy to get him on the plane."

April had no comeback for that. "You want the window?" she asked as she ducked her head to climb aboard. Oh, it was small.

"No, you take it." Mike slid in next to her, scrunching into the narrow space with zero legroom. "Isn't this fun?"

"Oh, yeah, this is great." She checked her watch. It was getting late. Nobody came to close the door. The other passengers had been smart enough to bring their coffee and bagels with them. They'd been too cool to think of food.

Mike's cell rang and he reached into his pocket for it. "Yeah? Oh, yeah, hi. Uh-huh, we're there. Yeah, looks like we'll be on time, maybe a minute or two late. Weather's good. Little bit of a breeze. Uh-huh, uh-huh, uh-huh. Okay." He hung up and gave April's arm a pat. "How ya doin', *querida*?"

"Who was that?" April asked, as if she didn't know.

"Bellaqua. Wendy hasn't moved or called anyone since last night. Ditto Louis. Tito's in the hot seat downtown. They'll work on him all day. She wants us to keep in touch and get with her later this afternoon at One PP."

April peered out the little window. Martha's Vineyard was about two hundred and forty miles, not that far, but ahead of her she could see a line of jets assembling for their eight o'clocks to wherever. *Let's*

go, let's go. They didn't have all day. Yesterday, she'd
taken a chance in the interview room and kept her
questioning real general because she hadn't wanted
to alert Wendy. Sometimes they talked around and
around a subject, never hitting the nail on the head.
In this case Wendy was holding out on them big-
time. April didn't want her calling her mystery assistant, or getting on the road in the BMW herself. She
hoped she knew what she was doing.

She turned to Mike with a little smile, remembering their search of Louis's place. They'd come up
with a few fancy sex toys, but nothing of a more sinister nature than that. The detectives who tossed
Tito's rented room in a small house found *Soldier of
Fortune* magazines, but no guns. He said he liked to
look at the pictures.

Let's go. Let's go. The nineteen seats filled up. Af-
fluent people with a certain look. Expensive khaki
clothes, expensive casual carry-on bags. Buff people,
Wendy's kind of people, fit and secure. And used to
the drill. Only April and Mike were tapping their
watches.

"Jesus, look at that. We're never getting out of
here." April pointed out the planes lining up on the
runway.

"We'll be fine." Mike squeezed her hand, always
the optimist.

Finally, the door was closed. The two propeller engines sputtered to life, and the Tinkertoy plane taxied
out sounding like something from World War II. Not
too many minutes later, the copilot rattled off safety
instructions and the little commuter took its place on
the runway between jumbo giants off to faraway
places.

Taking off, the plane teetered from side to side, fighting rising winds. At a hundred feet it hung there, engines throbbing. April watched the jets ahead of them soar up and away. Then the plane bounced a few times like a jeep off-road, losing altitude before it began to fight its way higher. Her empty stomach lurched. She clutched the arm of her seat and concentrated on the changing views: Rikers Island, the new Manhattan skyline, the George Washington Bridge receding behind them. Long Island and the coast opening out ahead.

Forty-seven

For forty-five minutes the little commuter bounced around in bumpy air. Then a patch of green appeared ahead in choppy, whitecapped water and grew larger until it reached the size of Manhattan. The turbulence increased as they went inland and down. The plane seesawed as it came down and connected hard with the ground twice before finally settling into a jerky taxi toward a toy-sized airport.

"Welcome to Martha's Vineyard, and thanks for flying American Eagle," the pilot announced.

April saw the police cruiser parked on the runway and unhooked her seat belt with a little sigh of relief. The local sheriff was waiting for them as he had promised. As soon as she and Mike broke away from the other disembarking passengers and headed his way, he stuck out a paw. If he felt any surprise by the New York team, he didn't show it.

"You got here right on schedule. Bert Whitmore, at your service." The sheriff was five-ten, heavy build, wearing a khaki uniform with a considerable belly protruding over his belt, bristly gray hair growing out well past the crew-cut stage, sharp blue eyes.

"Lieutenant Sanchez and Sergeant Woo. Thanks for coming out for us," Mike said.

"No trouble at all. We don't get too many requests from Nu Yawk. We have a lot of respect for you folks, what you did last fall. Anything to help." Whitmore smiled at April. "You the one who called me last night?"

"Yes, sir."

"You didn't tell me much." He waved his hand at the new-looking cruiser with the Commonwealth of Massachusetts seal on the front doors. It was real clean and neat, had a cage separating the front and back seats, and all the modern technology. "What's your time line?" he asked.

"We're going back out at fifteen hundred. You okay with that?" Mike asked.

"Anything you want is okay with me. I'm here to help." Whitmore glanced back at the wind socks on the runway, snapping hard in a rising wind and deepening haze. He shrugged big shoulders, then climbed stiffly into the car. "You'll be fine getting out if the weather holds."

"What if the weather doesn't hold?" Mike asked, checking his watch, then opening the front passenger door for April.

"Ferry to Woods Hole. Bus to Baaston or Hyannis. Or you can wait it out."

Cold, wet air gusted at them. April shivered and shook her head. Spring was several weeks behind here; maybe they wouldn't get home as easily as they got here. She chose the backseat, happy to let Mike do the talking for the moment. His hand grazed hers as she climbed into the back.

"You're here about those wedding shootings down there, huh? Terrible thing. One of you want to fill me in?" The sheriff started the engine and drove around a fortune in private planes parked in a grid next to the runway like cars in a big lot.

"How long have you been on the job, Sheriff?" Mike asked.

"Call me Bert. Going on nineteen years now," he said.

"You know a family up here called Lotte?"

"Oh, sure. Over on Lake Tashmoo. The little lady told me you wanted to go out there and take a look."

"You had a shooting incident there back about seventeen years. Do you remember anything about that?"

"Sure, I do. I went to grammar school with Barry Wood. We looked into it pretty carefully because of the sticky situation." The cruiser bumped off the field onto the service road and threaded through a bunch of buildings that looked like army barracks. At the entrance to the airport, he turned left onto a road that was empty but for cars leaving the airport.

"What kind of situation?"

"Missus Lotte took up with Barry's father, and there was a lot of bad feeling between the families over the divorce. Barry and Wendy went away to school. Then in college during the summers the two were running around the island together, getting into trouble."

"Oh, what kind of trouble?"

"Oh, you know, the usual kind of thing for here. Vineyard Haven is a dry town. They'd run into Oak Bluffs and get beer, drink out on the beach, light firecrackers. Once they set off a rocket across the cut. It set the beach grass on fire and burned out a couple acres." He thought about it for a few moments.

"They weren't malicious, though. They alerted the

fire department right away. Otherwise we could have lost a couple of houses out there. Everything's shingle on the beach, and pretty much everywhere else, too." He let out a chortle. "And they grew Mary Jane out in the vegetable garden. Those two were pretty wild for here, and their families, too."

He turned left again at a four-way intersection with a blinking yellow light. The weather was deteriorating fast. Fog rolled in at around a hundred feet. April could see it move forward like a wall. Unlike New York, where it just thickened the air until you couldn't see the tops of the buildings.

"What about the shooting?" Mike asked.

They passed a farm with fields just planted, houses, all gray shingle with shutters. Now they were on a main road with fancy SUVs and only white people driving them. April tried to imagine Wendy's life here as a kid growing up. A few miles on they turned left again, passed a cemetery, a grocery store, a couple of small strip malls. Then a sudden deep curve in the road brought them to a grassy hill overlooking a cove with bobbing sailboats below and they were in picture-postcard land.

"This here is the inland side of the lake."

They passed a horse farm with barns and an elegant white clapboard house, and soon turned onto a dirt road. Bert resumed his story.

"Wendy cleaned up pretty good after she went to college. No more trouble before the shooting. They had a twenty-eight-acre place and did trapshooting out there, target shooting. Harry Lotte had always been an enthusiastic sport shooter, and somebody was always complaining about him and the kids shooting out there in the dunes. Wendy was into it pretty big. Did you know she almost went to the Olympics her senior year of college?"

"Yeah, we heard something about it."

"Why did she shoot Barry?" April asked.

"The way they told it, Wendy was target shooting, didn't see Barry behind it. Bullet went through the target and hit him in the shoulder."

"What kind of target?" April asked.

"Old fashioned bull's-eye target," he replied. "Like for archery. Not much to it. It could have happened that way." He shrugged.

But that wasn't the way Wendy told it.

"Humph. Is shooting like that legal out here?" April asked.

"Nope, but as I told you, they did it."

"Did you compare the heights of the target and the victim to see if it could have been an accident?" April asked.

"I was pretty new on the job. I wasn't an investigator back then. That's what they said, and that's what they stuck to. It got in the paper, but it wasn't a real big deal, except those two broke up afterward, and the families moved away."

"What about the gun?" April, still asking from the backseat.

"AR-7."

"Takedown," Mike finished.

"Yep."

The classic survival rifle used first by the military and then on countless RVs, boats, and planes for the last forty years. Not much in favor on the market anymore, but hundreds of thousands of them were out there. It was a good gun for the wilderness, for shooting small game, and for plinking tin cans.

"Pretty neat little thing. The barrel, action, and eight-round magazine each have a compartment in the stock."

"Caliber .22," April said from the back.

"Yes, ma'am."

That's what they were looking for.

"Was the gun confiscated?" Mike asked.

"It was registered." Bert turned to Mike briefly. Up went his shoulder.

"Any complaints about shooting out there this season?" April asked.

"We have strict gun laws here in Massachusetts. We don't let anybody get away with any reckless shooting now." This he was sure about. "They can own, of course, but they can't just shoot anywhere."

The cruiser traveled down a deeply rutted, bone-jarring dirt road that wound through a dense scrub-oak forest, posted with NO HUNTING signs. Other signs pointed down branching roads to houses named Chateau, Swindle, Osprey Nest. Suddenly a deer with two tiny fawns crashed through the brush and crossed the road ahead of them. April caught her breath at the dazzling sight.

"Troublesome creatures." Bert didn't even slow down.

Mike turned around to smile at April. Nature. Unexpectedly lovely. Then he asked a question April didn't hear. Bert answered with a laugh. He was acting like a tourist guide, still hadn't asked how the old case pertained to the homicides in the big city. At twenty yards a .22 bullet might well travel through a soft target at close range, but it didn't play well to April, and it wasn't the story Wendy had told her. Why tell a different story now? She thought about it as the trees thinned and sand and sea grass filled the ruts that pretended to be road. Maybe Wendy's story changed in her mind over the years. Maybe she just lied all the time. They were almost there.

A tight turnaround with a scrub oak in the center formed a wheel off of which one road led out to beach and open water and two doubled back inland. The cruiser dipped into a pothole a foot deep and followed a crude hand-painted sign for Blueberry Farm, then turned again onto another bumpy road. He stopped in a clearing where the pine forest edged the lake.

"This is it?" April was surprised. The house was hardly more than a cottage.

"The main house is down the road. It was sold off years ago. The barn here, along with a few acres and about a hundred feet of waterfront, was kept, built at the same time. I think Wendy owns it. The water's brackish, so she can't rent."

So what Wendy had told her in the interview room was half truth. Sea grass was high in front of the house. A badly rusting van and a moped were parked there. April's heart spiked as they got out of the cruiser and hiked along a narrow path through the wet grass.

Bert went first and knocked on the door. Wet wind slapped at their clothes and faces as they waited. April shivered in her cotton jacket. It was downright cold up here.

"Open up, police," Bert said.

They waited some more. Bert turned the handle and the door opened. "Anybody home?"

A girl wearing a long flowered skirt and a sweat-shirt opened the door. Her hair was messy and her face didn't know it was morning.

"Who is it?" A male voice called from the other room.

"Lori Wilson?" April asked.

"Yes." Lori squinted out at them in sleepy surprise. "Hello. It's the police," over her shoulder. A warning.

"Sheriff Whitmore," Bert said.

April went next. "Sergeant Woo, Lieutenant Sanchez, NYPD."

"Jesus. What's going on?" Lori glanced around the small living room that was as folksy and American-country as Wendy's city apartment was urban-spare. At the moment it was in murky light and a mess. The faded, flowered sofas were littered with take-out food bags, empty beer bottles, and large soda cups. On the wood floor, the multicolored braided rugs were covered with sand. The fireplace was full of charred wood from many fires, and the room had a stale, smoky smell.

"You haven't heard?" Whitmore said, looking around.

"Heard what? We don't have a TV. She hasn't turned the phone on yet." She looked embarrassed when a young man in army fatigues emerged from one of two doors. One side of his face had a row of piercing on the eyebrow and another ringing the ear. Symmetry. A stud in his nose. The other side of his face was randomly pierced. His light hair was a huge nest of dreds. He appeared to be a young person trying to look as messed up as possible and succeeding very well. April guessed he had not reached legal drinking age, and Lori was a few years older.

"Hey, what's going on?" The kid raised his fingers in a peace sign at the sheriff.

"What are you doing here, Rod?"

"Just hanging with, uh, Lori." The kid shook spiderwebs out of a brain he didn't know how to use. "I was just on my way to work," he added, edging toward the door.

"I don't think so, Rod. It's Sunday."

"Already?" Rod seemed surprised by that and got defensive right away. "Whatever your problem is, I didn't do anything. We just hung out for a couple of days, okay? That's it." He gave the wash sign with his hands. Done. Could he go now?

"I'd like to talk to Lori," April said.

"Okay. You can tell me your life history, Rod." The sheriff moved him out the front door.

Mike moved inside. "Anyone else here?" he asked Lori.

"Uh-uh." She stuck a finger in her mouth.

Mike snorted and moved through the house, checking it for himself. April took out her notebook.

"Is Wendy all right?" Lori brushed the hair from her face and sank down on a sofa.

"How long have you been here, Lori?" April asked.

"About a week, I guess. Can't you tell me what's going on?"

April ignored the question. "Don't guess. Tell me exactly."

"I guess I came last Sunday."

"You guess? How did you get here?" April picked up a greasy Subway sack, then put it down.

"I took the bus to Woods Hole and then the ferry."

"Before or after the Schoenfeld wedding?" April turned on a light.

Lori squinted. "I didn't have to go. Wendy was doing it herself."

"I thought it takes a lot of people to pull off a wedding like that." April turned on some more lights.

"Not when it's only one site. That always keeps the glitches down, and sometimes Wendy likes to do them herself. She's very efficient. Why are you asking?" Lori twisted around to look at her.

April spun around, startling her. "She gave you these two weekends off, why?"

Lori recoiled. April noticed the hickey on her neck. A big one. She saw April looking at her and shifted uneasily; clearly she hadn't seen herself in the mirror.

"Why the two weekends off? Did you have another job Wendy wanted you to do?"

"Like what?" Lori was surprised by the question.

"Did you know Tovah Schoenfeld was murdered at her wedding last Sunday?"

Lori looked down at her hands. "Yes."

"How do you know if you don't have a phone?"

Her voice got very low. "I have a cell phone."

"And what else made you know?"

"She came up on Tuesday night."

Good. That was true. "Did she tell you she was coming?"

"Yes. I had to clean up for her. She would have killed me."

"Wendy's very particular, isn't she?"

Lori put her lips together and nodded.

"She wouldn't like to see her house like this. Why did she come, Lori?"

"She brought some things for the summer."

"In the middle of a busy week? What things?"

"I don't know."

"Where did she put them?"

"I don't know. I was asleep when she got here." Lori's eyes traveled up the wall to the ceiling.

"In the attic?" April said.

Silence. The thin girl got smaller, younger-looking. "I said I don't know."

"How old are you, Lori?"

"Twenty-four," she said softly.

"Twenty-four. Where were you yesterday?"

"Here." She frowned. "Why?"

"Lori, have you ever been in any kind of trouble before? Tell me the truth, because I can check it out."

"No," she said in a faint voice.

"You're in a lot of trouble now."

"I didn't know about Tovah until Wendy told me," she said, a plea in her voice.

"What about Prudence, did you know Prudence?"

"Prudence?"

"Prudence Hay. Another one of the weddings you didn't work. Prudence is dead, too."

"What?" Lori looked confused. "I didn't know about that. What happened?"

"Someone shot her on the way into St. Patrick's."

"God, I didn't know that." Her mouth fell open in amazement. "Is Wendy all right?"

"She's fine."

Mike came back into the living room. "Nothing in the bedrooms or the closets," he said. "There's a deck out back and an outbuilding of some kind, like a tool-shed. What about the kitchen cupboards? Let's do inside first."

"They're in the attic," April told him quietly. "Lori, get your things together. You're going back to New York."

Forty-eight

"Hey, Mike, take some gloves," April said. "Just in case."

She pulled some thin rubber gloves out of the bottom of her purse and handed them over. Mike stuffed them in his jacket pocket. This wasn't a crime scene. He cocked his head at the ceiling panel in the hall over his head. It had a handle at one end just out of his reach. A pole with a hook on the end rested in the corner, and Mike used that to lower the panel. Attached to the panel on the inside was a crude ladder on springs. He turned to the girl in the living room, twisting a handful of skirt in her hands.

"Anybody up there?" he asked.

She shook her tangled hair. "No, of course not."

"You sure?"

"Who'd be hiding? No one expected you. Can I pee?"

"Yeah, you can pee. I'll come with you," April said.

"Jesus," she muttered. "What do you think I'm going to do?"

"Flush the dope."

Mike changed his mind about the gloves. He pulled them on, then climbed the ladder. Upstairs, he pulled the string on the single bare lightbulb. It gave off just enough weak illumination for him to make out a surprisingly large and murky space. First thing he noticed was that it had been swept recently, so there were no footprints for him to disturb.

A pile of dust and mouse droppings filled a corner under the eaves. An ancient-looking broom lay beside it. The house wasn't insulated, so the dampness and smell of mold in exposed wooden beams was intense. Mike cast his eye quickly over the haphazardly placed contents. Closest to the stairs were ten oversize shopping bags filled with bulky tissue- and newspaper-wrapped objects. Beyond that, folded plastic deck chairs, a beach umbrella, two old suitcases, a hot-water heater, a clambake pot, a Weber barbecue, a trap machine and canvas bag filled with clay discs, and an old camp trunk with a broken lock.

Mike moved quickly, checking the shopping bags and suitcases first. While he worked, he could hear the murmur of voices downstairs. April's and the girl's. The sheriff must still be outside with the weirdo. Unwrapping the contents of the shopping bags as fast as he could, he found new candlesticks, crystal objects, glasses, linens, silver, small appliances in the bags. In the suitcases, quilts and pillows and summer clothes. The attic became a flea market, the evidence Wendy was a thief. But this was not what he was looking for.

When he heard the sound of rain falling on the roof above him, he checked his watch. One o'clock already. Over an hour had passed and he didn't hear voices downstairs anymore. Maybe April was outside with the sheriff searching the shed, the space under the deck. Finally he opened the trunk lid and exhaled. The gun cache was in the camp trunk: two revolvers, three shotguns recently cleaned and broken down, smelling of oil, variously emptied boxes of .22-, .38-, and .45-caliber ammunition, both regular and hollow-point. As well as ammunition for the shotguns and several homemade silencers. If Wendy had been shooting recently, the silencers would be the reason there hadn't been any complaints from the neighbors. He got to his feet, threaded through the mess he'd made, and climbed down the ladder.

While Lori sat sniveling in the cruiser with her duffel bag on her lap, April and Mike brought the trunk downstairs and cataloged its contents. Then they took two umbrellas from the stand by the front door and paced out the grounds in a steady downpour. They found a pile of discharged shell casings, bullet-pocked trees, and clay shards. They gathered some shell casings to see if there was a match with the one they had from the Tovah shooting.

Then paperwork, paperwork. Dealing with the law-enforcement issues surrounding the seizure and shipping of possible evidence of a crime committed in New York from a private residence in Massachusetts took a long time as the DAs and officials in BAFT were consulted. They missed their three P.M. flight.

Most disturbing to Sheriff Whitmore were the silencers, one of the most illegal things in the gun world—unless you had a permit. You could buy a machine gun or an assault weapon, but not even members of organized crime had silencers on their handguns. He'd never seen one for sale, and couldn't believe they might have been constructed in the cottage.

Most disturbing to April and Mike were three things: First, they did not find Wendy's takedown .22-caliber survival rifle or the .38 revolver that went with the ammunition boxes. Second, the next flight to New York was canceled. They finally got out at nine P.M. on a Cape Air flight to Boston in what looked like the smallest plane ever made. They caught the last shuttle back to New York and got into the city at midnight. Third, Lori Wilson was with them all the way so they had no time alone.

Forty-nine

Down at One PP in the Hate Unit when Lori Wilson finally understood she wasn't going home anytime soon, she broke down and admitted that she'd known about the guns.

"But I never shot one. They scare me shitless; I'm not kidding," Lori insisted.

Lori was bleary-eyed weary, but so was April, and she wasn't letting the girl loose until she gave up everything she had. April and Mike had split up. April was doing the questioning with the tape recorder on, for the record this time. Mike and Inspector Bellaqua were having a preliminary conversation with the Manhattan DA about the recovery of the guns and options vis-à-vis Wendy Lotte. Everything was heating up.

"When were the guns transported to New York?" April asked for the thirtieth time.

"I don't know. I told you. I didn't like them. I stayed away from the whole thing." Lori glanced at the tape recorder. Since the morning, she'd cleaned up. She was wearing jeans and a jacket now. April could see that she was a pretty girl with that WASP look so many Americans aspired to. Straight blond hair, blue eyes, pug nose, high cheekbones. She didn't know which end was up, though. The girl had no street smarts.

"How could you stay away from the guns if they were around all the time?" April tried not to tap her foot.

"I told you. They weren't around all the time. I never saw one in New York. Only on the Vineyard that one time." Lori yawned, then belatedly remembered to put her hand over her mouth.

"When was that?"

"Back in April."

"What were you doing on the Vineyard in April?"

"I told you that, too. We did a wedding there. At the Charlotte Inn."

"Who was *we*, Lori?"

"Wendy, of course. Louis, Tito, that creepy guy, Ubu. They decorated the whole first floor with lilies and roses and hydrangeas. White, red, and purple were the colors. They did the garden, too, and it was freezing even with the heaters on."

"So how many vehicles were involved?"

"I don't know. They had to bring everything in from the city. The Vineyard has nothing."

"How many vehicles traveled up?"

Lori threw her hands up. "I don't know. Ask Louis. I only saw his van. That's it. Maybe they shipped the rest."

"Okay, who else was with you?"

Lori rubbed her nose. "Only Kim."

"Kim?" April said.

"Kim Simone. He makes the dresses."

The new piece punched April in the gut. This late at night it was dead in the squad room, pretty dead in the whole building, in fact. She and Lori were sitting all the way in the back at a detective's desk by a window that overlooked some of the Wall Street area, and, beyond it, the Statue of Liberty.

"The wedding dress?" she said, taking it real slow.

"Uh-huh. It was a Tang Ling dress, but Kim copied it for her. Sometimes he did special orders for us as a favor. He wasn't supposed to knock off the dresses. I told you this already."

April didn't tell Lori that no, she hadn't mentioned this at all. Sometimes they had no idea what was important. Tang Ling. She shook her head. So Wendy stole some of the wedding gifts just to keep her hand in, Louis had the flower concession, and Kim knocked off the dresses for those clients who didn't go directly to Tang. A racket all the way around.

"Okay, but why did Kim go to Martha's Vineyard with you?" she asked.

"Umm." Lori stuck her finger in her mouth and sighed. "Am I supposed to tell you all this? I don't want to get anybody in trouble."

"We're way past that, Lori. What about the dress?"

"Ahh, well, Kim was supposed to make the dress and send it, like, on the Tuesday. The wedding was Friday. He sent it to Boston FedEx, but when the dress got there, it was too small. Kristen couldn't zip it up. By Thursday, of course, it was too late to send it back."

"The bride lives in Boston?"

"No, Kristen lives in New York, but she was in Boston at the time. And two of the bridesmaids' dresses needed work, too; so Kim just called in sick and came with us on Thursday."

"Did Kim make the bridesmaids' dresses, too?"

"No, but he said he'd do the alterations for Wendy."

"Sounds like Kim does a lot of things for Wendy," April remarked.

"Pretty much anything she asks."

"Why?"

Lori shrugged. "He likes her."

"Okay, so how did you travel up there?"

"We drove with Wendy. We had to, because Kim needed his sewing machine and all his, like, sewing stuff. It took up the whole trunk."

No one mentioned this before. Kim and his sewing stuff.

"Why did everybody stay at Wendy's?" April asked.

"The bride's father wouldn't pay for a hotel for everybody, and Louis complained it was too expensive for him. So she gave in. Believe me, Wendy wasn't happy about it."

"When did you start shooting the guns?" April moved on.

"I told you I didn't," Lori insisted.

April gave her a cold look. "Come on, Lori, you want to stay here all night?"

"I'm telling you. It was terrifying. That first night Wendy got so mad at Kim she shot a pistol into a pile of pillows right next to where he was sitting. I was never so scared in my life."

"And what did Kim do?"

"You better believe he stopped complaining and got to work. Who wouldn't?" Lori said this as if April were some kind of dummy.

"What had Kim been complaining about, Lori?"

"Oh, a thousand things. Marriage is terrible. His wife is mean to him. His sister is dead. Whatever. He's a real pain in the ass."

"Who else was there when Wendy fired the gun?" The recorder was taping, but April took quick notes. She always thought best with a pen in her hand.

"Ubu. Oh, my God, Tito! Louis. Everybody freaked. I thought Louis would have a stroke. The living room was just filled with these cans of water and all his flowers. And they were, like, leaping around insane, yelling at her to put the gun down."

"What kind of gun was it?"

"I don't know, a pistol gun."

"Did the gun have a silencer on it?"

"Hell no, it made a huge bang." Lori paused for a few moments, remembering that big bang. "And then the next day after the wedding everybody was out shooting in the woods. It started to rain and they put on these gray ponchos and kept shooting. It was just *weird*."

"Everybody except you."

"Yeah. Everybody but me. Wendy told me I better not say anything about it because shooting was illegal, or something."

April gave the time and turned off the tape recorder. She was bone tired and had had enough of Lori for the moment. She went out to confer with Poppy and Mike, and they all agreed that Lori was no flight risk.

"Okay, you can go home now. Here's my number. Call me if you think of anything else."

"I don't have any money," Lori said, tearing up.

"Someone will take you home. Oh, and Lori. Don't go anywhere tonight, okay?"

"Okay."

A uniform took Lori home in a squad car. Then, eighteen hours after they'd set out in the morning, April went home with Mike to his apartment in Forest Hills.

Fifty

Once again morning came too soon. Light and the racket of a ringing phone pierced April's sleep long before she'd had enough of it. Her first thought was that one of their suspects was on the move, and she jerked awake.

"Showtime," Mike grumbled and rolled over to pick up. "Sanchez." He listened for a moment; then his voice got sweet. "Hiya, babe, how ya doin'? No, of course not. No one's avoiding you."

Mike handed over the handset. "It's for you."

A babe for her? "Yes?" she said, hoping it wasn't her mother he was calling *babe*.

"April, didn't you get my messages?" Ching's frantic voice.

"Oh, Ching! What time is it?"

"Almost six. I didn't wake you, did I?"

"Almost six?" Was she nuts? April groaned. Four hours' sleep, less a half an hour for Latin meltdown.

"Look, I'm sorry to call so early, but I have to talk to you."

"Okay, you're talking to me. Speak." April closed her eyes.

"April, you told me you had him. You told me everything was fine. Oh, God, what happened?"

"You know I can't talk about it. We're working on it. That's all I can say."

"Oh, April, this is terrible. Can't you stop these killings?"

As if April were personally in control of the situation. So early in the morning the presumption of her power made April's head ache.

"There's a huge task force working on it," she said in as neutral a tone as she could manage, considering the hour, the amount of sleep she'd had, and the gravity of the situation.

She opened her eyes, lifted her head a little, and glanced over at her lover. He was out cold again with his face buried in the pillow.

"I thought this was your case," Ching said, accusing.

"It's never only one person; you know that. Hundreds of people are working on this." Okay, she was up.

"Well, look, I'm really worried. Tang called me a dozen times. I told her you were the head of it. Why didn't you call me back?"

"I've been working round the clock. I'm not the head of it; you know that." April didn't want to scold, but this was too much.

"April, Tang is a very important person! She's being hurt by this. Why didn't you talk to her? You're making me look bad."

"I'm going to talk to her today, I promise."

"Well, turn on the TV. She's on right now, offering a reward for the killer."

"Really?" That was news. April nudged Mike with her knee. Time to get up. He didn't stir.

"*Chico!*" No response.

"Everybody is terrified. No one knows who's going to be next. April, the city is going wild over this!"

"I know."

"Are you watching the news?"

April yawned. "Not yet."

"Hurry up! Oh, it's over. You missed it."

"I'm sure they'll show it again." April nudged Mike a second time. It was just as well that Ching called. They had to get going.

Ching sounded a little better. "April, my fitting is today. Ten o'clock. Should I still do it? Tang said I should come."

"Yeah, okay. I'll meet you there. And I'll talk to her then. Tell Tang I'll be there at ten, okay?"

"Thanks, April. I knew you could help."

April said her good-byes and hung up with a shiver of excitement. She'd never met Tang Ling before. She nudged Mike again. *"Mi amor. Vamos."* He rolled over the other way to avoid her.

Fifty-one

Late Saturday afternoon, the PC had officially named a Bride Homicide Task Force to link up the investigations of the two wedding homicides— virtually the same cast of characters. But the commissioner did not move the Tovah case from the Five-oh in the Bronx at that time.

By Monday morning, however, Sergeant Hollis had lost points for not having followed through on the Martha's Vineyard angle. And in the same war for detective supremacy Sergeant Woo and Lieutenant Sanchez had gained points for traveling up there and locating Wendy Lotte's gun cache.

Monday morning headquarters for the Tovah case was moved into the city, and the investigation had its focus. Wendy's trunk was in transit to the police lab in Jamaica, the movements of all the key players were being watched, and a search warrant for the residence of Clio Alma and Kim Simone was in process. Definitely they were material witnesses, if nothing else. Kim had to be questioned about his whereabouts Saturday. Clio as well. They were narrowing it down. Ubu was off the hook because he'd been in Bellevue when Prudence was killed.

April had already requested the first set of DD-5s

of Kim and his wife Clio Alma from the file up in the Bronx as well as the second set after Calvin Hill and his partner, Detective Moulder, went back to talk to them again. All the DD-5s were in the Hate Unit being studied by Mike and Inspector Bellaqua over coffee and doughnuts in Bellaqua's office. April had seen them all before.

The gist of it: Kim Simone, with his wife translating, told the two detectives that last-minute alterations on the wedding gown of Tovah Schoenfeld ordered by her mother meant he had to work overtime on the dress. It wasn't finished until late Saturday afternoon. Tang Ling had been out of town for the weekend. Since the shop was closed Sunday, Kim had taken the gown home with him on Saturday night, then personally delivered it to the synagogue on Sunday afternoon.

When asked if this kind of personal service was unusual, he said no, he had flown to France, to Hawaii, to Miami, and other places on the whim of wealthy clients. He said that he did not receive compensation for this and had to work extra hours to make up for his absences when he returned.

Clio Alma stated that she had driven him and the gown to Riverdale in her Saturn and waited for him while he fitted the dress. Kim Simone further stated that he had had to wait an hour before he could dress Tovah, but when he was finished, he immediately left the synagogue via the downstairs staff door and rejoined his wife in their car that was parked around the corner.

April chewed on her bottom lip as the other two read and reread both sets of statements. She was in a hurry. She had to get to Tang's shop by ten. Always do everything yourself, she was chastising herself. Kim and his wife were the only players in the Wendy game whom she and Mike had not interviewed personally. And the only one Iriarte hadn't checked out for her. Not good. She'd feel better if she'd cleared them herself.

The task force was putting together its case against Wendy, who was either the killer or the organizer. It wasn't clear yet which. But no one was making a move on her until every question was answered. Wendy would keep until the Kim piece was resolved. April clicked her tongue, causing Mike and the inspector to pause in their discussion.

April arched an eyebrow. "I have to talk to Tang Ling," she said. "And somebody has to go out to Queens and find Clio Alma, search their car and house. If Kim is at work, I'll bring him back with me and we all can have a go at him."

"I'm on it. I'll take the house and car," Mike said.

"Do you mind if I get someone from Midtown North to do a deep background on Kim and his wife?" April asked Bellaqua.

"We have enough computer whizzes right here, but if it makes you happy." Bellaqua lifted a shoulder.

"Yeah, it would make me happy." It wasn't good politics. But if there was anything to find, Hagedorn would find it.

"It's okay by me." Mike smiled.

"Mike, you're with me. We have DAs to do before you go anywhere," Bellaqua said.

"Fine." He rolled his eyes.

April nodded and grabbed her purse. She needed a car and driver. "Who can you give me? I need a car and a couple of bodies."

"Call in my people, will you? I'll let you know."
Bellaqua took her second doughnut of the morning.
In the stress of the situation she'd forgotten they were
just for the company.

Fifty-two

April's first thought when she went through the door to the famous Tang Ling shop was that she didn't want to alarm Ching in any way, but she didn't want her around today. She'd made a mistake involving her at all. She definitely wanted Ching way gone before she took Kim in the car with her. Her unmarked Ford was out front. She'd told the two detectives to watch all the entrances before she went inside.

"Is Ching Ma Dong here yet?" she asked the blond receptionist sitting at a desk on the first floor.

"No, she hasn't come in yet. Are you Sergeant Woo?"

"Yes."

"Miss Ling is expecting you in her office. Fourth floor."

"Thanks." April took a mirrored elevator and was immediately admitted to Tang's office. April had been expecting a bigger-than-life woman and was surprised to find that Tang Ling herself was a small, angry dragon wearing a fog-colored Armani suit with a pink silk blouse.

Tang was five-one, maybe five-one-and-a-half on a good day, probably not a hundred pounds. Still, she swept out from behind a huge glass-topped desk covered with sketches and swatches of fabric like a model taking a runway. "April Woo. You're Ching's sister. She's not here yet," she said, appraising April's figure and outfit. The first very good, the second only so-so.

"We're sister-cousins," April said, nodding. "Our mothers are friends." She tried not to be too awed by Ching's college acquaintance who was suddenly now such a close friend. She hated that Ching had told this superstar she was in charge of the case. So embarrassing and untrue.

"From the same town?"

"Ah, same borough. We all live in Queens." April knew that Tang Ling meant the same town in China, but no one cared to remember anymore what that town had been. April also knew that Tang Ling lived in several places, including Paris, Park Avenue, and L.A. And she did not come from the same planet that April and Ching did no matter how nice Ching said she was. That was pretty clear.

Tang Ling wore a circle of pearls around her neck the size of walnuts. The pearls were rare colors strung together—warm gold, cool silver, ink black, the pearl gray of her suit, lipstick pink, and the snowiest white. April had never seen a golden pearl before. On Tang's finger was a dazzling square-cut diamond, huge, next to a plain gold wedding band. On her right wrist was a fun watch with a pink plastic strap and diamond-studded face. The show of wealth reminded April of Rabbi Levi's remark about exciting envy.

"I have spoken to your boss," Tang said loftily,

giving April the distinct feeling she meant the police commissioner, not Lieutenant Iriarte.

April nodded politely.

"This is a terrible thing. I feel so keenly the loss of these girls. Both of them my clients. My lawyer is on the way."

Ah, did Tang know something? April felt a surge of excitement as Tang moved to a thronelike chair and sat, gesturing for April to sit on the bisque sofa opposite. April couldn't help noticing how the small woman moved in her suit, carrying her clothes, not wearing them. She crossed her legs, showing off shoes with no backs and long pointed toes made of exquisite gray-toned reptile skins. Slides so costly that even the copies had to be expensive, and these weren't copies. On a Monday morning Tang Ling was dressed to intimidate. Why?

"Did you see the newspapers all last week?" The woman's broad face flushed angry red, marring her perfect makeup, a lighter color than her own medium-dark skin.

"Photos of Tovah everywhere, all identifying my gown. And now Prudence! Same thing. Second bride murdered in a Tang Ling gown. I can't let this stand. I was on *Good Morning* today; did you see me?" she demanded.

"No, I'm sorry. I missed it. I understand you offered a reward," April said slowly.

"Yes, of course." Tang looked furious. "I couldn't just ignore it. This is a terrible thing for a special-occasion business. I had to do something to show my concern."

From the look on Tang's face April suspected a

publicity angle. "Has anyone threatened you, either directly or indirectly, recently?"

Tang gave her a blank look. "I don't know what you mean."

"An employee, for example, a customer, a vendor? Can you think of anybody who has a reason to be angry at you, to want to hurt you by putting you in the spotlight like this?"

"What? You're not suggesting this has something to do with me?" Tang looked stunned.

"Two of your clients have been murdered," April murmured.

"But—"

"And possibly a third a few months ago. Did you know Andrea Straka?"

"Oh, no. Oh, my God. Oh, don't bring this to my door." Tang clapped a manicured hand to her forehead. "This is outrageous. Yes, she was a client. But that was a subway accident, wasn't it? She fell."

"We're taking another look at the case."

"Oh, my." Tang's eyes widened in horror. "But this has nothing to do with me. I just make wedding gowns. You can't possibly think that someone . . . that someone I know—could possibly have . . . ?"

"We're looking for patterns, similarities. The two murdered girls and Andrea—their families are so different. We're looking for common threads that bring them together. Your gowns are one link. Even the press has picked it up."

"But there must be other links," Tang said angrily.

"Oh, yes, and we're following those, too. Is Kim Simone here today?" April suddenly shifted gears.

"Of course. He's upstairs in the sewing room."

Beads of perspiration sprouted on her forehead. "Why?"

"Tell me about him."

"Oh, well . . ." Tang opened her mouth. "He's my best fitter, my most loyal employee. Why?"

"I heard he has problems."

"Oh, well, he may have problems, but he's a very gentle person. He sent me flowers when Tovah was killed."

"Why?"

"Why did he send flowers? It was a thoughtful gesture. He knew I was upset. He wanted me to know he was thinking of me. He's that loyal. He's really unusually good. He would never do anything to hurt me." She tossed her head.

"What about his wife?"

"I've never liked the wife. She's another story." Tang rolled her eyes. "She's older than he. She's taken advantage of Kim in so many ways. Honestly, you know how it is. He needed to be legal; she wanted a slave. A lot of bad feeling there."

"Enough for her to want to hurt you?"

"To hurt me, yes, absolutely. But to murder two innocent young women . . . I would be very shocked. Do you suspect her?"

"It's a shocking case," April murmured, noncommittal.

Tang's buzzer sounded. "Yes?"

"Ching is here."

"Tell her to go to the second floor. I'll get her gown myself." Tang gave April a distracted smile. "We need to talk more, of course. But right now, would you meet Ching on the second floor? I'll be with you in a moment."

April hesitated. Ching first, or Kim first? She had the detectives outside, and the receptionist Melody downstairs at the front desk. Kim couldn't get away. She chose Ching. "All right. But please alert your security staff not to let Kim out of the building. I want to talk to him in a few minutes."

Tang nodded, and seconds later April was in the elevator.

Fifty-three

Ching was sitting on a pink silk slipper chair when April got off the elevator. All excited, she gave April a big hug.

"You won't believe this. Tang asked me to have dinner with her tonight. Her husband is in Hong Kong, and she canceled her dinner plans because of the publicity. Did you talk to her?"

"Yes, sweetie, where's your cell phone?" April was not interested in Tang's dinner plans. She was interested only in getting Ching out of the building.

"I left it home, why?"

"I tried to reach you. Let's go downstairs." April took Ching's arm and started moving her toward the stairs.

"What's the matter?" Ching was alarmed.

"Nothing. I just want to talk to you outside for a second."

"But what about my fitting?"

"Let's just leave the building. We can do it another time."

"What do you mean, another time? The wedding is this week!" Ching was moving her feet down the stairs, but hanging back. Almost a deadweight. "What's the matter, April?"

"Nothing, honey. Let's go. Stay with me on this."

"What the hell are you doing? You're treating me like a retard. Hi, Melody." She waved at the girl at the desk.

Melody waved back. "'Bye, Ching."

They moved through the doors out into the light.

"What was that about? April . . . April . . . talk to me."

"Just come outside and cool it a minute, okay?"

Fifty-four

Kim was working at his place in the workroom, in front of his sewing machine. He was doing the hem of a slippery silk jersey gown that had to be finished and sent out today. He wasn't feeling good, but he had come in to get away from his wife and because of his loyalty to Tang. He wanted to be with her in her time of trouble and show his respect. To give her flowers. He was wearing a white shirt and black pants, the uniform she required of all the sewers. The bright blue Hawaiian shirt he'd worn on the subway was in his carryall, along with his shoes and some leftover food from last night.

He was working on the gown, trying not to think about anything but keeping that stretchy silk from slipping through his fingers. He knew Tang was in the building. He knew she was upstairs in her office talking to a Chinese woman, a cop, the same one who was harassing Wendy. He didn't like that, but he wasn't thinking about the cop. He was thinking about Tang.

He hoped to have a chance to see her later. Sometimes the businesspeople and the telephone kept Tang so busy that she didn't come into the workroom for days at a time, even for a moment.

He was thinking about talking to Tang, telling her how sorry he was about Prudence, mouthing the same words over and over. He was stitching by hand when suddenly she came in. He looked up and was surprised to see her there, shaking all over. Her face was red, the way it got when she was really angry. What happened?

"You! Go upstairs to my office," she told the two other sewers, her voice crackling with anger. Their mouths dropped open at her tone, and they fumbled, trying to get out of their seats fast enough to please her.

"Right now. Hurry." She waved her hands, shooing them out.

Kim got up to go with them, his heart beating fast. Tang had a temper. He didn't want her to explode in his face like a hand grenade that blew apart everything that was near it. But he didn't move fast enough. She stepped in front of his table, her hand raised in a fist.

"Not you."

What? He cringed away from the hand darting out at him, but not far enough. She grabbed his ear as the other two scurried out, closing the door behind them. He'd wished that he and Tang could be alone, and now they were alone. He tried to find his voice to talk to her, but she pulled his ear hard, the way his mother used to when he was little, dragging tears out of his eyes and the sound from his voice. Tang took his voice away. He swallowed it in fear.

A grunt of pain was all he could manage. He couldn't tell her how sad he was for her troubles. How he planned to give her a plant, one of her favorites. She didn't give him time.

"Scandal," she hissed, shaking him the way Clio's dog shook his toy sock with the knot in it, to kill it and kill it again.

"You brought this scandal on me with that terrible wife of yours," she cried. "I could kill you with these two hands." She pushed him, knocking him against the corner of the table. The hard edge bit into the backs of his thighs. Tang was little, but she was strong. Kim's brain felt thick. What was she talking about?

"You wicked toad!" she cried, pushing, pushing.

He wasn't a toad. Not wicked. Everything he did was for her. He loved her, wanted her to protect him and love him like his mother used to. "What did I do?"

Her hot breath was in his face as she pushed him, hurting the bruises where the broom hit him yesterday. He could smell her perfume in her clothes, stale coffee and garlic in her mouth.

"Get out of here now. You have one minute. If you aren't out of this room in one minute, I'll throw you out that window. Don't think I can't. I'm so angry I could kill you. I hope you die a terrible death!"

He looked at her blankly. Throw him out the window? After all the things he'd done for her?

"And don't leave anything of yours behind. Do you hear me? Just get your things and get out now. There is a police detective here to talk to you."

He couldn't figure out what she was saying. His feelings were too hurt by the tone of her voice. He was just a sewer, but he had feelings. Get out! How could he get out? He had gowns to finish. He had things to do. People counted on him. No one could fit a gown the way he could; Tang said so herself.

"I have to fit Ching Ma Dong's gown. She's waiting for me."

"She is not waiting for you. The police are waiting for you. You don't belong here." Suddenly a funny look came over Tang's face and she slapped him hard.

Kim had seen Tang do that once before to a young saleswoman who'd made a mistake and given someone a fifty-percent discount on a dress that hadn't been on sale. The customer walked out with it, and later when Tang heard about the incident, she slapped the girl's face, then fired her on the spot. That's how he knew Tang really wanted him to go. His cheek stung with the insult. But his heart was where he really took the blow. He'd been so kind to her. He'd worked so hard and been so loyal, he didn't expect it.

"Meet the police *outside the building.* Do you hear me! And don't ever come anywhere near me again." She turned her back on him and walked out of the room.

He stood there alone in the workroom for a second, stunned and almost expecting Tang to come back and tell him she was sorry. Then he felt ashamed that Tang had treated him like a girl and trembled with the thought of telling Clio he'd lost his job.

Clio would just yell at him and tell him how much he owed her even though he'd paid for the wedding, the ring, and the party. And he'd made her dress. But she thought he owed her thousands and thousands more. It made him sick to think of her screeching at him now for losing his job.

Kim did not want to meet the detective outside

the building. He wanted to run away. He took the elevator to the basement, thinking that maybe he shouldn't go back to Clio's house in Queens. He got off the elevator and slipped up the back stairs to street level and exited the building from the back door. There, a narrow common area was shared by several buildings. He entered the building two doors down. It was a gallery with a back patio. The back door was open, and no one stopped him as he walked through. On Madison Avenue the sun was shining. He put on his sunglasses and quickly looked both ways. He froze, terrified for a second. A limo with a driver leaning against it. The driver was watching the shop door. April Woo, the cop he'd seen several times before, was talking with Ching, Tang's friend. The policewoman was pointing at a man standing on the roof of the building. Kim turned quickly and walked the other way.

Fifty-five

"April, I am not going anywhere until you tell me what's going on." Ching had planted herself on the curb by the car. Ever since she was a little girl she got upset when plans were changed.

"Okay, see that guy on the roof?" April pointed up.

"Uh-huh. So?"

"He's a cop. Just get out of the way. We're going to take someone in for questioning."

"Really?" Ching's eyes opened wide. Now she was going to see April be a cop. Her face told April this was something new and exciting. "Somebody from here?" she asked.

"Yes, and it's going to take a while. So you might as well head back to your office."

"Hey, why is Kim running down there?" Ching pointed at a man sprinting around the corner.

April spun around. "Where?"

"He was there a minute ago. I'm sure it was Kim."

"Looked like a girl to me," Detective Fray said.

"Go after him," April told him angrily. "I'll check inside." *Shit!* She didn't like losing both the suspect and face in front of Ching.

Fray took off at a run, and April radioed Grant on

the roof to come down and go through the building with her. "I thought I told you to watch the back," she accused Grant, who was hanging over the roof, gawking.

His voice crackled back. "I'm on my way."

April's face burned. *Shit.* "Don't say anything," she warned Ching. "Just don't say a word."

Ching raised her hands. She wasn't going to say anything.

Face still burning, April disappeared into the building and went through all six floors thoroughly. She didn't come out for a long time. When she did, Ching was still waiting there, leaning against the Ford with her face soaking up the sun.

"Hi," she said. "Any luck?"

April shook her head, disgusted with herself. She'd been too busy trying to be polite to Tang, trying to be a big shot to Ching. And couldn't even hang on to her witness. *Stupid.* This was what happened when friends were involved. *Shit.* "There's a back way. He must have used it."

"I don't think Kim is a killer," Ching said, as if she thought April's whole operation was nuts.

"Asking people what they know is not assuming they're killers." Shit, her sister-cousin thought she was an asshole. And maybe she was. She stopped to call in a BOLO from the radio in the car. Be-on-the-lookout-for. She gave a description of Kim: Asian male, five-one. Wearing a white shirt and black trousers.

"Sorry, Ching. You can go now."

"Thanks for everything," Ching said dryly.

Preoccupied, April and her two detectives got in their cruiser and drove around for an hour, looking for Kim in the hope that he was still in the area. When they didn't find him, they figured he'd gone down into the subway. And for all they knew, by now he could be anywhere.

Mike caught up with April at one o'clock on Madison and Fifty-ninth. She left the two detectives in their Ford, and got into Mike's Crown Vic. He handed over a wedding photo of Kim and Clio, and April studied it, cursing in Chinese because she didn't want to let her mood out in English.

"Don't say anything," she warned.

"How about I fill you in?"

"Okay, fill me in." She was pretty dejected, but as usual, he was not one for casting blame.

"FAS has confirmed a .22 rifle was used in both shootings. In Tovah's, the killer used both hollow-points and regular bullets. Both were found on the scene. For Prudence only the lighter load."

"Same gun?" April asked.

"Same for the light load."

Hollow-points could rarely be matched, since they exploded on impact. "Why the two kinds of bullets?"

"Maybe the gun was already loaded with hollow-points," Mike speculated. "And the shooter just added bullets, didn't know the difference."

"If the gun was stolen, that could explain Wendy's print on the casing," April said. "You said you found something interesting at Kim's place."

"Yes, a manual for making homemade silencers. It was Wendy's. Her name was in the flyleaf."

"Aw, jeez. She's in deep. What are we thinking? Wendy's gun. Wendy's print. Wendy's silencer. Wendy is the shooter. No?"

"Unclear. Wendy's at home, hasn't moved. The squirrel took off when you cornered him. What does that tell you?"

April didn't want to speculate. Tang had been completely surprised that Kim left without talking to them. Everyone said he was a gentle guy. Gentle and sweet. It was time to bring in the wife. Get Clio on the screen, see what she had to say.

"What did the DAs say? We can get Wendy on felony murder no matter what, right?" she said.

Mike was heading over to Lexington. "We'll have to see how much she'll squeal. Wendy's still the center of the wheel."

"We're going to Wendy's, I take it?" April was hungry, didn't want to admit it. Lunchtime. Guess they didn't have time to stop for lunch.

"Yes, ma'am."

"Right." She turned her attention to the wedding photo of Kim and Clio.

The first thing she noticed about the photo was the quality of Clio's dress. It was a stunner, as elaborate as one might expect from a groom who could copy a Tang Ling. And Clio herself was a beautiful woman. Slightly taller than her husband, with almond eyes like a cat's, she seemed very pleased with her catch.

Kim, on the other hand, looked very young, and handsome in a soft kind of way. In the photo, taken three years ago, he had punky gelled hair and was wearing a white suit. His sweet face was turned toward the bride, and he seemed to be smiling at the bouquet of pink roses clutched to her bosom. The half profile gave April a view of a child-sized ear, and she cursed some more.

Fifty-six

Wendy Lotte didn't answer her door when April and Mike rang her bell at one-twenty. The officers in charge of surveilling her maintained that she had not left the building since she'd arrived home early Sunday morning, but April was badly shaken after losing Kim Simone and didn't trust anybody's certainty about anything. There wasn't an elevator to a garage in this building, but maybe there were other ways out.

Still, Wendy had to have been exhausted. She could just be sleeping it off. April was wound tight as they stood there in the hallway waiting for her to rouse herself and come to the door. Five minutes passed. Mike tried her phone. Only voice mail answered. A gentle *ding-dong* sounded over and over. April felt the stillness inside the apartment as she kept her finger on the bell.

When a person was at home and the place was this quiet, something could be wrong. She glanced at Mike. The deep furrow between his eyes meant his thoughts were running on the same track. Saturday night, the last time they'd seen Wendy, she'd been feisty as hell, strangely unconcerned about her print on the spent cartridge that killed Tovah Schoenfeld.

Neither Mike nor April had pegged her for a suicide risk at that time. She could have crashed and done something stupid when she got home, or she could be a heavy sleeper. *Let it be that,* April prayed. Drunks were hard to rouse. *Let it be that.*

"Shit," Mike muttered.

"You want me to get the super?" she asked.

He nodded tensely. He could have tried his hand at the locks, but there were two of them, one a Medeco. It would take him a while. April was the one who'd lost Kim, so he gave her something useful to do.

A few minutes later, she returned with a worried young man who didn't speak much English but knew enough to unlock the door and get out of the way. The smell alone was chilling. It was clear that Wendy had been doing some pretty heavy drinking in the last thirty-eight hours. The lights were on, and even from the front door several empty large bottles of Gordon's vodka could be seen in the living room. One was upended on the sofa; one sat on the cocktail table.

A third bottle lay on its side on the rug. Quite a bit must have spilled out when it went over, because the room smelled as if a lit match would send it up. A loop in an electrical cord beside the sofa suggested that someone might have tripped over it. The lamp attached was shattered. Other things had been destroyed, too. Shards from many pieces of broken china made a blue and white abstract on the kitchen floor. The whole apartment was torn apart.

"Jesus." The super moved farther from the door.

April went in first, stepping over a broken teacup whose pattern she'd recognized a week ago as the

famous Chinese Willow. Mike followed in her footsteps. The quiet after what must have been quite a
storm was eerie and sad. It was the kind of scene where
one expected to find the worst and found it. There was
blood in Wendy's office. It was smeared on the walls
and stained the carpet. There was blood on her pink
quilt and on her pillow. A lot of blood on the floor of
her closet, along with piles of her clothes, as if she had
tried to get dressed before she died. They found her
lying on the floor of her bathroom awash in a pool of
vile-smelling vomit and clotting blood. They immediately called 911.

Three hours later they were sitting with Inspector
Bellaqua at a table for four in the back of the Metropolitan, across the street from the puzzle palace. At
five P.M. the day tour was over and the place was fill-
ing up with off-duty cops. Bellaqua was nursing a
diet Coke, her eyes punchy with dismay at all the
things that had gone wrong in a single day and the
fact that two of her detectives had played a part in
the worst of it.

"He did what?" she said of Mike Fray, who hadn't
been able to tell the difference between a boy's back
and fanny and a girl's.

"Kim's small. He's good-looking," April murmured.

Bellaqua studied the wedding photo. "Fray said
he walks with a wiggle. Jesus. What about that silencer book you found, Mike?"

"It has Wendy's name in it," he said, noncommittal. They were all noncommittal as hell.

"How about Wendy?"

"She's lost a lot of blood. The place looked like a

slaughterhouse. Ever seen an alcoholic hemorrhage? It's not a pretty sight. In her case everything went at the same time: esophagus, stomach lining. Just burned out by the booze. She had blood pouring out from everywhere. And she was so out of it she probably didn't even know how sick she was. She could have died if we hadn't come along," Mike said.

"Is she talking?"

"Uh-uh." April felt bad. They'd stayed in the ER at Lenox Hill Hospital for several hours waiting for word to come in. None had come. Finally they'd had to leave before finding out if she'd been stabilized. A uniform was posted at the hospital now, watching out for her.

Bellaqua sighed at the day gone bad. Then she picked up the wedding photo of Kim and Clio.

"I'll get this made up and we'll get Kim's face out there, all over TV. We'll get him."

"Good." Mike slapped the table and got up. He and April were heading out to Queens in case Kim had gone home.

Fifty-seven

Soon after Kim left Tang's shop, he put on his blue Hawaiian shirt in the men's room of a coffee shop near the Lexington Avenue subway. He put on his baseball hat and his sunglasses. He felt bad and needed to make a new friend. The empty place inside of him filled up when he made friends. He wanted to tell someone how Tang Ling had mistreated and misunderstood him, how she'd thrown him out like a stupid salesgirl.

Around Hunter College he looked over the students. Nobody gave him a second glance. The empty place inside him hurt as he got on the subway and traveled one stop south to Fifty-ninth Street. He had a handgun, but it made a lot of noise and wasn't one he could use for anything. The one he liked was in the Dumpster a block over on Fiftieth Street. He approached the street with high hopes because he could see that the Dumpster was still there. The only problem was that now it was piled much higher with rubble from a renovation going on there. A construction crew was dumping more stuff in it, raising a cloud of dust from crumbling chunks of old plaster. He couldn't get anywhere near where he'd dropped the black garbage bag on Saturday. He walked back and forth a few times but didn't get any attention from the men on the crew. He was hoping someone would talk to him, help him recover that garbage bag, but gave up after a little while when no one did.

With his glasses on and his shirt flapping around his hips, he started walking downtown on Lexington. The bar where he danced sometimes and picked up men was on Broadway in the Forties. He didn't get that far. At Fifty-sixth Street through the window of the Shamrock Inn, he saw Tang Ling on a big TV screen over the bar.

Immediately he knew that Tang had gone on TV as a way to speak to him. He knew her temper, knew that she was sorry about the way she had treated him. Kim was sure Tang Ling had a special feeling for him and was not really mad. He did not think he'd done anything bad. What happened happened, like the rain falling, like the water rising, like bad feeling and killing everywhere. People were killed all the time. Six thousand people at once. Bodies were everywhere. Two, three, four little angels were nothing.

Excited to see Tang on TV, Kim went into the bar and sat down on an empty stool to look at her and to hear what she had to say. Tang was not a beautiful woman, not like Clio. But she was so famous. She could be on TV whenever she wanted. On TV she was wearing the gray suit and her magnificent pearls she'd been wearing when she hit him. He studied her hair. It was no longer black like it used to be. It was getting redder every month. Now it was almost the color of red wine. On TV Tang had her glasses on. She looked serious, reading from a piece of paper.

"The viciousness of these murders of young

women at the very start of their lives has personally touched and horrified me," she was saying.

The sound was low, so Kim had to lean forward to hear her.

"At Tang Ling, we feel we can't stand by without offering our support. It is for this reason that I personally have set up a fund of ten thousand dollars for information leading to the arrest of the coward responsible for these unspeakably cruel crimes. Thank you." She put the paper down.

The person interviewing her started asking questions, but Kim couldn't understand what Tang was saying. All he could see was the sign in front of her. A sign in the shape of a check with the words on it: TANG LING, LTD., OFFERS $10,000 REWARD FOR ARREST OF THE BRIDE KILLER.

"I won't rest until I see the coward punished," she said.

The bartender finally came over. "What'll you have?"

Feeling all alone in the world and sadly misunderstood, Kim hugged his carryall and shook his head.

Fifty-eight

Clio's car was in the driveway. A yellow Saturn. Mike pulled in behind it, and April felt a warning jab from the ghost, Trouble, that sometimes burrowed in her stomach. She was still queasy from Wendy's thirty-six-hour crisis—the sick and threatened woman all alone and drinking herself to death. Maybe on purpose, but maybe not. Now this innocent-looking two-family house with the dog inside barking its head off. Trouble everywhere.

Mike killed the engine. April was doing her calculations. There were two of them in the car with four guns between them and no wish to die. There were possibly two people in the house and no telling how many guns. If Kim was there, she didn't want him either to shoot or run again.

"Plan?" she said.

Before Mike could answer, the front door opened, and the woman from the wedding photo stepped outside alone. Clio Alma had long, straight hair, all one length, red lips. She was wearing a beige linen dress that showed off her well-rounded figure. Her lovely face was annoyed, not frightened or anxious.

"You can't park there," she said. Matter-of-fact.

Mike and April got out of the car at the same time,

holding up their gold shields. "Clio Alma?" Mike took the lead.

"Yes?"

"I'm Lieutenant Sanchez. This is Sergeant Woo from the police department. We'd like to ask you a few questions."

"Is this about my husband?" she asked with a tense smile.

The two cops walked up the cement path. She stood in front of the door. "I can tell you he's all mixed up sometimes and doesn't always know what he's doing, but I'm fine. Everything's fine now. Nothing to worry about." She didn't want them to come in.

"Is your husband here now, Mrs. Alma?" April asked.

Clio gave her a sharp look. "I told you, everything's fine. We don't need you here." She tried to get back inside and close the door, but Mike's foot got in the way.

"We'd like to come in for a few minutes. It won't take long."

"Who called you, my tenant?" she demanded. "She's a liar; you can't believe anything she says."

"No, your tenant didn't call us. We're investigating two homicides. We're here to talk about that."

"Homicides!" Clio's fine eyebrows shot up. The distress in her voice caused the dog at her feet to start barking frantically. "I don't know anything about that. I told them before."

"Who did you tell?"

"The policeman who came here last week."

"Did you know there was another murder since then?"

"No . . . Maybe I heard something. I don't know."

She put her hand to her forehead as if trying to remember.

"Let me help you. Two young women, clients of Tang Ling, have been shot and killed," April told her.

"He's not here," she said quickly. "He's not here. Look for yourself." She shook her head, opened the door wider, and retreated into the living room, where she picked up her barking dog. "Shh," she told it. Unlike Dim Sum, the dog quieted instantly.

April entered the house, thinking fast in case Kim was really was there and she had to deck him. Stairs to the left. Click. Living room to the right. Click. In the back the kitchen, linoleum surfaces all clean and tidy. Wall-to-wall carpet, commercial grade. Sofa and recliner, stack of glossy magazines on the coffee table in the living room. Click. Nothing much on the walls. Home sweet home to Kim Simone. She prayed he was there and made a fast tour of the downstairs. Mike took the stairs two at a time and came down two minutes later shaking his head. April flipped the light switch for the basement, and they went down together. Nothing there either. When they returned to the living room, Clio was sitting on the sofa with the dog on her lap. Her pretty mouth sulked. "Too much trouble," she said.

"Your husband?" April went to the front window and looked out. Two officers were in a Con Ed van opposite. It was still light, and the street was quiet, except for some young roller boarders practicing on a curb.

"Yes. He's like a child. Sometimes he disappears. I don't know where he is." She heaved a sigh.

"On May ninth, Sunday a week ago, he delivered a gown to Riverdale and dressed Tovah Schoenfeld just before she was shot to death." April left the window and stood in front of her.

After the letdown of no Kim where she'd wanted him to be, her heartbeat finally began to slow. All the way out in the car, she'd been so full of hope that he'd be there. She'd prayed that he'd be there and more than half expected him to fall out of a closet, like a ghost in a funhouse.

Clio nodded. He'd delivered Tovah's gown and dressed her.

"You drove him there in your car?"

"He doesn't have a driver's license," she said, putting her face in the dog's soft fur.

"Did you drive him there and wait for him?" April asked.

Clio stroked the dog, hiding her lips in the dog's black fur, lowering her eyes.

"Did you use your car to drive to work?" April asked.

"No," she said softly.

"But you went to work that day, Mrs. Alma."

"No."

"Yes, you did. I spoke to your employer a few minutes ago. She told me they had a family party on May ninth. And you were there all morning, cooking." April struck a chord.

"I don't remember what day." Clio's eyes were in the dog's fur. "Maybe. I cook many parties for them."

"I understand. I get confused by dates, too. But we can straighten all this out. Did you know that Kim was driving your car to Riverdale?"

"No."

"Did you know when he returned?"

"No. I told you. As far as I know he didn't take the car."

"Why did you tell the detective that you drove him?" April asked softly.

"He doesn't have a license. I didn't want him to get in trouble." Clio spoke with a flat voice, then turned around to look at Mike. He was standing behind her by the front door, letting April talk. "He wouldn't hurt anybody, I know."

"Did you know he had a gun?"

"He doesn't have a gun," she said scornfully. "Where would he get a gun?"

April didn't answer. "Did he ever talk about any of the young women whose gowns he worked on?"

"He talks all the time. He has some crazy ideas," she said softly.

"What crazy ideas?"

"I don't know. I don't listen." She started rocking back and forth with the dog. "And he doesn't come home sometimes. It scares me."

"What scares you, Mrs. Alma?"

"The men he meets. He's doesn't understand anything about bad people."

April glanced at Mike. "What do you mean?"

"He's too trusting. He could get hurt."

"Does he have any particular friends he visits?" April asked. Maybe they could find him with a friend.

"Someone in a bar gives him money. . . ." Clio lifted her shoulders. "I told him to stay away from men who offer him money. He doesn't listen."

"What kind of crazy things does he say about brides?" April asked, back on the brides.

Relieved to be off the subject of Kim's friends, Clio

said, "He talks about angels. He loves angels," she said, smiling a little.

"Angels?" Click. April got a sick feeling. Hadn't Ching said something about an angel being embroidered in her gown?

"Yes, like that show on TV. He thinks when people die they become happy angels, like on TV."

Oh, shit! Ching a happy angel. April glanced at Mike. She needed to call the lab and check something about Prudence's gown. Tovah's. Andrea Straka's. Ching's. Her stomach churned.

"Did you ever hear him mention Tovah Schoenfeld?" April asked, just wanting to get this straight.

"I don't listen."

"How about Prudence Hay?"

"I told you. I don't know."

"Andrea Straka."

"Oh, yes, Andrea. That girl who died in the subway. He was very sad about that. Something's wrong with the lawn mower," Clio said suddenly.

"What's wrong with the lawn mower?" April asked, still horrified by that angel in Ching's wedding gown. Had Tang requested it, or was this Kim acting on his own? She didn't remember what Ching had told her.

"I don't know. Maybe somebody came in the gate and did something to it."

Mike went outside to take a look. Clio had a small patches of lawn in the front and back. The lawn mower was chained to the fence in the back.

April stayed in the living room. Her heart thudding over Ching. "What about Tang Ling?" she asked. "Do she and Kim get along?"

Clio's cat eyes narrowed down to slivers. "She's a

bad woman," she said. "Bad for Kim. You looking for him, he's probably hiding under her skirt."

"Thanks. Here's my card. If you get scared you can call me anytime."

April found Mike in the back puzzling over the small motor in the lawn mower. It looked all right to April until he stood up and brushed off his hand. Then she realized that Clio was right. Something was wrong with it. The muffler had been removed.

Fifty-nine

April was in a panic as they hurried back into Manhattan from Queens. Not since the attack on the World Trade Center had murder been something that could only happen to someone else. After thousands of people died in just a few minutes, everybody in New York felt close to death. For April, every murder since was personal. But the killings of Tang's brides brought death too close, way too close to home.

Clio's knowledge of Andrea Straka, Kim's driving the car for which he didn't have a license to Tovah's wedding. The missing guns still out there. The presence in Kim's house of the comic book for crooks that explained the items in his basement—the PVC pipe, the bottle caps, copper sponges, tennis balls, copper screen, metal washers, rubber stoppers. The muffler from the lawn mower. Kim had been making his own crude silencers from crude household materials to take the sonic boom of a heavy load down to subsonic whimper. Kim's past reliance on Tang when he was in trouble. The angel on Ching's gown. Ching's plan to have dinner with Tang that night. It was coming together way too close to her.

Ching had left her cell phone home. She'd already

left work. April wanted her safe and sound, somewhere far away from Tang. Her heart hammered in her chest. Her stomach churned. Why had Kim marked Ching? She wasn't a client of Wendy's or Louis's. She was just a girl, a plain girl! And the closest thing April had to a sister. It didn't matter why.

Her cell phone rang. She grabbed it. *Private* came up on caller ID. "Sergeant Woo."

"Where are you?" came the irritated voice of her boss.

"Lieutenant, thank God. Do you have something for me?"

"What's up with this guy Kim Simone?"

It was amazing from how many places in Queens you could see the skyline of Manhattan. You could be on the road, out in the borough, everything all quiet and low, on a highway or a back street, and all of a sudden you'd go up a little rise and there it was, Citicorp, Empire State Building, and everything in between, all spread out. The towers were gone, but New York was still there. At night the halo of lights still brightened the dark sky. It happened then just as the sky was fading to navy. The city loomed up ahead, and she was scared.

"We think he's the one," she said faintly. "What do you have?"

"Guy has a sheet. Joined a cruise ship as a steward some five years back. Jumped off at Cancún three and a half years ago. He was picked up on a local bus in El Paso, soliciting. Spent two months in an INS camp. His now wife, Clio Alma, helped him out with a lawyer."

The phone crackled for a moment as they hit a dead zone.

"April?"

"Okay now?"

"Yeah." He went on. "Simone's position at his deportation hearing was that he'd be in danger in the Philippines if he returned."

"Uh-huh, any particular danger?"

"His mother was denounced as a witch and stoned to death by neighbors when he was twelve. He and his sister were badly beaten and left for dead."

"True story?" April asked. Nothing surprised her anymore, but this was a new one. Witches now.

"True story."

"What about the sister?"

"She married a general or something. They had a dispute over a girlfriend. He shot her."

"Oh, God."

"There's more. Clio Alma paid his fine, and the two got married soon after he arrived in New York. And get this. He's been arrested several times since then."

"Let me guess," April said.

"You don't have to guess. I'm going to tell you. Indecent exposure, soliciting. And right here in Midtown North."

"No kidding. Does he have a favorite spot?"

"Forty-second Street, theater row, near the entrance to the Lincoln Tunnel. He's a repeater, so I've got people out there now."

"Any drug angle?"

"No, no, this guy is strictly sex, and no history of violence that we know of until now."

"What about the Straka case?"

"Okay. That occurred in the Nineteenth. At the

Hunter College subway station. Happened during rush hour, around seventeen hundred. Very crowded platform. A lot of people left right away."

It was the closest subway stop to Tang's shop. Another piece.

"You owe me," Iriarte growled.

"Yes, sir, I always owe you. One more question. How did Simone get his job at Tang Ling's?"

"Your florist met his bail twice. My guess is he and Kim first met up in the bars, or on the street. The florist definitely had him working in the shop for a while. After a dispute, he set Kim up with Tang because Kim knew how to sew. I'm going out now, and I'm staying out until we get him. I don't want him on my turf."

"Yes, sir. Be careful. He's A and D."

"Okay, are you with Sanchez?"

"Yes. We're coming in from Kim's home."

"You got someone watching out there?" he asked as if they were total dummies and he the one in charge.

"Yes, sir. Two."

"See you, then," were his last words.

Monday evening the traffic was still heavy getting onto the Fifty-ninth Street Bridge. April had plenty of time to tell Mike Kim's story. After she finished, he smacked the wheel angrily.

"We had him all along," Mike said. "We had his ear."

"A little ear, perfect seashell. I noticed it right away in the wedding photo, but I didn't want to jump on it until we knew it was him."

"Shit. We had him on day one. We could have put

this together in twenty-four if everyone around him hadn't covered for him. Wendy, Louis. His wife."

"They made it hard," April agreed.

"So he had a chance to kill somebody else. And still Wendy didn't say anything." He was furious.

"It was her gun," April said slowly. "She's a thief. She can't restrain herself. It's a sickness. That first day I questioned her I hit her with her weakness. She didn't want to get branded as a thief so she drove up to the Vineyard to get some of the stuff out of her apartment. But she also wanted to check out her guns. She wasn't absolutely certain one of her crew hadn't taken one. Remember when I asked her how many guns she had? She said she didn't know. She said they'd been stolen years ago. But after Prudence was killed, she knew she couldn't wiggle out. She just hit the bottle. Whether or not she wanted to die only she can say."

Traffic slowed almost to a stop on the bridge, and Mike hit the siren to open it up. "Bleeding to death like that is a hell of a way to die," he muttered.

"Maybe she didn't know what was happening." April didn't want to think about Wendy's lethal binge while they were on Martha's Vineyard.

"Yeah, Prudence Hay went that way, too. Wendy had that on her conscience." April's thoughts shifted to another member of the team, Louis the Sun King, not exactly an expert in pain management. He'd been Kim's first friend—after Kim had married Clio for citizenship. Maybe he was the man Clio was talking about, still Kim's special friend. Someone should check.

Mike hit the siren again, more insistently this time, and a little frantic maneuvering of the cars around them got them moving toward the off-ramp.

April punched some numbers in her phone. Mike glanced over at her.

"Who are you calling?"

"Tang. I'm worried about Ching."

"Why?"

"Mike. This thing has just been bothering me all day. Why is Kim doing this? How does he choose the girls? And then I realized Louis and Wendy have nothing to do with it. It's about the girls and their dresses. He's turning the girls into angels, dressing them in their white dresses, and marrying them to God so they don't have to marry men."

Mike whistled. "But what does Ching have to do with it?"

"Ching told me Saturday that Tang put an angel on her gown. But she must have been mistaken. My guess is that Kim did it on his own."

Sixty

After leaving the bar, Kim went back to the Dumpster on Fiftieth Street. Seeing Tang on TV offering so much money for the chance to punish him made him feel terrible. He was wandering around, dazed and wounded. When he got back to the Dumpster, there were policemen around it, and he left right away.

He didn't know what to do. Tang was his closest friend. He'd been so proud to have a friend, a boss, who was so famous and so rich. He told everybody about her house. He went out of his way to pass the fine brownstone just so he could show off and tell his friends, "This is where my boss lives."

Even when Tang wasn't home, Kim took every opportunity to deliver things and help out there. He knew how the alarm system worked and what her housekeeper looked like, much prettier and younger than Tang. He knew a lot of things about Tang. He knew that she did not get up early because she was out late every night. He knew that she did not like lunch or exercise, but at the end of every day she enjoyed an hour of relaxation in her beautiful pool. The maid told him Tang's pool had lavender oil in it and was kept very hot for her, almost as hot as a bathtub.

The pool was in a glass room on the roof. The room was full of plants and palm trees, and the pool was so heavy the ceiling of the floor above had to be reinforced with steel beams to support it. He'd seen the room on the top floor himself, that's how close to her he was.

Because Tang liked him, Kim thought of himself as a protector of hers. He'd pass her street in the evening before he went cruising just to see if she was home, to look through the windows into her rooms. He didn't want her as an enemy.

Kim felt sick and lonely and needed a friend to help him. Wendy wasn't answering her phone, so he went to see the old man, Bill, who bailed him out whenever he got in trouble. Bill was at home in his penthouse apartment, but he was busy and didn't want to be bothered. Bill Krauterman was his name. Bill buzzed Kim up, but as soon as he opened the door, he told Kim to go away.

"I don't have time for trouble now," he said with an angry face.

Kim started crying out in the hall. "Clio hit me."

"Well, I'm sorry she hit you. I told you not to stay with her."

"She hits me too much. I can't go back there."

"Okay, so leave her." Bill was big, very big. Over six feet tall, and he weighed too much. He had trouble getting in and out of bed, and sometimes he got very mad at Kim for nothing at all.

"I did leave." Kim was desperate and cried some more, letting his tears run down his face so Bill would feel sorry for him. He should have been an actor. "Tang fired me." He was pleading while the fat old man was trying to make up his mind.

"Kim, did anybody ever tell you you're too much trouble?"

"But you like me, Billy. We're friends, right? I need one thousand five hundred dollars for a new place. Then I won't bother you." Kim said the words quickly, working hard to get the order right in English.

Bill's angry face looked back inside his apartment as if someone were in there waiting for him. He wasn't letting Kim in.

"I'll pay it right back," Kim promised.

Bill snorted and pulled on his gray ponytail. "How are you going to pay it back if you've lost your job? Oh, never mind. Take it and get lost." He reached into his pocket, fanned out a fat roll of hundreds and gave Kim fifteen, then closed the door without saying anything more.

Kim's heart felt full. It made him so happy to get such easy money and be loved by a rich friend. Right away he went shopping. He wandered from store to store on Lexington and Third, looking for new clothes to look good for his friend. He spent all his shopping time thinking about the rest of the money in the old man's pocket and how he would get it later.

He was surprised when all his money was gone. He was wearing a green silk shirt and a fine suede jacket, new white pants, and Italian slip-on shoes. But he had nowhere to go, no plan. He felt poor and lonely again, and his memory flashed back to long ago. He thought of the village good-time girl who was so horribly burned when angry wives held her down and threw acid on her face for stealing their husbands. He could still hear the girl's screams in his head and see clearly the way she looked afterward.

Her body was still alive but she was dead. She called herself a living dead person.

Living dead person. Kim's sister, too. Kim thought of his sister, who was an angel now. He thought of Tang and the acid-throwing wives. Tang Ling was very vain; she liked to have her picture taken and see herself in the magazines. If acid spoiled her face, she would be ugly. She could never go on TV or hurt him again.

Kim was walking around Lexington Avenue, thinking about throwing acid on Tang for hurting him so much. He walked around for a long time, down to Forty-second Street and Grand Central Station. He was thinking how easy it would be to make Tang a living dead person. She would scream and roll around on the ground. Her husband wouldn't want her anymore. No more late nights in restaurants. Kim knew where acid was, but not here in Manhattan. He had to go back to Queens to get it. That would take a long time. Anyway, even if he was mad at Tang, he would never hurt her.

Kim thought of another dead person. A girl, only thirteen. He didn't know her when she was alive. But when the men pulled her naked body out of the river, his mother turned to him.

"Maybe someone raped her and she struggled too hard," she told him.

He was little then and didn't know what she meant. But he remembered later not to struggle too much when people hurt him. The girl in the river made him think of Tang drowning in her pool. A strong person could hold her under the water until she stopped struggling like the girl so long ago. Kim started walking to Tang's house. His feet in the hand-

some shoes were taking the familiar route back uptown. He wasn't thinking of taking the gun out and
shooting Tang. That was the furthest thing from his
thoughts. Wendy told him you couldn't shoot a gun
without fixing the bang first because people were so
afraid of guns. They got upset when they heard the
noise and called the police. He hated the police, who
always made trouble for him and tried to lock him up.

He had no plan to shoot anybody right then. The
gun with the muffler on it was buried in the garbage.
Because he was a forgiving person, he pushed his
bad thoughts about Tang away. He knew he would
never in a million years hurt Tang. He just wanted to
be near her and change her mind. He was good at
changing people's minds, never stayed in trouble for
long. He'd changed Billy's mind, hadn't he? The
closer Kim got to Tang's house the stronger was his
idea that if he had a chance to talk to Tang, she'd
change her mind. He'd get his job back and they'd
still be friends. That was all he wanted.

Sixty-one

April dialed Tang's private line at her office and was not surprised to hear her assistant say, "She's gone for the day."

"When did she leave?" April asked, relieved that anybody was there so late.

"Who's calling?"

"Sergeant Woo, police department. I was there this morning."

"Oh, yes, Miss Woo. Is there anything I can help you with?"

"I need to reach Miss Ling; it's very urgent." She had to find Ching and send her out of harm's way.

"Um. Miss Ling left the building a few minutes ago."

"In a car?"

"No, no, it's only a few blocks. She always walks home."

"What route does she take?"

The woman hesitated. "Oh, I'm sure you can reach her at home in half an hour."

"Well, that might be too late. Are you sure she's on her way home?" April asked.

"Well, I think so. Is something wrong? You could

call on her cell phone." The woman gave her the number.

"Okay, good. Thanks." April jotted it down.

"You know where the house is?" she asked, suddenly helpful.

"Yes. I know where the house is." April ended the call. "Tang is walking home," she told Mike.

Then she dialed Tang's cell number. It was turned off, so she left a message. Didn't important people like Tang Ling always keep their cell phones on? she wondered. Where was Ching? She was getting panicked.

"Shit." Mike had taken the Sixty-sixth Street crosstown, and now they were caught in the Lincoln Center traffic. He hit the siren and waited only a second before barreling through a red light at Lexington and bucking the oncoming traffic. A bus almost hit them, and the female driver gave them a horrified look as she jammed on the brakes.

April's stomach lurched as he kept going. She was in the death seat, her window open, perspiring heavily into the suit she'd worn for her visit to Tang Ling. Now she wished she'd never heard the woman's name. The cooling wind hit her in the face. Finally the temperature was dropping. April braced herself, thinking about Tang's town house on Seventy-first Street. Between Park and Madison Avenues, had a garage and a swimming pool.

She tried Tang's home number. Voice mail picked up on the first ring. April left another message. "The line's busy. She may be home already," she said.

"Hold on." Mike plowed through all six lanes of Park and turned up Madison. There was still a lot of life on the avenue. The ritzy crowd that lived there was walking home, walking out to dinner. Walking and turning to see what the noise was about.

"Let's not scare the horses," April murmured.

Mike turned the siren off, and she scanned the street, searching the pedestrians for a solo walker, a good-looking Filipino with a sweet face, just in case. . . .

They passed Tang's shop. At quarter to nine everything was shut tight. The lights on Madison illuminated dazzling clothes and accessories in boutiques only the very wealthy could afford. Once again April wanted out of the car. She wanted to run. For days she'd been wanting to run. Run and catch the killer. Knock him into hell. She didn't see Tang striding along in her Armani suit.

Mike cruised slowly past Seventy-first Street. Yves Saint Laurent was on the southeast corner. On the far side of the street was St. James. As they passed it, April saw that several homeless were camping on the front steps. No sign of Tang or Kim. Mike turned on Seventy-second Street. Ralph Lauren one corner. Around the block on Park he ran a light. April held her breath. Still nothing. They cruised down Park, then turned on Seventy-first Street with the light. It was a quiet street. As they headed back toward Madison, April could see the AA sign out on the side church door, indicating a meeting in progress. No one was outside.

Opposite the church, the town houses were grand. Tang's house was the grandest and widest of all. April detached her seat belt and scanned the area around the church. The west side of Madison on Seventy-first Street had its shady patches. Click. She scanned the dark areas back to the church where homeless were allowed to sleep on the steps and dozens of people were inside at an eight P.M. AA meeting. This was a perfect spot for a stranger. April's eyes went back to Tang's house, then ran east to Park Avenue. Two doormen, one on each side of the street, came out of their doors. One lit a cigarette. She had no sense of Kim's presence there. Maybe Clio, who knew Kim best, was wrong about him. Maybe he wasn't going to hide under Tang's skirt.

"I don't think he's out here," she murmured, trying to calm down. Mike slowed to a crawl.

"*Cuidado*," he warned as he pulled into the space in front of the garage door where the yellow sign said NO PARKING ANYTIME.

Upstairs on the second floor of Tang's house the lights were on. April opened her door. Mike put a hand on her arm. "I'm going," he said.

"She doesn't know you," April protested. She knew what he was thinking. She wasn't wearing a vest; her powder blue suit made her a perfect target. Too bad. She was going anyway. They were out of the car and moving at the same time.

April was troubled by the dark public spaces in the church behind her directly across the narrow side street. Homeless on the corner. What to check first, the house or the church?

But okay. Fine, they'd go in together. Mike nodded and chose the house. April moved first; he took a position behind her. There was no stoop. The front door was at street level. A security camera hung from above. April rang the bell. Almost instantly someone spoke through the intercom.

"Yes?"

"Lieutenant Sanchez, Sergeant Woo to see Miss Tang."

"She's out to dinner."

"Where?"

"May I see your ID?"

April showed her gold shield to the camera.

"She's at Willow Restaurant, on Lexington Avenue."

She gulped. Okay, that's where Ching was. "Let's go."

Sixty-two

Kim walked up Lexington Avenue. He walked so slowly it got dark outside long before he reached Seventy-first Street. At first he started looking in windows, jewelry store windows especially, moving his feet along in their new Italian shoes. He thought of the ring he'd bought Clio when they got married, the bracelets and the earrings. A real diamond and real gold to make her happy. He was good to her. But she was not good to him. Angry all the time. He didn't like that.

After a while he lost interest in stores and studied his shoes. Kim's new shoes had soles that were so thin he could feel every bump on the sidewalk. They were beautiful, but thin. His head drooped and he started feeling bad about the shoes and all the things he did for other people and the poor way they repaid him for his kindness.

It was not so far from Forty-second Street to Seventy-first Street, but Kim was not just walking up Lexington; he was walking through his whole life. By the time he reached Seventieth Street he was feeling so uncomfortable in his skin he wanted to break right out of it. Burst open and do something. Nothing he'd done yet had worked to make his life okay. Nothing was enough. Everything felt too tight inside him, and he didn't know what to do to make his skin fit again. He had no home, no job. His heart hurt and he thought it wasn't fair that people did so many bad things and only he should suffer, only he be singled out for punishment.

He was at Seventy-third Street before he realized he'd passed Seventy-first Street. He lifted his head. He saw the street sign and realized he'd gone too far. He turned to go across Seventy-third Street. There was a restaurant on the corner. He hesitated, suddenly alert to a familiar place. He knew this was a restaurant where Tang sometimes went with her husband, with important people he recognized.

Tables were set, and people were sitting outside. He stopped to look through the window, and there Tang was! But tonight she was not with an important person. His whole body felt the shock of seeing Tang with a customer. And it was not just any customer. Tang was sitting at a table inside the restaurant with the girl who was supposed to be his next angel. Ching Ma Dong!

Kim stared at them, horribly upset that Tang was taking the time to eat with a customer. She never did that. And the worst thing was that the two women—his boss and his next angel—were smiling and laughing as if he'd never existed. They looked completely happy, as if they didn't care about all the bad things that happened to him.

Sixty-three

Mike hurried back to the car, but April hesitated on the sidewalk, studying the street. Maybe they shouldn't move so fast. There were other choices here. That church, for one thing. Homeless on the front steps. The street was really quiet, a good place for action no one was expecting. April shivered and pulled out her phone to try Tang's cell number again. Still no answer.

"Let's go, *querida*." Mike was already back in the car.

"Right, let's be where she is."

He called for an address while she crossed the sidewalk.

"Hurry up. Get in the car. It's on Seventy-third Street."

Okay, okay. Back in the car April didn't attach her seat belt. Cops had special dispensation on the job. Some cops never wore seat belts. A macho thing. Right now Mike didn't do his either. He pulled out fast, and her heartbeat accelerated with the car. Upper East Side was about as high end as New York City got, and Mike was pushing it in a part of town he didn't know. Nineteenth Precinct. The radio crackled as he wove around one-way streets. Nothing was going down. It was a quiet Monday night.

He sped north on Madison. Up on Seventy-third

was another church. Homeless were gathered there, too. At Seventh-fourth the brakes squealed as he took the turn too fast and raced down the block, only to grind to a halt at Park, where four of the six lanes were moving fast.

A radio call came in. It was a nothing. Mike turned off the radio and neither said anything as they waited for the light to change. Ten thousand times every single day cops just got in cars and cruised around. Sometimes they were looking for something that hadn't even been thought of yet. Sometimes they were looking for a certain person, or a certain kind of person. Or certain activities in highly predictable locations. Sometimes you found what you were looking for, and sometimes you didn't.

April read the scene. At first there didn't seem to be much in the way of unpredictable on Lexington and Seventy-third Street. The restaurant they were looking for was a building that had once been a private house. A few tables covered with snowy tablecloths were set out on the sidewalk for spring dining, just a few for brave diners. They were decorated with candles and sweetheart roses. Five of the tables were filled.

Ching and Tang Ling were not sitting at one them. In the navy sky above the stars were coming out. It was a pleasant scene. Only one thing was out of place: Kim Simone was against the wall at the restaurant window. Mike and April both saw him at the same moment, saw the carryall over his shoulder.

"There he is. No fast moves," Mike said as he slid to a stop, double-parking on Lex before the intersection.

As if April didn't know. Adrenaline kicked in as they took a moment to observe him. Kim didn't seem to be doing anything except standing there. That was good. No one was paying him any attention. That was good, too. He wasn't nervous. The canvas carryall was hanging by its straps over his left shoulder. His back was to them, so his hands were not in view. Mike called Dispatch to give their location and to request backup.

They would take this real slow. The suspect didn't look jumpy, didn't appear to have a gun in his hand. Certainly not a rifle. They exchanged looks. Best case, they would get out of the car. They would cross the street. They would move across the sidewalk. There would be no sirens. They would not say, "Police, freeze." They would distress no diners. There would be no scene. They would get to Kim and each take a side of him. Then they would walk him quietly away from the restaurant, the diners—Tang Ling and Ching.

Mike broke the tense silence. "Did he see you today?" he asked.

"Don't know."

"Let's take it real easy."

Okay. Her vote was for easy. April nodded and popped open her door. Mike opened his. Then, as if he could read their minds, Kim started moving. He slowly slid down the side of the building in that narrow space between diners and building. He was walking, not a bit nervous. He didn't see them coming. He was completely cool, heading toward the door of the restaurant as if it were an everyday thing, but nothing about it was everyday to Mike and April. Kim's hand was in the bag, and he was going inside, where Ching was. April wanted to scream, but no sound came out of her mouth.

She was out of the car. She was running across the street into traffic. Horns honked as they dodged cars. People at the tables outside were startled. Kim disappeared through the door. Mike swore as April was the first to follow him in. Her hand was on her Glock. She did not want to unholster it. She did not want to have to shoot it in a crowded place. She wanted to grab the suspect and take him out quietly.

It didn't happen.

Lucky for her the light was the same inside and outside. She could see Kim moving into the restaurant. Then she saw where he was going. Tang Ling was in the back at a table for four. Ching was sitting beside her. They were drinking champagne. Between herself and Tang, the restaurant was filled with people. Diners, servers, people drinking at the bar. Lots of people. Mike was at her elbow. Kim was moving through the human traffic. Nothing stealthy about the way he was moving. April didn't see a gun. She still didn't see a gun. She thought they were all right. They were going to be all right. Mike was now ahead of her. She knew the plan.

"Excuse me, sir." Mike moved quickly toward Kim. He wanted Kim to turn around and focus away from Ching. He wanted to see if there was a gun. He wanted to take Kim's arm.

Kim turned around, surprised. "Me?"

"Do you have a reservation?" Mike asked.

Kim shook his head. "I have a friend here."

"Excuse me, watch your back." A waiter with a full tray got between them.

Kim turned away from Mike and started walking again. April was parallel to him, hurrying down the aisle between two rows of tables to get between him and Ching. She saw his hand go into the bag. She saw it come out with the gun.

"Police, freeze," she barked.

Tang Ling put her hand to her mouth and stood up. "Kim!" Ching stood up, too. She looked confused. Her body blocked Tang, but nobody blocked her.

"Get down! Down on the floor!" April screamed. She charged Kim. He raised the gun and fired at her. She felt the burn of the bullet and hit the floor, rolling between tables toward his feet. He lowered the gun to shoot her again.

Mike pushed the waiter to one side and the tray crashed to the ground. People were screaming, rising from their chairs, trying to get away. They blocked the area so Mike couldn't get through. Tang stood there, frozen with her mouth open. Then she found her voice.

"No. No," she screamed. "No, Kim, don't."

Kim spun around. April rolled again closer to him. Blood poured from her forehead, she felt the searing burn. Her heart knocked in her chest and her breath came hard. Blood ran into her eyes. She wiped it away with her sleeve.

"Police! Freeze!" Then, "Get down," April screamed. But no one was obeying her.

"No, Kim. Please." Tang stood there screaming and shaking her head at Kim as he raised the gun, aiming at Ching.

"Don't!" she shrieked.

But he was beyond noticing her, the people, the noise, the cop at his feet. His eyes, his whole concentration was right in front of him, his last angel.

April rolled one last time, aiming for his knees. She chopped him hard, then pulled him down. Kim was already toppling as he squeezed the trigger, firing off two more shots. Mike hurled himself on the two of them, reaching for the .38 as Kim tried to fire again.

"Get out of the way," Mike barked at April.

But she wasn't going anywhere. The three grappled on the slippery floor, fighting like dogs. April panted, kicked, and slipped in somebody's dinner. Ice scuttled through puddles of wine and blood. She kicked again, aiming for a sensitive place. Kim was twisting, twisting away from them like a practiced mud-wrestler, grunting as he fought to keep his weapon. Mike had him down. Kim twisted out, lashing out with a handful of spaghetti. He threw the long hot strings in Mike's eyes. Mike swiped at his face and sprang to his feet, holding on to Kim's silk shirt.

Then Kim was up, still waving the gun, kicking back. Mike grabbed his arm and hauled it behind Kim's back. Kim howled but didn't drop the gun. It was aimed now at the back of his head. People were screaming, and now the sirens were wailing, too. Blood was all over April's face. She was soaked with it. She'd lost her sight and was losing her grip. But she fought on. She didn't want Kim firing the gun again. He twisted one last time, almost into her arms. As he turned, she punched him in the gut and the gun dropped out of his hand. April and Mike landed in a tangle on the floor, pinning their man just as a dozen officers from the Nineteenth Precinct arrived on the scene, responding to a second call, a third one, everyone with a cell phone calling in. Man with a gun, woman with a gun, officer down. They came.

Sixty-four

One A.M. again. Tuesday, May eighteenth. Lenox Hill ER. Inventory. One brand-new powder blue pantsuit covered with blood and torn in five places. In other words, shot to hell. Likewise, one white blouse, not silk though, just linen blend. One well-loved leather jacket and contents of pockets, including several Rosario notebooks and cell phone. One pair of snakeskin cowboy boots. Trousers, formerly gray. Tie, indecipherable. Shirt, good, but bought on sale over two years ago. Still viable, two 9mm Glocks, one shoulder holster. One wallet with credit cards and driver's license. Two gold shields. One cop shot in the head who'd been removed from the scene in an ambulance at nine-thirty-seven P.M.

The nurses cleaned April up before a team of doctors came to look at her. That meant washing the blood out of her face and hair while not messing with the four-inch swath that oozed from her temple and the side of her head. She was awake enough to know that she was being handled by a lot of people, her clothes were removed, and she had a headache worse than any migraine. She wanted Mike and Ching to know that she was all right. She wanted to go home, but she was seeing funny and she wasn't going anywhere until everything was checked out. That was what they told her at eleven.

At midnight the hospital was alerted that the mayor was en route. After that, no way she was going to be released until they were through with her. If the mayor wanted a photo op with a fallen cop in a hospital gown, with some major hair loss and a huge bandage on her head, he would get it.

Night from hell. TV cameras don't roll anymore; the red light comes on and they record. The mayor was recorded with the police commissioner standing behind him as usual. Sergeant April Woo looked dazed in her hospital gown as she and Lieutenant Mike Sanchez received the city's official thanks. It wouldn't be aired tonight, but by morning the whole world would know that wedding guru Tang Ling, targeted by a deranged member of her own staff, had been saved by two of New York's finest.

At one-thirty-five April and Mike departed from the hospital wearing sweatsuits with the Lenox Hill logo. April's top was the zip-up kind with a hood, because nothing would go over her head. Somebody had driven the unmarked vehicle with her purse in it to the hospital. She was moved from the wheelchair into the backseat of it. She and Mike were being driven home. Mike got in beside her and cradled her in his arms.

"*Querida, qué tal?*" he whispered as soon as they got under way.

Qué tal? *What's new? Ha.* The good side of April's head lolled against his chest. *Qué tal*, that was Spanish, right?

"I almost lost you," he murmured, kissing her bandage, her hand, whatever he could reach.

"Nah, bad shot," she mumbled. She loved him so much it almost took her past the pain. Almost.

"Oh, baby. *Te amo.*"

"Uh-uh. No, you *te amo. Mí te amo,*" she said, as if they were arguing about it.

Oh, God. She didn't feel good. She'd missed lunch and dinner. Again. Nausea rolled over her. Her head hurt. Her vision was impaired. Would he love her if she couldn't see? "Where's Ching?" she mumbled.

"Matthew took her home."

"She okay?" she asked five minutes later.

"Yeah, she's fine. How about you?"

She nodded off.

"Did they check the other gowns?" she asked, reviving for a second when they hit the bridge.

"For angels? Yeah, the lab picked it up right away."

"Could have told us sooner," she muttered. Then, "I love Ching."

"I know you do, *querida.*" He stroked her arm, her cheek. "I love her, too."

"I love my mom," some minutes after that.

"I know you do."

"You guys okay back there? The temp okay?" the driver asked. Somebody from the Nineteenth.

"Oh, yeah, everything's fine." Mike gazed out the window. They were on the LIE. They'd already passed Astoria. He'd ordered some food and planned to take April home to his place. She was used to eating late at night. But he'd figured if she was too tired to eat, he'd just put her to bed. Now he wondered if he ought to take her home to her mom, who must be worried sick.

"But I love you most, *chico*. You're my only home. I want to be with you forever." She interrupted his thought. Her arms were around him. She was holding on tight. Her eyes were closed, but maybe she wasn't asleep.

"Is that a proposal?" Mike was surprised. They'd been through a lot, but he hadn't expected the gunshot wound to unscramble her brains.

"Uh-uh, that's your job. You have to get on your knees and give me a ring. That's the way it has to be."

"Okay. I was saving up for a new car, but I can get a ring instead. What kind do you want?" He thought he'd better get it tomorrow before she changed her mind. But she didn't answer. She slept the rest of the way home.

Epilogue

After an intense family debate about her wedding gown, Ching Ma Dong finally decided to be married in a traditional Chinese suit of lucky red and gold, with a huge dragon on it. Her wedding to Matthew Tan at the Crystal Palace in Chinatown had nearly three hundred guests and went off without a hitch. Ching and Matthew said their vows over a microphone so everyone could hear them. Then the food and music began. By the fourth of twelve courses the guests, many of whom had flown in from California, were pie-eyed with happiness and too much drink.

Ching wore her hair up and looked like a movie star in each of the jade, gold, and pink-and-gold cheongsams she changed into. But the real star of the show was wearing a startling purple-and-red cheongsam, a large bandage on her head, and a diamond engagement ring on her finger. Her birthstone.

April Woo was only a little drunk and grinning from ear to ear when she gave her loving-sister speech and was royally toasted for her own engagement in return. As the glasses were raised April called Mike Sanchez, her intended, up to the microphone to be introduced to the crowd. Wearing a tuxedo, a red scar on his hairline with his bruises yellowing, Mike said a few hastily learned words of congratulation to Matthew and Ching in Chinese, ending in English with his deep appreciation for April Woo, the love of his life. It was very touching and the applause was thunderous.

The one abstainer was Skinny Dragon. Even at this magical moment, April's mother could not stop talking. How could she, when she was aloft with pride for her daughter? April the immortal was so powerful that she could be shot in the head and survive with just a scratch. Her daughter, April Woo, was so important in the police department that no crime could be solved without her. Skinny happened to be seated at a huge table that included Matthew Tan's Mexican-American and Caucasian sisters and brothers-in-law from California and their many children. Skinny was so happy that she nodded and smiled at them constantly, as if she'd known them all her life. Her husband, Ja Fa Woo, was seated next to Gao Wan, the chef from Hong Kong. The two chefs drank and laughed and talked China and cooking until they couldn't see straight.

April Woo returns!

Turn the page for a
special preview
of the next
Leslie Glass crime novel,

A KILLING GIFT,

a thrilling homicide
investigation
coming soon from NAL.

"Well, I've had about all the nostalgia I can take." Lieutenant Alfredo Bernardino's retirement party was still going strong when he abruptly pushed away from the bar at Baci and called it a night. "I'm outta here."

"Hey, what's the rush?" Sergeant Marcus Beame, his second whip in the detective unit of the Fifth Precinct, protested. "The night's young."

"Not for me." Bernardino raised two fingers at his famous protégé, Sergeant April Woo. Woo had her eye on him while she sipped tea with Poppy Bellaqua, another girl star. It made him sad. He was going. The girls were taking over. He snorted ruefully to himself about the way things were changing and how he wouldn't be there to gripe about it anymore.

Poppy didn't look up, but April nodded at him. *Coming in a second.* Her body language told him she wasn't walking away from an inspector for nobody. Bernardino snorted again. He hated this girl ganging-up thing. They were getting to be a pack. Then he smiled and let up on the resentment.

Even if April didn't jump for him now, he knew she was a good girl. She'd planned the event tonight, had chosen his favorite restaurant, had made sure that the invite was up all over the puzzle palace so everybody knew. Made sure enough brass was there.

It was a nice party, and she hadn't even worked for him in five years! Yeah, April was a good girl, and she had a good guy now, too.

Bernardino glanced over at Lieutenant Mike Sanchez, April's fiancé. The good-looking CO of the Homicide Task Force was having his third espresso with Chief Avise, commander of the Department's six thousand detectives who never hung around anywhere for more than a minute or two.

Bernardino was aware that a lot of important people were there to give him a nice send-off, but he was feeling drunk and more than a little sorry for himself. He couldn't help feeling that it was all over for him—not just the job to which he'd devoted his whole life, but his life itself.

What does a man think about when he has a premonition that he's on the very last page of his story? Bernardino was a tough guy, a bruiser of a man. Not more than a hair or so over five nine, he was barrel chested. Always an enthusiastic feeder, he had quite a corporation going around his midsection. He still had a brush of gray hair on top, but his mug was a mess. His large nose had been broken a bunch of times by the time he was thirty; and his face, deeply pitted from teenage acne, was creased and pouchy with age. He was sixty-two, not really old in the scheme of things. His father had lived past ninety, after all. Bernardino wasn't as old as he felt.

"Thank you guys for everything. That's about all I can say," he muttered to the detectives nearest him. Charm was not exactly Bernardino's middle name. He was done. He was goin' home. That was that. No pretty good-byes for him. He took a quick survey. The dark Greenwich Village hole-in-the-wall where he'd spent so many happy hours was so full of old friends that he actually had to blink back his emotions.

Thirty-eight years on the job could make a man a lot of buddies who wouldn't want to call it a day, or a lot of enemies who'd barely stop in for a free feed. Bernie had been surprised to see that he'd collected the former. At eleven forty-five on a Wednesday night, the speeches were long over. His awards were sitting on the bar, and the buffet of heavy Italian favorites—the lasagne and ziti, the baked clams and calamari fritti, the eggplant parmigiana—had been picked clean and cleared away.

A lot of the guys had gone to work, or gone home, but the pulse of the party was still beating away. More than two dozen cronies—bosses and detectives and officers with whom Bernardino had worked over the years—were eating cannolis and drinking the specialty coffees, vino, beer, and free sambuca. They were hanging in there as if there were no tomorrow, telling those stories that went back, way back to when Kathy and Bill were just kids and Lorna had been a beautiful young woman.

Bernardino shook his head at what time had done to him. Now Kathy was an FBI special agent, working Homeland Security out in Seattle. She couldn't make the party. Bill was a prosecutor in the Brooklyn DA's office. He'd come and gone without either stuffing himself too much or drinking more than half a beer. With Becky and the two kids at home and court tomorrow, Bill was out the door in less than an hour. A real straight arrow. But what could he expect? Bernie couldn't blame his son for turning out to be a grind just like him. He'd wanted to take off with his son. The party was like a wake—everyone reminiscing over his life as if he were already dead or gone to Florida.

"Hey, congratulations, pally. You watch yourself in West Palm." His successor, Bob Estrada, patted him on the back on his way. "Lucky bastard," Estrada muttered.

Bernardino snorted again. Yeah, real lucky. His wife, Lorna, had won the lottery, literally, then died of cancer only a few weeks later. You couldn't get any luckier than that. Lorna had finally gotten the millions she'd prayed for for all those years so they could retire in the sunshine and finally spend time together. Then she had to go and die and leave him to do it alone. What was Florida to him without her? What was anything?

He slipped out the door, thinking about all the others who'd passed before they should have. In thirty-eight years he'd seen quite a parade of dead. Each human who'd passed away too soon had been a little personal injury to him that he'd covered with macho humor.

The worst of all were the bodies of cops and civilians all over the place in the World Trade Center attack. Smashed fire trucks and police cars. And the fire that had gone on and on. In Chinatown, you couldn't get the smell of smoke and dead out of your nose for months. Refrigerators in apartments down there had had to be replaced. Thousands of them. The smell wouldn't fade. And that was the least of it.

When the unthinkable happened, Bernardino had been CO of the detective unit in the Fifth Precinct on Elizabeth Street in Chinatown for over a decade. Too close to ground zero for comfort. Everyone in the precinct worked around the clock because nobody wanted to go home, or be anywhere else. They'd stayed on the job twenty-four/seven for weeks longer than they had to. People who'd retired years ago came back on the job to help. And they came from other agencies, too. Retired FBI or CIA agents manned the phones, directed traffic. Whatever had to be done. He shook his head, thinking about it.

All through those long, long days, the cops who worked the front lines were waiting with the rest of the world for the second shoe to drop. They'd responded to hundreds of bomb threats a day, telling themselves they were fine. Doin' okay. But the truth was none of them was okay. The worst for Bernardino was that he'd let Lorna down. He'd been out fighting a war on New York and hadn't been home for her.

Amazing how one thing could tip a person over. He hadn't been there for Lorna before she'd gotten the cancer. That was what ate away at him. He hadn't been there where she was well. Then as soon as things were back to "normal," people were out the door. Retiring left and right. And now he was out the door.

Bernardino was a retired cop on a familiar street on a warm spring night, immediately enveloped by a deep warm fog. He looked around and was startled by it. You didn't see real pea soup in New York that often anymore. The thickness of it was like something in a movie. Downright dreamy. While he'd been inside, the haze had droppped low over the Washington Square area, blurring figures, lights, and time. Maybe that was what got to him. Bernardino dipped his head, acknowledging to himself the spookiness of the night. But maybe he was just drunk.

He shuffled his feet a little as he headed north on a side stree he knew as well as his own home. On the other side of Washington Square was his car. He walked slowly, muttering his regrets to himself. Lively, funny, rock-solid Lorna had faded in a few short months. He remembered a social worker's warning to him at the time. "Denial isn't a river in Egypt, Bernie." But he just hadn't believed she would die.

The smell of Italian cooking followed him down

the block. He was a warhorse, a cop who'd always looked over his shoulder especially on really quiet nights. But tonight he wasn't a cop anymore. He was done. His thoughts were far away. He was feeling sluggish, old, abandoned. All evening his buddies had punched and hugged him, told him they'd visit. Told him he'd find a new honey in Florida. He'd be fine. But he didn't think he'd ever be fine.

Out of the fog came an unexpected voice. "You made your million, asshole. What about your promise to me?"

Like a blind dog, Bernardino turned his big head toward the sound. Who the hell—? Instantly his guilt about the money was triggered. Someone hit the nail right on the head. But who did he owe? He puzzled over it only for a nanosecond. Then he burst out laughing. Harry was pranking him. Ha ha. His old partner from years ago following him to his car to say good-bye.

"Harry, you old devil!" Bernardino had been un-nerved for a moment but now felt a surge of relief. "Come out here where I can see you." He spun around to where he thought the sound originated.

"Nopey nope. Ain't going to happen." An arm snaked around Bernardino's neck from behind and jerked hard.

Bernardino didn't even have time to lean forward and flip the guy before the grip was set. Despite Bernardino's size and heft, he was positioned for death with little effort. After only a very few pan-icked heartbeats, his neck was broken and he was gone.